IN
FULL
VIEW

THE
UNVEILING

ROBERT AUSTIN MOWBRAY

IN FULL VIEW – THE UNVEILING

PUBLISHED BY: ROBERT AUSTIN MOWBRAY

Book Cover design by Robert Austin Mowbray
(credit to Canva)

ISBN 979-8-9921306-0-7

PRINTED IN THE UNITED STATES OF AMERICA

TABLE OF CONTENTS

INTRODUCTION

In the high-stakes world of art crime, accomplished art historian Julian Taylor races against time to dismantle a notorious underground art crime syndicate while uncovering the truth behind a stolen masterpiece that could change everything.

Julian Taylor, a dedicated art historian and restoration expert, finds himself embroiled in a dangerous game as he seeks to locate Victor Salvatore, the mastermind behind the largest art crime syndicate in history. When a high-stakes auction features Leonardo da Vinci's 'Salvator Mundi', Julian must navigate a treacherous landscape filled with deception, betrayal, and unexpected alliances. As the auction approaches, he discovers that the art world is fraught with secrets, and the stakes are higher than he ever imagined.

With the help of a diverse team—including law enforcement and fellow art enthusiasts—Julian races to expose Salvatore's operations while grappling with his growing feelings for his partner, Marco, who stands steadfastly by his side. Their relationship deepens as they confront the perils of their world, each moment drawing them closer together.

However, when the carefully orchestrated trap at the exclusive Christie's auction house spirals into chaos, tragedy strikes. In the midst of the turmoil, Marco is shot, leaving Julian desperate and heartbroken as he watches the love of his life fall victim to the violence surrounding them.

With Marco in critical condition and the chaos of the auction fresh in his mind, Julian is propelled into a relentless pursuit of vengeance. As law enforcement scrambles to piece together the events of the night, he grapples with his own fears and moral dilemmas, torn between seeking justice for Marco and protecting the integrity of the art world they both cherish.

'The Unveiling' explores the complexities of love, the value of art, and the moral gray areas that arise in the pursuit of justice. It delves into how ambition and greed can corrupt even the most passionate of pursuits, ultimately questioning what it means to truly possess art. As the dust settles and Marco lingers near death, Julian is left to confront the haunting reality of their choices, setting the stage for a gripping continuation of their story.

1.

'The Starry Night'

The operation began with meticulous planning, a symphony of precision orchestrated by Victor Salvatore and his handpicked team of specialists. For months, they had scoured the Van Gogh Museum in Amsterdam, scrutinizing every detail, and any vulnerabilities. Victor, a man whose life had been shaped by the thrill of the heist, knew that the museum was preparing to loan the famed 'Starry Night' for a special exhibition at the Metropolitan Museum of Art in New York City.

This wasn't just an opportunity; it was a golden ticket, a chance to execute a high-stakes heist that could cement his legacy.

"Are you sure about this, Victor?" Conrad Mercer, the field operative, asked, his voice low as they reviewed plans in a dimly lit café nearby. "It's a high profile piece. If we get caught—"

"We won't get caught," Victor interrupted, his confidence unwavering. "We've done our homework. With the right distraction, we'll slip in and out like shadows."

Conrad nodded, though a flicker of doubt crossed his face. "Alright, but I'm counting on you to handle the timing perfectly."

On the evening of the private viewing event, Conrad blended seamlessly into the opulent surroundings of the museum. Dressed impeccably in tailored attire, he struck up conversations with museum staff, posing as a wealthy collector eager to acquire rare pieces.

"Beautiful collection you have here," he said to a curator, his charm turning heads. "I've always admired Van Gogh's work. Any chance you can tell me about 'The Starry Night'?"

The curator smiled, pleased to share, "Ah, it's a masterpiece, isn't it? We're actually preparing for its transport to New York soon. It's a significant moment for us."

"Transport?" Conrad feigned surprise. "I'd love to know more about the security measures in place. I wouldn't want anything to happen to such a treasure."

Meanwhile, in a makeshift lab, Simon Leduc was hard at work, his fingers flying over high-resolution digital imaging equipment. "Victor, I'm almost done," he communicated through a secure line, his focus unwavering. "This forgery will be indistinguishable from the original.

Just a few more details."

"Make it flawless, Simon," Victor urged, his voice steady. "We can't afford any mistakes."

As the day of the transfer approached, Victor and his team synchronized their efforts like clockwork. Clara Jensen, their insider at the museum, relayed crucial information. "The guards will be distracted during the routine check at 3 PM," she informed them. "That's your window."

"Perfect," Victor replied, a grin spreading across his face. "Let's make this happen."

On the fateful day, the museum buzzed with energy. Staff members scurried about, preparing for the transfer of 'Starry Night'. Victor stood a safe distance away, his heart racing as he observed the chaos unfold. Conrad discreetly signaled to him, his expression calm but focused.

"Remember, just create the distraction and I'll handle the rest," Conrad whispered, adjusting his cufflinks.

"Trust me," Victor replied, his eyes locked on the loading area.

With a subtle flick of his wrist, Victor's associate, posing as a museum intern, activated a small smoke bomb hidden in a nearby corner of the gallery. As the device hissed to life, a sudden haze filled the air, swirling around the room like a ghostly shroud.

"Smoke! Over there!" a staff member shouted, panic creeping into her voice.

Museum staff rushed to address the unexpected commotion, their faces a mix of confusion and concern. Their attention was diverted from the loading area, creating the perfect opportunity for Victor's team.

"Now, Conrad!" Victor urged, almost breathless with anticipation.

Conrad moved swiftly, his heart

pounding. "Just like we practiced," he murmured to himself. He approached the original painting, his hands steady as he expertly swapped it with Salvatore's forgery. "This will do," he whispered, carefully securing the forgery in the original's protective casing.

As the museum staff scrambled to comprehend the chaos unleashed by the smoke-filled room, Victor felt a surge of exhilaration. Conrad slipped away, seamlessly merging into the throng of panicked employees, each one unaware of the true nature of the emergency. "We did it!" Victor exclaimed, visualizing the adrenaline coursing through his veins like wildfire, igniting a thrill that energized him.

Outside, the transport truck—arranged by their legitimate logistics company—sat poised and ready, a silent accomplice in their audacious plan. Victor's heart raced as he watched the vehicle, its engine idling softly, prepared to depart without raising a hint of suspicion. The weight of the moment bore down on him; inside that truck lay a stolen masterpiece, the authentic Van Gogh, its vibrant colors now concealed beneath layers of deception.

"Did it go smoothly?" Clara's voice crackled through the earpiece, cutting through the tension as Victor stepped into the shadows, his pulse quickening with each passing second.

"Like clockwork," he replied, a triumphant grin breaking across his face as he envisioned the masterpiece safely nestled within the truck. "'The Starry Night' is mine, and we've successfully replaced it with our replica, all while keeping the swap hidden from anyone. The original now rests with us, while the forged 'Starry Night" takes its place unnoticed."

With the game plan complete, the team

ensured that the truck carrying the forgery left without raising suspicion. Victor had arranged for a legitimate transport company to handle the delivery to The Met, using Anton Petrov's logistics expertise to cover their tracks.

But as they disappeared into the bustling streets of Amsterdam, Victor could not shake the feeling that their victory was only the beginning. The art world was a labyrinth of hidden treasures and dangers, and they had just ignited a fire that could consume them all. With the 'Starry Night' now in his possession, Victor knew he had to tread carefully, for in the realm of art theft, every masterpiece had its price, even a $500 million masterpiece like 'The Starry Night'.

In the vibrant art scene of New York City, Julian Taylor was a renowned art historian and restorer, celebrated for his meticulous attention to detail and profound love for the masterpieces he worked with. Julian was a chief historian and restorer at The Metropolitan Museum of Art in New York City. His days were spent in the sunlit studios of The Met and, from time to time, in other prestigious galleries throughout Europe, carefully restoring damaged artworks and immersing himself in their histories. With a sharp mind and an eye for authenticity, he had garnered respect in both academic and artistic circles. Julian's passion for art was not just professional; it was personal. He believed that every piece had a story to tell, and he dedicated his life to uncovering those narratives.

Julian Taylor stepped out of the Metropolitan Museum of Art, the crisp New York air filling his lungs as the cacophony of the bustling city enveloped him. The towering skyscrapers loomed overhead, casting long shadows across the sidewalk as taxis honked and pedestrians hurried past, each one lost in their own world. It was a typical day in 'the city that never sleeps'—a relentless pulse of energy that matched the rhythm of Julian's own heart.

With a tattered leather portfolio under one arm and a mind buzzing with thoughts of art restoration, he rounded the corner onto Fifth Avenue. Just as he was about to lose himself in the beauty of a nearby street mural, a loud crash shattered the familiar hum of the city. Julian's instincts kicked in as he turned abruptly, noticing a small delivery van had come to a sudden halt, its side door partially open.

A crowd was quickly gathering, voices rising in alarm. Julian felt a surge of urgency as he approached. Was someone hurt? The driver, a young man with wide eyes, stumbled out of the van, panic etched across his face.

"Help! I need help!" he shouted, gesturing wildly.

Julian's heart raced as he pushed through the swelling crowd of onlookers, his focus razor-sharp. As he caught sight of the van, he noticed something had shifted within its interior. Nestled precariously among packing crates, what appeared to be a major masterpiece—a canvas draped with a protective tarp that was now torn, revealing its dynamic colors beneath.

Julian could hardly believe his eyes. It was a painting by renowned artist Vincent van Gogh, a piece worth millions, and it appeared damaged. The sight sent a chill through him. If this was indeed what he suspected, this was not just a mere accident; it was a crisis that could ripple through the art world, impacting countless lives.

Outside the Metropolitan Museum of Art, near their loading dock, the air is chilly, and the sounds of the city buzz in the background. Eyes wide with concern, Julian approaches the scene, his heart racing. "What just happened here? Are you okay?" Julian asked.

The driver, a young man with tousled hair and a distracted demeanor, stepped towards him, unaware of the chaos about to unfold.

Suddenly, a woman in her early forties burst onto the scene, her expression a volatile mix of anger and disbelief. "You hit me with your van!" she shouted, jabbing an accusing finger at the driver. "You weren't paying attention, you idiot!

The driver, taken aback, raised his hands defensively. "I didn't see you! I swear, I wasn't trying to—"

"Liar!" she interrupted, her voice cutting through the air like a knife. "You hit me on purpose! Do you think this is a joke?"

"Look, I'm sorry! It was an accident!" he protested, frustration creeping into his voice. "I was just trying to get through—"

"Trying to get through?" she barked, stepping closer, her eyes blazing. "You think you can just bulldoze your way around here without a care? This isn't some stupid game!"

"I wasn't speeding! I wasn't even close!" he shot back, his own anger rising. "You came out of nowhere! Maybe you should watch where you're going!"

"Watch where I'm going?!" she exclaimed, incredulity etched on her face. "You're the one who needs to learn how to drive! This is exactly why you should be more careful—"

"Careful? I was minding my own business!" he retorted, his defensiveness turning into irritation. "How about you take a breath and realize it was an accident?"

The tension between them crackled in the air, both unwilling to back down, each convinced they were in the right.

The sound of sirens grows louder as police arrive, blue and red lights flashing, casting an eerie glow on the scene. Just then, two police officers arrived, their presence commanding immediate attention. One of the officers, said with a no-nonsense attitude, as she stepped forward, "I am Sgt. Erin Michaels, and this is my partner, Sgt. John Pierce, his demeanor serious as he moved closer and asked, "What's going on here?"

Pointing to the woman, Julian Taylor answered, "I arrived right after the accident occurred. The driver claimed the woman had dashed in front of him and now she appears injured, while hurling a stream of colorful insults."

"Miss, please calm down," Sgt. Michaels said firmly. "We can't have language like that here. I won't tolerate it."

The woman narrowed her eyes, her indignation boiling over. "Calm down? I was just hit by a van! You expect me to be calm?"

Sgt. Pierce, tried to interject as the injured woman continued to rant, "Let's take a step back and figure out what happened. Can you tell us your side of the story?"

Julian stood off to the side, observing the unfolding drama with a mix of curiosity and concern. The woman noticed him and turned her ire in his direction. "You're a witness! Tell them he hit me!"

Julian raised an eyebrow, uncertain how to respond. "I just got here. I didn't see the accident happen."

The van driver, 24 year old Mark Tolkin, standing outside of the van, panic etched on his face, his hands trembling. Breathless and agitated,

"No," he said. "I swear, I didn't even see her until she was right in front of me. It was an accident!"

Sgt. Michaels turned to the driver, her tone firm but measured. "We'll need your information and a statement. Let's keep this civil, alright?"

The woman holding her side, her frustration still palpable, "Civil? I have a sharp shooting pain in my side! Something is broken or ruptured! This isn't just a minor issue! This is bullshit! That's what this is! Fucking ridiculous!"

"Miss," the officer interjected again, "I understand you're upset, but shouting and swearing won't solve anything. Let's take a deep breath and figure this out."

Julian watched, sensing the tension in the air. As the police worked to calm the situation, he couldn't help but wonder how this chaotic encounter would ripple through the next few days ahead.

Julian's gaze was fixed on the masterpiece, now laid bare to the harsh realities of the street. A crack ran horizontally across its surface, marring its beauty. It was a moment of collision--not just between a van and a pedestrian, but between two worlds, the realm of art and the gritty reality of life, both precariously intertwined.

Mark, the van delivery driver, gestured frantically toward the van, as he exclaimed, "I was just delivering art to the museum when that woman dashed right in front of my van, and the side door flew open!"

Julian's gaze was fixed on the masterpiece, as he moved closer to the open side door. His heart sinks as he has a better view of the crate, the faint outlines of masterpieces he knows are now at risk. An edge of urgency in his voice, he said, "Sgt. Pierce, those paintings are arriving from Amsterdam for a new exhibition! They must not be damaged any further!" Julian moved closer to get a better look, his heart pounding with the urgency of a restorer faced with the possibility of saving a work of art in peril.

The sirens wailed in the distance, growing louder as he assessed the damage, knowing that this was only the beginning. The stakes were rising, and the art world was about to be shaken to its core.

Looking intently at Julian, Sgt. Pierce said, "Let's take it one step at a time. Sir, speaking to the van driver, can you give me your license and registration please?"

Nervously rummaging through his pockets, Mark said, "Sure, here you go."

Turning towards the woman, Sgt. Pierce said, "And you, ma'am, an ambulance is just a block or two away."

Sgt. Michaels said, "An ambulance has arrived. EMS will take care you now. I do need to see your identification please for my report. Do you need my help?" As she reached into her purse, she handed the Officer her driver's license ID. Sgt. Michaels recorded her information and handed back the ID to her. She had noted that her name was Joanne Brunetti, 46 years old, living in Brooklyn Heights, New York, just across the Brooklyn Bridge from lower Manhattan.

EMS quickly took over attention to Ms. Brunetti. She seemed to be slightly more calm now that she had medical attention. Tears welling up in her eyes, with a trembling voice, she said, "I am in severe pain."

Julian shifts his focus back to the van, his heart racing. He knows the significance of the paintings—their history, the stories they tell.

Julian's voice urgent but composed, said,

"Sgt. Pierce, I saw several paintings in the back of the van. They're not just any pieces; they are van Gogh originals. This exhibition is crucial for the museum!"

Raising an eyebrow, intrigued, Sgt. Pierce said, "Thank you for that information. We'll need to check the contents of the van."

Panic rising in his voice, Mark said "No! Those are for the museum! They're really important!"

Reassuringly, trying to calm Mark, Julian said, "I'll make sure they're handled properly. I'm the art restorer for the museum. This is my responsibility at the museum."

Julian's mind races as he thinks of the meticulous restoration work he's done on other van Gogh masterpieces. He feels a deep sense of duty to protect them.

Sgt. Pierce nods, while taking notes, and said, "Alright, we'll secure the area. Can you tell me more about the paintings, Mr. Taylor?"

Determined, with a steady voice, Julian said, "Yes, this is a shipment of four Vincent van Gogh paintings from The Van Gogh Museum in Amsterdam for a new exciting upcoming exhibition here at The Met. If there's damage to the painting inside the van, I need to assess it immediately. Each painting has its own story, and they deserve to be preserved."

Looking back at the van, his expression serious, Sgt. Pierce said, "Understood. Once we get the situation under control, I'll let you follow the van to the loading dock."

His voice trembling with remorse, Mark the van driver said, "I'm really sorry! I didn't mean for this to happen."

Trying to keep the mood calm, Julian sighed, "Accidents happen, but we need to make sure no one else gets hurt, and that those paintings are safe."

As the police continued to gather information, Julian's thoughts drift to the exhibition opening. He envisions the crowd, the anticipation, and the beauty of the artwork. He can't let this moment be ruined.

Sgt. Pierce, firmly, but kindly, said "Thank you, everyone. Let's get this wrapped up."

As the officers begin to direct traffic, Julian takes a deep breath, preparing himself for what lies ahead. He knows the importance of his role—both for the museum and for the art itself.

Throughout Julian's illustrious career, he has stumbled upon discrepancies in the provenance of several major masterpieces that had been displayed in world-renowned museums. Intrigued and concerned, Julian has worked with teams of people to dig deeper, uncovering sophisticated theft and forgery schemes that threatened the integrity of the art he loved.

Julian paced the floor of his office at the Metropolitan Museum of Art, his mind racing. He picked up his phone, heart pounding, and dialed Marco Rossi's number in Florence. The call connected with a few rings, and Marco's familiar voice broke through.

"Julian! What's going on? You know its after midnight here in Florence?" Marco sounded both slightly perturbed at the late hour and curious, even though through an open window the bustle of Florence was evident in the background.

"Marco, you won't believe what just happened," Julian began, his voice taut with urgency. "There was an accident outside the museum involving a delivery van. They were bringing in paintings for the upcoming van Gogh exhibition."

"Is everyone okay?" Marco asked, his tone shifting to concern.

"Yeah, the driver's fine, but…" Julian hesitated, taking a deep breath. "One of the paintings—'The Starry Night'—it's here, but there's a serious gash across in the middle of the 'sky'. I need your expertise to repair it."

"The Starry Night?" Marco echoed, a mix of excitement and worry in his voice. "That's a major piece. How bad is the damage?"

"Marco, I could really use your help here in New York," Julian implores. "The painting is in the museum now, but it needs immediate attention. At first look, it appears the other three paintings did not suffer any damage."

Julian rubbed his temples, trying to steady his thoughts. "It looks significant. I've seen worse, but this needs immediate attention. I can handle the initial assessment, but I want you here to oversee the restoration—especially given its importance."

"Of course! I'll book a flight right away," Marco said, his resolve clear. "How soon do you need me?"

"Tomorrow, if possible. I'll arrange for a car to pick you up at the airport," Julian replied, glancing at the clock. Time was of the essence. "I'll be waiting for you at the museum. We need to start on this ASAP."

"I'll get on it," Marco assured him. "What about the other restorations? Is everything else okay?"

"For now, yes," Julian said, though a hint of unease lingered. "But this is a priority."

"Got it. I'll text you the details of the flight as soon as I have them. I'll pack a bag and head to the airport. There is usually an early morning flight to JFK," Marco said, his determination palpable. "I'll be there as soon as I can."

"Thanks, Marco. I appreciate it," Julian replied, relief washing over him. "I'll talk to you soon."

Marco Rossi was born and raised in Florence, Italy, a city steeped in art and history. From a young age, he was captivated by the Renaissance masterpieces that adorned the city's museums and churches. His passion for art led him to study at Columbia University in New York City, where he met Julian Taylor. Graduating together, their shared enthusiasm for art history and restoration forged a strong bond that would carry them into their professional lives.

Now back in Florence, Marco serves as Julian's trusted assistant, managing logistics and assisting with restorations mostly in Europe, but sometimes in the U.S. His keen eye for detail and understanding of traditional techniques make him an invaluable asset to Julian's work. While he often works remotely, Marco frequently travels to New York to support Julian during critical projects, especially when major exhibitions are on the horizon.

Marco is known for his warm and approachable demeanor, often acting as the bridge between Julian and the various artists, curators, and dealers they collaborate with. His enthusiasm is infectious, and he possesses a natural curiosity that drives him to learn more about every piece he encounters. Though he admires Julian's expertise, Marco is determined to carve out his own identity in the art world.

The friendship between Marco and Julian goes beyond professional boundaries. They often share late-night conversations about art, philosophy, and their dreams for the future. Although they are the same age, Marco looks up to Julian as a mentor and strives to emulate his dedication to authenticity and preservation in art.

After hanging up with Marco, Julian took a moment to collect his thoughts. He knew he needed additional support for this situation. With Marco on his way, his next call had to be to Kamil Russo in Paris. Julian took a deep breath and dialed Kamil Russo's number, heart racing as he prepared to explain the situation. As the phone rang, he glanced out the window, watching the chaos of New York City unfold below. The weight of the situation pressed heavily on him, and he hoped Kamil would be able to help.

"Bonjour," Kamil's voice came through, warm and familiar.

"Kamil! It's Julian," he replied, trying to keep his voice steady. "I hope I'm not interrupting your sleep or anything important."

"Not at all! I was just wrapping up for the day. What's going on?" she asked, her tone shifting to concern.

"I wish it were under better circumstances," he began. "There was an accident outside the museum. A delivery van collided with a pedestrian crossing the street, and they were bringing in paintings for the van Gogh exhibition."

Kamil's breath caught. "Oh no. Is everyone all right?"

"Yeah, the driver is fine, but… one of the paintings—'The Starry Night'—it's here, and there's a significant gash through the 'sky' part of the painting," Julian explained. He could hear the tension in Kamil's silence. "I've already contacted Marco Rossi; he's flying in early morning, your local time, to help with the restoration."

"The Starry Night? That's a major piece! Are you sure it can be repaired?" Kamil asked, her voice filled with urgency.

"I believe so, but I want to make sure we handle it properly. This painting is too important to take any chances," Julian said. "That's why I'm calling you. I'd love for you to join us here in New York. Your expertise has been invaluable in our past projects, and I could really use your insight on this one."

Kamil paused for a moment, contemplating. "I'd be honored to help, Julian. You know how passionate I am about van Gogh. I'll book a flight as soon as we're done here. Do you have a timeline for how long you'll need me?"

"I'm not sure yet, but the sooner we can assess the damage and start the restoration, the better. I'll arrange for a car to pick you up from the airport," he replied, relief flooding through him at her willingness to assist.

"Thank you, Julian. I'll get on this right away," Kamil said, her determination evident. "I will text you my flight details. Let's save 'The Starry Night'."

The soft glow of the skyline light filtered through the glass ceilings of the Louvre, casting a warm light on the masterpieces that adorned its hallowed halls. Among them stood Kamil Russo, a Parisian art historian whose presence seemed to blend seamlessly with the elegance of the artwork surrounding her. Dressed in a chic, tailored outfit that echoed her sophisticated taste, Kamil exuded an air of confidence and knowledge that drew the attention of both visitors and fellow scholars alike.

Born into a family of passionate art enthusiasts, Kamil grew up amidst the vibrant cultural tapestry of Paris. Her childhood was filled with visits to galleries, conversations about brushstrokes and color palettes, and stories of the great masters that shaped the art world. This upbringing instilled in her a profound appreciation for French Impressionism, a movement that she had dedicated her academic career to studying. Her expertise was not merely academic; it was deeply personal, fueled by a desire to uncover the hidden narratives behind each brushstroke and to share these stories with those who wandered through the museum's corridors.

Kamil's sharp intellect and impeccable taste made her a respected figure among her peers. She often collaborated with other art historians across Europe, her closest ally being Alexander Murray, a fellow scholar based in Rome with offices in Vatican City. Their shared passion for Renaissance art forged a bond that transcended professional admiration; they often spent hours discussing the intricacies of artists like Caravaggio and Michelangelo over coffee at quaint Parisian cafés.

As Kamil stood before a Monet in the Louvre, contemplating the delicate interplay of light and water, she felt a familiar thrill of inspiration. Little did she know, her world was about to be turned upside down. A whisper of forgeries and deceit rippled through the art community, and Kamil would soon find herself drawn into a mystery that would challenge her passion and test her dedication to preserving the integrity of art.

When she met Julian Taylor during their freshman year at Columbia University in New York City it was 2010. Their shared passion for art sparked an immediate connection. Kamil was drawn to his determination to uncover the truth behind so many forgeries, and she quickly offered her expertise in French art to assist him. Now in

2024, fourteen years later, together, they work to unravel the web of deception that continuously threatened the art world.

In the bustling streets of Florence, Marco Rossi weaved through the crowd, his keen eyes scanning the art scene for opportunities. Working also at times as Kamil's trusted assistant in Europe, he is tech-savvy and resourceful—a perfect complement to her scholarly pursuits. With a mop of curly hair and a casual yet stylish wardrobe, Marco was approachable and charismatic, often disarming the most skeptical of art lovers with his charm.

Growing up in a family of artisans, Marco developed a love for art from a young age. Although Marco's skill sets includes exceptional restoration and painting abilities, his background in technology and digital archiving makes him invaluable to Kamil as he assists her with research and logistical planning. He had a knack for uncovering obscure details that often eluded even the most seasoned historians.

After they exchanged a few more details, Julian hung up, feeling a renewed sense of hope. With both Marco and Kamil on their way, he was ready to face the challenges ahead.

Julian's call marks the beginning of Marco's pivotal role in the restoration of the masterpiece, as he flies to New York to assist Julian. While preparing his luggage, Marco finds himself drawn deeper into the unfolding mystery, navigating the complexities of friendship and loyalty amidst the looming threat of deception in the art world.

2.

Marco and Kamil in Manhattan

As Marco stepped off the plane at JFK, the time difference weighed heavily on him. It was a very sunny morning at 8AM. Six hours from the crowded streets of Florence to the bustling, often chaotic atmosphere of New York City morning traffic. He felt disoriented, the remnants of jet lag tugging at his energy.

After collecting his luggage, he pulled out his phone to check for messages from Julian. They had spoken the night before, and Marco couldn't shake the feeling that Julian's tone had been slightly off—perhaps it was just the late hour in Florence or something more. He set the phone down and took a deep breath, reminding himself that this trip was about the exhibition, not personal complications.

As he made his way to through the

arrivals terminal, he spotted Julian waiting for him, a mix of excitement and nervousness evident in his posture. "Marco!" Julian called out, his voice cutting through the clamor of the airport.

Marco felt a flutter of warmth at the sight of him, but it was tinged with confusion. Why had Julian seemed so distant on the phone? "Hey, Julian," Marco replied, forcing a smile as they embraced briefly. It felt both familiar and awkward, as if they were grappling with unspoken feelings that had yet to surface.

"Did you have a good flight?" Julian asked, stepping back to look at Marco, his eyes searching.

"Long, but fine. I'm just glad to be here," Marco said, trying to keep the conversation light despite the weight of their recent exchanges hanging in the air. "Thank you so much for surprising me! I didn't think you would actually be here at the airport to pick me up," he said with a happy smile.

They walked toward the taxi stand, the city's early-morning energy buzzing around them. Julian began to explain the plans for the next few days, but Marco's mind drifted. He wondered about the hotel Julian had arranged or if they were headed straight to the museum. "So, which hotel am I staying in?" Marco asked, attempting to regain focus.

"Oh, I booked a place near the museum," Julian replied. He seemed more animated now, the excitement of the exhibition bringing out a spark in him. But Marco couldn't shake the lingering unease. Was it just the fatigue, or was there something unresolved between them?

As they waited for a taxi, Marco glanced at Julian, noticing how the morning sun caught the edges of his face, illuminating his features. "Thanks again for picking me up," Marco said, sincerity threading through his words.

"Of course! I wouldn't miss it," Julian replied, his gaze steady. In that moment, Marco felt a flicker of hope that maybe they could navigate whatever tension had built up between them.

The taxi ride was filled with small talk, but both men could sense the undercurrents. Marco wondered if Julian felt it too—the weight of possibility and the remnants of past conversations that hung between them like a bridge waiting to be crossed.

As the taxi wove through the vibrant streets of Manhattan, the city unfolded around them, a whirlwind of sights and sounds. Julian glanced at Marco, who was gazing out the window, lost in thought. "You know, I was thinking... it might be easier for you to stay at my place instead of the hotel," Julian suggested, his voice casual but his eyes searching Marco's reaction.

Marco turned to face him, surprise flickering across his features. "Are you sure? I don't want to impose."

"Not at all! I have plenty of room that includes a guest suite. My apartment is just a few blocks away from the museum. Plus, it'll be more convenient for us to go over the exhibition details," Julian replied, his tone light, but there was an underlying urgency, as if he was eager to bridge the gap between them.

After a moment of contemplation, Marco nodded. "Okay, that sounds great. It'll be nice to catch up, just like old times." There was a hint of nostalgia in his voice, and Julian couldn't help but smile, the memory of late-night conversations and shared dreams flooding back.

Once they arrived at Julian's apartment, Marco was struck by how familiar it felt, despite the years that had passed since college. The walls were adorned with art, much of it reflecting Julian's own style—bold and expressive. "Wow, it looks amazing in here," Marco remarked as he stepped inside.

"Thanks! After a little over a year, it's still a work in progress," Julian said, shrugging with a hint of pride. "Make yourself at home. I'll grab us something to drink."

As Julian moved to the kitchen, Marco took a moment to absorb his surroundings, his heart racing at the proximity. Memories of late-night study sessions where they'd get lost in conversation filled his mind. He could almost hear their laughter echoing off the walls.

"Here we go," Julian said, returning with two cups of coffee. He handed one to Marco, their fingers brushing briefly, sending a jolt of electricity between them. "To old friends and new beginnings," Julian toasted, his gaze steady. "I hope I remembered correctly how you like your coffee; a little milk and no sugar."

"How thoughtful for you to remember. To old friends," Marco echoed, clinking his coffee cup against Julian's, but their eyes lingered on each other longer than necessary. The air felt charged, thick with unspoken words and lingering glances.

As they settled onto the couch, the conversation flowed easily at first—reminiscing about professors who had inspired them, the late-night debates that had turned into passionate discussions. But as the laughter faded, a more serious tone crept in.

"Do you ever think about those days?" Julian asked, his voice softer. "About what we had?"

Marco's heart raced. "I do. Sometimes I wonder if we missed something back then... if we were just too caught up in everything."

Julian leaned forward, his expression earnest. "I felt it too. There was always something between us, wasn't there? But we never acted on it."

The tension in the room shifted, becoming more evident. Marco looked into Julian's eyes, searching for answers. "Do you think it's too late?"

Julian's gaze held steady, a mix of hope and uncertainty. "I don't know. But I'd like to find out."

In that moment, the past and present collided, and the possibility of rekindling something deeper hung in the air. Marco's pulse quickened as he realized that perhaps this trip to New York wasn't just about the exhibition—it was a chance to explore what they had left unresolved.

Julian earned his undergraduate degree in Art History at Columbia University in New York City. Here, he was introduced to a diverse group of passionate individuals, including Marco Rossi, who shared his enthusiasm for art restoration and history and became one of his closest confidants and friends.

Pursuing a Masters Degree in Art History at Yale University, in New Haven, Connecticut, Julian honed his skills and deepened his knowledge of art movements. It was at Yale University where Julian met Harper Thompson, forming a long-term friendship that would last throughout his career.

After completing his education, Julian became a renowned art historian and restorer in

New York City, known for his meticulous work and deep understanding of art. His expertise led him to collaborate with various investigation teams on art crimes, establishing connections across Europe with curators, museum directors, and law enforcement, including the FBI and Interpol.

As first year freshman at Columbia University, Julian and Marco meet during orientation week. Both share a passion for art, quickly bonding over their mutual interests. They discover they have similar backgrounds and ambitions, leading to late-night discussions about their dreams in the art world.

During their first semester classes, they take introductory courses in art history, forming a study group with other students, including Kamil Russo who becomes a key friend in their lives.

Julian begins to notice a deeper connection with Marco, feeling a mix of admiration and confusion about his feelings. Both enjoy the vibrant college atmosphere, attending art exhibitions and social events, often accompanied by female friends. They flirt and date casually, but an underlying tension remains between them.

During their sophomore year, Julian and Marco collaborate on a joint project for an art history course, exploring the influence of Impressionism. This deepens their bond and artistic appreciation for each other's perspectives. They start volunteering at local galleries, gaining hands-on experience and building connections in the New York art scene.

Julian and Marco each grapple with their sexuality, experiencing attraction to women but also feeling an undeniable chemistry between them. They confide in each other about their struggles, creating a safe space for vulnerability.

They attend a LGBTQ+ event on campus, which helps them explore their identities but also leaves them feeling conflicted.

Julian and Marco meet Isabella Rossi during a lecture and quickly become friends, bonding over shared interests in Renaissance art. Isabella introduces them to influential figures in the art world.

An art dealer in Venice, Isabella Rossi, navigated the vibrant art scene with a keen eye and an unyielding passion for Italian masterpieces. As a prominent art dealer, Isabella specialized in Renaissance art, her gallery a treasure trove of paintings and sculptures that attracted collectors from around the world. Known for her charm and persuasive skills, she forged strong relationships with both artists and clients, ensuring that each piece found its rightful home.

When whispers of a forgery scheme reached her, Isabella felt a deep sense of urgency. The thought of counterfeit artworks infiltrating the market was a threat to her reputation and the integrity of the art world she loved. Having crossed paths with Julian Taylor during art fairs and exhibitions, they discussed the importance to protect her gallery and the artists she represented against art crimes of any nature.

As Julian and Marco delve into more specialized courses, the pressure of academics increases. They support each other through late nights studying and preparing for critiques. Julian begins to explore restoration techniques, while Marco focuses on art history research, complementing each other's strengths.

They curate a student exhibition that garners attention, catching the eye of local art critics. This leads to internships and opportunities for both. Julian and Marco navigate the complexities of their feelings, with moments of tension and unspoken attraction, yet remain platonic.

The group, including Kamil and Harper, takes a trip to Europe during spring break. They visit major art museums, deepening their appreciation for the works they study. This trip solidifies their friendships and broadens their perspectives.

During their senior year, as graduation approaches, Julian and Marco discuss their future plans, dreaming of careers in art restoration and curation. They encourage each other to pursue their passions. Julian considers applying for graduate programs, while Marco contemplates working in art galleries.

They work on a capstone project together, possibly restoring a piece of art or curating a final exhibition. This project showcases their growth and deepens their collaborative spirit. The tension between them escalates during a late-night work session, but they ultimately decide to keep their feelings unspoken, valuing their friendship above all.

Graduation day arrives, filled with mixed emotions. They celebrate their achievements with friends, but an underlying sense of uncertainty lingers about their relationship. Julian and Marco promise to stay in touch, knowing their paths will diverge but hopeful that their friendship will endure.

3.

True Friends

Outside a cozy tapas bar in Midtown Manhattan, the late afternoon sun dips low in the sky, casting a golden hue over the bustling street. Julian, Marco, and Kamil all planned to meet outside of the charming tapas bar adorned with colorful tiles and green plants. The air is fragrant with the scent of spices and sizzling food.

Julian, spotting Kamil and waving excitedly, shouts "There she is! Ready to feast?"

While attending Yale from 2014-2018, Julian and Kamil collaborated on projects about French Impressionism. Their professional respect blossomed into a close friendship, with Julian often seeking Kamil's insights on European art.

Kamil, grinning, her eyes sparkling says, "Always! I can't believe we're finally tackling this 'Starry Night' situation."

Marco, playfully nudging Julian, said, "Just don't let your excitement overshadow the disaster at hand. We need to focus on the restoration."

Julian sighs, running a hand through his hair, "I know, but I can't help it. It's "Starry Night", you guys. This isn't just any painting; it's a piece of history. Let's grab some tapas and head to the museum. Your expertise will be invaluable."

Kamil nodding "Absolutely. I can't imagine how stressful this must be for you, Julian."

Marco smirking, "Yeah, don't worry— we've been through worse. Remember the time we had to fix that sculpture from the gallery?"

Julian chuckling, "True, but this feels different. It's van Gogh."

They place their order and, with food in hand, head towards the museum. While walking through the busy sidewalks in Manhattan, the conversation flows easily, filled with laughter and shared memories.

It is nearing lunchtime as they enter The Met, and Julian leads them to the main art restoration workshop. The familiar scent of paint and varnish envelops them. The space is a blend of organized chaos, with tools and art supplies strewn about. But their focus immediately shifts to the center of the room: the damaged 'Starry Night' painting, leaning against a very large worktable, shrouded in a heavy silence.

Julian, setting the tapas down on a nearby table said, "Welcome back to my creative chaos."

Kamil, her eyes widening as she approaches the painting, says "Oh no... it looks worse up close."

Marco, studying the gash remarks, "This is a serious tear in the canvas. How did this even happen? "

Julian, exhaling sharply, said "It was

during transport. The van was packed with the other three van Gogh paintings, and somehow this one got jostled. When I took a closer look inside the van, I saw it—this gash right across the sky of the painting."

Kamil, gently touching the edge of the canvas, says, "It's heartbreaking. This isn't just some artwork; it's a 130 year old masterpiece, painted only one year before van Gogh's death in 1890."

Julian, his voice trembling slightly said, "I've always admired van Gogh's ability to capture emotion. This piece has so much history and beauty. I can't believe it's damaged."

Marco nodded, expressing confusion about what could have caused such a significant gash. "What was in the back of the van that might have caused this? It doesn't add up. We need to approach this cautiously," he said. "We aren't just undertaking a major restoration; this looks like it might require an investigation."

Kamil then turned to Julian and asked, "Have you spoken to any conservators?" Julian shook his head and replied, "Not yet. I wanted us to assess the situation first. I trust your judgment; we've worked on many projects together, but this one feels different."

Leaning closer to the painting, Marco added, "We need to document the damage— photos, measurements, everything. Then we can formulate a plan. Do you think we can get a copy of the police report? The conservators will definitely want to see it." Julian took a deep breath and acknowledged, "You're right. I guess I just wanted to resolve this as quickly as possible."

He then recalled the scene of the accident—the side door of the van had been ajar, and the driver had acted suspiciously. "I suspect there was someone else in the van with him, trying to do something with that painting. When the accident happened, that person jumped out and ran off, and amid all the chaos, it seems like no one noticed."

Kamil, smiling reassuringly, said, "We'll figure it out together. Let's eat first; we need our energy for this challenge." Neither Marco nor Kamil had eaten anything except a snack on the plane since their departures from Florence and Paris many hours ago.

As the three friends gather around the table filled with colorful tapas, the atmosphere lightens momentarily. The initial tension eased as they share laughter and stories, ready to tackle the emotional and practical task of restoring 'The Starry Night' together. Julian's anxiety, however, lingers just beneath the surface.

Taking a deep breath as he bites into a patatas bravas, Julian said "Okay, we need to get our ducks in a row. I will make the call to the conservatorship in about an hour, and I want to have everything ready."

Nodding, a piece of chorizo halfway to her mouth, Kamil says "Right. Let's start with the basics. We need photos of the damage, measurements, and details about the painting's history."

Marco, focusing intently, but somewhat anxiously, said "We've done this before—remember the sculpture from the gallery? We can get this done faster than you think."

Julian, fidgeting with his napkin "I know, but this is van Gogh." he said. "I just don't want to mess it up. What if they need more information than we anticipate?"

Reassuringly, Kamil said "They'll appreciate that you're being thorough. Let's just outline everything clearly. We can divide the tasks."

Marco, gesturing with his fork, "I'll handle the measurements and take detailed photos of the painting. We need to capture the gash from different angles to show the extent of the damage and maybe determine how it was caused."

Julian, nodding, feeling a bit more at ease, said "Great. I can start compiling the history of the painting—when it came into the collection, past restorations, anything we can dig up."

Kamil, smiling, said "And I'll set up a document to organize our findings. We can create a timeline of events leading up to the damage including the shipping of the van Gogh art from The Van Gogh Museum in Amsterdam to here in New York City. Julian, can you please call the police officer from the accident and ask for a copy of the accident report? All of this will be helpful for the conservators."

Julian, finally relaxing a bit, says "Thanks, you guys. I really appreciate it. I just want to make sure we present ourselves well."

Marco, grinning, says "Just keep your phone close. You'll feel better once you've made that call."

Kamil, teasingly, says "And once we're done with the tapas! This is the best part."

They dig into the food, laughter filling the workshop as they share stories from their college days at Columbia and Yale, reminiscing about late-night study sessions and their first art projects together.
Julian, smirking, asks "Remember that time we almost set the studio on fire trying to create that mixed media piece?"

Marco, laughing hysterically said, "How could I forget? I still have a scar from where I burned my arm!"

Kamil, giggling, "I think we all learned our lesson about fire safety that night."

Julian, lovingly grinning, said "And it's those experiences that have made us better artists. We can handle this restoration; we've faced tougher challenges."

Marco, raising his glass of water, says "A toast to teamwork then! Let's get this done and save 'The Starry Night'!"

Clinking her glass with theirs, Kamil said, "To our friendship, which always helps us overcome any hurdles!"

With renewed determination, they finish their tapas, energized for the task ahead. They quickly gather materials, documenting the damage and preparing for Julian's call. The atmosphere in the workshop transforms from anxiety to focused collaboration, each friend contributing to the mission at hand.

4.

Inside The Met

After compiling their findings, Julian stood up and walked to a quiet corner of the room, phone in hand. He was about to call Dr. Lila Thorne, the Director of Restoration and Conservation at the museum. Dr. Thorne is a renowned art conservator with over 20 years of experience in the field. Lila was known for her expertise in restoring 18th-century artifacts, and her reputation for meticulous work preceded her. She specializes in the preservation and restoration of Impressionist and Post-Impressionist works, making her an invaluable asset to the Art Institute. Lila received her PhD in Art History from Columbia University, where she focused on the techniques of 19th-century painters like Vincent van Gogh.

Known for her meticulous attention to

detail and her innovative restoration techniques, Lila has worked on several high-profile exhibitions, including retrospectives on van Gogh and Monet. She is respected in both academic and practical circles, often collaborating with museum curators and restoration experts across Europe. Lila is also a close friend of Julian, having shared many late-night brainstorming sessions about art and preservation.

As he dialed, Julian mentally prepared himself. He needed to convey the urgency of the situation.

"Dr. Thorne, it's Julian Taylor," he began when she answered. "I wanted to inform you about the van Gogh painting 'The Starry Night' that has been damaged in an accident outside of The Met loading dock. As you know, four van Gogh paintings were being transported from Amsterdam to The Met for exhibition." He paused, allowing her to absorb the information. "The painting is in delicate condition, and we need your team to assist in the restoration process immediately. We've gathered all the relevant details and photographs from our initial assessment, and I can send those over to you right now, if you like."

Julian could hear Lila's excitement on the other end. "This is incredible news! We'll need to discuss the specifics and the resources required. When do you want us to start?"

"I'd like your team to begin tomorrow— the sooner, the better," he replied. "We can't afford to lose any more time, especially if this is as significant as we believe."

Lila agreed, her voice brimming with enthusiasm. "Absolutely, Julian. I'll gather my team and we'll be ready in the morning. Please send over the details as soon as possible."

As they wrapped up the call, Julian felt a mixture of anxiety and relief. With Lila and her team on board, he knew they would do everything possible to restore the damaged van Gogh.

After finishing his call with Dr. Thorne, Julian took a deep breath and dialed the number to reach Dr. Samuel Grant who is the Director of The Metropolitan Museum of Art and has been instrumental in shaping its mission to promote art education and accessibility. Samuel is very well respected in the art world and is currently curating the highly anticipated Vincent van Gogh exhibit. With a PhD in Art History focusing on American and European Art, Samuel has a deep understanding of the cultural significance of the pieces in the museum's collection.

Before taking on the director role, he served as the Chief Curator for several years, where he was known for his visionary exhibitions that often pushed the boundaries of traditional art presentation. Samuel is pragmatic and strategic, often focusing on the museum's reputation and public relations. His leadership style is collaborative, and he values input from his team, particularly regarding sensitive situations like the current forgery crisis.

"Dr. Grant, it's Julian," he said when Samuel answered. "I hope you have a moment to discuss the upcoming exhibit."

"Of course, Julian. What's on your mind?" Samuel replied, his tone professional yet warm.

"I wanted to inform you about an urgent matter concerning the upcoming van Gogh exhibit. We have four pieces in hand, but there's been an incident with the "Starry Night." It was damaged during transport due to the delivery van accident just outside the museum's loading dock on 5th Avenue," Julian explained, trying to keep his voice steady.

There was a brief silence on the other end before Samuel responded, his concern evident. "That's troubling news. 'The Starry Night' is the centerpiece of the exhibit. What's the extent of the damage?"

Julian took a deep breath. "We're still assessing the full impact, but Dr. Lila Thorne and her team will begin the restoration process tomorrow morning. I will oversee the restoration along with my assistants, Marco Rossi and Kamil Russo. I wanted you to be aware of this before we move forward."

Samuel sighed, clearly worried about the implications. "Thank you for letting me know. We're on a tight schedule, and this could affect our opening timeline. I'll need to inform the board and discuss contingency plans."

"I understand completely," Julian replied. "We'll do everything we can to expedite the restoration. I'll keep you updated as soon as we have more information."

"Please do," Samuel said. "I appreciate your transparency in this matter. Let's hope for the best." As they wrapped up the call, Julian felt the weight of the situation pressing down on him. He was determined to ensure that the exhibit went on as planned, despite the challenges ahead.

5.

Julian's Team

With a hint of autumn in the air, it is a beautiful September morning in New York City when Julian, Marco and Kamil meet at the museum at 8AM sharp. None of the three had much sleep last night fueled by their excitement about the work ahead of them.

As they entered the bright, airy lobby of the museum, Julian spotted Dr. Lila Thorne waiting by the entrance, flanked by her team of expert restorers, Timothy Johnson and Rose Cantor. The atmosphere buzzed with anticipation.

Timothy Johnson is a graduate student pursuing his master's degree in Art Conservation from the Pennsylvania Academy of Fine Arts in Philadelphia. He works as an assistant to Dr. Lila Thorne and is eager to learn from her expertise. Passionate about art restoration, Timothy is meticulous and detail-oriented, often spending long hours in the lab analyzing pigments and techniques. Timothy received his undergraduate degree in Art History from the School of the Art Institute of Chicago.

Timothy is enthusiastic and somewhat idealistic, often bringing fresh ideas to the table. His dedication to preserving art is evident, and he looks up to Lila as a mentor. While he is still learning the intricacies of the field, his keen observations and insightful questions make him a valuable part of the team.

Rose Cantor is a Columbia University graduate working under Dr. Lila Thorne. She focuses on the historical context of artworks, providing essential research that informs restoration decisions. With a background in Art History, Rose brings a wealth of knowledge about various artists and movements, particularly in the 19th century.

She is analytical and articulate, often engaging in discussions about the implications of restoration versus preservation. Rose is also known for her collaborative spirit and ability to connect with others, making her a natural team player. Her relationship with Timothy is friendly, and they often bounce ideas off each other while working.

"Good morning, everyone!" Julian greeted, his voice echoing slightly in the high-ceilinged space.

"Good morning, Julian!" Lila replied with a warm smile. "I hope you're ready for a busy day."

"Absolutely," he said, glancing at Marco and Kamil, who were equally eager. "We've been looking forward to this."

Lila greeted both Kamil and Marco,

"Bonjour and bienvenue!" They both replied simultaneously, "Good morning and thank you."

Timothy, a tall, built young man with a calm demeanor, stepped forward. "We are eager to see your initial assessment of 'The Starry Night'. It's a challenging restoration, but I believe we can bring it back to its former glory."

Rose, with her short curly light brown hair and keen eyes, nodded in agreement. "It's essential we approach this carefully. We'll need to document every step for both preservation and future reference."

"Let's move to the restoration lab," Lila suggested, leading the way. "We can discuss the plan while we set up."

As they walked through the museum's corridors, Julian felt a mix of excitement and nervousness. 'The Starry Night' loomed large in everyone's mind—its damaged canvas a stark reminder of the stakes involved.

Once they reached the lab, the team gathered around a large worktable where the painting was being carefully displayed. Julian took a moment to absorb the sight of the beloved artwork, its vibrant swirls now marred by the accident.

"Okay, team," Lila began, her tone turning serious. "We have a limited timeframe before the impending van Gogh exhibit opens. Our goal is to stabilize the painting and begin the restoration process as quickly as possible."

"Timothy and I will handle the initial restoration analysis," Rose added, pulling out a set of magnifying glasses and tools. "We'll assess the damage and determine the best methods for repair."

Marco looked at Julian, a hint of concern in his voice. "Are we sure about the timeline?

What if the restoration takes longer than expected?"

Julian nodded thoughtfully. "That's a valid point, Marco. We'll need to keep Dr. Grant updated and possibly prepare for any changes in the exhibit schedule."

"Communication is key," Lila emphasized. "Let's work efficiently but meticulously. We owe it to the artwork and to the public."

As the team settled into their expert roles, Julian felt a surge of determination. This was more than just a restoration; it was a mission to preserve a piece of art history.

"Let's get started," he said, taking a deep breath. "We have a lot of work ahead of us."

Julian started working alongside Lila to make the first assessment of the painting. As the lead restorers at The Met, both understood the gravity of the situation, especially after the delivery van accident the previous evening. The excitement in the room was palpable, but so was the tension.

"Let's take a close look at the canvas," Lila suggested, her brow furrowed in concentration. They leaned in examining the vibrant swirls and colors that characterized van Gogh's style.

The other members of the team—Timothy, Rose, Marco, and Kamil—stood back, allowing the two experts the space they needed. As they worked side by side, Julian felt the weight of responsibility on his shoulders. He had been involved since the moment they learned of the damage, and now he was determined to uncover the truth.

"Just a bit more light here," Julian said, adjusting the lamp to illuminate the canvas better. He gently shifted the edge of the painting, his fingers brushing against the surface. Almost immediately, he felt a sudden jolt of realization.

He took a step back, his breath catching in his throat. "This can't be! This is not an original van Gogh," he gasped, his voice rising in disbelief. "It's not 'The Starry Night'… it's a forgery, just a copy!"

The room fell silent, the weight of Julian's words hanging heavy in the air. Lila's eyes widened, disbelief etching across her face. "Are you sure?" she asked, her voice steady but laced with urgency.

Julian nodded, his heart racing. "I can see the brushwork is inconsistent with van Gogh's technique. The colors lack the depth and vibrancy that are signature to his pieces."

Timothy stepped forward, curiosity and concern in his expression. "Let's not jump to conclusions. We should verify this with a more detailed analysis."

Rose moved closer, her eyes narrowing as she inspected the edges of the canvas. "Julian might be right. We need to look at the layering and the under-painting closely."

Marco and Kamil exchanged worried glances, the shock of the revelation sinking in. "If it's a forgery, what does that mean for the exhibit?" Kamil asked, her voice barely above a whisper.

"It means we need to re-evaluate everything," Lila said firmly, her mind racing. "If we're dealing with a forgery, we have to inform Dr. Grant immediately."

Julian took a deep breath, trying to steady his thoughts. "Let's document everything we find. We need to gather evidence and prepare for what comes next."

As the team rallied around him, the

atmosphere shifted from one of excitement to urgency. They knew they were on the brink of uncovering a much larger issue than they had anticipated.

"Okay, everyone, let's get to work," Julian said, feeling the weight of the task ahead. "We need to conduct a thorough examination and get to the bottom of this."

With that, the team dove into action, the stakes higher than ever as they began to peel back the layers of the mystery surrounding the painting.

As Julian and his team delved deeper into their examination of the painting, the atmosphere in the room shifted from uncertainty to a focused determination. Each expert brought their unique skills to the table, and the weight of their collective knowledge felt palpable.

"Let's start with the texture analysis," Rose suggested, pulling out a magnifying glass. She began examining the brushstrokes, her brow furrowed in concentration. "The way the paint layers are applied here is inconsistent with van Gogh's technique. It's almost too smooth."

Timothy nodded, leaning over to get a closer look. "I agree. The impasto technique—where he applied thick layers of paint—is noticeably absent. This doesn't have the same depth."

Julian stood back, watching as the team worked. He had seen forgeries before, but the stakes felt particularly high with this piece. "I've worked on similar cases around the world, and I can assure you, the signs are clear. If anyone knows a forgery, it's me."

Lila, who had been quietly assessing the painting from a different angle, chimed in. "The colors are also off. Van Gogh was known for his vibrant yellows and blues, but these hues lack both vibrancy and the emotional resonance he typically achieved."

"Exactly," Julian said, stepping closer. "And look at the canvas itself. It doesn't have the same weave pattern as the originals we have in storage. This is a reproduction."

When the whispers of forgery reached his ears, Marco was excited to dive into the depths of the art world's underbelly. He quickly became an integral part of the team, using his local connections and digital skills to gather crucial information that would help expose the syndicate operating in the shadows.

Marco, who had been taking notes, looked up. "So we're all in agreement, then? This is definitely a forgery?"

Marco's involvement with Julian as his long-term friend and in his professional career, his assistant, adds to the tension. He's torn between loyalty to Julian and the allure of the forgery world, which adds complexity to their relationship that has been kindling over the years since their graduation from Yale University in 2018.

"Yes," Rose confirmed, her voice steady. "I believe we can all stand by that conclusion."

Julian felt a mix of relief and concern wash over him. "Then we need to inform Dr. Grant immediately. He needs to understand the gravity of this discovery before the exhibit opens."

Lila nodded. "I'll call him. We need to be ready to present our findings clearly and concisely. This could change everything for the exhibit."

Let's gather our notes and make sure we have all the evidence we need," Timothy added. "We should document every detail of our examination to support our claim."

Marco moved to the whiteboard, jotting down key findings as the group discussed their observations. "We should also prepare for questions. Dr. Grant will want to know how we reached this conclusion," he said, glancing at Julian for confirmation.

"Absolutely," Julian replied, feeling a sense of urgency. "We need to present a united front. This is our professional reputation on the line as well."

As Lila stepped out to call Dr. Grant, Julian felt the weight of responsibility settle back onto his shoulders. They were on the cusp of revealing a significant truth, and he knew they had to handle it with care.

Moments later, Lila returned, her expression serious. "Dr. Grant is on his way. We need to be ready."

The team gathered around the worktable, their collective focus sharp. Julian took a deep breath, preparing himself for the conversation that lay ahead. This was more than just a restoration project; it was a turning point that could reshape their understanding of art and authenticity.

As the door opened and Dr. Grant stepped into the room, Julian felt the tension rise. They were ready to present their findings, and the truth would soon be presented to the world – a major art piece determined a forgery.

The room was thick with tension as Dr. Samuel Grant entered, his expression a mix of curiosity and concern. The atmosphere shifted palpably; the excitement that had once filled the air was now replaced with apprehension. Julian stood at the forefront, ready to take charge.

"Thank you for coming on such short notice, Dr. Grant," Julian began, his voice steady despite the weight of the moment. "We have crucial findings regarding the painting you designated for the exhibit."

Dr. Grant nodded, his brow furrowed as he took in the scene. Lila, Rose, Timothy, Marco, and Kamil stood nearby, each exchanging nervous glances. "What have you discovered?" he asked, crossing his arms, a sign of both authority and unease.

"This painting is not an original van Gogh," Julian stated, his voice clear. "It's a forgery—a replica."

The room fell silent, the gravity of Julian's words settling like a dense fog. Dr. Grant's expression shifted from concern to disbelief, and he struggled to process the revelation. "A forgery?" he repeated, his voice barely above a whisper. "Are you certain?"

Lila stepped forward, her tone firm. "We've conducted a thorough analysis, Samuel. The brushwork, color quality, and canvas weave do not match van Gogh's originals. We're confident in our conclusion."

Rose added, "We've documented every aspect of our assessment, and we're prepared to present the evidence."

Dr. Grant inhaled sharply, glancing at each member of the team, his shock evident. "This is a disaster. The van Gogh exhibit is set to open in just a few weeks. What does this mean for the others?"

Kamil, who had been quiet until now, found her voice. "What will you do about the announcement of the exhibit? How do we explain this to the public?"

Dr. Grant ran a hand through his hair, clearly overwhelmed. "I have no idea. We need to assess the three other van Gogh pieces that arrived with this one. If they're forgeries too, we're in serious trouble." He paused, looking at Julian. "And we have one more piece coming from The British Museum in London. Once that painting arrives, we need an assessment of the painting's authenticity as well."

Julian nodded, feeling the weight of responsibility pressing down on him. "We need to act quickly. I suggest we conduct a thorough examination of the other pieces immediately. We can't risk another potential forgery being presented to the public."

Timothy interjected, "I can lead the analysis on the additional van Gogh paintings. We need to have a clear understanding before we make any announcements or decisions."

Dr. Grant's eyes narrowed as he considered the implications. "The museum's reputation is at stake. If we confirm more forgeries, we need to be prepared for the fallout. The art community and the public will demand answers."

Rose chimed in, "We must also prepare a statement for the press. Transparency will be key, but we should frame it as a commitment to authenticity and integrity in art restoration."

Lila nodded in agreement, her expression resolute. "We can't shy away from the truth. If this is a broader issue, we need to address it head-on."

As the discussion continued, Julian felt a sense of urgency wash over him. They were standing on the precipice of something monumental. The discovery of this forgery could send shockwaves through the art world, and he knew they had to handle it with care.

"Let's gather our findings and prepare for the next steps," Julian suggested. "We need a plan to verify the authenticity of the other pieces, and we should start drafting a statement for Dr. Grant to present."

Dr. Grant looked around the room, his expression shifting from shock to determination. "You're right. We need to move quickly. I'll coordinate with the museum's communications team to draft a statement and prepare for a press briefing."

With that, the team sprang into action. Julian felt a renewed sense of purpose as they began to document their findings and discuss the next steps. The weight of the discovery hung heavy in the air, but they were ready to face the challenge head-on.

As they worked, the reality of the situation began to settle in: they were about to expose a major art forgery, and the world would soon know the truth. The path ahead would be difficult, but together, they were determined to uphold the integrity of art restoration and ensure that authenticity prevailed.

The team moved with a sense of urgency, each member focusing on their assigned tasks. Julian felt the adrenaline coursing through him as he gathered the documentation of their findings. He knew that every detail mattered; the integrity of their work depended on it.

"Let's start with a timeline of our assessment," Julian suggested, stepping closer to the whiteboard. "We need to outline when we made our observations and the specific evidence that led us to conclude this is a forgery."

Lila took a seat beside him, reviewing the notes. "We should categorize the evidence by its significance. Highlight the differences in brushwork and color application compared to known van Gogh pieces. This will help us present a clear case."

Rose joined them, her laptop open and ready to compile the data. "I'll photograph the painting in detail, capturing the inconsistencies we've noted. Visual evidence will be crucial for our report."

Meanwhile, Timothy and Kamil set up a separate area for the additional van Gogh pieces. "We'll need a controlled environment for their analysis," Timothy instructed, carefully unpacking the artworks. "No distractions. We have to approach this fastidiously."

As the minutes turned into an hour, the sense of urgency only intensified. Dr. Grant returned from a brief meeting with the museum's communications team, his expression somber but determined. "They're drafting a statement, but we need to finalize our findings first. I want to ensure we're all aligned before we go public."

"Agreed," Julian said, glancing at the notes they had compiled. "We'll need to be prepared for questions, especially regarding the authenticity of the other pieces."

Kamil spoke up, her voice steady. "What if the press demands to see the forgery? How do we handle that?"

Dr. Grant sighed, contemplating the implications. "We'll need to balance transparency with caution. If we reveal the forgery, we have to be ready for the backlash. But we must also reassure the public about our commitment to authenticity."

Lila nodded in agreement. "We should emphasize our dedication to preserving art and that this discovery is part of our responsibility as restorers. It's an opportunity to educate the public about the complexities of art authentication."

Just then, Rose called out, "I've finished photographing the painting! The images show clear discrepancies in texture and color." She quickly pulled up the images on her laptop, projecting them onto the large screen in the room.

The team gathered around, studying the visuals closely. "Look at this comparison," Rose pointed to a side-by-side of the forgery and a known original. "The brushstrokes here are far too uniform. Van Gogh's technique was much more chaotic and expressive."

Julian felt a sense of resolution wash over him. "This is it. We have a solid case. Now we just need to prepare for what's next."

Dr. Grant nodded, his demeanor shifting to one of leadership. "Let's finalize our findings and get ready for the press announcement. We'll present a united front and make it clear that our priority is the integrity of art."

As the team continued to refine their statement, Julian's mind raced with thoughts of the implications. This was more than just about one painting; it was a pivotal moment for the museum, the art community, and the public's trust in authenticity.

"Once we've confirmed the authenticity of the other van Gogh pieces, we'll need to issue a follow-up statement," Timothy added. "We can't leave any stone unturned."

"Exactly," Julian said, feeling the weight of responsibility. "And let's ensure that we provide a clear path forward for the museum. We need to establish protocols for verifying future acquisitions to prevent this from happening again."

Kamil, who had been taking notes, looked up. "I think we should also include a message of gratitude for the support of the museum staff and the art community during this process."

As they finalized their statement, Julian felt a sense of purpose solidifying within him.

They were not just responding to a crisis; they were setting a standard for accountability and integrity in the art world.

With the press announcement looming, the team felt a mix of anxiety and determination. They knew that the world was about to learn of the forgery, and they were prepared to face the challenge head-on. Together, they would ensure that the truth was told, and that art, in all its forms, would be respected and preserved.

As the team settled into their rhythm, the reality of the situation began to crystallize. They needed to determine the authenticity of the three other van Gogh pieces that had arrived alongside the forgery. Julian called a meeting to address this pressing concern.

"Alright, everyone," he began, looking around the room at the faces of his colleagues, each reflecting a mix of anxiety and determination. "We need to prioritize the assessment of the other van Gogh paintings. We can't afford any surprises."

Lila nodded, her expression serious. "Which pieces are we dealing with?"

Julian glanced at the notes he had prepared. "We have 'Irises' c.1889, he paused to insert placeholders for the names of the paintings, Irises c.1889,' 'Red Vineyards at Arles, c.1888,' and 'The Church at Auvers-sur-Oise c.1890.' We need to examine each of them thoroughly to ensure they're authentic. 'House and Figure c.1890' is due to arrive soon. These are the five paintings slated for the Vincent van Gogh exhibit here at The Met.

"Let's divide and conquer," Timothy suggested. "If we work in pairs, we can speed up the process. Lila and I can take "Irises" while Julian, you partner with Rose on 'Red Vineyards at

Arles'. Kamil and Marco can handle 'The Church at Auvers-sur-Oise'. "Of course, when 'House and Figure' arrives later today, we can complete the review. Does anyone have any idea why this was shipped separately, and when is it due to arrive," Timothy asked.

"Sounds like a plan," Julian agreed. "The sooner we verify their authenticity, the better. We need to be prepared for any further inquiries from Dr. Grant or the press. It is my understanding that 'House and Figure' is due to arrive later this afternoon from London."

As the team organized their assignments, Lila's phone buzzed, interrupting the discussion. She glanced at it and frowned. "I just received a message from the communications team. They're drafting a press release that needs our input."

"Let's get to it," Julian said, feeling the pressure mount. "We need to clearly articulate what we've discovered and outline our next steps."

The team gathered around the whiteboard, brainstorming the key points for the press release. Julian took the lead, jotting down essential elements:

1. Confirmation of the forgery: Clearly state that the painting believed to be van Gogh's 'The Starry Night' has been determined to be a forgery.
2. Commitment to authenticity: Emphasize the museum's dedication to preserving the integrity of art.
3. Ongoing investigations: Mention that an immediate examination of the other van Gogh pieces is underway.
4. Future plans: Outline steps to ensure thorough vetting of new acquisitions.

After some back-and-forth, they crafted a statement that felt both transparent and reassuring.

"Okay, here's the draft," Julian read aloud to the team:

"Today, the museum confirms that the painting previously attributed to Vincent van Gogh, titled 'The Starry Night', has been determined to be a forgery. We take this matter very seriously and are committed to maintaining the highest standards of authenticity in all artworks within our collection. We are currently conducting thorough examinations of four additional van Gogh pieces, and we will keep the public informed as we proceed. Our dedication to art preservation remains unwavering."

"Let's add a note about our investigative team," Rose suggested. "We should mention that we'll be exploring the provenance of artworks across multiple cities in Europe."

"Good point," Julian agreed. "We can also highlight our collaboration with international experts."

Once they finalized the press release, Dr. Grant stepped in, ready to address the media. "We will hold a press conference tomorrow morning. I want everyone to be prepared for questions. The art community and the public will want to know how we're handling this situation."

As the team disbanded to prepare for the next day's press conference, the air was charged with anticipation. They knew the news would break soon, and the weight of its potential fallout loomed heavily over them. Each member felt the gravity of the moment, aware that their hard work and meticulous planning were about to be thrust into the spotlight. With a shared sense of purpose, they exchanged determined glances, silently acknowledging the challenges ahead. Before parting ways, Julian gathered everyone for a final huddle. "Let's regroup at 8 AM at the museum, tomorrow," he said, his voice steady. "We need to be ready for whatever comes our way." With that, they all left the workroom, each carrying the resolve to face the storm together.

In a quiet corner of the museum, away from the bustling crowds and the watchful eyes of colleagues, Timothy Johnson and Rose Cantor found refuge in a small, dimly lit storage room filled with crates and unmounted artworks. The air was thick with the scent of varnish and old wood, but to them, it felt like a sanctuary.

"Are you sure we won't get caught?" Rose whispered, glancing nervously at the door. Her heart raced, both from the thrill of their secret and the fear of discovery.

Timothy stepped closer, his blue eyes sparkling with mischief. "Let them gossip. I'd rather be here with you than worrying about what they think." He reached out, tucking a loose strand of hair behind her ear, his touch sending shivers down her spine.

Rose smiled, her anxiety melting away in the warmth of his gaze. "You always know how to make me feel better," she said softly, her heart swelling with affection.

"Good," Timothy replied, his voice low and sincere. "Because I don't want to hide this anymore." He took her hand, their fingers intertwining as he drew her closer. "I want everyone to know how much you mean to me."

With that, he leaned in, capturing her lips with his in a gentle but passionate kiss. Rose melted against him, feeling the world outside disappear. She kissed him back, the warmth of his body igniting a fire within her.

"I've wanted this for so long," she murmured against his lips, breathless. "But what if it complicates things at the museum? What if Lila finds out?"

Timothy sighed, his brow furrowing slightly. "I know it's risky, but I don't care. I can't pretend we're just colleagues anymore. You're too important to me."

Rose pulled back slightly, searching his face. "Are you sure? I don't want to jeopardize our jobs, especially not yours. You've worked so hard."

"I'd risk it all for you," he declared, his voice steady and resolute. "We'll figure it out together. I'm not letting you go."

With a renewed sense of determination, Rose leaned in again, capturing his lips with hers, pouring all her fears and hopes into that kiss. They lingered in their embrace, the outside world fading into oblivion. For that moment, nothing else mattered—only the love they shared in the shadows of the museum.

As they finally pulled apart, both breathless and flushed, Rose looked into Timothy's eyes. "Let's be careful. I can't lose you."

"Then we'll take it one day at a time," he replied, brushing his thumb across her cheek. "But I won't hide how I feel about you. Not anymore."

With a shared smile, they took a moment to collect themselves before stepping back into the world outside, their secret safe—for now, at least. The thrill of their hidden romance added a spark to their everyday lives, even as the complexities of their work loomed ahead.

6.

It's a Forgery!

As Marco stood in the living room, he felt the weight of the day pressing down on him. "I'm going to take a shower and head to the guest bedroom," he said, his voice barely masking his unease.

"Sounds good," Julian replied, offering a reassuring smile. "The bathroom is all yours. It's a suite, so you can take your time. Get some rest."

"Thanks, Julian," Marco said, forcing a smile as he made his way to the bathroom.

"I'll see you in the morning. I plan to be at the museum by 7 AM. Too early for you?" Julian teased lightly.

Marco managed a weak chuckle. "We'll see what happens when I wake in the morning. Have a good night."

As he stepped into the bathroom, Marco

turned on the shower, letting the warm water wash over him. He closed his eyes, trying to relax, but his mind was anything but calm. Images of the day's events flashed through his thoughts—the discovery of van Gogh forgery, the impending press release, and the weight of being part of the task force.

After a few moments, he turned off the water and dried himself off. He stood in front of the mirror, staring at his reflection, grappling with a growing sense of dread. Working on the task force felt exhilarating, but the reality of the situation was starting to sink in.

He was now entwined in something much larger and more dangerous than he had anticipated. The thought of being involved in a forgery ring without anyone's knowledge sent a chill down his spine. What if the forgers found out he was on their trail? Would he become a target?

He stepped out of the bathroom and into the guest bedroom, where he found a neatly made bed. The room felt refreshing and comfortable, a stark contrast to the chaos swirling in his mind. He sat on the edge of the bed, trying to gather his thoughts.

"I have to put this together," he murmured to himself, a sense of determination rising within him. He knew he had to figure out how to move forward, not just for himself, but for the entire team. They needed clarity, a path to follow in this tangled web of forgeries.

Pulling out his phone, he began to jot down notes. He listed the paintings that had been confirmed as forgeries, the connections he had made with the team, and the experts they had contacted.

Forged Paintings:
- The Starry Night, V. van Gogh, The Van Gogh Museum, Amsterdam
- House and Figure, V. van Gogh, The British Museum, London

Task Force Members:
- Julian Taylor, Art Historian and Restorer, NYC
- Marco Rossi, Asst. to Julian Taylor, Restorer and Historian, Florence
- Kamil Russo, Art Historian, Louvre, Paris
- Dr. Lila Thorne, MET Conservator, NYC
- Timothy, MET Asst. to Dr. Thorne, Restorer, NYC
- Rose Cantor, Johnson, MET Asst. to Dr. Thorne, Restorer, NYC
- Harper Thompson, Art Historian, NYC
- Isabella Rossi, Art Dealer, Venice
- Det. David Cortez, FBI, NYC
- Det. Claire Bertrand, Interpol, Lyon
- Alexander Murray, Art Historian, Vatican Museum
- Antoine DuBois, Auction House Director, Sotheby's Paris Auction House
- Jonathan Walters, Art Crime Specialist, Scotland Yard

Next Steps:
1. Analyze the provenance of the forged painting.
2. Connect with the experts for additional insights.
3. Investigate any links to the art market in New York and Europe.
4. Determine how to expose the forgery ring without compromising their safety.

As he wrote, Marco's heart raced. He needed to uncover the truth, but the stakes were higher than ever. The urgency of the situation pressed on him, and he felt the weight of his responsibility to the team.

After finishing his notes, Marco set his phone down and took a deep breath. He lay back on the bed, staring at the ceiling. The silence of the apartment felt heavy, filled with unspoken fears and uncertainties. He closed his eyes, trying to quiet the storm in his mind.

"Tomorrow," he whispered to himself. "Tomorrow, we'll figure this out."

With that thought, he finally allowed himself to drift off to sleep, hoping that clarity would come with the dawn.

Julian's alarm blared at 6 AM, startling him awake. He groaned, rubbing his eyes, realizing he had only managed six hours of sleep. But the urgency of the day ahead pulled him from his bed. He had asked the team to arrive by 7 AM, and he couldn't afford to be late.

After a quick shower and dressing, he hurried out the door, but as he reached the entrance, he paused. Marco hadn't emerged from the guest bedroom yet. "Let him sleep," Julian thought, remembering how exhausted Marco had looked the night before. He quickly scribbled a note: 'Hey Marco, sleep in if you need to. Come to the museum when you're ready. No need to rush!'

As he turned to leave, he noticed the weather outside. "Oh no, it's pouring," he muttered to himself, realizing he'd forgotten his umbrella. He quickly stepped back into the apartment, only to find Marco standing in the kitchen, completely nude, filling a glass with water.

"Wow, you freaked me out!" Marco exclaimed, turning to face Julian, surprise evident in his eyes.

"Sorry about that," Julian said, trying to

maintain composure despite the unexpected sight. "I came back for my umbrella. There are others in the closet if you want to grab one before you head out. It's pouring rain.

Marco chuckled awkwardly, his cheeks slightly flushed. "Right, I will need an umbrella. I guess I didn't expect to see you so soon."

Julian couldn't help but notice the way Marco's body glistened in the subdued lighting, the tension in the air palpable between them. "I hope I didn't wake you. You looked like you needed the sleep," he said, trying to keep the conversation light.

"Yeah, it's been a long couple of days," Marco admitted, leaning against the counter. "I was just trying to hydrate before I head out. You know, jet lag and all."

Julian nodded, feeling an undeniable chemistry lingering in the space between them. "Take your time. I'll see you at the museum. Just don't forget to take an umbrella," he laughed, his voice a mix of casualness and underlying warmth.

"Thanks, Julian," Marco replied, his gaze lingering for a moment longer than necessary. "I appreciate it. You know, for always being there."

Julian felt a flutter in his chest, remembering their long history together. They had known each other since they were eighteen at Columbia, navigating the ups and downs of life side by side. Now, at thirty-two, those years felt both distant and immediate, like a tapestry woven with shared experiences, laughter, and unspoken feelings.

As Marco turned back to the refrigerator, Julian felt a surge of affection mixed with desire. "Hey, Marco," he called softly, making Marco pause. "You know, if you ever want to talk about… well, anything, I'm here."

Marco glanced over his shoulder, a hint of vulnerability in his eyes. "I know. And I appreciate that more than you realize. Sometimes it's just hard to figure everything out."

"Life's complicated," Julian said, stepping closer, his heart racing. "But we've always got each other's backs, right?"

"Right," Marco replied, his voice steady, but there was something more in his gaze—a flicker of connection that had always simmered beneath the surface.

"Well, I'll let you get ready. I'll be at the museum," Julian said, forcing himself to step back, aware of the tension that hung in the air.

"See you soon," Marco replied, and as Julian turned to leave, he couldn't shake the feeling that something significant had shifted between them.

7.

Under Pressure

As Julian stepped out into the rain, umbrella in hand, he felt a mix of anticipation and uncertainty. The day ahead promised challenges, but the unspoken bond with Marco lingered in his mind, a thread connecting their past to an uncertain future.

The city was alive with the morning rush at 7 AM. Umbrellas lay scattered on the ground, mangled by the wind, while others flapped wildly as pedestrians navigated the sidewalks, trying to avoid collisions. Julian maneuvered through the chaos, grateful that his apartment was only a few blocks away. He had made a wise choice in location, especially on such a stormy morning.

At 9 AM sharp, the press conference began with Dr. Grant reading their carefully crafted statement:

"For Immediate Release: Today, the museum confirms that the painting previously attributed to Vincent van Gogh, titled 'The Starry Night', has been determined to be a forgery. We take this matter very seriously and are committed to maintaining the highest standards of authenticity in all artworks within our collection. We are currently conducting thorough examinations of four additional van Gogh pieces, and we will keep the public informed as we proceed. Our dedication to art preservation remains unwavering."

As Dr. Grant concluded, the room erupted with questions.

"How do you plan to handle the other van Gogh paintings?" a New York Times reporter asked, thrusting a microphone forward.

"We're conducting thorough assessments as we speak," Dr. Grant replied, maintaining composure. "We take this matter very seriously and will ensure that all pieces are authenticated."

"What does this mean for the exhibit?" another reporter pressed.

"We are currently reevaluating our plans," Dr. Grant said, his tone firm. "Our priority is the integrity of the artworks and their history."

After the conference, Julian, Lila, and the rest of the team gathered to discuss their next steps. The fallout from the announcement was already starting to ripple through the art community, and they knew they had to act quickly.

"Given the recent discovery, we need to think bigger," Julian proposed. "If there are forgeries here, it's likely they exist elsewhere. We should consider a broader investigation into suspected forgeries across Europe."

Timothy raised an eyebrow. "You mean to look into artworks that might be counterfeit? That could be a massive undertaking."

Julian nodded, feeling the weight of the task ahead.

"Who are you planning to include on your call list?" Lila asked, intrigued.

"I'll need to gather some data on artists with artwork on the scale of van Gogh, the locations of their masterpieces—what museums or private collections," Julian replied. "I'll compile a list of potential artwork that needs to be evaluated and the museums where they can be found. But I want to lead this entire investigation."

As they brainstormed, Julian felt a fire ignite within him. This was a chance to not only address the current crisis but to make a real impact on the art world. They would expose forgeries, protect authentic works, and uphold the legacy of artists who deserved recognition.

The team began discussing logistics, potential locations, and how to coordinate their efforts. They were stepping into a world fraught with uncertainty, but together, they were determined to uncover the truth—no matter the cost.

As the team gathered in the conference room, Julian had a sense of urgency come over him. The recent revelations about the forgery had opened up a broader conversation about the integrity of the art worldwide. He knew they had to think beyond just the immediate situation.

"Everyone, I've been considering our next steps," Julian began, pacing slightly as he gathered his thoughts. "Instead of just compiling a list of potential forgeries, I think we should establish a task force—a coalition of experts from various fields dedicated to combating art forgeries globally."

Lila leaned forward, intrigued. "What do you envision for this task force?"

"We need a diverse group of professionals," Julian explained. "Art historians, curators, restorers, auction house directors and art dealers, but with utmost urgency, we also need law enforcement. This includes special agents from the FBI, Interpol and even Scotland Yard."

Kamil raised an eyebrow. "That sounds ambitious. Where do you want to start?"

"Let's consider a central meeting point—perhaps Paris for Europe and here in New York for the U.S.," Julian suggested. "Both cities are hubs for the art community and have the resources we'll need. We can bring together experts to discuss strategies and develop a coordinated approach to identify and combat forgeries."

Timothy nodded, clearly onboard. "We'll need to outline the specific roles of each member. The art historians and restorers will be crucial; they have the trained eyes that can spot discrepancies in style and technique."

"Exactly," Julian said. "And we can enlist the help of auction house directors and art dealers to provide insight into market trends and potential counterfeit hotspots. They often see firsthand the pieces that raise suspicion."

"Not to mention the legal aspects," Lila added. "We'll need legal experts to navigate the complexities of art provenance and ownership, especially if we're looking at significant pieces."

Julian took a moment to collect his thoughts before continuing. "We'll also want to reach out to educational institutions—art schools and universities. They often have emerging talent who can assist with research and documentation."

"Do you have a list of potential members in mind?" Marco asked, ready to contribute.

"I can start compiling names," Julian replied. "But I'd like each of you to think of contacts you might have within your networks. If we can create a coalition that spans multiple countries, we'll have a much better chance of uncovering forgeries."

The discussion shifted to logistics, with Kamil suggesting, "We should draft invitations for our potential members, outlining the purpose of the task force and the importance of their involvement. We need to convey urgency and collaboration."

Rose chimed in, her enthusiasm evident. "We could also collaborate with law enforcement from various countries. Having agents from Scotland Yard, for instance, would give us a robust framework for investigating international cases."

"Let's also set an agenda for the initial meeting," Rose added. "We should discuss the current situation, share findings about the 'Starry Night' forgery, and outline our goals for the task force."

"Perfect," Julian said, feeling energized by the group's enthusiasm. "I want to emphasize the need for transparency and communication. This task force will need to operate as a cohesive unit, sharing information and strategies across borders."

As they continued to brainstorm, the excitement in the room grew. Julian could envision the task force—a coalition of passionate experts united by a common purpose. They would tackle the issue of forgeries head-on, preserving the integrity of artworks that deserved to be celebrated and protected.

"Let's aim for a preliminary task force meeting this month, as soon as feasibly possible," Julian suggested. "Time is of the essence to contact potential members and organize logistics. We can secure a venue in Paris and seek accommodations for New York right here in the MET. Let's start gathering materials for discussion."

Timothy smiled, his eyes sparkling with enthusiasm. "I can reach out to some of my contacts in the European art community. I know a few art historians who would be invaluable."

Rose looked up at him, her heart swelling with affection, "Oh, Timothy, I'd be thrilled to help! Let's compare our list of contacts—I bet we know some of the same people."

Timothy's smile widened, warmth radiating from him. "Of course, Rose, That sounds fantastic. Thank you!"

As they exchanged knowing glances, a few colleagues in the room raised their eyebrows, exchanging curious looks. It was clear that the chemistry between Timothy and Rose was more than just professional, and the subtle tension in the air hinted that their connection hadn't gone unnoticed.

"Great," Julian said, feeling a surge of optimism. "And I'll connect with law enforcement agencies to see who might be interested in joining our efforts."

As they wrapped up a long 4-hour, fast paced planning session, the sense of purpose was substantial. They were no longer just reacting to the immediate crisis; they were taking proactive steps to tackle a much larger issue.

"Together, we can make a difference," Julian said, his voice steady with conviction. "This is about more than just art; it's about preserving history and ensuring that future generations can appreciate authentic masterpieces."

With that, the team dispersed, each member energized and ready to take action. Julian felt a renewed sense of purpose as he prepared to reach out to potential collaborators. They were about to embark on a significant journey, one that would challenge them but also offer the chance to reshape the art world for the better.

8.

An Evening with Friends

The sun dipped below the horizon, casting a warm golden glow through the windows of Julian's apartment. After a long second day at the museum working solely on the discovery of the van Gogh forgery, Julian felt a sense of relief wash over him as he prepared to unwind. The day had been filled with meetings and strategic planning for the newly formed task force, and the air was thick with both urgency and camaraderie.

As he set the dining table, Julian glanced at the clock. It was nearly 7 PM, and he was looking forward to spending some quality time with his friends. He picked up his phone and texted Kamil: 'Hey, would you like to join Marco and me for dinner tonight?'

Moments later, his phone buzzed with a reply. 'Absolutely! What's on the menu?'

Julian smiled, knowing that Kamil's enthusiasm would add to the evening, 'Just pasta and salad with a good bottle of red wine. Hope you're hungry!'

He set the phone down and moved to the kitchen, where the aroma of simmering garlic and tomatoes filled the air. He had always enjoyed cooking, finding it a therapeutic way to unwind after long days. The soft clinking of dishes echoed as he prepared the meal, his mind wandering back to the events of the day.

Just then, there was a knock at the door. Julian quickly wiped his hands on a towel and opened it to find Kamil standing there, her face illuminated by a bright smile.

"Hey, you!" she exclaimed, stepping inside. "The savory aroma of garlic and herbs is intoxicating Julian! It smells amazing in here!"

"Thanks! I hope you're hungry," Julian replied, ushering her in. "Marco has prepared a delicious Italian meal, and he should be back any minute."

Kamil took a deep breath, savoring the pleasant scent. "I can't wait! It feels like ages since we've all had dinner together."

"Almost like old times," Marco chimed in as he entered, carrying a couple bottles of red wine. "I bought some wine to celebrate!"

"Perfect timing!" Julian said, taking the bottles from Marco. "Let's get this opened."

As they settled around the dining table, the atmosphere was warm and inviting. Julian poured wine into three glasses, the rich crimson liquid catching the light as he raised his glass in a toast. "To friendship and solving our crimes!" he declared with a playful grin.

Kamil and Marco echoed, clinking their glasses together before taking a sip. The conversation flowed easily, punctuated by laughter and the clinking of silverware against plates.

"So, Kamil, how's life in Paris treating you?" Marco asked, leaning back in his chair with a hint of nostalgia in his voice.

Kamil smiled, her eyes sparkling. "Oh, it's been wonderful! Paris is as enchanting as ever, but there's something even more exciting happening in my life."

Intrigued, Julian leaned forward, his curiosity piqued. "Oh? Do tell!"

With a playful grin, Kamil replied, "I've been seeing someone—his name is Luca Rinaldi. He works in the international art crime division of Interpol in Lyon." Her voice was filled with warmth as she spoke, clearly smitten.

"Luca Rinaldi?" Julian interjected, his interest sharpening. "Isn't he the international crime specialist? I've worked with him on other art crime cases."

Kamil nodded enthusiastically. "Yes! We met at an art symposium in Paris six months ago. We hit it off immediately. He's as charming as he is knowledgeable. It's getting pretty serious between us."

Marco leaned closer, intrigued. "What's he like?"

Kamil's smile widened. "He's got this calm demeanor that puts everyone at ease. His background in both law enforcement and art history gives him such a unique perspective. He truly understands the cultural significance of the artworks at stake, which I find incredibly attractive."

"Sounds like a great match," Marco said, raising his glass in a toast. "To love and art!"

"To love and art!" Julian echoed, clinking his glass against theirs. "So, do you see him often?"

Kamil's eyes sparkled as she continued. "We try to make it work despite the distance. He stays with me when he's in Paris, and if I have time, I go to Lyon to see him. By car, it takes close to 5 hours to drive from Paris to Lyon. It's almost 485 kilometers or 300 miles away, but sometimes it feels like an ocean apart."

Julian nodded thoughtfully. "I can imagine. Balancing work and a relationship in this field can be tricky."

"Absolutely," Kamil agreed, her expression turning a bit more serious. "But with Luca, it feels different. We share this passion for art, and he understands the stakes of our work. He's been incredibly supportive of my career."

"Have you talked about the future?" Marco asked, a hint of curiosity in his tone.

Kamil hesitated for a moment, her smile faltering slightly. "We have, but I don't want to rush things. I love what we have now, and I'm just enjoying every moment."

Julian leaned back, reflecting on their conversation. "It sounds like you've found someone special. Just be sure to keep your own ambitions in mind, too."

Kamil nodded, her expression softening. "I will. It's important to have that balance. But right now, I'm just grateful to have him in my life."

As they continued to share stories and laughter, the bond between them deepened, each moment infused with the vibrancy of their connections—both personal and professional. The warmth of friendship mingled with the thrill of budding romance, creating an atmosphere that felt alive with possibility.

"I've been working on a few exhibitions.

It's exhausting, but I love it. Every day feels like an adventure."

"I can imagine," Marco said, leaning forward, intrigued. "I've spent the last five years in Florence, and there's something breathtaking about it. Remember, I was raised in Venice. The history and creativity in the air in both cities abounds—it's truly magical."

"Florence is beautiful," Kamil agreed, her smile widening. "I've visited several times over the years, but what was it like actually living there?"

Marco's expression softened as he reflected on his time in Italy. "Living in Florence has been incredible. The culture, the people... I feel inspired every day. I even made some great friends there." He paused, a flicker of vulnerability crossing his face. "It was a time of self-discovery for me."

Kamil watched him, sensing the weight of his words. "It sounds like a remarkable experience, Marco. I wish I could have been there with you."

As they continued their meal, Kamil's demeanor shifted slightly, a hint of seriousness replacing her earlier lightheartedness. "But I have to tell you both something," she said finally, her voice steady but tinged with emotion. "I'm going back to Paris tomorrow evening. It's time for me to return home."

Julian and Marco exchanged glances, the warmth of the moment suddenly feeling bittersweet. "So soon?" Julian asked, trying to mask his disappointment.

Kamil nodded, her gaze unwavering. "Yes. I've got projects lined up and responsibilities waiting for me. It's hard to leave, especially after reconnecting with you both, but I need to embrace this next chapter."

Marco leaned forward, concern etched on his face. "Are you sure? You've just gotten here. We could use your help with the task force. It's a pleasure to have you with us at the museum too.

Kamil smiled softly. "I know, and I want to help. But I also need to take care of my life in Paris. You both understand, right?"

Julian sighed, a mixture of pride and sadness in his eyes. "Of course we do. Just promise you'll keep in touch. You're part of this journey, Kamil."

"Always," she replied, raising her glass again. "To friendship, no matter the distance. You can always contact me in Paris if you need my help with any exhibitions in Paris or anywhere in Europe. I would be proud to collaborate with you Julian, and you too Marco."

As their glasses clinked once more, the weight of the moment lingered in the air, a reminder of the bonds they had forged and the paths that lay ahead.

Julian caught the nuance in Marco's words but decided to keep the mood light. "And what about the food? I bet you have some great stories about that!"

"Oh, the food is heavenly!" Marco laughed. "I still dream about the fresh pasta and gelato. I've tried to recreate some of those dishes, but it's just not the same as a good Italian restaurant with their master chefs preparing scrumptious Italian cuisine."

As they continued to share stories and laughter, Julian sensed a shift in the atmosphere. Kamil's perceptive nature seemed to pick up on the subtle tension between Marco and Julian. She glanced between the two of them, a knowing smile playing on her lips.

"Julian, do you think all this forgery business will affect the art scene in New York?" Kamil asked, bringing their focus back to the pressing issue at hand.

Julian nodded, his expression turning serious. "It already is. With two confirmed forgeries, people are starting to question the integrity of the pieces we have. It's crucial that we act quickly to restore public confidence."

Marco chimed in, "And we need to ensure that no other pieces are circulating that could put the museum's reputation at risk."

As they finished their meal, Kamil glanced at her watch. "Wow, time flies! I should probably head back to my hotel soon."

"Are you sure?" Julian asked, a hint of disappointment in his voice. "We were just getting into the good stuff."

Kamil smiled warmly, "I'd love to stay longer, but I have an early morning meeting. I must keep focus on my job at the same time working with you guys on the Task Force. Compliments to the chef! The meal was heavenly. Let's not let it be too long until the next dinner."

"Definitely," Marco agreed, his eyes lingering on Kamil. "It's always a pleasure to have you around."

As Kamil stood to gather her things, Julian felt a sense of camaraderie wash over him. "Thanks for joining us tonight, Kamil. It was great to catch up."

"Thanks for having me, Julian. And Marco, it was wonderful to hear your stories," she said, giving Marco a playful nudge. "You two take care of each other, alright?" "See you tomorrow, bright and early," all three said in unison as Kamil stepped out the door.

After Kamil left, the atmosphere shifted

again. The door clicked shut, leaving Julian and Marco alone in the apartment.

"Did you notice how Kamil seemed to sense something between us?" Marco asked, breaking the silence.

Julian leaned against the counter, arms crossed. "Yeah, I felt that too. It's hard to hide anything from someone who knows us both so well."

Marco ran a hand through his hair, looking thoughtful. "Do you think… do you think we've crossed a line from just friendship to something more?"

Julian took a moment to consider. "I've been feeling that way too. There's definitely a deeper connection between us, but what does that mean, especially with everything going on?"

"It complicates things," Marco admitted, his expression earnest. "But I can't deny that I care about you, Julian. A lot."

Julian felt warmth spread through him. "I care about you too, Marco. We've been through so much together—maybe it's time we acknowledged that."

As they stood in the quiet apartment, the air was thick with unspoken feelings and possibilities, both men aware that the road ahead would require honesty, vulnerability, and the courage to embrace whatever came next.

9.

Authentic or Not?

The large conference room at the Metropolitan Museum of Art is an impressive space, featuring high ceilings adorned with intricate moldings and large windows that flood the room with natural light, illuminating the polished wooden table at its center. Elegant chairs surround the table, each upholstered in rich fabric, inviting collaborative discussions. On the walls, framed art pieces and photographs of past exhibitions serve as a reminder of the museum's storied history and its commitment to the arts. A state-of-the-art projector hangs from the ceiling, ready to display presentations, while a sleek whiteboard stands ready for brainstorming sessions. The atmosphere is charged with anticipation, reflecting the importance of the meeting to address the pressing issues surrounding the ongoing investigation into art forgeries.

The atmosphere in the conference room was charged with urgency as the team gathered around the large oak table. Papers and laptops cluttered the surface, each member keenly aware of the gravity of the situation. Julian stood at the head, his expression serious.

"Let's get back to it," Julian said, glancing down at his notes. "'House and Figure' is scheduled to arrive later today, so we will be able to wrap up our review on the four van Gogh pieces and determine if they are authentic."

Dr. Lila Thorne leaned forward, her brow creased in thought. "The first four paintings came from The Van Gogh Museum in Amsterdam, but 'House and Figure' was shipped from the British Museum in London," she paused, glancing around the room for comments.

"Who will be the scribe here?" Timothy asked, nodding as he scribbled notes. "I can take the minutes from this meeting, unless someone else prefers to do so," Timothy offered.

"Great, thank you, Timothy," Julian replied. "Now, the first order of business: our restoration team needs to analyze the remaining van Gogh paintings for authenticity."

Lila spoke up, her determination evident, "I'll handle the analysis myself, but I'd like Timothy, Rose, Kamil, and Marco to assist me so we can go through the additional paintings quickly today. Julian, you're welcome to join us, but I understand if you're too busy forming the task force."

Julian glanced at Kamil and nodded, signaling for everyone's attention. "I have a short message to announce to the team. Kamil will be going back to Paris this evening. She has her obligations there and needs to return to her life in that fabulous city."

Kamil looked around at her friends, a bittersweet smile on her face. "I've enjoyed myself here so much," she said, her voice warm yet tinged with nostalgia. "But like Julian said, I must get back to Paris and my work there."

Julian hesitated, weighing his responsibilities. "I'll assist where I can. Please call me to the restoration workroom for your final results prior to letting any information leak out. Let's make sure we get this right."

"Alright then," Lila said, her enthusiasm contagious. "Let's head to the workroom. We have three paintings to review. And, Julian, I will still assist making calls to invite people to our forgery task force." Julian, somewhat agitated, said "Ok, but your task at hand is more important at the moment."

As the group of expert art aficionados moved to the workroom, the atmosphere shifted from tension to focus. The five gathered around a large table, where the three van Gogh paintings awaited their scrutiny.

"Alright, let's break into pairs," Lila suggested. "Marco and Kamil, you take the first painting, van Gogh's vibrant landscape, 'Red Vineyards at Arles' was laid out in front of them. Timothy and I will handle the other landscape, 'The Church at Auvers-dur-Oise.' And, Rose, you can assist me. We'll rotate through the pieces, and handle his painting 'Irises' last.

"Sounds good," Marco said, leaning closer to van Gogh's masterpiece "Red Vineyards at Arles, "Let's see what we can find."

Kamil nodded, her eyes scanning the brush strokes. "I can already tell the texture is consistent with van Gogh's technique. Look at the way the paint is layered."

As they worked, Marco pointed out details, "See how the light plays off the colors? That's classic van Gogh. I'd be surprised if this one is a forgery."

Meanwhile, Lila, Timothy and Rose examined the other landscape, 'The Church at Auvers-dur-Oise' painted in 1890, their conversation punctuated by observations.

"Timothy, look at the signature," Lila said, her finger tracing the edge of the painting. "It matches the style and placement of van Gogh's other works."

Timothy leaned in closer, nodding. "And the palette—he often used these hues of blue and yellow together. I think we're in the clear."

After a thorough examination, the team shifted to the third painting, a magnificent creation painted in 1889, so aptly entitled 'Irises'.

"Let's be methodical," Rose suggested, taking notes as they began their analysis. "We should check the provenance and any previous restoration work documented."

Kamil chimed in, "I've seen this portrait in other exhibitions. The brushwork here is too precise to be a fake. Vincent van Gogh had a distinct way of blending colors that's evident."

As they compared notes, Lila's confidence grew. "All signs point to authenticity. We should document everything we've found to support our conclusions."

After an intense two hours of scrutiny, they gathered their findings.

"Okay, team," Lila announced, a smile breaking across her face. "It seems we can confidently say all three paintings are authentic. No forgeries here!"

Marco let out a breath he didn't realize

he was holding. "That's a relief. I was starting to feel the pressure."

Timothy nodded, his expression lighter. "Let's prepare our report and present it to Julian. This is a significant win for the team."

As they wrapped up, Julian entered the room, curiosity etched on his face. "How did it go?"

"Great news!" Lila exclaimed, her excitement palpable. "All three paintings are authentic. We've found no signs of forgery."

Julian felt a wave of relief wash over him. "That's excellent. Let's document our findings and keep the momentum going as we prepare for the 'House and Figure' painting's arrival later this afternoon from London."

10.

The Heist of a Masterpiece

The theft of Vincent van Gogh's 'House and Figure' from the British Museum was yet another audacious operation orchestrated by Victor Salvatore and his meticulously chosen team of thieves and forgers. This iconic piece, celebrated for its artistic significance, was set to join four other van Gogh paintings already delivered to The Metropolitan Museum of Art for a high-profile exhibition. The stakes were high, but for Victor, the thrill of the heist was more than just a financial gain; it was a twisted love affair with art itself.

Victor stood in front of the painting in his dimly lit underground fortress, a sly smile creeping across his face. "This masterpiece will be mine," he murmured, stroking the edge of the canvas with a reverence that bordered on obsession. "An original, stolen, and replaced with a perfect forgery. The world will never know, and I will possess beauty that is denied to so many." His passion for art was a sickness, a compulsion that drove him to outwit the very systems meant to protect it.

Clara Jensen, a key member of Victor's team, had leveraged her expertise to analyze the security protocols of the British Museum. She had discovered a gap in their alarm system during a scheduled maintenance window, a crucial detail that would dictate the timing of their operation. "This is it, Victor," Clara had said, her eyes gleaming with excitement. "We strike when the alarms are down. It's the perfect opportunity."

Martin Falcone, the team's master forger, had worked tirelessly on a flawless replica of 'House and Figure.' His meticulous craftsmanship ensured that the forgery captured the original's essence, down to the most intricate brush strokes. "I've aged it perfectly," Martin said one evening, applying the final touches. "It'll fool even the most seasoned experts. Van Gogh would be proud, in a twisted way."

On the day of the heist, Victor's team executed their plan with the precision of a well-rehearsed symphony. Outside the museum, Conrad orchestrated a diversion—a staged protest involving passionate art students advocating for increased funding for the arts. The rallying cries of "Save Our Art!" echoed through the streets, drawing a crowd and diverting the attention of security personnel.

"Remember, keep it chaotic but peaceful," Victor reminded Conrad as they watched the scene unfold from a distance. "We need their focus elsewhere."

With museum staff distracted by the

chaos outside, Victor and Anton swiftly navigated the labyrinthine corridors of the British Museum. The air inside was thick with anticipation and tension. "There's no turning back now," Victor whispered, adrenaline coursing through his veins.

They located 'House and Figure' in a secure storage area, its vibrant colors and emotional depth calling to Victor like a siren. "It's beautiful," Anton said, almost reverently. "Are you sure about this?"

"Absolutely," Victor replied, his voice low but firm. "This piece deserves to be appreciated, not locked away in a museum. We'll set it free."

In a matter of moments, they replaced the original with Martin's expertly crafted forgery, carefully securing the authentic piece in a transport crate meant for a traveling exhibition. As Victor sealed the crate, a thrill surged through him. "Another van Gogh for my collection," he declared, his voice a mix of triumph and madness.

Outside, the protest grew louder, art students chanting fervently, oblivious to the crimes being committed just within the walls of the museum. Victor relished the chaos; it was a perfect cover for their audacious act. "Let them fight for their art," he thought. "Meanwhile, I will possess it."

As they executed the final steps of their plan, Anton coordinated the logistics, ensuring the transport of the original was whisked away for safe storage in one of Victor's secluded hiding places. The team moved with a practiced efficiency, each member playing their role to perfection. Meanwhile, the replica was put back in its place, making it seem as if it had never been disturbed.

Evelyn Sinclair, the curator at the British

Museum, would later swear she had signed off on the authenticity of 'House and Figure' when it left her possession. This assertion became a focal point of investigation, as the task force began to piece together the timeline of events surrounding both thefts. The connections between the two high-profile paintings raised suspicions about a coordinated effort, leading to deeper inquiries into Victor's syndicate.

Victor's actions were not merely driven by greed; they were rooted in a complex web of passion, ambition, and a desire to outsmart a system he believed was fundamentally flawed. Each successful heist was intoxicating, reinforcing his belief that he was reclaiming art for the people, even as he operated from the shadows. "Art is meant to be experienced, not hoarded," he would tell himself, justifying his actions, his mind spiraling deeper into rationalizations.

As the task force began their investigations, the pieces of the puzzle slowly came together. They recognized that Victor was not just a common thief; he was an artist in his own right, manipulating the art world to fulfill his twisted vision. With each stroke of his brush—a brush that had once painted forgeries—he was both creator and destroyer.

The tension mounted as law enforcement delved deeper into Victor's world. They understood the complexity of his operation, the audacity of his actions, and the danger that loomed with each passing moment. Victor Salvatore remained one step ahead, confident that his team could navigate the treacherous waters of the art world, while continuing their pursuit of beauty and deception.

11.

Gathering Forces

Meanwhile, in New York City, the team exchanged satisfied glances, the tension of the earlier meeting fading as they celebrated their collective success. They knew the road ahead was still fraught with challenges, but for now, they had uncovered a small victory in the tangled web of the art world.

"Alright, let's keep moving. We need to prepare for the upcoming discovery. As I mentioned, we should immediately begin assembling a task force to tackle suspected forgeries. We need to move quickly now that the press release has been published." Julian said, trying to shake the tension that had formed in his chest. He glanced at Marco, who was casually scrolling through his phone. Julian was starting to feel worrisome doubts about Marco's loyalty, which left him feeling conflicted. He needed to trust his team, as the stakes felt higher than ever.

"First, I'll reach out to Harper Thompson from New York. We go way back to Columbia, and her insights into 19th Century art will be crucial."

"Is she available?" Marco asked, a hint of skepticism in his voice.

"I'll contact her," Julian replied, the weight of Marco's gaze heavy on him. He pushed his doubts aside. "Next up is Isabella Rossi from Venice. We've developed a strong friendship through our shared passion for Renaissance art. Her connections could lead us to significant information."

"And for law enforcement?" Timothy pressed.

"David Cortez from the FBI and Claire Bertrand from Interpol," Julian said, feeling the pressure mount. "David and I have a solid relationship from previous investigations, and I met Claire at an international art conference. They'll provide vital support as we navigate this complex case. And last, but not least, I will reach out to my acquaintance Jonathan Walters, an art crime specialist at Scotland Yard."

"Good," Timothy said, jotting down names. "But remember, we need to contact them separately. Repeating the story will take time."

Julian sighed, knowing the challenges ahead. "I want to invite them to participate on our Task Force. These are the experts that I personally know and trust. I have worked with them on several art crime cases:

Harper Thompson, Art Historian, NYC

Isabella Rossi, Art Dealer, Venice

Agent David Cortez, FBI, NYC

Det. Claire Bertrand, Interpol, Lyon, France

Antoine DuBois, Art House Director, Sotheby's Paris Auction House

Alexander Murray, Art Historian, Specializing in Renaissance Art,
Vatican Museum

Jonathan Walters, Art Crime Specialist, Scotland Yard."

"I can handle these calls and provide my notes from the conversations," Julian offered. "Again, I cannot emphasize the urgency of this matter."

"Thank you Lila. You and the team can take the remainder of the list of names and makes those calls. Please divide the list according to personally knowing the individual and their expertise. Personal contact is critical for these calls. Of course, if you have anyone that we should also include, please let me know.

As the team began discussing strategies, Julian's mind raced, filled with lingering doubts about Marco. Could he trust him fully? The tension between them was palpable, and the internal conflict was becoming increasingly difficult to ignore.

"Let's make this happen, team," Lila urged, her enthusiasm infectious. "We will uncover the truth behind this forgery scheme."

Julian nodded, but as he looked at Marco, uncertainty loomed over him. The investigation was a delicate dance of trust and suspicion, and he knew that every member's unique background and expertise would be essential in peeling back the layers of deception in the art world.

12.

The Outreach

Julian gathered his papers and proceeded out the door to make the calls from his private office. Julian decided that Dr. Anneke Vermeer at The Van Gogh Museum should be notified first, as word will spread fast with the press release looming.

Julian sat at his desk, the urgency of the situation weighing heavily on him. He picked up the phone and dialed Dr. Anneke Vermeer, the Chief Curator at The Van Gogh Museum in Amsterdam. The line rang a few times before she answered.

"Van Gogh Museum, Dr. Anneke Vermeer speaking."

"Dr. Vermeer, it's Julian Taylor from The Met in New York. I hope you're well," he said, attempting to keep his tone professional despite the gravity of the situation.

"Julian! Yes, I'm well, thank you. What can I do for you?" she replied, her voice warm but curious.

"We need to discuss a serious matter concerning the van Gogh exhibition shipment we received yesterday of four van Gogh paintings. I am sorry to tell you, but our expert team here confirmed 'The Starry Night' is a forgery," Julian stated, his heart racing as he prepared to dive into the details.

There was a brief pause on the other end. "A forgery? That's incredibly concerning. What do you know about it?"

Julian took a deep breath. "The paintings were in an accident outside of our loading dock here at the museum. The delivery van was involved in an accident with a pedestrian. No one was seriously injured. At first, we were distraught because 'The Starry Night' was damaged with a gash across the skyline of the painting. We thought that was our main concern and our restoration team and myself reviewed the damage to determine how to restore the gash. That is when we discovered something even more distressful. We discovered many inconsistencies in he brushstrokes and the blue and yellow hues used in the sky did not match van Gogh's brilliant colors making it obvious to anyone familiar with van Gogh's work that it was not the original and authentic painting. It doesn't match the original piece at all."

"Given your position, I'm surprised it could leave your museum without proper scrutiny." Julian's voice was firm but respectful.

"Julian, I can assure you that we have rigorous protocols in place for all outgoing pieces," Anneke responded, her tone defensive.

"Each artwork is meticulously documented, and the details are cross-verified before they leave. I will need to look into this matter thoroughly."

"I understand. But how could a significant detail like that slip through? Anyone with a basic understanding of art could see that discrepancy," Julian pressed, feeling a mix of frustration and concern.

"Art forgery is a complex issue, and even the most experienced professionals can sometimes be fooled," she said, her voice steadying. "I will investigate how this happened. But let's not overlook the fact that this forgery could be part of a larger scheme."

Julian nodded, though she couldn't see him. "Exactly. That's why I'm reaching out. We've formed a task force to address this situation, and I believe your expertise is crucial. We need to coordinate our efforts to ensure no other forgeries are circulating."

"Of course, I'd be happy to join the task force," Anneke replied, her demeanor shifting to one of cooperation. "I have extensive records on all van Gogh pieces that have left our museum recently. We can compare notes."

"Great. I think it would be beneficial to start by reviewing all van Gogh artworks sent out over the last few years," Julian suggested. "We need to identify any patterns or discrepancies."

"Absolutely. I'll pull all relevant documentation, including shipping logs and authentication papers, for the pieces sent to your museum and others," Anneke confirmed. "I'll also contact the other institutions that have received shipments from us."

"Thank you, Anneke. I appreciate your willingness to collaborate on this," Julian said, feeling a sense of relief. "It's critical that we tackle this head-on. The integrity of our institutions is at stake."

"Julian, I share your concern. I will ensure that we approach this with the seriousness it deserves," she replied, her passion for the art evident in her tone. "Van Gogh's work represents so much cultural heritage. We cannot let forgeries undermine that."

Julian felt a sense of solidarity building between them. "Let's coordinate a meeting for the task force as soon as we can. I'll keep you updated on our findings and any developments on our end."

"Please do. I'll make this a priority," Anneke said, her voice firm. "Together, we can work to resolve this issue and restore confidence in our institutions. Thank goodness the other three paintings are safe and are the original paintings."

As they wrapped up the call, Julian felt a renewed sense of determination.
With Anneke's expertise and commitment, he was confident they could uncover the truth behind the forgeries and protect the integrity of van Gogh's legacy.

He took a deep breath and picked up his phone, dialing Harper Thompson's number. As the phone rang, he mentally prepared himself for the conversation ahead.

Julian and Harper have known each other since their time at Columbia. They share a mutual admiration for their work and often collaborate on exhibitions at the Metropolitan Museum of Art.

Harper serves as a link to the New York art scene from London and can provide insights into the forgery's implications within the massive world of art. Her involvement adds depth to the investigation.

The phone rings, then connects:

"Hello?" Harper's warm voice came through the line.

"Harper! It's Julian. How have you been?" Julian started, trying to keep the tone light.

"Julian! It's great to hear from you. I've been well, busy with a few projects at the museum. What's going on?" Harper replied, curiosity evident in her tone.

"I wish I were calling with better news," Julian said, his voice turning serious. "I'm reaching out because our team has encountered a potential forgery case involving several van Gogh paintings. The implications could be extensive, and I believe we need to investigate further across Europe and the U.S."

"Forgery? That's alarming. What do you have so far?" Harper asked, her professional tone shifting to concern.

Julian leaned forward, gathering his thoughts. "We recently discovered a painting damaged in transit to The Met turned out to be a forgery, which led us to believe that there may be others. We've examined three additional pieces, and thankfully, they're authentic. However, van Gogh's 'House and Figure' is still on its way from The British Museum in London, and I'm worried it might not be what it seems."

"Have you traced the provenance of these works?" Harper inquired.

"Yes, we've been tracking the shipments. The first four paintings came from The Van Gogh Museum in Amsterdam sent by their Chief Curator, Dr. Anneke Vermeer, but 'House and Figure' was shipped from the British Museum in London sent by curator, Evelyn Sinclair. It's a tangled web, and I think we need more eyes on it.

That's why I'm reaching out to trusted experts like you."

Harper paused, digesting the information. "I'd be happy to assist. What do you need from me?"

"I'd like your insights on the market trends and any recent forgeries you've encountered. Your experience will be invaluable in understanding the broader implications of this case," Julian explained.

"Of course! I can start pulling together recent case studies and any known forgers that might be operating. I'll also reach out to some contacts in Europe to see if they've noticed anything unusual," Harper offered, her enthusiasm evident even over the phone.

"Thank you, Harper. I knew I could count on you. We need to coordinate a strategy to track down any potential forgeries before they spread further," Julian said, feeling a sense of relief.

"Absolutely. I'll make this a priority. When do you want to regroup?" Harper asked.

"Let's touch base in a few days. I'll be calling other experts on my list, and I want to compile our findings together. If we can align our efforts, we might stand a better chance of uncovering the entire operation," Julian suggested.

"Sounds like a plan. Keep me updated on your end, and I'll do the same. We'll get to the bottom of this," Harper replied confidently.

"Thanks, Harper. I appreciate your help. Talk soon!" Julian ended the call, feeling a renewed sense of purpose.

At Harper Thompson's last visit to the Metropolitan Museum of Art in New York City, she examined the striking van Gogh masterpiece, 'Vincent's Chair' c.1888, her fingers gently brushing the frame. An accomplished art historian with a focus on American art, Harper was known for her innovative exhibitions and ability to connect modern audiences with historical pieces. With her vibrant personality and sharp wit, she was a beloved figure in the New York and London art scene.

When Julian Taylor reached out to Harper for her expertise, she was intrigued by the mystery of the forgery scheme that had begun to unfold. Recognizing the potential impact on the art community, Harper eagerly joined forces with Julian and the Task Force. Her knowledge of American art and contemporary practices would offer a fresh perspective as they worked to expose the deception threatening the integrity of museums worldwide.

Julian finished documenting his call with Harper, and next on his list is Isabella Rossi. He knew that each expert he reached out to would bring unique insights, and every conversation would help piece together the puzzle of the art forgery scheme.

Isabella and Julian met during an art symposium in Europe. Their shared passion for Renaissance art led to a strong professional friendship, and they often consult each other on significant artworks. Julian dialed Isabella's number.

The phone rings, then connects:

"Pronto?" Isabella's vibrant voice came through the line, full of energy.

"Isabella! It's Julian," he said, a smile creeping onto his face at the sound of her familiar voice. "How have you been?"

"Julian! Always a pleasure. I'm well, just wrapped up a hectic exhibition in Venice. What's on your mind?" she replied, her tone shifting to curiosity.

"I'm reaching out because we've encountered a forgery case involving van Gogh's 'The Starry Night' painting," Julian said, his voice taking on a serious tone. "We're concerned that there may be more forgeries circulating, especially given the art market's current climate."

Isabella's interest piqued, "Forgery of van Gogh's work? That's alarming. What do you have so far?" Isabella's knowledge of the European art market will be crucial as they investigate the forgery. Her connections in Venice may also provide leads on art forgery and theft crime teams.

"We discovered the forgery of a van Gogh painting that was involved in a van delivery accident outside the museum's loading area. It was delivered to The Met with three other van Gogh paintings, and we've examined three others that turned out to be authentic, thankfully. However, the van Gogh painting 'House and Figure' is still en route from London, and I fear it might not be what it seems," Julian explained, feeling the weight of the situation more acutely.

"Given the reputation of van Gogh and especially 'The Starry Night' with an estimated worth of over $450 million, this definitely has significant implications. Have you traced the provenance of the pieces?" Isabella asked, her analytical mind already at work.

"That's the next step. The first four paintings came from The Van Gogh Museum in Amsterdam, but 'House and Figure" was shipped from the British Museum in London," Julian replied. "I'm worried there might be a network of forgers operating across Europe."

Isabella paused, her voice steady. "I've heard whispers of some suspicious dealings in

Venice lately. There have been rumors of forgeries being sold as originals, particularly among lesser-known dealers. I can tap into my contacts and see if anything emerges."

"That would be incredibly helpful," Julian said, a sense of relief washing over him. "Your connections in Venice could provide critical leads. If anyone can sniff out the truth, it's you."

"Leave it to me. I'll start reaching out to my sources and see if there's been any chatter about new forgeries or any art pieces that seem off," Isabella assured him, her determination solid. "We need to stay ahead of this before it spirals out of control."

"Absolutely. Let's stay in close contact. I'll be calling other experts as well, and I think it would be beneficial for us to compile our findings together," Julian suggested, feeling a renewed sense of purpose.

"Agreed. I'll have my notes ready, and we can strategize on our next steps. We can't let these forgers undermine the integrity of the art world," Isabella replied, her passion evident.

"Thank you, Isabella. I really appreciate your help. Let's touch base in a few days, and I'll keep you updated on our end and the timing for the Task Force group meeting here in Manhattan," Julian said, feeling a surge of confidence in their collaboration.

"Anytime, Julian. I'm always here to help. Talk soon!" Isabella concluded, her voice warm as they wrapped up the call.

As Julian hung up, he felt a sense of fellowship and support—the connections he had forged over the years were proving invaluable in the fight against art crime.

Julian stepped out briefly to the

restroom, and returned immediately with a bottle of water ready to place his next call to his friend, FBI Agent, David Cortez.

Julian met David during a previous investigation into art theft, establishing a professional relationship that has grown into a friendship. David will play a critical role in the investigation, providing FBI expert law enforcement support as Julian and his team navigate the complexities of the forgery case.

In the dimly lit New York offices of the FBI, Agent David Cortez reviewed evidence collected from a recent art heist. With a sharp suit and an air of authority, David had earned a reputation as a relentless investigator in the world of art crimes. He was known for his keen instincts and unwavering dedication to justice; qualities that had propelled him through the ranks of law enforcement.

David's path crossed with Kamil's during a high-profile investigation into a series of art forgeries that had shaken the art community as recent as two years ago. He admired Kamil's expertise and passion, often relying on her insights to navigate the complex web of art dealings. Their professional relationship grew into a partnership, each motivated by a desire to expose the truth and protect the integrity of the art world.

Phone rings, then connects:

"Cortez here," David answered, his tone steady and professional.

"David, it's Julian Taylor from The Met," Julian said, feeling the familiar weight of urgency in his voice. "I hope you're doing well."

"Julian! Good to hear from you. What's the situation?" David replied, his interests peaked.

"I'm reaching out because we've uncovered a forgery case involving van Gogh's

'Starry Night' painting. We're concerned that there might be a network of forgers operating across both the U.S. and Europe," Julian explained, his mind racing with the implications.

David's tone shifted to serious. "Forgery is no small matter, especially with van Gogh's work. It's critical we gather all relevant information."

"We discovered the forgery while examining a van Gogh painting that was damaged in a delivery van accident outside of our loading dock entrance. Thankfully, we've examined the other three van Gogh paintings and they were determined to be authentic. However, van Gogh's 'House and Figure' is still on its way from London, and I'm worried it could be compromised," Julian said, the tension palpable in his voice.

"Do you know who has the police report for the delivery van accident?" Agent Cortez inquired.

Julian answered swiftly, "Yes, two officers came to the scene and filed an accident report because a woman was struck by the van as she crossed directly in front of it. There was some back-and-forth between the van driver and the injured woman. Thankfully, she's okay, but both the driver and pedestrian were understandably shaken. The officers were Sgt. John Pierce and Sgt. Erin Michaels."

Julian continued, "They took the report, spoke with the van driver and the injured woman, and briefly spoke to me as well. They also checked inside the van to ensure everything was in order before it was unloaded at the museum. I haven't requested the police report yet, but I can follow up on that."

David nodded on the other end. "Great, I can easily obtain the report as soon as we are finished. I will get you a copy and send it over. It could provide vital information for our investigation."

"Have you traced the provenance of the pieces?" David asked, his investigative instincts kicking in.

"Yes, the first four paintings came from The Van Gogh Museum in Amsterdam, while 'House and Figure' was shipped from the British Museum in London. We're currently trying to piece together how this forgery happened," Julian explained, feeling the weight of the investigation on his shoulders.

"Sounds like you're dealing with a complex web here. I'll check our recent cases to see if there have been any similar forgeries reported," David replied, his voice firm. "We've been tracking some suspicious art sales in the city that might connect."

"Exactly what I was hoping for," Julian said, feeling a sense of mutual support. "Your insights will be invaluable. If we can share information, we might be able to identify any potential leads."

"Absolutely. I'll dig through our files and get back to you. If there's a network involved, we need to act quickly before more pieces slip through the cracks," David assured him.

"Thanks, David. I appreciate your support," Julian said, a wave of gratitude washing over him. "It's good to have someone like you on our side."

"No problem. Just make sure to keep me in the loop. If I find anything that could help, I'll reach out immediately," David replied, his tone resolute.

"Will do. Let's touch base again in a few days once we've gathered more information," Julian suggested, feeling a renewed sense of determination.

"Sounds like a plan. Stay safe out there, Julian," David said, his voice warm as they wrapped up the call.

"Thanks, David. Talk soon!" Julian concluded, hanging up with a sense of purpose.

As he sat back in his chair, he felt reassured that with the support of trusted colleagues like David, they could tackle the daunting challenge of uncovering the truth behind the forgeries.

David admired Julian's passion for art and was determined to support him in protecting the integrity of the masterpieces they both cherished. With Julian's expertise in art history and David's investigative skills, they set out to uncover the truth behind the forgeries.

Julian picked up his phone again, and this time dials Claire Bertrand at Interpol in Lyon, France.

Phone rings, then connects

"Claire Bertrand," she answered, her voice crisp and professional, a hint of warmth underlying her tone.

"Claire, it's Julian Taylor from The Met in New York. I hope you're doing well," Julian said, feeling a mix of urgency and mutual support.

"Julian! It's always a pleasure. What's going on? You sound serious," Claire replied, her tone shifting to one of concern.

"I need your expertise on a potential forgery case involving van Gogh's painting 'The Starry Night'. We've hit a critical point, and I fear we may be dealing with a larger network of forgers," Julian explained, trying to convey the gravity of the situation.

"Forgery? Involving van Gogh? Now, that's a significant issue. What do you have so far?" Claire asked, her investigative instincts kicking in.

"After close examination of 'The Starry Night', we have determined it is a forgery. While we've verified that three other pieces are authentic, Van Gogh's 'House and Figure' is still on its way to New York. I'm worried it might not be legitimate," Julian shared, his voice tense with the weight of the investigation.

"Have you traced the origin of the artworks?" Claire inquired, her mind racing through the possible implications.

"Yes, the first four van Gogh paintings were sent from The Van Gogh Museum in Amsterdam, but van Gogh's 'House and Figure' was shipped separately from The British Museum in London. It's a tangled web, and I'm concerned about how deep this could go," Julian said, his frustration noticeable.

"I'll start checking our Interpol databases for any suspicious activity related to these shipments. If there's a forger operating internationally, we need to know who they are," Claire said with an assured and demanding tone.

"Thank you, Claire. Your expertise in international art crime is exactly what we need. If we can connect the dots, we might uncover a larger scheme at play," Julian replied, feeling a sense of relief.

"Absolutely. I'll pull together any relevant cases we've encountered over the last two years. It might help to cross-reference with what you find on your end," Claire suggested, her voice focused.

"Let's make a plan to reconvene in a few

days. I'll keep you updated on our findings as well," Julian said, his optimism rising.

"Sounds good. And Julian, remember to stay cautious. Art crime can be unpredictable," Claire reminded him, her concern evident.

"I will. Thanks for looking out for me, Claire. I appreciate your support," Julian said sincerely.

"Always. We're in this together. I'll be in touch soon," Claire concluded, her voice warm as they wrapped up the call.

"Thanks, Claire. Talk soon and will probably see you when we have our first Task Force meeting!" Julian said, his heart lighter as he hung up.

Inspector Claire Bertrand stood at the forefront of an Interpol investigation, her steely gaze focused on the intricacies of the art world. With a sharp mind and a deep sense of justice, Claire was known for her tenacity in uncovering the truth. Her background in criminology, combined with a passion for art, made her a formidable force against art crime.

Having worked alongside various art institutions across Europe, Claire was well aware of the delicate balance between art preservation and criminal activity. Her path converged with Harper Thompson several times as they both sought to expose art criminal rings threatening the integrity of the art world.

Claire's instincts told her that the case was far more complex than it appeared. As the investigation begins to unfold, she found herself drawn into a network of deceit and danger. Knowing the team of Harper Thompson and FBI Agent David Cortez, Claire is ready to confront the powerful figures behind the operation, and she is determined to bring them to justice.

Claire recognized the importance of Julian's insights and connections within the art world. Julian, as the Task Force leader, has begun to organize a highly skilled team to form a formidable alliance, determined to expose the powerful syndicate behind the forgeries and restore justice to the art they loved.

Sitting back in his chair, Julian felt a renewed sense of determination. With the collaboration of trusted allies like Claire, he knew they could navigate the complex world of art forgery and bring the truth to light.

Julian finished up his notes from his conversation with Claire, and picked up the phone to dial Antoine Dubois's number. Mr. Dubois is the Auction House Director at Sotheby's Auction House in Paris, France.

In the elegant setting of Sotheby's in Paris, Antoine Dubois curated auctions that celebrated the rich heritage of French art. As the auction house director, he was known for his charm and persuasive skills, drawing in collectors from around the world. Antoine's passion for art was evident in every auction he orchestrated, making each event feel like a grand celebration of creativity and culture.

When news of the forgery scheme reached his ears, Antoine felt a strong sense of responsibility. He had built his career on trust and authenticity, and the thought of counterfeit artworks infiltrating the market was unacceptable. With a history of collaboration with Julian Taylor, he wasted no time in offering his expertise and support, ready to delve into the shadows of the art world to protect the integrity of his auctions.

"Bonjour, Antoine Dubois speaking," he said, his voice rich with a French accent, exuding a blend of authority and warmth.

"Antoine! It's Julian Taylor from The Met in New York. I hope you're doing well," Julian replied, relieved to hear his friend's familiar tone.

"Julian! It is a pleasure to hear from you. What brings you to call?" Antoine asked, his curiosity evident.

"I need your expertise regarding a serious matter. We've come across a forgery case involving van Gogh's painting 'The Starry Night'. I believe we might be dealing with a larger operation," Julian said, his tone turning serious.

"Forgery? That is indeed troubling. What do you need from me?" Antoine inquired, his professional instincts kicking in.

"We received the van Gogh painting 'The Starry Night' and after inspection we determined it to be a forgery, and meanwhile we've verified the other three van Gogh pieces are authentic. 'House and Figure' is still in transit from London. I'm concerned it might not be legitimate," Julian explained, the weight of the investigation pressing down on him.

Antoine paused, thinking, "Have you traced the provenance of these artworks? The auction houses may have additional records that could shed light on this situation."

"Yes, the first four paintings came from The Van Gogh Museum in Amsterdam, while 'House and Figure' was shipped from the British Museum in London. I suspect there could be connections to various auction houses across Europe," Julian said, frustration creeping into his voice.

"Let me check our auction sales records. I'll see if any recent sales have raised red flags. It's crucial we identify any patterns or anomalies,"

Antoine offered, his tone firm and reassuring.

"That would be incredibly helpful," Julian replied, feeling a sense of respect. "Your insights could uncover connections we might not have considered."

"Of course. I have my contacts in Paris and beyond. I will reach out to them as well. The art market can be a labyrinth, and we must navigate it carefully," Antoine assured him.

"Thank you, Antoine. I knew I could count on you," Julian said, gratitude flooding his voice. "Let's keep in close contact as we gather more information."

"Absolutely. I will have my findings ready soon. We cannot allow these forgers to undermine the integrity of the art world," Antoine replied, his passion evident.

"Let's plan to regroup in a few days. I'll update you on our progress as well," Julian suggested, feeling hopeful about their collaboration.

"Sounds like a plan. Take care, Julian, and keep your eyes open," Antoine concluded, his tone both friendly and protective.

"Thanks, Antoine. Talk soon!" Julian said, hanging up with a renewed sense of purpose.

As he sat back in his chair, Julian felt a wave of determination wash over him. With trusted allies like Antoine on his side, he knew they could tackle the complex challenge of uncovering the truth behind the forgeries.

Julian sits back in his chair and positions himself for yet another call. This time he will call Alexander Murray in Rome.

In the heart of Rome, amidst the grandeur of ancient ruins and vibrant piazzas, Alexander Murray meticulously examined a newly uncovered fresco in a small gallery. A respected art historian specializing in Renaissance art, he had a knack for uncovering hidden gems that others often overlooked. With tousled hair and a well-worn leather satchel slung over his shoulder, Alexander embodied the spirit of a scholar. His passion for art was obvious, igniting conversations with fellow historians and art lovers alike.

Alexander's friendship with Kamil Russo had flourished over years of shared interests and spirited debates about art. Their late-night discussions often turned into philosophical explorations, delving into the emotional depth behind each piece. He admired Kamil's sharp insights and her unwavering dedication to revealing the stories behind the artworks.

However, Alexander carried a weight of responsibility on his shoulders. He had recently stumbled upon rumors of a forgery ring operating covertly in the shadows of the art world. As whispers of deception grew louder, he felt compelled to delve deeper, knowing that the integrity of the art he cherished was at stake. Little did he know that his pursuit of truth would intertwine with Kamil's journey, igniting a thrilling adventure that would test their friendship and their resolve.

While in Rome, Alexander Murray examined a recently restored fresco, his mind racing with ideas. An esteemed art historian specializing in Renaissance art, Alexander had a reputation for uncovering hidden narratives within works of art.

Phone rings, then connects:

"Alexander Murray here," he answered, his voice authoritative yet approachable, with a hint of British charm.

"Alex! It's Julian from The Met in New York. I hope you're doing well," Julian said, feeling a mix of urgency and friendship.

"Julian! I am happy to hear from you. What's on your mind?" Alexander replied, his curiosity piqued.

"I'm reaching out because we've encountered a forgery case involving van Gogh's painting 'The Starry Night'," Julian explained, the gravity of the situation weighing on him. "I believe we may be dealing with a larger network of forgers operating across Europe and possibly here in the U.S."

"A forgery of van Gogh's work? That's quite humorless. What details do you have so far?" Alexander asked, his professional demeanor shifting to one of concern.

"We recently discovered through the expert examination of a damaged van Gogh painting, that it is a forgery. Thankfully, we've verified that three other pieces are authentic, but I'm worried about van Gogh's 'House and Figure' that's still en route from London," Julian said, his voice steady but laced with tension.

"Have you traced the provenance of these works? It's essential to understand their journey," Alexander inquired, already considering the implications.

"Yes, the first four paintings came from The Van Gogh Museum in Amsterdam, while van Gogh's 'House and Figure' was shipped from the British Museum in London. The connections seem tenuous, and I fear we might be missing something crucial," Julian explained, frustration edging into his tone.

"I will dig into our records at the Vatican Museum and see if we have any recent acquisitions or suspicious activity that aligns with these shipments," Alexander offered, his expertise shining through. "It's important to cross-reference anything that seems off."

"Thank you, Alex. Your insights will be incredibly valuable for our shared peace," Julian responded, experiencing a profound sense of relief.

"Absolutely. If there's a network involved, we need to expose it before more art falls victim to forgery," Alexander assured him, his determination clear.

"Let's plan to touch base again in a few days. I'll keep you updated on our findings as well," Julian suggested, feeling hopeful about their collaboration.

"Good plan. Remember, Julian, these forgers often operate in the shadows. We must shine a light on their activities," Alexander advised, his tone both serious and supportive.

"Will do, Alex. I appreciate your help. Talk soon!" Julian concluded, hanging up with a renewed sense of purpose.

As he leaned back in his chair, Julian felt invigorated; with trusted allies like Alexander by his side, he was confident they could navigate the complexities of the art world and uncover the truth behind the forgery scheme.

Julian decided a call to Scotland Yard would be his last call for today. He wanted to check on the rest of the team for an update.

Jonathan Walters is a seasoned investigator with Scotland Yard, specializing in art crime. With over 20 years of experience in law enforcement, Jonathan has built a reputation as a thorough and resourceful detective. He holds a degree in Criminal Justice and has undergone extensive training in art theft and forgery investigations. His keen analytical skills and attention to detail have allowed him to solve several high-profile cases, making him a respected figure in both the police force and the art community. Jonathan has a particular passion for uncovering the intricacies of art fraud, often working closely with museums and galleries to ensure the integrity of their collections.

Jonathan's connections within the art world run deep, thanks to his collaborative approach and ability to foster relationships with curators, historians, and law enforcement agencies globally. He has worked on cases that span across Europe and the United States, often liaising with international organizations like Interpol. Known for his calm demeanor and strategic thinking, Jonathan navigates complex investigations with ease, making him an invaluable ally in the fight against art crime. His impending partnership with Julian and the task force is critical as they tackle the emerging threats posed by forgery and theft, and he remains committed to protecting the legacy of art and culture.

Phone rings, then connects:

"Scotland Yard, Jonathan Walters speaking," he said, his voice firm yet approachable, exuding confidence.

"Jonathan! It's Julian Taylor from The Met in New York. I hope you're doing well," Julian replied, feeling a mix of necessity and respect for his colleague.

"Julian! Hello my friend! What's the situation?" Jonathan asked, his tone shifting to one of professional concern.

"I'm reaching out because we've uncovered a forgery case involving van Gogh's 'The Starry Night' painting, and I believe it may be part of a larger scheme," Julian explained, the weight of the investigation adding a sense of seriousness to his voice.

"Are you serious? A forgery involving a

van Gogh painting? That's quite astounding news. What have you discovered so far?" Jonathan inquired, his interest piqued.

"We recently identified van Gogh's painting 'The Starry Night' as a forgery. Fortunately, we've confirmed that three other van Gogh pieces included in the same shipment are authentic, but another van Gogh 'House and Figure' is still on its way from London, and I fear it might not be legitimate," Julian detailed, anxiety creeping into his tone.

Jonathan paused, processing the information. "Have you traced the provenance of these pieces? You understand their origin is crucial in art crime investigations."

"Yes, the first four paintings came from The Van Gogh Museum in Amsterdam, while the 'House and Figure' was shipped from the British Museum in London. It's a complex situation, and I'm concerned there may be connections to other forgers operating in the market," Julian said, frustration evident.

"I can check our records at Scotland Yard for any recent art crime cases that might correlate with your findings. If there's a network involved, we need to identify it quickly," Jonathan assured him, his voice steady and determined.

"Thank you, Jonathan. Your expertise in art crime is exactly what we need. If we can pool our resources, we stand a better chance of uncovering the truth," Julian replied, feeling a surge of optimism.

"Absolutely. I'll make this a priority. I'll also reach out to other detectives who specialize in art crimes to see if they've encountered any similar cases lately," Jonathan offered, his commitment clear.

"Let's plan to reconvene in a few days to

share our findings. I'll keep you updated on our progress as well," Julian suggested, feeling encouraged by their collaboration.

"Just so you aware. Jonathan, I called Claire Bertrand at Interpol in Lyon earlier today. She is fully aware of the same details I have given to you on this call. She said she would also touch base with you," Julian explained.

"That sounds great, Julian. And remember, these forgers can be clever. We need to be one step ahead," Jonathan reminded him, his tone both serious and supportive.

"I will, Jonathan. Thanks for your help. Talk soon!" Julian concluded, hanging up with a renewed sense of determination.

As he leaned back in his chair, Julian felt invigorated by the conversation. With trusted allies like Jonathan by his side, he felt confident they could bring the perpetrators to justice.

Not even time for Julian to catch his breath, Julian's phone rang and it was Agent Cortez calling.

"Julian, I managed to obtain the police report from the van accident, and there's some rather alarming information," he began, his voice serious. "It appears that the van driver was using a fake ID, and there was someone else in the van with him."

Julian's interest piqued. "What do you mean? Why didn't we know this before?"

David continued, "While everyone was focused on the injured woman, that second person swung open the side door and escaped during the chaos. It seems they were working for the mastermind behind the forgery operation, which many suspect is the notorious Victor Salvatore, although that's not confirmed yet."

"That's a significant development,"

Julian replied, his mind racing. "So, what happened in the van?"

"According to the report, the guy who disappeared kept insisting he wanted to see the paintings. The driver repeatedly told him not to open the box, saying it was meant for delivery. But the guy pulled out a knife and slashed the box open. That's likely what caused the driver to hit the woman—distracted by the commotion in the back."

Julian felt a chill run down his spine. "So the damage to the painting was a result of that? The knife went too deep?"

"Exactly," David confirmed. "The slash in the painting corresponds with the timing of the accident. This whole thing is starting to unravel, and it points directly to Salvatore's operation, even if we can't confirm his involvement just yet."

"Thanks for the update, David. This changes everything," Julian said, his mind racing with possibilities. "We need to dig deeper into both the driver and this accomplice. There's a bigger picture here that we can't ignore."

"Agreed," David replied. "Let's coordinate our next steps."

As they hung up, Julian couldn't shake the feeling that they were on the brink of uncovering something monumental, a web of deception that reached further than they had ever anticipated.

13.

Two Out of Five

The clock on the wall ticked to 1:30 PM as Julian stepped out of his office, feeling a sense of urgency in his chest. He headed toward the workroom where his team was gathered, determined to check on their progress and find out if the much-anticipated Van Gogh painting from London had arrived.

As he entered the workroom, he found Lila, Timothy, Marco, Kamil and Rose huddled around a large table strewn with papers, their expressions focused. The room was filled with the soft rustle of notes being shuffled and the faint sound of typing.

"Hey, team," Julian greeted, a sense of solidarity washing over him. "How's everything going?"

Lila looked up, a smile breaking through

her concentration. "We're just refreshing our notes and compiling everything we've gathered so far for the forgery task force. It's coming together."

"Good to hear," Julian replied, moving closer to the table. "I just finished calling several experts, including art historians, curators, and detectives. I think we're on the right track, but we need to act quickly."

Timothy leaned back in his chair, curiosity glinting in his eyes. "What did they say? Any leads?"

Julian took a deep breath, gathering his thoughts. "Harper Thompson is digging into market trends for us, and Isabella Rossi is reaching out to her contacts in Venice. Detective Cortez from the FBI is reviewing recent art crime cases, and Claire Bertrand at Interpol will look into any international connections. Alexander Murray, Vatican Museum, and Jonathan Walters, Scotland Yard, are also on board to help us piece everything together."

As he spoke, Marco scribbled notes furiously, while Rose nodded, absorbing the information. "Sounds like a solid network. It's good to have those connections," she said.

Julian continued, "We need to be prepared for anything. These forgers might be more organized than we realize." After a brief call with FBI agent David Cortez, the police report from the van accident revealed much more intrigue and crucial information. There was another person in the van, and the driver was using a fake ID. The second man jumped out during the accident, which is how the side door was opened. He was determined to check out the paintings in the crate, despite the driver's frantic protests as he tried to stop him. That distraction caused the driver to hit the pedestrian. Meanwhile, the man who escaped used a knife to open the crate, and the impact of the crash drove the knife deep, tearing into the box and damaging the painting. The FBI will conduct a thorough investigation of the accident and will update me with any findings.

Before they could delve deeper into their discussion, the door swung open, and Samuel Grant stepped into the room, a mix of excitement and urgency in his demeanor.

"Everyone, we've just received a crate from London!" he announced, his voice ringing with enthusiasm.

Julian's heart raced at the news; "The painting 'House and Figure'? Is it here?"

"Yes! It just arrived. The delivery was a bit delayed, but it's finally here," Samuel confirmed, his eyes sparkling with anticipation.

"Let's get it opened!" Julian said, his adrenaline pumping. "This could be the breakthrough we need."

The team sprang into action, gathering around Samuel as he led them to the receiving area. The crate was large and heavy, marked with the insignia of the British Museum. Julian felt a mix of excitement and apprehension as they prepared to unveil whatever lay inside.

"Everyone ready?" Dr. Grant asked, lifting a crowbar to pry open the crate.

"Ready as we'll ever be!" Julian replied, his heart pounding.

With a few swift movements, Dr. Grant broke the crate open, and the team leaned in closer. As the lid creaked open, they were greeted by layers of protective padding, slowly revealing the wrapped painting within.

"Careful now," Lila cautioned, her eyes

wide with anticipation.

Julian's gaze was fixed on the painting as they unwrapped the layers. "This is it. Let's see if it's authentic."

As the final layer fell away, the team collectively gasped.

"Wow," Marco breathed, taking a step closer. "It's stunning."

Lila reached out, her fingers brushing against the surface of the painting. "The brushwork... it looks consistent with van Gogh's style."

Julian stepped forward, inspecting the piece closely. "We need to analyze this immediately. If it's authentic, it could change everything for our investigation."

As they gathered around the painting, the atmosphere shifted from excitement to focused determination. This was the moment they had been waiting for, and they were ready to uncover the truth behind the forgery scheme.

As the final layer of protective wrapping fell away, Julian's excitement quickly turned to dread. He stared intently at the canvas, his expression freezing in disbelief. The vibrant colors of the painting seemed to blur as he focused on a specific detail.

"Julian? What's wrong?" Lila asked, noticing his blank stare. The room was thick with anticipation, and the atmosphere shifted almost immediately.

"Look at the 'Figure's' left foot, in the bottom right corner," Julian finally managed to say, his voice barely above a whisper.

"What do you mean?" Marco replied, leaning in closer. The rest of the team followed suit, their eyes shifting to the foot of the 'Figure' depicted in the painting.

"That's not right," Julian said, his heart racing. "It's turned to the right too far compared to the original painting. Look at the photographs we have of the actual piece!"

Lila quickly moved the easel with the reference image closer to the original van Gogh painting. As she compared it to the piece before them, her eyes widened. "Oh no... you're right. The angle is completely off!"

"Let me see," Rose said, stepping in to get a better look. "This doesn't match at all. If the foot is turned incorrectly, it raises serious questions about the authenticity."

Julian felt a wave of frustration wash over him. "Absolutely, Rose. This is definitely a forgery; once again. It's another van Gogh forgery, but shipped from the British Museum in London, not from Amsterdam."

Timothy shook his head in disbelief. "But how? The British Museum is reputable. How could they let a forgery slip through?"

"It's not just about them," Julian replied, his voice growing more intense. "This has something to do with a larger operation. I suspect there's a forgery team in Europe trying to move stolen artworks, hiding them while they're sent to places like The Met in New York."

The room fell silent as the gravity of Julian's words sank in. "How many paintings like this are out there?" Marco finally asked, his voice laced with concern.

"It's becoming increasingly clear that we're dealing with a well-organized network," Julian said, pacing back and forth. "If they've managed to replace this piece, who knows how many others have been altered or forged?"

Lila looked at Julian, her expression a mix of determination and fear. "What do we do next?"

"We need to escalate this immediately," Julian replied, his adrenaline pumping. "Interpol and the FBI were put on notice with my telephone conversations earlier today. This isn't just a forgery case anymore; it's part of a larger art crime syndicate. It has been suggested that Victor Salvatore and his notorious team may be behind these forgeries, if not many more."

"What if they're already moving more pieces?" Rose interjected, her brow furrowed. "We could be running out of time."

Julian nodded, his mind racing. "Exactly. I'll reach out again to Claire Bertrand at Interpol and Detective Cortez at the FBI right away. They need to know that this is a coordinated effort to infiltrate major art institutions."

Timothy leaned forward, urgency evident in his voice. "We should also document everything we've found here. This needs to be airtight when we present it to the public and to our Task Force."

"Right," Julian said, feeling the weight of leadership settle on his shoulders. "Let's compile our notes and findings about the forgeries, the provenance of the paintings, and this new lead about the stolen artworks. We need to be ready to present a compelling case."

As the team sprang into action, gathering their notes and preparing for the calls, Lila paused, looking at Julian. "Are you alright? This is a lot to take in."

Julian met her gaze, determination hardening his features. "I'll be fine. We can't lose sight of what's at stake here. The integrity of the art world is on the line, and we can't let these criminals win."

"Let's do this," Marco said, his voice

adamant.

Julian took a deep breath, feeling the support of his team around him. "Alright, let's get to work. I will reach out to David Cortez, Claire Bertrand and Jonathan Walters again right now. Time is of the essence."

As they gathered their materials, the atmosphere shifted from shock to focused determination. They were ready to dive into the depths of this investigation and uncover the truth behind the art forgery scheme, no matter how far it took them.

After the startling discovery that the recently arrived painting revealed, Julian continued, "We need to be prepared for anything. These forgers might be more organized than we realize." After a brief call with FBI agent David Cortez, the police report from the van accident revealed much more intrigue and crucial information. There was another person in the van, and the driver was using a fake ID. The second man jumped out during the accident, which is how the side door was opened. He was determined to check out the paintings in the crate, despite the driver's frantic protests as he tried to stop him. That distraction caused the driver to hit the pedestrian. Meanwhile, the man who escaped used a knife to open the crate, and the impact of the crash drove the knife deep, tearing into the box and damaging the painting. The FBI will conduct a thorough investigation of the accident and will update me with any findings." Julian continued, "We need to be prepared for anything. These forgers might be more organized than we realize." Now that the van Gogh 'House and Figure' has been confirmed a forgery too, Julian felt this was now top priority. He hurried back to his office, his mind racing with the implications of this new revelation. He needed to inform the law enforcement teams immediately.

He sat down at his desk, taking a deep breath to steady himself. His fingers hovered over the keyboard as he dialed David's number first.

"Cortez here," David answered, his tone professional and alert.

"David, it's Julian calling again," he said, urgency threading through his voice. "We've just confirmed that the van Gogh painting 'House and Figure' we received from the British Museum is a forgery."

"Another forgery? That's alarming," David replied, his interest piqued. "What do you have on it?"

Julian leaned back in his chair, running a hand through his hair. "We were examining the painting closely, and it became clear that it doesn't match the original. One foot of the 'Figure' is turned incorrectly, and the brushwork lacks the authenticity we expect from van Gogh's pieces."

"Have you notified the press yet?" David asked, his voice steady.

"Yes, we're finalizing a press release at this moment. Dr. Grant, the Director of The Met, is handling that with our Communications people. But I wanted to give you a heads-up before it goes public. This is the second forgery linked to van Gogh, and I believe it's indicative of a larger operation," Julian explained.

David paused, considering the implications. "You might be right. We need to track this down. Any leads on where the forgeries were born?"

"Not yet, but we're planning to investigate the provenance of all recent acquisitions from the Van Gogh Museum and the British Museum," Julian replied, determination evident in his voice. "I think we might need to set up a joint task force meeting to address this urgently."

"Good idea. I'll coordinate with my team and see what we can dig up on our end," David said. "Let's meet later today to discuss our next steps."

"Absolutely. I'll keep you posted on any developments. Thanks, David," Julian said, feeling a sense of relief in having the FBI's support.

"Talk soon," David replied before hanging up.

Taking a deep breath, Julian quickly dialed Claire Bertrand's number at Interpol, his heart still racing from the previous conversation.

"Bertrand here," Claire answered, her voice sharp and clear.

"Claire, it's Julian from The Met once again. I need to inform you about a second forgery we've discovered," he said, urgency evident in his tone.

"Another one? What can you tell me?" Claire replied, her professionalism shining through.

"We've confirmed that the van Gogh painting 'House and Figure' we received is a forgery," Julian explained, pacing slightly as he spoke. "It was delivered from the British Museum, and we found discrepancies in its authenticity."

Claire's voice turned serious. "What kind of discrepancies are we talking about?"

"One foot on the 'Figure' in the painting is turned incorrectly compared to the original, and the brushwork lacks the depth and texture typical of van Gogh's style. This is the second forgery linked to him, and I suspect there's a larger scheme at play," Julian said, determination fueling his words.

"I'll need all the details you can provide. This could be part of an international operation," Claire replied, her tone shifting to one of urgency. "Have you reached out to the FBI yet?"

"Yes, I just spoke with David Cortez. We're both aligned on the need for a coordinated effort," Julian confirmed. David mentioned that he suspects Victor Salvatore may be behind the recent spate of forgeries.

"Good. We need to act quickly. I'll mobilize our resources and see if there are any similar cases reported in Europe," Claire said, her voice steady. "We'll want to compare notes and see if we can find any patterns."

"Exactly. I think we should set up a joint task force meeting to address this situation comprehensively," Julian suggested, feeling hopeful about their collaboration. "I also spoke to Jonathan Walters at Scotland Yard earlier today. I mentioned that you would be reaching out to him. Do you mind letting him know about this second van Gogh forgery and the details? Also, can you please fill him in on Agent Cortez' suspicion of Victor Salvatore's proposed involvement?"

"Absolutely, no problem. I will reach out to Jonathan today. Let me know when you plan to have our first Task Force meeting. I hope it will be soon, so the group can strategize," Claire replied.

"Thank you, Claire. I'll keep you updated with any new information as we finalize our press release," Julian said, relieved to have her support.

"Stay safe out there, Julian," Claire said before hanging up.

As Julian set the phone down, the day ahead would be critical, and with both the FBI and Interpol in the loop, he felt more prepared to tackle the challenges ahead. With the task force coming together, they were one step closer to uncovering the truth behind the forgeries.

With a sense of seriousness coursing through him, Julian picked up the phone again, this time dialing Evelyn Sinclair's number at the British Museum. As one of the most respected curators in England, Evelyn had been instrumental in numerous prestigious exhibitions. Her expertise in Impressionist art, particularly van Gogh, had garnered her recognition throughout Europe.

"British Museum, Evelyn Sinclair speaking," her voice came through, confident and professional.

"Evelyn! It's Julian Taylor from The Met in New York," he said, feeling a rush of relief at her familiar tone. "I hope you're well."

"Julian! What's going on?" Evelyn replied, her curiosity evident.

"I'm calling because we've just confirmed that the van Gogh painting 'House and Figure' you sent to us is a forgery," he stated, his voice steady but urgent.

There was a brief silence on the line. "A forgery? That is very troubling news, to say the least. Who made this determination, and what are the specifics, please?"

Julian leaned back in his chair, preparing to explain. "My team and I discovered discrepancies in the painting's details, particularly in the 'Figures' foot positioning in the bottom right corner of the painting compared to photographs of the original. It doesn't match van Gogh's authentic style. This is the second forgery linked to a van Gogh in the past two days."

Evelyn sighed, her professionalism not masking her concern. "This is particularly alarming, especially since we've been preparing for the upcoming van Gogh exhibition. We've put a lot of effort into showcasing his work, and this could tarnish that."

"I know how much work you've put into it. Your reputation as a curator precedes you," Julian replied, recalling her extensive background. Evelyn had been a curator at the British Museum for over a decade, known for her meticulous attention to detail and her ability to connect with artists and institutions across Europe and the U.S. Her ties to Kamil Russo and other prominent figures in the art world had further solidified her status.

"Thank you, Julian. It's been a journey, to say the least," she said, her tone shifting to one of determination. "What's the next step? We need to address this immediately."

"I plan to involve the task force we've formed, including the FBI and Interpol. We need to investigate the provenance of not just this piece but any recent acquisitions from the British Museum and other significant institutions," Julian explained.

"That sounds like a prudent approach. I'll assist in any way I can. We can start by reviewing all Van Gogh pieces that have been sent out recently, especially those linked to the exhibition," Evelyn replied, her mind already racing with ideas.

"Thank you, Evelyn. Your expertise will be invaluable. I know you have experience navigating these kinds of situations," Julian said, recalling how she had dealt with similar challenges in previous exhibitions.

"Absolutely. I've dealt with forgeries before, and I know how quickly they can spiral out of control," she affirmed. "I'll also reach out to Kamil. She has insights into the market that could help us track down where these forgeries might be coming from."

"Good idea. Kamil arrived in New York a few days ago. She is well aware of what is taking place. I will ask her to give you a call. She is actually heading back to Paris this evening. The more connections we have, the better," Julian said, feeling a surge of hope. "I'll keep you updated on our findings and the press release we're preparing."

"Please do. We need to act fast to protect the integrity of the art community," Evelyn replied, her voice resolute.

"Thanks, Evelyn. I appreciate your support. Goodbye," Julian said before ending the call.

With Evelyn on board, they would be better equipped to tackle the challenges ahead. Her knowledge and connections would be crucial in navigating the complex web of art forgeries. He knew the road ahead would be fraught with difficulties, but with a strong team behind him, he felt ready to face whatever came next.

14.

Evelyn Sinclair, Art Curator

In the shadow of the iconic British Museum, Evelyn Sinclair meticulously curated an exhibition that celebrated the rich history of ancient artifacts. Known for her discerning taste and deep knowledge of art history, Evelyn had dedicated her career to making the museum's vast collection accessible and engaging to the public. With her polished demeanor and sharp intellect, she commanded respect from colleagues and visitors alike.

When whispers of a forgery scheme began to circulate, Evelyn became concerned about the integrity of the artifacts under her care. Her connections with Julian Taylor and Kamil Russo, forged during previous collaborations on exhibitions, made her a valuable ally in the investigation. With her expertise in ancient art, she was determined to uncover the truth and protect the heritage of the museum.

Julian stepped outside the museum for a breath of fresh air. It was a gorgeous afternoon in the city. As Julian took in the hustle of Fifth Avenue, he suddenly had a thought that made him jolt back to his office.

Julian, hurriedly, dialed Evelyn Sinclair's phone hoping that she had not left her office as it was quite late in London.

Evelyn was sitting her corner office in The British Museum, with the darkness completely engulfing London as the last rays of sun disappeared beyond the horizon through the tall windows covered in a magnificent tapestry of drapery.

"Evelyn speaking, may I help you?" much less formal at this hour.

Leaning forward, "Evelyn, this is Julian calling again." His voice low and urgent sounding. "Evelyn, I've been thinking about the van Gogh piece you sent to The Met. The one that was supposed to be an original."

Evelyn, maintaining a composed demeanor, said "Yes, I remember our discussion. The exhibit was a significant opportunity for both institutions."

Julian, becoming frustrated "Yes, but how could this happen? The foot on the bottom of the painting—it's pointing in the wrong direction! How did your team not catch this?

Evelyn, sighing, her brow furrowing, "Julian, we have rigorous protocols. The painting was authenticated before being shipped."

Julian interrupting "Rigorously authenticated? This is van Gogh we're talking about! You're telling me there wasn't a single person who compared it against high-resolution

136

photos or examined it in detail?"

Defensively Evelyn spoke "We did use photographs, Julian. But sometimes, things slip through the cracks. Art is complex, and even the slightest detail can mislead."

Julian, leaning back in his chair, visibly upset said, "This isn't just about a detail, Evelyn. This is a potential switch. I can't shake the feeling that when the shipping company picked up the painting, they could have easily swapped it out."

Eyes narrowing, Evelyn said, "You think someone would do that?"

Julian shaking his head at her ridiculous comment, "I need to know who picked it up. What shipping company handled the logistics? There could be a trail we can follow."

Evelyn, pausing, considering, said, "I'll have to look into the records. But Julian, jumping to conclusions without evidence could be damaging."

Julian, voice rising, "Damaging? This is about integrity! If this is a forgery, it's not just damaging to us; it undermines the entire art world!"

Calmly, Evelyn said, "I understand your passion, but we need to approach this methodically. Let's gather facts before we make any accusations."

Julian sighs, running a hand through his hair, says, "I just can't believe this happened. I trusted your expertise, and now I feel like we've been mislead."

Evelyn, softening her tone, "Julian, I share your concern. I've dedicated my career to protecting art, and I won't let this slide. Let's work together. I'll get the shipping documents. We can investigate this further."

Reluctantly nodding, Julian said, "Alright.

But we need to act fast. If there's a switch, time is not on our side."

Determined, Evelyn said, "Then let's get to work. I'll pull the records and meet you back here in an hour. We'll figure this out."

Julian, standing up, calmness returning, said, "Thank you, Evelyn. I know it is late there, but if you just send me the shipment records and start work here and reconvene tomorrow afternoon your time. I appreciate it. We can't let this go unnoticed."

Evelyn, smiling faintly, said, "We won't. I promise."

Evelyn Sinclair is a distinguished curator at the British Museum, specializing in Impressionist and Post-Impressionist art. With nearly 20 years of experience, she has organized numerous exhibitions that have garnered critical acclaim. Evelyn is well connected in the art world, with ties to institutions across Europe and relationships with many prominent artists and curators.

Her expertise in van Gogh's work has made her a sought-after figure for exhibitions, and she has a strong understanding of both the historical context and the current art market. Evelyn is known for her attention to detail and her ability to navigate the complexities of exhibition planning. Her relationship with Julian and Kamil adds depth to her character, as they often collaborate on projects and share insights.

As Julian leaves the museum, the weight of uncertainty lingers in the air. He knows the stakes are high, and he feels a renewed sense of purpose. The world of art is not just about beauty; it's about authenticity, and he's determined to uncover the truth behind the van Gogh that might not be what it seems.

15.

Another Press Release from The MET

Upon entering the workroom, Julian was surprised to see Dr. Samuel Grant and Dr. Lila Thorne already seated in the workroom, their heads bent over a laptop. The atmosphere was serious, and the press release was clearly a priority.

"Good morning!" Julian called out, shaking off the rain as he stepped inside.

"Morning, Julian!" Lila replied, looking up with a smile. "We're just finalizing the press release. Dr. Grant is determined to get it out by 9 AM."

"Absolutely," Dr. Grant said, his brow furrowed in concentration. "We need to preempt any speculation about why this news wasn't conveyed sooner. It's crucial for maintaining public trust."

"Can I read it while I get myself situated?" Julian asked as he began to unpack his things.

"Sure, here it goes," Samuel replied, clearing his throat.

FOR IMMEDIATE RELEASE

'The Metropolitan Museum of Art regrets to announce that a recent acquisition, a painting attributed to Vincent van Gogh, was found to be a forgery. This discovery follows the identification of another forged piece from the same artist delivered to our institution in a separate shipment two days ago. We are taking this matter seriously and are investigating the provenance of our recent acquisitions to ensure the integrity of our collections. Further updates will be provided as we work closely with law enforcement and art experts.'

'We appreciate the public's understanding as we navigate this situation.'

Julian nodded as he listened, feeling the weight of the words. "This is a solid start, but we really need to start thinking about what this means for the museum. Now we have two pieces from the same artist that are not authentic."

"Do you think we should pursue looking into other paintings we've received over the last year?" Julian continued, leaning against the table. "I'm talking about significant pieces, not every little thing that comes through the door."

Lila glanced at Samuel, then back at Julian. "I think that might be jumping to conclusions. We can't assume this is as widespread as you're imagining."

Julian shook his head, his expression serious. "I don't feel comfortable thinking there could be multiple pieces of art in this place that are forgeries. We need an investigation. The task force we put together here and in Europe is going to want to add this to their list of cases."

"Where do you suggest we start?" Samuel asked, his interest piqued.

"Two obvious places would be The Van Gogh Museum and the British Museum," Julian replied. "We should look at everything we've received from both of those institutions over the last two or three years. After that, we can expand our search to other museums in Europe and the United States."

Lila frowned slightly. "That's a lot of work. We need to be methodical."

Julian nodded, undeterred. "The Boston Museum of Fine Arts, the Art Institute of Chicago, the Los Angeles County Museum of Art, and the National Gallery of Art in Washington, D.C.—they all receive pieces from museums from around the world as well. We need to determine if any forgeries have been brought into the country."

Samuel considered Julian's words. "It sounds like we need to compile a comprehensive list of all recent acquisitions from those museums. If there's a pattern, we might be able to trace these forgeries back to their origin."

"Exactly," Julian said, feeling a sense of purpose. "I'll start drafting a plan for our investigation. We have to be proactive about this. The integrity of our collection is at stake."

Lila nodded, her expression serious. "Let's make sure we're thorough. If we're going to tackle this, we need to be united in our approach."

"Agreed," Julian said, feeling a surge of determination. "We'll set up a meeting with the task force as soon as we can. This isn't just about our museum; it's about protecting the entire art community."

As they continued to discuss the logistics of the investigation, the atmosphere in the room shifted from urgency to resolve. They were ready to face the challenges ahead, knowing that the truth was their only path forward.

Julian stood at the front of the workroom, glancing around at his team. They had just finished discussing the press release, and now he felt the weight of the next steps pressing down on him.

"Alright, everyone," Julian began, his voice firm but encouraging. "I need to write a blast email to the newly formed task force members I spoke to yesterday. Although I have called the FBI, Interpol and Scotland Yard directly, we need to notify them about the second forgery."

Samuel nodded, tapping a pen against his notepad. "Once we finalize the press release and make our announcement, are you ready to send that email?"

"Yes," Julian replied. "After we announce it to the press, I'll send off the email to the team. I want to emphasize that this situation is becoming increasingly urgent. We need to convene the task force as soon as possible."

Lila raised her hand slightly, catching Julian's attention. "What are your thoughts on where to hold the meeting? Should we meet here in New York City, or would it be better to pick a city in Europe, like Paris?"

Julian considered this. "We need to decide soon. The meeting can't just be another delay. We've been searching and wondering for over 48 hours. The FBI and Interpol are likely going to want to act quickly, especially with the stakes getting higher."

"Paris has great resources and connections," Rose chimed in. "Plus, it's a central location for many of the experts we'll need."

Timothy nodded, a thoughtful expression on his face. "But New York is also significant given that the forgeries are affecting our museum directly. Wouldn't it be more impactful for the task force to meet here at The Met in New York?"

"I see both sides," Julian replied, pacing slightly as he contemplated their options. "We need to weigh convenience against the symbolism of the location. If we're meeting to discuss these serious issues, being in New York could show our commitment to resolving them."

"Let's not forget about logistics," Lila added. "Traveling to Paris might complicate things for some team members, especially on short notice."

"True," Julian said, nodding. "I think we should take a vote on it. Let's see how everyone feels about it."

As Julian wrapped up his thoughts, he noticed Timothy and Rose walking toward Lila. "Lila," Timothy said, a hint of urgency in his voice. "Would you mind filling us in on the details while Julian drafts that email?"

"Of course," Lila replied, her eyes brightening. "I'll summarize everything we've discussed so far and highlight the key points from the press release."

"Thanks, Lila," Julian said, feeling grateful for the teamwork. "I'll work on getting that email out as quickly as I can. We need to keep the momentum going."

As he settled down at a nearby desk to

draft the email, he could hear the quiet hum of conversation as Lila began to outline the situation for Timothy and Rose. He focused on the words he needed to convey to the task force: urgency, collaboration, and the need to act decisively.

Just then Marco arrived, the room buzzed with energy as they all prepared for the challenges ahead Lila motioned for Marco to join her as she filled the team in on what took place thus far this morning, knowing that every moment courted in their pursuit of the truth.

Julian nodded a hello towards Marco as they joined Lila's outline of where the team is at so far this morning.

16.

The Invitations

As the sun rose over New York City, casting a warm glow through the window of Julian's office at the Metropolitan Museum of Art, he felt a mix of excitement and apprehension. Today marked an important milestone—the first official announcement of the first meeting of the task force to tackle the burgeoning forgery crisis. Julian had been busy coordinating the logistics, and now it was time to finalize the details.

He sat at his desk, fingers poised over the keyboard, ready to draft the email that would invite key members to the meeting. The chosen location is the museum itself, with a live broadcast streaming for those who might not be able to make the journey from Europe and Asia. He felt a sense of urgency as he recalled the importance of having everyone on board.

Metropolitan Museum of Art
1000 Fifth Avenue
New York, New York 10028

September 19, 2024

Subject: Invitation to Task Force Conference
          International Art Theft and Forgeries

Dear Esteemed Colleagues,

I am writing to invite you to the inaugural meeting of our 'International Art Theft and Forgeries' task force conference dedicated to addressing the recent surge in art theft and forgeries affecting our institutions. The meeting will take place on Thursday, September 26 beginning at 8 AM with a welcome breakfast at The Metropolitan Museum of Art, 1000 Fifth Avenue, New York City.

For those unable to attend in person, a live broadcast will be available from your location via Zoom.

This task force is comprised of experts in art history, restoration, curators and law enforcement, and your insights will be invaluable as we work together to uncover the truth behind the forgeries and protect the integrity of our collections. We are pleased to provide accommodations for your stay at The Carlyle, 35 East 76th Street, New York, NY 10021, located conveniently near the museum.

Please confirm your attendance and complete your registration at your earliest convenience so we can finalize arrangements. You may do so by going to our website and search for 'MET Conference July 26, 2024.'

Looking forward to our collaboration.

Best regards,
Julian Taylor
Chief Historian and Art Restoration Specialist
The Metropolitan Museum of Art

As Julian finished the email, he felt a wave of willpower. He knew that the people gathered for this meeting would play crucial roles in the investigation. At the time of the meeting, the task force consisted of twelve key members:

1. Julian Taylor – Task Force Chairman, The Met, NYC
2. Victoria Harrington – Auction House Director, Christie's London
3. Antoine Dubois - Auction House Director, Sotheby's Paris
4. Dr. Lila Thorne, The Met Conservator, NYC
5. Harper Thompson, Art Historian, NYC
6. Dr. Samuel Grant, Director, The Met, NYC
7. Alexander Murray, Art Historian, The Vatican Museum
8. Evelyn Sinclair – Director, The British Museum, London
9. Dr. Anneke Vermeer – Director, The Van Gogh Museum, Amsterdam
10. Det. David Cortez – FBI, NYC
11. Det. Claire Bertrand – Interpol, Lyon
12. Jonathan Walters – Art Crime Spec, Scotland Yard, Westminster

Each member brought unique expertise, and Julian felt confident that their combined knowledge would yield significant results. As he prepared to send the email, his phone buzzed with a text from Kamil: 'Can't wait for the meeting! Let's make sure we cover everything we need to. Are you ready?'

Julian smiled, typing back quickly: 'Absolutely! Just finalizing the details now. Excited to see everyone together. Are you returning for the meeting or joining Zoom? I have completed the agenda and the guest speakers are confirmed.'

Kamil texted back, 'I will decide tomorrow. It's tough after being back only a couple days, but I want to be there.'

Julian texted back, 'It's your decision. It is understood that some people would rather join via virtual meetings. No worries Kamil.'

He clicked "send" on the text and leaned back in his chair, taking a moment to reflect on the challenges ahead. Just then, there was a knock at the door, and in walked Lila, her expression bright.

"Hey, Julian! How's the prep going?" Lila asked, crossing her arms in a casual stance.

"Just sent out the invitations for the task force meeting. It's all coming together," he replied, feeling a surge of energy. "Before you ask, the internal task force staff will be given the details of the Conference today or tomorrow. You know who they are, I presume."

"Great! I think it's important that we emphasize collaboration among everyone involved. We must make sure that everyone feels welcome and valued, including our internal team," Lila suggested, her passion for teamwork evident.

Julian nodded. "I agree. I think bringing in people from various backgrounds will enrich our discussions. It's not just about solving the forgeries; it's about rebuilding trust in the art community."

"Exactly! And speaking of trust, I hope everyone is on the same page, especially Evelyn," Lila said, her tone serious. "After what happened with the van Gogh shipment from London, we need to be cautious."

Julian sighed, recalling his own suspicions about Evelyn's thoroughness. "We'll have to keep a close eye on her involvement. Her expertise is valuable, but we must ensure transparency."

As they continued discussing the meeting logistics and the list of internal staff that should be invited to the conference, Julian felt a mix of anticipation and anxiety. The task force would be a pivotal moment in their investigation, and he hoped it would lead them to uncover the truth behind the forgeries and the crime ring threatening their world.

As Julian entered the workroom, he noticed his staff busily preparing for the upcoming conference. He gathered everyone's attention and began to speak.

"Team, I want to thank you all for the incredible effort you've put into organizing this conference. The agenda is already in place, and now it's time for me to take charge of a few important tasks.

First, I need to extend invitations to you to attend the conference. This includes Marco, Timothy, Rose, and of course, Dr. Thorne and Dr. Grant. Your expertise and presence will be invaluable as we tackle the pressing issues surrounding international art theft and forgery.

In addition, we need to invite key representatives from law enforcement in New York who have been instrumental in combating art crime. I'll compile a list of those individuals to ensure we have a diverse group of perspectives.

Lastly, I'll outline the guest speakers we've confirmed for the event. These include:

- Dr. Emily Harper, an expert on art crime trends.
- Mark Thompson, a forensic art analyst.
- Sarah Chen, a digital security expert.
- Dr. Robert Sinclair, an art recovery consultant.

If you have anyone in mind that should attend the conference, please let me know. I'd like to assign someone to take the lead on internal invitations and compile a list from our group," Julian announced.

Lila immediately spoke up. "I'd like to prepare that list along with my two assistants, Timothy and Rose."

Julian replied to Lila, "Great! One note for you is Kamil remains undecided if she will return after only two days back to Paris. If not, she will join via Zoom. Let's ensure we reach out to everyone promptly so they can prepare for an engaging and productive event. Thank you all for your hard work. I'm truly excited to see everything come together.

Now, one more important item on the agenda: we will have two roundtable breakout sessions. The first is 'Authenticating Art,' facilitated by Laura Mitchell, an art historian. The second will focus on 'Collaborative Strategies for Art Institutions,' led by Tom Sullivan, a museum director. I've already secured both facilitators, and they're actively developing their presentations. Conference attendees will have the opportunity to choose one roundtable session to attend."

As the sun dipped below the horizon, casting a warm glow through the tall museum windows, Julian wrapped up his presentation to the team. The room buzzed with excitement about the conference tomorrow, a significant event that promised to bring the art world together to fight theft and forgery and foster new connections within the art community.

"Thank you all for your hard work," Julian said, glancing around the room at his colleagues. "I know we have a lot to prepare, but I believe our participation in the round table sessions will really elevate our presence. I encourage each of you to consider which sessions you'd like to attend. It's a great opportunity to engage with experts and share our insights."

He could see the enthusiasm in their eyes as they began discussing which topics intrigued them the most, the room filled with lively chatter. Julian felt a swell of pride at the thought of representing the museum alongside such dedicated individuals.

Once the meeting concluded, he gathered his notes and headed to his office, ready to call it a day. As he organized his things, he pulled out his phone and texted Marco: 'Hey, I am just wrapping up here. Are you finished? Let's meet at five?'

A moment later, Marco replied, 'Almost done. See you soon!'

17.

A Bond Between Two

Feeling a sense of anticipation, Julian smiled as he left the museum. He had been looking forward to spending more time with Marco, and the idea of sharing a drink and dinner together filled him with warmth.

They decided to try a new bar downtown, a cozy spot known for its artisanal cocktails and relaxed atmosphere. As they settled into a booth, Julian poured himself into the conversation, the laughter flowing as easily as the drinks.

"I can't believe you almost forgot to mention that artist's talk," Marco teased, a playful glint in his eyes. "You know that's the best part of the conference!"

Julian chuckled, shaking his head. "I swear, I have so many details swimming in my mind that I lose track. But seriously, it's going to be a great event. I'm glad we're doing this together."

"Of course! It's way more fun to navigate this with you," Marco replied, his gaze lingering on Julian a moment longer than necessary.

After a delightful meal, they strolled back to Julian's condo, the evening air crisp and refreshing. The conversation continued to flow easily, a comforting rhythm between them. As they reached the entrance, Julian felt a mix of contentment and something deeper stirring within him.

Once inside, they both retired to their respective bedroom suites, the earlier energy of the night still hanging in the air. Julian changed into his pajamas, feeling a pleasant exhaustion settle over him. He reflected on the evening, the laughter, the shared glances—everything that had brought them closer.

When the clock struck one, Julian was jolted awake by a soft knock on his door. Heart racing with a mixture of excitement and apprehension, he recognized the familiar silhouette of Marco outside his door.

"Julian?" Marco's voice was barely above a whisper, yet it carried the weight of all the unsaid words between them.

Julian, opening the door, slightly surprised, says "Hey, Marco. Everything okay?" It's 1AM. The living room is dimly lit, casting soft shadows against the walls. A gentle hum of the city can be heard outside.

Marco, rubbing the back of his neck, looking down, "I... I'm having a hard time sleeping. Mind if we talk a bit?"

Julian, smiling softly, said "Of course,

Marco."

They decide to move to the living room, both settling onto the couch. The atmosphere is thick with unsaid words.

Nervously glancing at Julian, Marco said "It's just... I keep thinking about us. Why we're not... you know, moving forward."

Julian sighs, "Yeah, I've been thinking the same. It feels like we're stuck, doesn't it?"

Leaning forward, Marco in low sigh said, "I want more, Julian. I really do. But every time I think about saying something, I freeze. What if it ruins what we have?"

Julian, looking into Marco's eyes, says, "Listen...What if it doesn't? What if it makes it better?"

They share a moment of silence, the weight of their feelings hanging in the air.

Marco, somewhat apprehensively, "Just... I can't imagine not having you in my life. It scares me."

Julian, reaching out to Marco, placing a reassuring hand on Marco's. "You're not going to lose me," he replied softly. "But we need to be honest with each other."

As they settled into the couch, the weight of their unspoken feelings hung heavily in the air. Julian searched Marco's eyes, wanting to convey the depth of his own emotions. "I've been feeling this tension between us for a long time," he admitted, his voice barely above a whisper. "Every time we're together, I feel it. Like there's something more we're both afraid to touch."

Marco nodded, his heart racing. "I know exactly what you mean. It's like we're dancing around each other, afraid of what might happen if we take that step. But the truth is, I want to take that step. I just... I don't want to ruin what we have."

Julian took a deep breath, his gaze steady. "What if taking that step is what makes us stronger? What if it brings us closer instead of tearing us apart?"

The air between them crackled with possibility, and Marco felt the tension shift. "You really think so? I've been so scared of losing you as a friend that I've pushed my feelings down."

"Me too," Julian confessed, a hint of vulnerability in his voice. "But I'm tired of pretending. I want to know what it's like to explore this... whatever this is between us."

Marco felt a surge of hope. "So, what do we do now?"

Julian squeezed Marco's hand, a smile breaking through the uncertainty. "We take it one step at a time. Let's be open with each other. No more hiding."

They shared a moment of silence, both feeling the weight of their past and the promise of their future. As they talked, their connection deepened, the tension and yearning that had built up between them transforming into something beautiful and undeniable.

"I care about you, Julian," Marco said, his voice steady. "More than I've ever let on."

"And I care about you," Julian replied, his eyes sparkling with sincerity. "This doesn't have to be scary. We can figure it out together."

In that moment, the barriers that had kept them apart began to crumble, leaving room for the love they had both longed for. They leaned closer, the world around them fading as they embraced the possibilities that lay ahead.

"Now, let's try to sleep," Julian said to Marco as they walked to their rooms. "I need to be at the museum no later than 7AM.

Goodnight!"

18.

Final Touches

As the conference day drew nearer, the anticipation among the attendees was noticeable. In the bustling preparation room at The Met, Julian gathered the seven esteemed presenters to discuss their upcoming contributions.

Based in the bustling offices of the FBI in New York City, Special Agent Sophia Roberts was the head of the Art Crime Team, known for her sharp instincts and unwavering dedication to justice. With a background in criminal psychology and a passion for art, Sophia expertly navigated the complexities of art theft, forgery, and illicit trade. Her reputation for solving high-profile cases made her a respected figure in both law enforcement and the art community.

Sophia first crossed paths with Julian Taylor during an investigation into a series of art thefts. Their mutual respect blossomed into a professional partnership as they worked together to protect the integrity of the art world. When whispers of a forgery scheme began to surface, Sophia recognized the potential threat to both the museum collections and the artists involved. Eager to collaborate with Julian and his team, she was determined to bring the criminals to justice and ensure that authenticity in art was upheld.

Next to speak was Mark Thompson, a forensic art analyst from New York. With a background in chemistry and a passion for art, Mark had carved out a niche for himself in the world of art authentication. He specializes in analyzing pigments and materials to determine the legitimacy of artwork.

"Thank you, Julian," Mark said, adjusting his glasses. "I'll be discussing the scientific techniques we use to authenticate artworks. Many people don't realize how much science goes into determining an artwork's provenance. My goal is to demystify the processes involved and show how collaboration between scientists and art historians can lead to more accurate appraisals."

"Your expertise will definitely shed light on the importance of scientific methods in our discussions," Julian replied, appreciating Mark's enthusiasm.

Sarah Chen, a digital security expert based in Washington, D.C., chimed in next. Her work focused on protecting artworks through technology, an increasingly crucial aspect of art preservation.

"I'm excited to join the conversation," Sarah said, her eyes sparkling with passion. "I'll be presenting on how digital tools can help us track stolen art and enhance security measures in galleries and museums. With the rise of cybercrime, it's vital that we integrate technology into our strategies for protecting cultural assets."

Julian smiled. "Your perspective on technology will be a game-changer for many attendees. It's important that we adapt to the evolving landscape of art crime."

David Rosen is a seasoned law enforcement officer with over 15 years of experience in the New York City Police Department. Currently serving as a detective in the Major Crimes Unit, David specializes in art theft and cultural property crime. His commitment to protecting New York's rich artistic heritage has led him to collaborate with various museums and galleries in the city, where he works to recover stolen artworks and educate the public on art crime prevention. David has been recognized for his investigative prowess and has played a critical role in several high-profile cases, utilizing innovative technologies to bring criminals to justice. As a panelist at the conference, he will share insights on the intersection of law enforcement and the art world, discussing the latest trends in recovery and the importance of collaboration between institutions and law enforcement agencies.

Dr. Laura Mitchell is a distinguished art historian with a focus on the documentation and authentication of artworks. With a Ph.D. in Art History from Columbia University, Laura has spent over a decade researching and teaching about the complexities of provenance and the significance of proper documentation in the art market. In addition to her academic contributions, she has worked with various museums and galleries to develop best practices for authenticating artworks, ensuring that both collectors and institutions can trust the integrity of their pieces. As the facilitator of the workshop "Documenting and Authenticating Art," Laura aims to equip participants with essential tools and methodologies for verifying the authenticity of artwork, highlighting the critical role that accurate documentation plays in the art world today.

Tom Sullivan is the esteemed Museum Director of the Guggenheim Museum in New York City, where he has served for over a decade. With a background in art history and museum studies, Tom has been instrumental in curating groundbreaking exhibitions that highlight both contemporary and historical artworks. His leadership has fostered innovative educational programs and community engagement initiatives, making the Guggenheim a vibrant hub for art lovers and scholars alike. Tom is a strong advocate for the integration of technology in the museum experience, championing digital initiatives that enhance visitor interaction with art. As the facilitator of the workshop 'Collaborative Strategies for Art Institutions' at this conference, Tom will share his insights on the evolving role of museums in the art recovery landscape and the importance of collaboration with law enforcement and private collectors.

Dr. Robert Sinclair is a renowned art recovery consultant with over 20 years of experience in the field. He holds a Ph.D. in Art History from Boston University and has advised numerous museums, galleries, and private collectors on best practices for recovering stolen and lost artworks. Dr. Sinclair combines his deep knowledge of art provenance with innovative strategies for tracking and verifying artworks, making him a sought-after expert in art recovery. He has successfully led several high-profile recovery cases and has collaborated with law enforcement agencies worldwide to reunite artworks with their rightful owners. At the conference, Dr. Sinclair will discuss the intricacies of art recovery and the critical role of expertise in navigating the complex landscape of art theft and restoration.

"I'm looking forward to sharing some of my case studies," Robert began, his tone serious yet hopeful. "Art recovery is often a long and complicated process, but I believe it's essential to highlight successful recoveries to inspire others. I'll also discuss the challenges we face when dealing with international thefts and how collaboration can enhance our efforts."

Dr. Emily Harper, a renowned expert on art crime trends, stood confidently at the center of the room. Her extensive research into the methods employed by art thieves and forgers had made her a sought-after speaker at international conferences. With a Ph.D. in Art History from Columbia University, she had spent over a decade studying the evolution of art crime.

"Art theft is not just a crime; it's an assault on our cultural heritage," Emily began, her voice steady. "I plan to highlight the latest trends we're seeing in the field, including the rise of online marketplaces for stolen art. Understanding these trends will empower us to develop more effective prevention strategies."

Julian nodded, impressed. "Your insights will be invaluable, Emily. I'm sure everyone will benefit from your expertise."

Julian nodded appreciatively. "Your insights into the recovery process will be crucial for our discussions. It's important for attendees to understand the complexities involved and the need for a united approach."

As they wrapped up their discussion,

Julian felt a surge of excitement. With such a diverse and knowledgeable group of presenters, the conference was sure to spark important conversations and foster collaborative efforts in combating art crime. The presenters brought a unique perspective, and their combined expertise would help pave the way for a brighter future in the protection of cultural heritage.

19.

The Task Force Conference

Grace Rainey Rogers Auditorium at The Metropolitan Museum of Art
Thursday, September 26, 2024 - 8AM

    As the bright light of morning filtered through the tall windows of The Met's Grace Rainey Rogers Auditorium, a sense of urgency filled the air. Julian has gathered a diverse group of art professionals, each recognized in their respective fields, to confront the escalating threat posed by an international crime syndicate that specializes in stealing and forging the world's most valuable precious art masterpieces. The atmosphere was charged with anticipation as the distinguished guests started to take their seats around the perimeter of the expansive stage.

    The meeting agenda is being handed out

by museum staff as they check in and pick up their welcome package, which contains the meeting agenda, their name badges and information on The MET and surrounding hotels and restaurants for their information. The meeting agenda:

CONFERENCE AGENDA
Inaugural International Conference
The Theft and Forgery of World Art Masterpieces

September 26, 2024
The Metropolitan Museum of Art
Grace Rainey Rogers Auditorium
1000 Fifth Avenue, New York, New York 10028

8:00 AM - 9:00 AM
Registration and Welcome Breakfast

9:00 AM - 9:15 AM
Opening Remarks
Speaker: Julian Taylor, Task Force Head & Chief Historian and Restorer,
Metropolitan Museum of Art, New York
Topic: Welcome and Introduction to the Conference

9:15 AM - 10:00 AM
Keynote Address
Speaker: Special Agent Sophia Roberts, Art Crime Specialist,
 FBI, New York
Topic: "The Rise of Art Theft: Trends and Implications"

10:00 AM - 10:45 AM
Panel Discussion
Topic: "Innovative Technologies in Art Recovery"
Panelists:
- Mark Thompson, Forensic Art Analyst
- Sarah Chen, Digital Security Expert
- David Rosen, Law Enforcement Officer

10:45 AM - 11:00 AM
Coffee Break

11:00 AM - 12:30 PM
Workshops (Choose One)
1. Workshop A: "Documenting and Authenticating Art"
Facilitator: Dr. Laura Mitchell, Art Historian

CONFERENCE AGENDA, p.2
Inaugural International Conference on the Theft and Forgery of World Art Masterpieces

2. Workshop B: "Collaborative Strategies for Art Institutions"
Facilitator: Tom Sullivan, Director of the Guggenheim Museum

12:30 PM - 1:30 PM
Networking Buffet Lunch

1:30 PM - 2:15 PM
Case Study Presentation
Speaker: Dr. Robert Sinclair, Art Recovery Consultant
Topic: "Successful Recoveries: Lessons Learned"

2:15 PM - 3:00 PM
Roundtable Discussion
Speaker: Dr. Emily Harper
Topic: "Building a Global Alliance Against Art Theft"

3:00 PM - 3:15 PM
Closing Remarks
Speaker: Julian Taylor
Topic: Next Steps and Call to Action

3:15 PM - 4:00 PM
Informal Networking Session

Thank you for attending! Let's work together to protect our cultural heritage.

Victoria Harrington was the first to arrive. With a background in art history and a strong business acumen, Victoria navigated the competitive world of art sales with grace. "Thank you for bringing us all together, Julian," she said, her voice smooth yet assertive. "This situation is more pressing than I initially thought."

Julian nodded, appreciating her timely arrival. "I'm glad you're here, Victoria. Your insights will be invaluable."

Victoria Harrington, Auction House Director at Christie's in London, commanded the auction house with poise and sophistication. As the director, she was known for her keen eye for valuable artworks and her ability to create buzz around high-profile auctions. Victoria expertly navigated the competitive world of art sales, earning respect from collectors and artists alike.

When whispers of a forgery scheme began to surface, Victoria's instincts told her that the integrity of her auctions was at risk. Having previously collaborated with Julian Taylor on several exhibitions and auctions, she recognized the importance of his findings. Determined to protect the reputation of Christie's and the trust of its clients, she eagerly joined forces with Julian and his team to uncover the truth behind the deception.

As they exchanged pleasantries, Antoine Dubois, the Director of the prestigious auction house Sotheby's in Paris, joined the meeting. Known for his expertise in French Impressionism, Antoine's charm and extensive network made him a key player in the art market. "I've heard whispers of this forgery scheme," he remarked, leaning forward with interest. "It seems our world is more interconnected than we realized."

"Absolutely," Julian replied. "We need to share information across borders to combat this effectively."

Dimitri Ivanov, the esteemed art curator from the Hermitage Museum in Saint Petersburg, Russia entered. With a deep passion for preserving cultural heritage, Dimitri was renowned for his expertise in Russian art.

Amidst the grandeur of the Hermitage Museum in St. Petersburg, Dimitri Ivanov, a distinguished curator, was renowned for his expertise in Russian art. With a passion for preserving cultural heritage, he dedicated himself to showcasing the masterpieces of the past while fostering appreciation for contemporary artists. Dimitri's deep understanding of art history and charismatic personality made him a sought-after figure in the international art community.

When news of the international forgery scheme reached the Hermitage, Dmitri felt an urgent need to act. His longstanding friendship with Julian Taylor, developed during collaborative projects, prompted him to offer his assistance. Dimitri's knowledge of the intricacies of the art world would be crucial in navigating the challenges ahead as they aimed to expose the syndicate threatening their beloved art.

"Julian, my friend!" Dimitri greeted warmly, extending his hand. "I'm eager to contribute. This kind of deceit must be exposed."

"Thanks for reaching out to me and offering to be here, Dimitri. Your knowledge of art history will help us navigate this difficult situation. We will regroup later today," Julian said, feeling the camaraderie grow among them.

Next to enter the auditorium, Akiko Tanaka, the curator at the Tokyo National Museum, bringing a refreshing energy to the room. Akiko is known for her innovative exhibitions that bridged the gap with her stunning displays of traditional Japanese art, and historical and contemporary art.

At the Tokyo National Museum, Akiko Tanaka stood surrounded by stunning displays of traditional Japanese art. As a highly respected curator, her dedication to preserving Japan's artistic legacy was matched only by her enthusiasm for engaging diverse audiences.

When Akiko learned of Julian Taylor's investigation into the theft and forgery of a precious van Gogh masterpiece, she felt compelled to contribute her expertise. Having collaborated with Julian on several projects in the past, she understood the importance of safeguarding authenticity in art. With her keen insights into the cultural significance of artworks, Akiko joined the team, ready to uncover the truth and protect the integrity of the art world from the looming threat.

"I'm honored to be part of this discussion," she said, her enthusiasm evident. "We must safeguard the authenticity of our cultural artifacts."

"I am happy you are able to attend with such short notice, I am glad to have you here, Akiko," Julian replied. "Your insights into contemporary practices will be crucial as we move forward."

Olivia Chang Phillips, the dynamic auction house director from Christie's New York City, entered with a confident stride. Known for her innovative approach to art sales, Olivia had revitalized the auction experience to attract a diverse range of clients. "I've been following the developments closely," she said, her tone serious. "This situation has the potential to impact the entire New York art scene."

Julian raised an eyebrow. "Exactly! That's why I felt it was essential to gather everyone here.

I am glad that you could make it under such short notice. We need to coordinate our efforts to uncover the truth behind this forgery ring."

Walking into the auditorium alone, Evelyn Sinclair was the head curator of the British Museum, known for her discerning taste and deep knowledge of art history. With over 15 years in the field, she had dedicated her career to making the museum's vast collection accessible and engaging to the public. Her polished demeanor and sharp intellect commanded respect from colleagues and visitors alike. Evelyn had a reputation for organizing captivating exhibitions that showcased the cultural significance of the artifacts under her care.

As whispers began to circulate about the integrity of the museum's collections, particularly following the discovery of the forgery linked to the van Gogh paintings, Evelyn became increasingly concerned. Her connections with Julian Taylor and Kamil Russo, forged during previous collaborations on exhibitions, made her a valuable ally in the investigation. However, Julian harbored suspicions about her thoroughness in reviewing the van Gogh painting before it was shipped to The Met. He couldn't shake the feeling that there was more to Evelyn's involvement than met the eye.

Evelyn had been involved in various high-stakes exhibitions across Europe, often collaborating with renowned art historians, including Alexander Moretti. Their mutual respect for each other's expertise had led to successful projects, but the current crisis threatened to unravel that trust. Additionally, Evelyn had previously dealt with issues of art theft, having been part of a task force that investigated the smuggling of artifacts from war-torn regions. This experience, while valuable, left her wary of scrutiny, and she was determined to protect the heritage of the museum at all costs.

Evelyn approached Julian with a sense of determination. "Good morning Julian, I made a last-minute decision to attend in person because this matter is extremely important to me and the British Museum. I spoke with Alexander Moretti the other day, and he mentioned he would be here in person as well. Our conversation prompted me to come—especially after the forgery incident at the museum--which left the British Museum an authentic van Gogh painting intact while we now face a forgery here at The Met. Have you seen Alex?"

In the hallowed halls of the Vatican Museum, Alexandre Moretti carefully studied a recently restored fresco. As an esteemed art historian specializing in Renaissance art, he was known for his deep understanding of the intricate narratives woven into each masterpiece. His Italian heritage and extensive training made him a respected authority in the field.

When rumors of a forgery scheme reached Alexandre's ears, he felt compelled to join the investigation led by Julian Taylor. Their shared dedication to preserving the integrity of art brought them together, and Alexandre's insights into Renaissance works would prove invaluable as they navigated the dark underbelly of the art world.

Julian, with a sigh of relief, murmuring to himself, "I could not get a word in edgewise." Evelyn scurried away on a mission to find Alexander Moretti before the conference began.

As Julian turned back around, he was pleasantly surprised to see David Cortez and Claire Bertrand approaching him.

"Good morning, Julian!" David said with a warm smile, his FBI badge glinting on his belt. "It's great to see you here."

"Hello, Detectives. Good to see you both," Julian replied, extending his hand for a firm handshake with David before turning to Claire. "Claire, it's a pleasure, and thank you for making the trip to New York."

"Likewise, Julian," Claire said, her demeanor professional yet friendly. As an Interpol detective, she carried an air of authority, and her experience in international art crime was well known. "I wouldn't miss this conference. The exchange of information is crucial for us right now."

Julian nodded, appreciating their presence. "Absolutely. The collaboration between our agencies is vital, especially with the rise of international art thefts. How are things on your end?"

David leaned in slightly, his expression serious. "We've been following a few leads related to recent high-profile thefts. It's evident that there's a coordinated effort among several syndicates. We need to share intelligence and strategies to combat this."

Claire added, "And we're hoping to gather more insights from the presentations today. The more we understand each other's methods, the better equipped we'll be to tackle these challenges."

Julian felt a surge of optimism. "I'm glad you're both here. Your expertise will greatly enrich our discussions. Let's make sure to connect during the breakout sessions. I'd love to hear your thoughts on the workshops."

"Definitely," David said. "We should also consider setting up a follow-up meeting after the conference to discuss specific cases and strategies in more detail."

Claire nodded in agreement. "That sounds like a plan. Sharing our findings will only strengthen our efforts. I booked two extra days in NYC to visit a few museums and take in a show perhaps, so I will be available."

As they continued their conversation, Julian felt reassured knowing that such dedicated professionals were engaged in the fight against art crime.

Anneke Vermeer, the Director of The Van Gogh Museum, strode into the room with purpose, her gaze quickly locking onto Julian. She approached him, her expression a mix of concern and determination.

"Julian! It's good to see you," Anneke said, her voice steady despite the weight of the situation. "I'm glad to be here, though I wish it were under better circumstances."

"Anneke, it's a pleasure to see you," Julian replied, extending a hand. "I share your sentiment. The thefts have cast a shadow over the art community, especially with the forgeries circulating."

"Yes, particularly the forgery that was taken from our museum," Anneke said, her brow furrowing. "Out of the four pieces we shipped, van Gogh's 'Starry Night' is the most troubling. The implications for our reputation are serious."

Julian nodded, understanding her concerns. "I can only imagine. That painting was a significant piece in your collection. Have you had any leads on how it was stolen?"

Anneke sighed, running a hand through her hair. "We believe it was a coordinated effort from an international syndicate. The security footage was compromised, which raises more questions than answers. It's crucial that we collaborate with law enforcement and other institutions to recover it."

"Absolutely," Julian agreed. "The conference is a perfect opportunity to share insights. It's essential that we pool our resources and intelligence. The more we know, the better equipped we'll be to combat this threat."

Anneke's expression softened slightly. "Thank you, Julian. I appreciate your support. It's reassuring to know we have allies in this fight. We need to protect our cultural heritage, and it starts with collaboration."

"Let's make a point to connect during the breakout sessions," Julian suggested. "I'd love to hear your thoughts on the strategies we can implement moving forward."

"Definitely," Anneke replied, her resolve renewed. "Together, we can make a difference. I'll see you during the sessions."

As they parted ways, both felt a sense of purpose, knowing that their collective efforts could lead to the recovery of not just one painting but the integrity of the art world itself.

It appears that Evelyn tracked down Alexander Moretti and they had already secured their seats close to the stage. Julian was somewhat relieved to not have to speak with Evelyn again before the conference started.

In the hallowed halls of the Vatican Museum, Alexander Moretti painstakingly studies the recently restored frescoes, blending his keen eye for detail with a profound understanding of Renaissance art. An esteemed art historian, Alexander specialized in the intricate narratives woven into each masterpiece, often delving into the socio-political contexts that shaped their creation. His Italian heritage, steeped in a rich cultural legacy, combined with extensive training in art history, had earned him a respected authority in the field.

When rumors of a forgery scheme reached Alexander's ears, he felt compelled to join the investigation led by Julian Taylor. Their shared dedication to preserving the integrity of art brought them together, and Alexander's insights into the workings of the art world, particularly its darker underbelly, would prove invaluable. He had crossed paths with various experts in the field, including Kamil Russo, with whom he had collaborated on exhibitions showcasing the Renaissance's influence on modern art. As the investigation unfolded, Alexander's connections would be crucial in navigating the intricate web of art theft and forgery, and he was determined to uncover the truth behind the rising tide of deception.

Dr. Grant, Dr. Thorne, Timothy and Rose entered together. Kamil and Marco followed a few steps behind.

They waved to Julian and attempted to find seating next to each other. The room was quickly filling up with the keynote speakers, other key essential players and important guests.

As the group settled in, Julian took his place at the podium to welcome everyone to the inaugural International Conference on the Theft and Forgery of World Art Masterpieces!" The crowd erupted into applause, the magnitude of this event and the presence of such esteemed attendees nearly overwhelmed Julian with gratitude and hope.

As the applause subsided, Julian smiled warmly at the audience and began his introduction.

"Welcome, everyone, to this pivotal gathering on the theft and forgery of world art masterpieces. We are here today not only to address the alarming rise of these crimes, but to forge a united front in protecting our cultural heritage. Our goal is to share insights, develop strategies, and create collaborations that will empower us to combat these threats effectively.

As you can see, today's agenda is packed with engaging discussions and expert panels. We will start with a keynote address by a leading investigator in art crime, followed by a series of presentations highlighting innovative technologies and methods to track and recover stolen art. After a break, we will dive into workshops that encourage collaboration among our diverse professionals, culminating in a roundtable discussion where we can brainstorm actionable solutions.

Together, we can make a difference in safeguarding our masterpieces for future generations. Thank you for being here, and let's get started!"

As the conference was on a coffee break, several attendees gathered in a room with Julian to provide some important updates:

Victoria took the lead. "We should first share what we know about the forgeries. I've heard rumors that they are not only happening in the UK but are also spreading across Europe and into the United States."

Dimitri nodded in agreement. "I've seen an uptick in inquiries about Russian works that seem suspicious. It's possible that this ring is more extensive than we initially thought."

Akiko added, "In Japan, there's been an increase in counterfeit traditional art as well. It's becoming a trend that could undermine the efforts we've all made to preserve our cultural heritage."

"I believe we all share a common goal," Olivia said, her voice firm. "We need to protect the integrity of our collections and our reputations."

Julian leaned forward, feeling the momentum building. "Exactly. I suggest we document all findings and we provide that information to the newly formed Task Force so there is a central location of all information and leads from representatives from each of our institutions. We can share intelligence, coordinate our investigations, and ensure that no piece of art is sold without thorough authentication."

Victoria raised a hand. "I can provide access to our auction records and any suspicious sales we've encountered. We should also look into recent shipments from our galleries to identify any patterns."

Antoine chimed in, "And I can coordinate with my contacts in Paris to gather information on any artworks that may have crossed borders recently."

Dimitri added, "I'll reach out to my colleagues at the Hermitage to compile data on any recent acquisitions that might be related to this scheme."

Akiko nodded enthusiastically. "And I will collaborate with museums in Japan to see if they've noticed similar forgeries."

Olivia smiled, her eyes sparkling with determination. "Together, we can uncover the truth behind this deception. I'll also leverage my connections in New York to gather insights from local galleries and collectors."

As they began to outline their action plan, Julian felt a surge of hope. This diverse group of experts, each with their unique strengths, was united in their mission. The stakes were high, but so was their commitment to preserving the integrity of the art world.

"Let's keep each other informed and meet regularly," Julian said, a sense of purpose in his voice. "I will establish a central email address to be used for information and documentation gathering. I will have a couple people on my staff monitor the email and compile the data. We have the potential to make a significant impact."

With that, the meeting commenced, and the atmosphere shifted from uncertainty to collaboration. Together, they would navigate the complexities of the art world and confront the looming threat of the forgery ring.

Before lunch, the conference attendees engaged in two informative workshops that aimed to equip them with practical skills and strategies for addressing art crime.

The first workshop, "Documenting and Authenticating Art," was facilitated by Dr. Laura Mitchell, an accomplished art historian from Boston. With a deep knowledge of art provenance and an impressive background in museum curation, Laura led the session with passion and expertise. She emphasized the importance of thorough documentation in the authentication process, illustrating her points with vivid examples from her own experiences at the Boston Museum of Fine Arts. Attendees learned about the various techniques used to verify the origin and authenticity of artworks, including the use of scientific analysis and historical research. Laura encouraged participants to engage in hands-on activities, allowing them to practice the skills necessary for documenting art accurately. The workshop was interactive, fostering lively discussions as attendees shared their own challenges and successes in the field.

Meanwhile, the second workshop, "Collaborative Strategies for Art Institutions," was facilitated by Tom Sullivan, the esteemed Museum Director of the Guggenheim Museum here in New York. Tom's extensive experience in managing art institutions made him a valuable resource for attendees looking to enhance their collaborative efforts. He opened the session by discussing the critical role of partnerships between museums, galleries, and law enforcement in combating art theft. Tom shared case studies that highlighted successful collaborations, inspiring attendees to consider how they might implement similar strategies in their own institutions. The workshop included group exercises where participants brainstormed potential partnerships and developed action plans to strengthen their networks. Tom's engaging approach fostered an atmosphere of cooperation and innovation, encouraging attendees to think beyond traditional boundaries in their quest to protect cultural heritage.

As the workshops concluded, participants left with newfound knowledge and a sense of camaraderie, eager to apply their insights to the pressing challenges faced by the art community. The combination of Laura's focus on the intricacies of documentation and authentication, alongside Tom's emphasis on collaborative strategies, set a strong foundation for the discussions that would follow in the afternoon sessions.

After lunch, the conference resumed with a compelling case study presentation by Dr. Robert Sinclair, an esteemed art recovery consultant. His presentation, titled "Successful

Recoveries: Lessons Learned," focused on real-world examples of recovered stolen artworks. Dr. Sinclair shared invaluable insights into the complexities of the recovery process, detailing specific cases where collaboration among various agencies and institutions led to the successful return of priceless pieces to their rightful homes. His expert analysis highlighted the importance of persistence, strategy, and the power of networking in the art recovery community.

Following Dr. Sinclair's presentation, the conference moved into the highly anticipated roundtable discussions, commencing at 2:15 PM. The topic, "Building a Global Alliance Against Art Theft," was moderated by Julian Taylor. Attendees gathered in smaller groups, eager to exchange ideas and explore collaborative efforts to combat the rising tide of art crime. Julian facilitated the discussions, encouraging participants to share their experiences and propose actionable strategies for enhancing international cooperation.

As the discussions wrapped up around 3 PM, Julian delivered the closing remarks, expressing gratitude to all the speakers and attendees for their contributions to a successful conference. He emphasized the importance of continuing the dialogue and maintaining the connections made during the event.

As the afternoon sessions progressed, Marco sat in his workshop, absorbing the discussions and the energy in the room. Inspired by the insightful presentations and the collaborative spirit of the conference, he decided to send a quick text to Julian.

'Hey Julian! Just wanted to say how great the meeting has been so far. The workshops were incredibly informative, and I love the direction we're heading. I was wondering if we could continue our conversation from last night—maybe talk about our ideas over coffee later? I feel like there's a lot to explore between us, both professionally and personally. Let me know your thoughts.'

After sending the message, Marco felt a mix of anticipation and nervousness. He appreciated his growing connection with Julian and hoped it could evolve into something more meaningful.

As the conference drew to a close, attendees began to filter into the networking area, where coffee and pastries awaited them. The atmosphere buzzed with excitement as people mingled, exchanging ideas and forging new connections. Laughter and animated conversations filled the room, creating an inviting space for collaboration.

At 4 PM, Julian stepped back onto the stage for the final wrap-up. He looked out at the gathered crowd, a sense of accomplishment washing over him. "Thank you all for being here today," he began, his voice steady and warm. "Your participation and insights have made this conference a resounding success. Together, we've taken significant steps toward building a global alliance against art theft."

He continued, "I encourage everyone to continue these conversations during our networking session. It's not just about sharing knowledge; it's about forming partnerships that can lead to real change in our field."

As he concluded, Julian felt a sense of gratitude toward everyone who had contributed to the day's success. "Let's keep the momentum going. Thank you once again for your dedication and passion. I look forward to seeing you all at future events!"

Julian stepped down from the stage, a satisfied smile lingering on his lips. The meeting had gone exceptionally well—he could feel the electric buzz of connections made, both professional and personal, as he navigated through the throng of attendees. The air was thick with the scent of polished wood and fresh paint, and the murmurs of excited conversations swirled around him like a warm embrace.

After the formalities concluded, everyone was invited to stay for an informal networking session. Attendees mingled, sharing their thoughts on the day's discussions and exchanging contact information. The atmosphere was lively, filled with laughter and animated conversations as professionals from different backgrounds connected over their shared passion for art preservation. Julian moved through the crowd, engaging with individuals and fostering new partnerships, fully aware that the relationships formed today would play a crucial role in the ongoing fight against art theft.

As he wandered through the crowd, his thoughts drifted back to Marco's text. The memory of their earlier conversation filled him with optimism. Marco had a way of seeing potential where others saw obstacles, and Julian couldn't help but feel that their paths were destined to intertwine further. He imagined the two of them over coffee, discussing everything from art to life, their laughter mingling with the clinking of cups.

"Hey, Julian!" a voice called, pulling him from his reverie. It was a colleague, waving enthusiastically. Julian paused to exchange pleasantries, but his mind was only half on the conversation. He nodded, smiled, and murmured the expected responses, all the while his thoughts danced back to Marco.

As the crowd began to thin, Julian made his way to his office, the familiar surroundings offering a sense of comfort. He gathered his belongings—his tethered leather briefcase, a few scattered notes, and a well-worn sketchbook filled with ideas he'd yet to explore. The hustle and bustle of the museum faded into the background as he focused on the evening ahead.

Once he was settled, Julian pulled out his phone and typed a quick message to Marco: 'I'm leaving now, and heading back to the apartment. We'll figure out what we can do for dinner when you arrive. Take your time; I'll be at home when you get to my condo.' He hit send and felt a flicker of anticipation.

20.

Moments with Marco and Julian

With a final glance around the office, Julian turned off the lights and stepped out into the Manhattan rush hour chaos, the cool air refreshing against his skin. As he began his short walk—only two blocks to his condo, thoughts of Marco filled him with a sense of possibility. Julian couldn't shake the feeling that this was just the beginning of an unexpected adventure.

Julian arrived back at his apartment, the familiar scent of polished wood and fresh linen greeting him as he stepped inside. Julian remembering his cleaning lady, Maria Reyes, was there today. He let out a sigh of relief, the energy of the day slowly ebbing away. The bustling crowd of The Metropolitan Museum of Art felt like a distant memory now. He tossed his briefcase onto the couch and wandered into the kitchen, glancing at the clock. It was still early, and he felt a flutter of excitement at the thought of Marco joining him soon.

Twenty minutes later, just as he was pouring himself a glass of water, he heard a knock at the door. A smile spread across his face as he opened it to reveal Marco, his eyes bright and a casual grin on his face.

"Hey! You made it!" Julian exclaimed, stepping aside to let him in.

"Of course! I wouldn't miss this," Marco replied, shaking off the chill of the evening air. "So, what's the plan? Coffee? Dinner? I'm starving."

Julian leaned against the doorframe, considering. "I could go for some coffee, but I'm also in the mood for something more filling. What do you think?"

Marco ran a hand through his hair, a thoughtful look on his face. "How about we grab some food and bring it back? There's that great sushi place just a few blocks away. We can get those sushi bowls you love."

"Perfect!" Julian replied, his enthusiasm matching Marco's. "Let's do it."

As they stepped out into the New York night, the streets came alive with the sounds of the city—honking cars, laughter, and the distant hum of music. Julian felt a sense of ease walking beside Marco, their conversation flowing effortlessly.

"So, how did you think the meeting went?" Marco asked, nudging him playfully with his shoulder.

"I thought it was a success. I mean, we made some solid connections," Julian said, his mind briefly flashing back to the earlier discussions. "But honestly, I'm even more excited about us getting to hang out like this."

"Me too," Marco said, his smile widening. "It's nice to unwind after all that hustle. Plus, I've been looking forward to catching up. Even though I have been staying at your place for a week now, we are so busy we don't have a lot of time to talk about anything other than art theft and forgeries."

They reached the Japanese sushi restaurant, the neon sign glowing invitingly. Inside, the air was fragrant with the scent of rice and fish. They placed their orders quickly—Julian opting for a spicy tuna bowl while Marco chose a salmon bowl, both eager to indulge.

As they walked back, the bowls cradled in their arms, Julian felt a warmth building between them. Once inside the apartment, they settled at the small dining table, the bowls very inviting before them.

"Cheers to good food and good company," Marco said, raising his bowl in a playful toast.

"Cheers!" Julian echoed, clinking his bowl against Marco's before digging in.

Between bites, their conversation turned more introspective. "You know," Marco began, "I've always valued our friendship. It's important to me, especially now that we're working together."

Julian nodded, his gaze steady on Marco. "Same here. I don't want our personal feelings to interfere with business. But I also can't deny that there's something... more between us."

Marco paused, looking thoughtful. "I feel it too. But I worry about how it might complicate things. We've been friends for so long."

"I get that," Julian said, setting down his

bowl. "But it's also why I think we should be open about it. We can't ignore this connection, right?"

"Right," Marco replied, a hint of relief in his voice. "I just think we should take it slow. We don't want to jeopardize what we have."

Julian smiled, feeling a sense of understanding pass between them. "Agreed. Let's just enjoy the moment and see where it leads us."

They continued to eat, laughter and easy banter filling the room, the tension easing as they shared stories and dreams. In that cozy space, surrounded by the warmth of their friendship, Julian felt hopeful about what lies ahead.

Feeling somewhat exhausted from the whirlwind of the day, Julian let out a soft sigh and leaned against the doorframe. "I'm heading to my bedroom, Marco. I really need to rest and clear my mind after everything that's happened today. You understand, right?" He managed a weary smile, hoping to convey his need for solitude without sounding dismissive.

"Of course, Julian," Marco replied, rubbing the back of his neck as he glanced toward the window, where the city lights illuminated the skyline. "I'm feeling a bit worn out myself. I think I'll head to my room too and check my emails. There are responsibilities waiting for me in Florence, and I need to stay connected." He paused, a hint of concern touching his voice. "Just make sure you take care of yourself. We've got a lot ahead of us."

Julian nodded appreciatively. "Thanks, Marco. It's good to know we're in this together. Good night."

"Good night," Marco echoed, a faint smile crossing his lips as he turned to make his way down the hall.

As Julian closed the door to his

bedroom, he leaned against it for a moment, allowing the silence to envelop him. His thoughts immediately turned to Marco, a whirlwind of emotions swirling within him—deep affection mixed with a nagging suspicion. He admired Marco's determination and passion, yet there was an undeniable tension that lingered between them. 'Why can't I just tell him how I feel? Julian pondered, running a hand through his hair. They had shared countless moments over the years, their friendship deepening with each encounter, but the weight of unspoken words hung heavily in the air.

Now, the thought of crossing that line both excited and terrified him.

'What if he doesn't feel the same way?' Julian's heart raced at the thought. They had shared a few fleeting touches—hugs that lingered a moment too long, glances that felt charged with unspoken longing—but those were mere hints of intimacy he craved. Each time they brushed against the possibility of exploring their feelings, an invisible wall seemed to rise between them, leaving Julian yearning for clarity.

In the adjacent room, Marco sat on the edge of his bed, staring at his laptop, but the screen blurred as his thoughts drifted. 'I need to check my emails, but what's the point?' he mused, frustration creeping in. His mind was consumed by thoughts of Julian. He admired Julian's determination and passion, qualities that had always drawn him in, but he couldn't help but feel a sense of unease. There were things he hadn't shared—secrets that weighed heavily on him.

'What if I push him away?' Marco wondered. He had always been the more guarded of the two, reluctant to take risks with his heart. Even though he wanted to explore the depth of his feelings for Julian, the fear of jeopardizing their friendship loomed large. They had danced around their emotions for so long, and now it felt like they were teetering on the edge of something profound.

Maybe it's better this way, he thought, but deep down, he knew that avoiding the truth wouldn't erase the longing he felt. The memories of their shared laughter, their adventurous days at Columbia, and that fleeting embrace haunted him. 'Can I really keep pretending that everything is fine?'

As the night deepened, both Julian and Marco lay in their separate rooms, each wrestling with their thoughts. The silence was thick with unspoken words, and the distance between them felt both comforting and painfully isolating. They were at a crossroads, caught between friendship and something more, both yearning for connection but held back by their own fears and uncertainties.

Tension charged with unspoken desires, Marco knocks on Julian's bedroom door.

Julian, opening the door, surprised says "Marco? What's wrong?"

Before Julian can say more, Marco steps inside and, in one swift motion, pulls Julian close to him and pushes him gently onto the bed.

Breathless, leaning over Julian, Marco whispered "I can't take it anymore. I need you."

Julian's heart races as he looks up at Marco, a mix of shock and excitement in his eyes.

"Marco...Julian" they said.

Marco, voice low, intense, said "I've been holding back for too long. I want you. All of you."

He leans down, capturing Julian's lips with his, the kiss igniting all the feelings they've both been suppressing. It's passionate and raw, filled with longing. Julian, pulling back slightly, breathless "Are you sure about this?" Marco, gazing into Julian's eyes "I've never been more sure of anything."

As the door closed behind them, the air crackled with unspoken tension. Marco and Julian stood close, their breaths mingling, each heartbeat echoing in the charged silence. With a swift, almost primal instinct, they tore off each other's boxers, shedding the last remnants of restraint. The world outside faded away, leaving only the two of them in their dimly lit sanctuary.

Their bodies collided in a fever of wild, animalistic passion. Every kiss ignited a fire that had long been simmering beneath the surface, fueled by years of pent-up desire. They lost themselves in each other, surrendering to the intensity of the moment. Each touch was electric, every whisper a promise of the connection they had both yearned for. The boundaries of their friendship blurred, morphing into something deeper and more profound.

As the night unfolded, they explored the depths of their emotions, intertwining their souls in a dance that felt both exhilarating and liberating. The years of hesitation melted away, leaving only the raw vulnerability of their love. They moved together with an urgency that spoke of their shared history, their bodies speaking the words they had never dared to say.

Finally, as the waves of ecstasy subsided and silence enveloped them, they lay entwined in each other's arms. The intimacy of the moment settled around them like a warm blanket, and in that peaceful aftermath, they felt a deep sense of fulfillment. The connection they had craved for so long now felt tangible, solidified in the quietude of their shared breath. They gazed into each other's eyes, the promise of a new beginning shimmering in the air between them as they drifted off to sleep.

21.

The Morning After

The light of early morning spilled into the apartment, casting a warm glow on the carefully curated chaos of the night before. Julian stood by the window, sipping his coffee, the city awakening beneath him. He took a moment to appreciate the stillness before the day's whirlwind began. Last night replayed in his mind—the warmth of Marco's body next to his, the intimacy of their lovemaking, and the way they had drifted into sleep wrapped in each other's arms. Julian felt a smile tug at his lips as he recalled the softness of Marco's touch and the laughter they shared.

Reluctant to disturb him, Julian rose quietly from the bed, careful not to wake Marco. He slipped out of the sheets, feeling the cool air against his skin, and gathered his clothes from the floor. After a quick shower to shake off the remnants of sleep, he dressed, the anticipation of the day ahead mingling with the lingering warmth of their night together.

Julian glanced at the note he'd left on the kitchen table for Marco: 'Heading to the museum. Looking forward to seeing you later, and looking forward to an incredible weekend. P.S. You're mine!' With a little smile, he grabbed his bag and stepped out, the door clicking shut behind him.

As he walked down the bustling streets of Manhattan, Julian stopped at his favorite café. The aroma of freshly brewed coffee filled the air, mingling with the scent of warm bagels. He ordered his usual—a plain bagel with cream cheese and a large coffee. The barista, recognizing him, offered a friendly nod, and Julian felt a sense of comfort in the routine.

With his breakfast in hand, he arrived at The Metropolitan Museum of Art, the grand facade looming before him like a guardian of history. Inside, the halls were still quiet, footsteps echoing in the vastness. Julian headed straight to his office, a small, organized space filled with art books and sketches, remnants of the conference swirling in his mind.

Settling at his desk, he opened his laptop, ready to tackle the influx of emails that awaited him. Questions from the conference attendees flooded in, ranging from logistics to artistic inquiries. He methodically began responding, each keystroke a reminder of the vibrant discussions from the night before.

As he typed, a thought struck him—he needed to connect with Dr. Samuel Grant. The Director of the Met had to be in the loop regarding the staged auction at Christie's. Julian knew the stakes; they couldn't afford any leaks, especially with such a small circle of trust. He grabbed his phone and dialed Dr. Grant's number.

"Good morning, Julian," Dr. Grant answered, his voice steady and professional.

"Dr. Grant, I hope I'm not interrupting. I wanted to discuss something important regarding the auction," Julian began, keeping his tone measured. "Could we arrange a meeting today? There are a few details I'd like to share, and I believe Lila should also be involved."

"Of course," Dr. Grant replied. "I'm free in an hour. Will that work?"

"Perfect. I'll have Lila join us then. Thank you, Samuel."

As he hung up, Julian felt the weight of the day settling on his shoulders. He knew adding Lila to the mix would only increase the number of people privy to their plans, but it was essential for the project's success. He leaned back in his chair, considering the implications.

His phone buzzed with a message from Eleanor Byrne. 'Ready to discuss the auction when you are. Let's keep this under wraps.' Julian's heart raced; he had to remind Eleanor and Liam of the utmost confidentiality. He quickly typed back, 'Absolutely. This must remain between us for now.'

With a sigh, Julian turned his attention to the view outside his office window. The city was alive, yet he felt an urgent need to contain the excitement brewing around the auction. He picked up his notebook, jotting down key points for their meeting, emphasizing the need for discretion.

22.

The Sting Operation

As Julian settled into his office, the anticipation of the upcoming auction buzzed in the air, intertwining with the vibrant energy of The Metropolitan Museum of Art. Today marked a pivotal moment, and he knew the path ahead would require careful navigation, trust, and above all, discretion.

Before he could gather his thoughts or make any calls, his phone buzzed with a text from Dr. Samuel Grant. 'Lila and I are on our way to your office.'

Julian took a deep breath, knowing this meeting would set the tone for everything that followed. He adjusted his tie, mentally preparing to bring Samuel and Lila into the loop about the staged auction at Christie's in London.

He glanced at his notes, which detailed

the auction plans and the key points he needed to cover. It was crucial to explain that he had already reached out to Eleanor about the logistics and that he intended to call both Det. Eleanor Byrne and Liam Chen after this meeting. They needed to understand the significance of keeping this information confidential, especially as more people became involved.

Moments later, there was a gentle knock on the door. "Come in!" Julian called, his heart quickening as Samuel and Lila entered.

"Good morning, Julian," Samuel greeted, his expression serious yet open. Lila followed, her demeanor calm, but focused, ready to engage in the discussion.

As Julian settled back into his chair, he glanced at Samuel and Lila, both of whom were leaning forward with keen interest. "Thank you for being here on such short notice," he began, feeling the weight of what he was about to share. "I want to discuss the staged auction we're planning at Christie's. This isn't just any auction; it's a strategic move to catch the person behind the recent theft and forgery of the two van Gogh paintings sent to The Met for inclusion in The Vincent van Gogh Exhibition."

He watched as their expressions shifted to one of curiosity. "Eleanor Byrne, a detective in London, is already in the loop about our investigation. She's been instrumental in tracking leads and has a wealth of experience in art crimes."

Julian paused to gauge their reactions, then continued, "Additionally, I've consulted with Liam Chen. He's well-known in the European art community and has collaborated with law enforcement, including Eleanor. He brings significant credibility to our efforts."

Lila nodded, her brow furrowing slightly. "What about the international aspect?"

Julian pressed on, encouraged by their engagement. "We're also involving two individuals from Interpol—Jonathan Walker, a specialist in art crime from Scotland Yard, and Det. Claire Bertrand from Interpol who's been instrumental in similar cases. There is one more person at this time that must be brought into the loop and that is Victoria Harrington, Auction House Director of Christie's London. These five individuals will play a strategic role in the staged auction. I believe we have a robust team ready to handle this operation."

He leaned back, letting the implications sink in. "This auction will not only help us identify the culprit but also reaffirm the museum's commitment to protecting its collection. We need to ensure everyone involved understands the gravity of this situation and the necessity for strict confidentiality."

"I need your insights on how we can approach this," Julian said, looking between Samuel and Lila. "I plan to reach out to Eleanor and Liam afterward to keep them in the loop, but I want your thoughts first. We need to ensure everyone understands the gravity of this situation."

Samuel nodded thoughtfully. "It's a significant opportunity and something we must be involved in, but we must tread carefully. The fewer people who know about this initially, the better."

Lila chimed in, "Agreed. We can't risk any leaks. It's essential that we present a united front with Eleanor and Liam."

Julian felt a sense of relief wash over him. "Exactly. I want to ensure that everyone involved understands the importance of discretion. This isn't just another project; it could redefine how we approach our exhibitions."

As the three of them discussed the logistics and potential challenges, Julian felt a growing sense of purpose. Today was just the beginning, and with Samuel and Lila on board, he was more confident than ever that they could navigate the complexities ahead while safeguarding their vision.

With their shared commitment to confidentiality, Julian knew they were laying the groundwork for something truly remarkable. He could already envision the impact of the auction, and he was eager to take the next steps—carefully, of course.

Samuel and Lila excused themselves, offering reassuring smiles as they left Julian's office, gently pulling the door closed behind them.

As Julian settled down for the calls he needed to make, he jotted down notes documenting his meeting with Samuel and Lila. First on his list was Detective Inspector Eleanor Byrne from London. He hoped to discuss the van Gogh painting shipped from the British Museum under Evelyn Sinclair's direction to The Met. Eleanor was sharp and resourceful, known for her tenacity in solving complex cases. Julian envisioned a conversation where he could glean insights into the current climate of art crime, which would be invaluable as they prepared for the "high-stakes" auction.

Next, he turned his attention to Dr. Alexander Fischer, the esteemed curator from the Hermitage Museum in Saint Petersburg. Julian had long admired Fischer's expertise and hoped to collaborate with him on sourcing pieces for the auction. He imagined discussing the potential of showcasing lesser-known treasures alongside the more famous artworks, creating a narrative that would captivate bidders.

As he typed out notes, a thought struck him about Liam Chen, the district art dealer. Chen was a well-known figure in the art community, celebrated for his connections and keen eye for valuable pieces. Julian made a mental note to reach out to him as well; he could be instrumental in curating a diverse collection that would draw significant interest at the auction.

With his mind racing, Julian began drafting an email message to Eleanor. 'Hello Detective Byrne, this is Julian Taylor from the MET in New York. I'd love to discuss some recent developments in art theft with you—do you have time for a call this week?' Email sent.

After sending the message, he turned his attention to Dr. Fischer. 'Dear Dr. Fisher, I hope this message finds you well. I'm reaching out to explore the possibility of collaborating on an upcoming auction. I believe your expertise would be invaluable in putting together a remarkable collection. Would you be available for a call me?' Julian pushed send.

Feeling accomplished, Julian leaned back in his chair for a moment, glancing out the window at the city beyond. He could already feel the thrill of the auction house scenario—the excitement of potential deals and connections. The stakes were high, and he was determined to make this worthwhile, not just for the museum but also for himself and colleagues in the art world.

His thoughts drifted to the undercurrents of the art world, where crime and intrigue often lurked just beneath the surface. The upcoming high-stakes auction was not just an opportunity to showcase exceptional pieces; it was also a magnet for those who might try to exploit the situation. Julian's mind raced with the possibilities—art theft, forgeries, and underhanded dealings. He knew that the darker side of the art world was always lurking, and he felt the thrill of the challenge.

He envisioned the auction floor, crowded with eager bidders, each one hoping to secure a masterpiece. But among them could be those who sought to manipulate the event for their own gain—a black market art network, perhaps, looking to slip a forgery into the mix or steal a coveted piece in the chaos. Julian's heart quickened at the thought; this was a game of high stakes where every piece of art told a story, and every bidder had a secret.

Determined to stay ahead, he began brainstorming strategies. He needed to gather not just art, but also information—who might attend, who might have ulterior motives, and how to safeguard the integrity of the auction. He reached for his notebook, jotting down names of contacts who could provide intel, including Eleanor Byrne, who had her finger on the pulse of art crime in London.

Julian felt a mix of excitement and trepidation. This wasn't just about selling art; it was about navigating a treacherous landscape filled with ambition, deception, and the allure of danger. As he prepared for the day's tasks, he knew he had to be vigilant. The auction might just be the most thrilling chapter of his career, but it was also a potential battleground.

With renewed focus, Julian returned to his notes, ready to tackle the calls that lay ahead. He was determined to uncover every lead, to connect the dots in the complex tapestry of the art world, all while keeping an eye out for the shadows lurking in the corners.

Just then, his phone buzzed with a message from Marco. 'Hey Julian! Just woke up. Thank you for the very nice note. I appreciate that very much. Thinking of grabbing some breakfast outside. Let's figure something out for this weekend!'

Julian smiled, feeling happy to receive Marco's text. He quickly replied, 'Marco, I hope you know how enjoyable last night was and I have been thinking about you today. I will reach out around 4pm to discuss our plans for the evening.'

As he settled back into his work, Julian's mind raced with ideas and possibilities, each call and connection bringing him closer to the high-stakes auction that was fast approaching. The thrill of the art world was calling him, and he was ready to answer.

Julian's phone rang, pulling him from his thoughts. He glanced at the screen and saw Liam Chen's name flashing. The mere sight of it sparked a mix of excitement and apprehension. Liam was a well-known figure in the art community, straddling the fine line between legitimate art dealing and the underground market with a charm that often disarmed even the most skeptical.

"Good afternoon, Liam!" Julian answered, trying to keep his tone light despite the seriousness of their ongoing discussions.

"Julian! Good to hear from you," Liam's voice came through, smooth and confident. "I hope I'm not catching you at a bad time."

"Not at all. I was just jotting down some notes about the upcoming auction, potentially in London, that we would like your collaboration on," Julian replied, leaning back in his chair. "I could use your insight, actually, and your strictest confidentiality here. As you have probably read, we encountered two van Gogh forgeries last week, one arriving from The British Museum, curated by Evelyn Sinclair; and, the other from The Van Gogh Museum in Amsterdam, curated by Dr. Anneke Vermeer. Both are reputable in the art world, but I am still shaken that they both could sign off on forgeries to be used in a prestigious exhibition at The Met. There must be something else. I am thinking, perhaps, a switch during shipping on their end or the arrival city."

"Ah, the murky waters of the art world," Liam said with a chuckle, but there was an edge to his voice. "You're right to be cautious. The stakes are high, and those who play with fire often get burned."

Julian could sense the underlying tension in Liam's words. The art world was a double-edged sword, and Liam's connections often placed him in morally ambiguous situations. "I know you have your ear to the ground in London's vibrant art district. With your street smarts and knowledge of the darker side of the market, you could be a valuable ally in this."

"Or a liability," Liam interjected, his tone shifting slightly. "I respect your dedication to uncovering the truth, but you should know that crossing paths with powerful figures in this game can be dangerous. My connections could help you, but they could also lead you into deeper waters than you bargained for."

Julian considered this. He appreciated Liam's transparency but felt the weight of his warning. "I get that, but I believe we need to navigate these treacherous waters carefully. If there's a forgery ring out there, we need to expose it before it wreaks more havoc with more stolen pieces. I know you have a knack for spotting the real from the fake."

"True," Liam replied, his voice thoughtful. "But you have to remember that not everyone in this game plays by the rules. Some of the best pieces are found in the shadows, and the same goes for the players involved. You need to decide where your loyalties lie."

"I'm committed to the integrity of the art world," Julian said firmly. "But I can't do it alone. I need someone who knows the ins and outs like you do."

Liam paused, weighing his response. "I'll help you, but let's tread carefully. I'll set up a few meetings with some contacts who might have information on the forgeries. Just be prepared for the unexpected—things can get complicated."

"Thanks, Liam. I appreciate it," Julian said, feeling a surge of hope. "I know we can make this work. Just let me know when we can meet."

"Will do. Just remember, Julian, in this business, trust is a rare commodity. Keep your wits about you."

As the call ended, Julian leaned back in his chair, reflecting on Liam's words. With allies like Liam by his side, he felt equipped to navigate the intricate web of the art world. Yet, he knew the shadows ran deep, and vigilance was essential. The excitement of the upcoming auction, fraught with the shadow of forgery and theft, mingled with a discernible threat of deception, Julian was resolute in his mission to uncover the truth, no matter how perilous the path ahead might be.

As Julian pondered his next steps with Liam Chen, his phone buzzed with a new voicemail notification. He glanced at the screen and saw it was from Inspector Eleanor Byrne. The clock on his desk read 11:00 AM—4 PM in London on a Saturday afternoon. He quickly pressed play, her voice coming through with a sense of urgency.

"Julian, it's Eleanor Byrne. I hope you're still available to talk. I have some important updates regarding the art theft case. Please call me back when you can."

Julian felt a stir of excitement. He typed a quick response: 'Yes, I'm still in my office. Would you like me to call you now, or is it too late? I don't want to take up your weekend.'

Her reply came almost instantly: 'No, I'm really anxious to speak with you. Please call now.'

Without hesitation, Julian picked up the phone and dialed her number. She answered immediately, her tone professional yet warm. "Julian, thank you for getting back to me so quickly."

"Of course, Inspector Byrne. I appreciate you reaching out. What's the update?" Julian asked, leaning forward in his chair, ready to absorb whatever information she had.

"I've been reviewing the recent art thefts and the potential connections to the forgeries we discussed. It appears that there's a network operating between London and New York," Eleanor explained, her voice steady.

"I'm considering an operation where we arrange a staged auction to catch the thieves in the act. We'd need to create an environment that could lure them in, and an auction at Christie's in London would be the perfect setting."

Julian's mind raced as he processed Det. Byrne's words. "As they say, 'two great minds think alike.' I just hung with Liam Chen and we also discussed the idea of a staged auction in London to catch the art crime syndicate in action.

Now it makes more sense than ever to put this urgently in motion. The downside is the auction could attract all the wrong attention. Are there specific leads you want me to be aware since this is such a bold move. How do you envision this working?"

Eleanor paused for a moment before responding. "We'd need to involve key players who have connections to the art underworld, including Liam Chen. His knowledge of the darker side of the market could help us understand how to set the bait. We'd also need to ensure the right security measures are in place."

"Absolutely," Julian agreed. "Liam has a unique perspective and can navigate those waters better than most. But what about the logistics? How do we keep this under wraps while ensuring the right people are there?"

"I have a few contacts within the London police force who specialize in undercover operations," Eleanor said. "They can help us manage the security and surveillance aspects without raising suspicion. We'll need to keep this tight-lipped to avoid alerting the thieves. Have you discussed this plan with anyone other than Liam Chen?"

Julian could feel the weight of the plan developing. "Yes. For obvious reasons, I had to bring into the loop, Dr. Samuel Grant, Museum Director of The Met, and our colleague, Dr. Lila Thorne, Director of Restoration and Conservation. At this point, we have five individuals that know about this plan. I can handle the auction details and ensure everything appears normal. I will need to bring Victoria Harrington into the loop. I don't believe we can pull this off without her. She is the Auction House Director for Christie's London. We'll just need to be strategic about the artwork we showcase."

"Precisely," Eleanor confirmed. "And we should also consider any other potential partners who might have insights or connections to these criminals. The more intelligence we can gather, the better our chances of catching them."

Julian nodded, feeling a mix of excitement and apprehension. "I'll reach out to Liam again to bring him on board to assist. It's a risky plan, but it might just work."

"Risky, yes, but necessary," she replied. "We're working against some dangerous individuals, Julian. But if we can catch them in the act, we can put a significant dent in their operations."

"Understood, Inspector. I'll start making calls to get the "auction" set up and keep you updated. Of course, other than you and Liam, I will not divulge this plan to anyone," Julian said, determination fueling his voice.

"Thank you, Julian. I'll be waiting to hear back from you. And remember stay safe. This isn't just about art; it's about navigating a treacherous world," Eleanor warned.

"Absolutely. I'll be careful," he assured her before hanging up.

As he put down the phone, Julian felt the weight of the situation settling over him. Arranging a staged auction was no small feat, but it was a necessary step in exposing the truth behind the forgeries and thefts that plagued the art world. With allies like Eleanor and Liam, he felt a flicker of hope amidst the shadows.

Julian took a deep breath and dialed Liam Chen's number. He felt a rush of urgency; they needed to work on their plans now that Eleanor was on board.

"Julian!" Liam answered, his voice lively.

"What's the news?"

"Eleanor is on board for the staged auction," Julian said, cutting straight to the point. Eleanor suggested we stage the auction at Christie's in London."

"Christie's? That's a prime location," Liam replied, his intrigue evident. "What's the plan?"

Julian leaned back in his chair, excitement mingling with apprehension. "Eleanor mentioned she's come across some significant leads regarding a couple of paintings—one that was shipped from the British Museum to New York and possibly the van Gogh that was sent from Amsterdam. We believe these could be tied to the forgery ring."

"Interesting," Liam mused. "I can see why we're moving quickly. The stakes are high, and if they catch wind of our intentions, it could get messy."

"Exactly," Julian said. "We need to keep this under wraps. I was thinking we could frame it as a collaborative effort with both Victoria Harrington, the Auction House Director at Christie's London and Eleanor Sinclair, the curator at The British Museum. It'll give us a legitimate front while we set the stage."

"Clever," Liam replied, his tone shifting to one of consideration. "But how do you think they will feel being part of a potential sting operation? They might not take kindly to being used as bait."

Julian rubbed his temples, contemplating the challenge. "I am fully on board with approaching Victoria Harrington. I do not think we could pull off a staged auction without Christie's Auction House Director involved. However, quite honestly, I was hoping to not make Evelyn aware of our plans at this time. I'll make sure to approach her as if I want to collaborate on an auction with her and Christie's. The idea is to create a genuine auction atmosphere, so we'll need her expertise and credibility. It is not a good idea to include anyone else in our plan unless they are fully vetted."

"Good point," Liam agreed. "Evelyn Sinclair is well-respected. If we can get her on board, it adds a layer of legitimacy. But we also need to ensure she understands the risks involved. I also thoroughly agree that we cannot stage an auction without the Auction House director fully involved. Victoria Harrington is well respected and is well-known throughout the European art community."

"Right," Julian said, feeling the weight of the plan. "I'll reach out to her and discuss how we can frame it. We need to present it as an opportunity for her to curate an exciting auction that showcases rare pieces. I want to make it sound appealing. I do not want Evelyn to know our real intentions at this time."

"Let me know how that goes," Liam said. "And keep me in the loop. I can help with the logistics and make sure we have the right pieces lined up to draw in the right crowd—both legitimate buyers and those with less honest intentions."

"Thanks, Liam. I'll touch base with you after I speak with Evelyn Sinclair," Julian replied, feeling the momentum building. "I will not reach out to her until early Monday. Contacting her on the weekend to discuss an auction may arise her suspicions."

"Looking forward to it. Just remember, Julian, this is a delicate dance we're doing. One misstep could blow everything wide open," Liam warned.

Julian nodded, even though Liam couldn't see him. "I understand. I'll be cautious. We're in this together." He paused, then added, "Just to clarify, it's understood that for now, the three of us—Victoria, you, and I—are the only ones fully aware of the plan we're putting into motion."

Liam responded, "Agreed, Julian. We will speak soon.

Julian paces as he processes the high stakes of the upcoming auction.

After wrapping up his calls with Liam and Eleanor, Julian felt a surge of anxiety. The stakes were higher than he had anticipated, and the complexity of the auction was becoming overwhelming. With so many influential players involved, he couldn't afford to let any mistakes slip through the cracks.

In a moment of clarity, he realized that a more focused approach was necessary. He grabbed his phone and dialed Samuel Grant and Lila Thorne, requesting an urgent meeting. Just 90 minutes had passed since their last discussion, but Julian's instincts told him that time was of the essence.

Julian, on the phone, "Samuel, Lila, I know we just met not long ago, but I need to see you both again. There are too many moving parts in this auction, and I feel we need to regroup. Can you meet me in 15?"

Samuel replied "Of course, Julian. We will be in your office soon."

Lila and Samuel walked into Julian's office since he was waiting with the door slightly ajar. Samuel said, "What can we do for you Julian?

"I want to fly to London and hold a planning meeting," Julian stated firmly. "We need to gather everyone involved—Evelyn, Victoria, Liam, Eleanor… It's crucial that we align our strategies before things spiral out of control."

Lila nodded, interjecting her agreement. "That makes sense. The more minds we have in the room, the better."

Julian hesitated, glancing between them. "I didn't think either of you would attend in person. If you feel it's necessary, please say so. I just assumed that with all the work here and the reworking of the van Gogh exhibit needing your expertise, it would be too much for all of us to go to London at the same time."

Samuel replied, "You're correct, Julian. Neither Lila nor I will be able to leave the museum at this delicate time, especially after the van Gogh forgery press releases. We think you should go as soon as possible. If you need someone to assist you, why don't you take Marco Rossi? He's mentioned that he doesn't know how much longer he can stay in New York before returning to his work in Florence. This trip could get him closer to home."

Julian paused, considering the suggestion. "That's something to think about. Marco is talented, and having him with me could provide additional support. Plus, it might give him a chance to reconnect with the art scene in London and be closer to his home in Florence."

Julian, continued, "He has a keen eye for details, and I could use that perspective in the meeting. Marco's passion for art is infectious. Having him there could boost morale and help keep the energy up during the planning. With Marco's familiarity with our projects, he can help bridge any gaps and ensure we're all on the same page. I, certainly, don't want him to feel stuck in New York when he has a life waiting for him in

Florence. This trip might be just what he needs."

"I will reach out to Marco and see if he's available. I think it could work out well for both of us. Thank you so much for your confidence. I will do my best."

Lila spoke up, "Well, that sounds like a solid plan. It should be easy for you to discuss this with Marco since he's staying at your place while he's in New York, right?"

Julian seemed momentarily lost in thought. "Julian?" Lila called again.

"Sorry, Lila," he said, shaking off his distraction. "I was just considering everything I need to prepare. I think I should book a Sunday night flight—tomorrow night, actually. It'll just be the two of us traveling. We need to arrange everything tonight when I get home."

The clock ticking closer to noon as the bustling sounds of the city filter through the window, Julian picked up his phone and dialed Marco's number, feeling a mix of excitement and urgency about the upcoming trip. As the phone rang, he briefly reflected on how much he valued Marco's perspective.

Marco, picking up, "Hey, Julian! What's up?"

"Hi, Marco. I wanted to talk to you about something important. I've decided to fly to London for a planning meeting regarding the auction. We need to gather everyone involved, and I think it would be beneficial for you to come along."

Marco, somewhat surprised, "Really? That sounds exciting! What's the timeline?"

Julian said, "I'm looking to leave tomorrow night. I know you're staying at my place, so it'll be convenient for us to make arrangements together. Can you come to my office as soon as possible? We need to discuss the details and finalize everything."

"Absolutely! I'll be there in twenty minutes. What should I bring?" Marco asked.

"Just your notes and any ideas you have for the auction. I want us to hit the ground running in London. And let's make sure our travel plans are all set before tonight."

Marco said "Sounds good! I'll see you soon."

Julian replied "Great, hey Marco? If you don't mind, can you run out and pick up lunch; a sandwich or something. We can have a working lunch here in my office."

Marco agreed, "A working lunch it is! Great idea Julian."

While Julian waited for Marco to come with their lunch, Julian decided to call Liam and Eleanor to begin the process to set up the meeting as soon as possible for an arrival in the next couple of days. 'I want to hit the ground running as soon as we land, he mumbled to himself.

Julian takes a deep breath and dials Liam's number.

"Liam, it's Julian. I hope I'm not catching you at a bad time?"

Liam said, "Not at all Julian. Did you find out something new?"

"I've realized we need to have a planning meeting in London. I want to gather everyone involved in the planning of the auction—Victoria, Eleanor, and you. I think we should wait to bring Evelyn into the meeting. Can we coordinate schedules for the next couple of days," Julian asked.

"Absolutely," Liam said. "I think that's a great idea. We need everyone on the same page, especially with the stakes this high. When do you want to meet?"

"I'm thinking of flying to London Sunday night." Julian said. "Let's aim for the day after, if that works for everyone. I'll reach out to Eleanor next."

Liam: "Sounds good. I'll make sure to clear my schedule."

Julian: "Perfect. I'll keep you updated once I hear back from Eleanor."

Julian hangs up and immediately calls Eleanor.

Julian: "Eleanor, it's Julian. I hope you're doing well. I wanted to touch base about the a planning meeting regarding the auction in London."

Eleanor: "Hi, Julian! Everything's good on my end. What days?"

Julian: "I'm flying to London tomorrow on an overnight flight. I thought we should hold a planning meeting, in person, with everyone involved. Can you confirm your availability for all day Tuesday and Wednesday, if possible?"

Eleanor: "Absolutely. I'm very much on board. It's crucial we get everyone together, especially with all the complexities we're facing."

Julian: "Great! I'll reach out to Victoria as well. Liam is already on board. Let's make this happen."

Eleanor: "Looking forward to it. Let's make sure this auction is a success? Safe travels Julian!"

Julian hangs up, feeling a sense of relief wash over him. The urgency of the situation hadn't diminished, but now, with the team coming together, he felt a flicker of confidence. He was happy that Marco would be going with him to London. He knew that the next few days would be critical, and he was determined to steer the auction toward success.

Marco returned with their lunch. "I bought two Italian subs and some chips. I hope that is ok with you," Marco asked.

"That's perfect, Marco," Julian began, leaning forward with a sense of urgency. "We can eat and work. Hence, a working lunch." Julian let out a little chuckle and smile. "We need to get organized for our trip to London. I want to make sure we're on the same page before we leave."

Marco nodded, his eyes bright with enthusiasm. "Absolutely! What's the plan?"

Julian: "First off, we need to book our flights. I'm thinking we should leave Sunday afternoon or evening. That way, we can arrive early Monday morning."

Marco: "Sounds good. That'll give us some time to settle in. I can check the airline options right now."

Julian: "Perfect. Also, we need to find a hotel near the museum. I want us to be close to where the action is."

Marco: "I can look up some options while we're on the call with the airline. Do you have a preference for hotels?"

Julian: "Something comfortable but not too extravagant. We'll be busy, and I want to keep our expenses in check."

As Marco pulled out his phone, Julian continued, "Once we land at Heathrow, we'll need to arrange transportation to the hotel. We should look into car services or taxis."

Marco: "I can check the rates for that, too. Should we plan to stay three nights? We'll need at least Monday through Wednesday to handle everything with the team."

Julian: "Exactly. We'll be dead tired on Monday after the flight, so we won't be very functional. We'll need all of Tuesday and Wednesday to finalize the auction details."

Marco: "Got it. I'll make sure we have everything lined up. Let's start calling the airline."

Julian watched as Marco dialed the number, feeling a sense of companionship and relief. They worked well together, and he appreciated Marco's attention to detail. After a brief hold, Marco spoke with the airline representative, efficiently securing their tickets.

Marco: "Hello, yes, I'd like to book two tickets from New York to London for tomorrow evening... Yes, that's right, two seats... Thank you!"

After hanging up, Marco turned to Julian, a triumphant smile on his face. "We're all set for the flight! We leave at 6 PM and arrive in London at 6 AM. That gives us some time to rest on the plane."

Julian: "Excellent! Now, let's look for hotels."

As Marco searched on his phone, Julian pulled out a notepad to draft their agenda for the meeting. "We should outline what we want to cover with the team—allocation of roles, timelines, and any specific issues we need to address."

Marco: "Definitely. We should also include a section for any potential challenges we might face during the auction."

Julian: "Good thinking. And we'll need to connect with Eleanor, Liam, and Victoria once we're settled in. I want to make sure everyone's on the same page before the meeting."

With the hotel secured, they finalized their transportation from Heathrow and mapped out a tentative agenda for their discussions. The atmosphere was charged with excitement as they readied themselves for the challenges that lay ahead.

Marco: "Okay, we've got the flights, hotel, and transportation sorted. What about the meeting venue? Do you have any ideas?"

Julian: "I think Eleanor and Liam have arranged something. We'll find out more once we're in London. I'm hoping to meet up with Evelyn, the curator at the British Museum, too, though she won't be part of the planning meeting just yet."

Marco: "That makes sense. It'll be good to get her insights on the auction, even if she's not directly involved."

As they wrapped up lunch, Julian felt a mix of anticipation and anxiety. The next few days would be critical, and he was grateful to have Marco by his side.

Julian: "Alright, let's finish up here and begin work on the agenda for our meeting. We need to double-check everything here before we leave."

Marco: "Absolutely! I can't wait to get this trip underway."

"I have one more quick call to make," Julian told Marco as they opened their sandwiches. Julian dialed Victoria Harrington's number.

"Hello, Victoria Harrington here," she said.

"Good evening Victoria, Julian speaking. I just wanted to inform you that I will be arriving in London on Monday morning, with my assistant Marco Rossi, to have a planning session with Eleanor Byrne, Liam Chen and, hopefully you, if you are available Tuesday and Wednesday for the majority of both days," he asked.

Victoria immediately replied, "I will clear

my calendar to make sure to be there. This is of utmost importance and we need to get underway without further delay. Please send me the location and the time the meeting starts on Tuesday morning."

Julian answered, "I knew we could count on you Victoria. Liam and Eleanor are working on the meeting location and will know in plenty of time. I will get that information to you as soon as we have it from Liam. Have a good weekend!"

23.

London: Marco and Julian's Journey

As the sun dipped below the horizon, casting a warm golden hue through the windows of Julian's condo, Marco and Julian settled into the evening after a long day of phone calls and planning a draft agenda for the auction planning committee. The tension from their busy workday faded, replaced by a comforting intimacy that filled the air.

"Do you think we covered everything for the meeting?" Marco asked, leaning against the kitchen counter, a playful smirk dancing on his lips. He poured himself a glass of wine, the rich red liquid swirling elegantly in the glass.

Julian chuckled, his eyes sparkling. "I think we've got a solid foundation. But you know how these things go—there's always something we'll forget." He wiped down the counter, his mind already shifting from work to something much more personal.

"Maybe we should celebrate a little," Marco suggested, leaning in closer. "After all, it's not every day we plan an auction in London together."

Julian raised an eyebrow, a teasing smile forming. "Celebrate? You mean with more work? Or do you have something else in mind?"

"Definitely something else." Marco stepped closer, the warmth of his body radiating a sense of security. "How about we order some dinner, then we can watch a movie? Just the two of us."

"Sounds perfect." Julian reached for his phone, almost giddy at the thought of a quiet evening together. "What are you in the mood for? Thai? Italian?"

"Let's go with Italian," Marco replied, his voice low and inviting. "It feels more… romantic."

As Julian placed the order, the air thickened with anticipation. They settled onto the couch, the soft cushions encircled them as they turned on a classic movie. The flickering light from the screen danced across their faces, creating an intimate atmosphere.

Halfway through the movie, Julian turned to Marco, his expression softening. "You know, I'm really glad we're doing this together. It's nice to have someone by my side."

Marco smiled, his heart swelling at the sincerity in Julian's words. "I feel the same way. It's been a whirlwind, but I wouldn't want to share it with anyone else."

The movie faded into the background as they leaned closer, their fingers intertwining.

Marco's gaze dropped to Julian's lips, and without a word, he closed the distance, capturing Julian's mouth in a gentle, lingering kiss. It was a kiss full of promise and warmth, igniting a spark that had been building between them.

"Let's not stop there," Julian murmured, pulling Marco closer, their bodies fitting perfectly together. The world outside faded away, and all that remained was the soft glow of the TV and the rhythm of their heartbeats.

They were both startled back to reality when the doorbell rang. Marco scurried to the door and pushed the intercom and said, "Yes..." Food delivery for Julian Taylor." Marco buzzed the deliveryman inside the building. In what seemed less than a minute, there was a knock at the door. Marco opened the door, the deliveryman handed him the bag of food and Marco slipped a $10 bill in the man's hand. The deliveryman smiled, and said, "Thank you!"

Julian sprang up to assist Marco with the food, his heart racing at the delicious aroma wafting through the air. There was a steaming array of Italian dishes—pasta, bruschetta, and a rich tiramisu for dessert. "Dinner is served!" he announced with a flourish, setting the table for two. Marco's eyes lit up as he took in the feast.

"Wow, you really went all out," he said, pouring more wine into their glasses. "This looks incredible."

Julian grinned, taking a seat across from Marco. "I figured we deserved a little indulgence after a long day. Plus, what's better than Italian food for a romantic evening?"

"True, you can never go wrong with pasta and wine," Marco replied, twirling a forkful of spaghetti. "And the company isn't half bad either." He winked, and they both laughed, the tension of the day melting away as they savored each bite.

"Here's to our upcoming adventure," Julian said, raising his glass, "May it be as delicious as this meal."

"To new beginnings," Marco echoed, clinking his glass against Julian's, their eyes locking in a moment that felt both fleeting and eternal, a promise of the journey they were about to embark on together.

As the evening deepened, they found themselves lost in each other, the conversation flowing as easily as the wine. They shared dreams, fears, and laughter, their connection deepening with every word, every touch.

The next morning, sunlight streamed through the window, waking Julian to a peaceful scene. He turned to find Marco still asleep, his features relaxed and serene. A smile crept onto Julian's face as he admired the man beside him, feeling grateful for the moments they shared.

"Hey, sleeping beauty," Julian whispered, gently nudging Marco awake. "We have a flight to catch."

Marco groaned, stretching lazily. "Can't we just skip the airport and stay here?" He cracked one eye open, a playful grin spreading across his face.

"Tempting, but I'd rather not miss our flight to London," Julian replied, chuckling as he swung his legs off the bed. "We need to finish packing."

"Fine, fine. I'll be up in a minute," Marco said, feigning annoyance but unable to hide his smile. Julian headed to the kitchen to prepare coffee, the rich aroma filling the air as he focused on the task at hand.

A few moments later, Marco joined him,

hair tousled and eyes still heavy with sleep. "You make the best coffee," he said, accepting a steaming cup with a grateful nod.

After picking up fresh bagels, salmon, and cream cheese on their way home from work last night, Marco and Julian barely had to prepare their brunch. They sat down to enjoy their delicious homemade meal. "This is fantastic, Julian! We really need to get on the ball," Marco said with a grin, his smile infectious. As noon approached, they realized they still hadn't finished getting ready for their trip. Once they polished off their meal, they quickly tidied up the kitchen, making sure all the small appliances were unplugged. "Now, let's tackle that suitcase," Julian said, nodding toward the half-packed bag on the floor. The next hour flew by as they moved around each other, laughter and playful teasing filling the space while they folded clothes and packed essentials.

"Did you really pack three pairs of shoes for a three-day trip?" Julian teased, holding up Marco's stylish loafers.

"What? You never know when you'll need the right pair!" Marco shot back, his tone light as he reached for the shoes. "Besides, they match my outfits."

Once their bags were ready, they checked the time. "We should call for the car now," Julian said, glancing at the clock. "We need to be at the airport by 4 o'clock."

"Right," Marco agreed, pulling out his phone. He arranged for a car to pick them up at 3pm, ensuring they had plenty of time for check-in and security. Both Julian and Marco are well aware of how long security can take for International flights, especially at JFK International Airport.

As they waited, Julian looked at Marco, his heart fluttering with excitement for the adventure ahead. "Are you ready for this? London, the auction, everything?"

"Absolutely," Marco replied, a determined glint in his eye. "With you by my side, I feel like we can take on anything."

Their car arrived promptly at 3pm, and they slid into the backseat, the city whizzing by outside the window. "You know," Marco said, glancing over at Julian, "no matter what happens at the planning meeting, I'm just glad we're in this together."

Julian smiled, feeling sultriness spread through him. "Me too. Let's make some memories."

As the car began their just under an hour trip, the driver expertly navigated through the bustling streets of Manhattan on to the Van Wyck Expressway toward JFK Airport, the two shared quiet moments, hands intertwined, each glance filled with unspoken promises of what lay ahead. Excitement buzzed in the air, blending with the sweet thrill of new beginnings.

As Marco and Julian arrived at JFK International Airport at 4 PM, a wave of excitement washed over them. The bustling terminal was alive with travelers, but they navigated through the crowds with purpose, eager to reach the British Airways check-in for their international flight.

"This is it! London, here we come!" Julian exclaimed, his eyes sparkling with anticipation.

"Can you believe we're finally doing this?" Marco replied, his grin wide as they approached the check-in desk. To their surprise, the process was smooth and efficient, and soon they found themselves standing at the counter, ready to check in.

"Actually, I have great news for you," the agent said, tapping away at her computer. "It looks like you both have enough frequent flyer miles to be upgraded from business class to first class!"

"Wait, what?" Julian gasped, his excitement bubbling over. "Did you just say first class?"

"Yes! Congratulations!" the agent beamed.

Marco and Julian exchanged incredulous looks, their hearts racing. "This trip just got a whole lot better," Marco said, laughing as they made their way through security, reeling with happiness at the upgrade.

Once on board, they settled into their spacious first-class seats, the plush leather enveloping them in comfort. "This is amazing!" Julian said, adjusting his seat and grinning at Marco. "I could get used to this."

"Just imagine the champagne and hors d'oeuvres," Marco replied, his eyes lighting up. "And we'll have a full dinner service after takeoff. I feel like we're living the high life."

As the plane prepared for takeoff at 6 PM, a flight attendant approached with a tray of hors d'oeuvres and flutes of champagne. "Welcome aboard! Can I offer you some appetizers?"

"Yes, please!" Julian replied, accepting a glass. "Cheers to our adventure!"

"Cheers!" Marco echoed, clinking his glass against Julian's. They savored the moment, the tension from their busy lives melting away as they toasted to their journey.

After takeoff, they received the dinner menu, which featured an array of gourmet options. "Look at this!" Julian said, scanning the choices. "I can't believe we're eating like this at 35,000 feet flying over the Atlantic."

The meal was surprisingly delicious, and they couldn't help but marvel at the quality. "I could get used to flying first class like this," Marco said, leaning back in his seat, content.

"Definitely. But we should try to get some sleep too," Julian suggested, stifling a yawn. "With the almost seven-hour flight, we'll need all the rest we can get to adjust to the time difference."

"Good idea," Marco agreed, adjusting his seat into a more comfortable position. "Let's see if we can wake up refreshed for our first day in London."

Julian stirred awake. The cabin lights were dimmed, and he glanced at his watch—5 AM local time. "Hey, we made it!" he whispered, nudging Marco awake. "Time to get ready for landing." Marco rubbed his eyes, a sleepy smile spreading across his face. "I can't believe we're finally here. Just think, we will be in our hotel in London very soon!"

Approximately one hour before landing time, the flight attendant asked if they would like a light breakfast. They both accepted and one after another they entered the two small first class restrooms to freshen up a bit before landing. The flight attendant brought out an array of pastries and muffins with coffee for their breakfast. The looked at each other and smiled and then laughed out loud. "I love this," Marco exclaimed in pure excitement!

As the plane began its descent into Heathrow the 'Fasten Your Seatbelt' sign was illuminated, and the flight attendants hurriedly asked everyone to please return to their seats so they could come through the aisle to pick up any trays and items to be thrown away.

After the amazingly smooth landing of their flight, and navigating through Customs, they collected their luggage and headed outside to meet their pre-arranged car. The cool London air hit them as they stepped out, invigorating and fresh. "What a difference from New York," Julian remarked, taking a deep breath.

"Right? I love it already," Marco replied, his excitement evident as they hopped into the car.

During the drive to their hotel, they marveled at the sights. "Look at those buildings! The architecture is incredible," Julian pointed out, snapping pictures with his phone.

"Definitely different from home," Marco agreed, his eyes wide. "I can't wait to explore more."

It didn't take long to reach their hotel near the British Museum. They checked in quickly, and luck was on their side with an early check-in. "Your room is ready!" the receptionist said with a smile, her British accent apparent.

Once inside, they dropped their bags and collapsed onto the bed, the exhaustion of travel catching up with them. "I can't remember the last time I was this tired," Julian sighed, sinking into the plush heavenly pillows and mattress.

"Me neither," Marco replied, chuckling softly. "But let's not waste our first day here. We should at least take a quick shower and freshen up."

After a refreshing shower, they took a moment to gather their energy. "Alright, let's go see what London has to offer," Julian said, pulling on a jacket.

Stepping outside, they were immediately overtaken by the vibrant sounds of city life. "It's so alive here," Marco remarked, taking in the diverse mix of people and cultures bustling around them.

"Let's head toward the museum; I want to see how close we are," Julian suggested, confidently leading the way. Having visited London several times over the past five years, he felt somewhat familiar with the area. "Just be careful crossing the streets and navigating the sidewalks," he added, glancing at Marco. "The traffic runs the opposite way here, and I've noticed that drivers don't seem to pay as much attention to pedestrian crossings. Jaywalking is illegal here." Marco nodded, still captivated by the stunning architecture of the London buildings. For some reason, he had never made it to London, even though his sister lived just outside of London, and it is about 1,000 miles from Florence—barely over 16 hours by car in light traffic.

As they strolled, they chatted about their plans for the next few days. "Liam is handling the meeting arrangements, right?" Marco asked.

"Yeah, I'll call him once we find a place to eat," Julian replied. "I'm sure he'll have everything set up."

They wandered through the streets, soaking in the sights, the excitement of their surroundings fueling their energy. "Look at that café! It looks so charming," Marco said, pointing to a quaint spot with outdoor seating.

"Let's check it out!" Julian exclaimed, leading them inside. As they settled in with a menu, he pulled out his phone. "Time to get in touch with Liam."

While Julian made the call, Marco admired the café's cozy ambiance. "This place has a great vibe," he said, glancing around at the art on the walls and the aroma of fresh pastries.

After Julian hung up, he smiled. "Liam said everything is set for the meeting tomorrow. He will send me the logistics in a text. Now, let's enjoy some food and explore the area."

As they waited for their meals, they couldn't help but feel the thrill of adventure in the air. "Here's to our first day in London," Marco said, raising his glass of water.

"To new beginnings and unforgettable memories," Julian replied, clinking his glass against Marco's, both of them eager for the experiences that lay ahead.

Julian received a text from Liam, 'The meeting will be held at The Montague on the Gardens in a private conference room, situated right next to The British Museum. We will meet at 8:30am. I have notified Eleanor and Victoria.' Marco and Julian were thrilled that the meeting place was only a couple blocks from the Hilton London West End where they were staying.

After finishing their meal, Julian and Marco felt a surge of energy. "Let's explore a bit!" Julian suggested, his eyes sparkling with excitement. They stepped out into the bustling streets of London, eager to soak in the sights and sounds around them.

As they strolled, they noticed a distinct difference in the pace of life compared to New York. "People here seem less frantic," Marco observed, watching a group of locals chatting leisurely at a bus stop. "It's like they have a purpose, but it's more controlled. Not as erratic as in Manhattan."

"Exactly!" Julian replied, glancing at

Marco with a smile. "It feels relaxing, even amidst the hustle. I love it." Marco nodded, feeling a sense of contentment wash over him. "This is totally different from Florence or New York. I'm so happy to be here for the first time, especially with you by my side."

As they wandered through the magnificent streets, they stumbled upon a contemporary art gallery. "Let's check this out," Julian suggested, pointing to the sleek entrance. They stepped inside, greeted by the cool air and vibrant artwork.

Inside the gallery, they perused the exhibits, captivated by many famous paintings. "Look at that one!" Julian exclaimed, pointing to a striking piece by Banksy, one of the world's most famous and celebrated graffiti artist. "It's so provocative." Marco nodded, admiring a large panorama by Tracey Emin. "And this one by British painter, David Hockney—it's simply stunning," he said, his gaze sweeping over the colorful landscape. They continued to admire works by artists like Damien Hirst and Lucian Freud, discussing the emotions and stories behind each piece.

After their gallery visit, they found themselves in the theater district, surrounded by the luminous marquees of famous shows. "Wow, look at all these productions," Marco said, glancing at the vibrant posters. "It's amazing how many of these will end up on Broadway."

"Yeah, most of the significant shows premiere here before crossing the pond," Julian added, scanning the listings. "If only it weren't Monday night—the theaters are dark tonight."

"Such a shame," Marco replied wistfully. "I would've loved to catch a show. But it's still thrilling to be in this area."

As the evening began to settle in, they decided to head back to their hotel. The hotel boasted a lovely restaurant, but Julian had a different idea. "Let's ask the concierge for a recommendation," he suggested.

"Good thinking!" Marco agreed. They approached the concierge, who provided them with a fantastic list of nearby eateries. "You can't go wrong with any of these," the concierge said with a smile.

After a brief discussion, they settled on a cozy Italian trattoria known for its homemade pasta. "Perfect choice!" Marco said, his mouth watering at the thought.

Once they arrived at the restaurant, they were greeted warmly and shown to a charming table by the window. As they perused the menu, Julian looked up with a grin. "I think I'm going to try the pappardelle carbonara with arugula—far from ordinary. Do you agree? How about you?"

"I'm leaning towards the chicken cacciatore," Marco replied, excitement evident in his voice. They placed their orders and settled in, enjoying the ambiance and each other's company.

Over a couple of drinks, they shared stories and laughter, the atmosphere buzzing with warmth. "I can't believe how lucky we are to be here," Julian said, raising his glass. "To new adventures and good food!"

"To us," Marco replied, clinking his glass against Julian's. "I wouldn't want to share this trip with anyone else."

After finishing dinner, they strolled back to their hotel, the streets of London illuminated by soft lights. Once they were back in their room, they changed into comfortable clothes and flopped onto the bed, feeling a sense of peace wash over them.

As they lay side by side, talking about everything and nothing, their conversation slowly turned tender. Julian wrapped his arms around Marco, pulling him closer. "I feel so connected to you," he murmured, their eyes locking in an intimate gaze.

"Me too," Marco replied softly, leaning in for a kiss. Their lips met gently at first, then deepened as passion ignited between them. Julian's hands explored Marco's strong back, feeling the warmth of his skin beneath the fabric of his shirt.

The kiss grew more intense, their bodies instinctively pressing against one another. "I want to feel you," Julian whispered, his breath hot against Marco's ear.

"Then let's not wait," Marco replied, his voice filled with desire. They frantically removed all of the clothing and embraced tightly. They became completely entwined, each touch sparking a flame that engulfed them both.

As they made love, it felt as if they were becoming one—two souls intertwined in a dance of intimacy and passion. They savored each moment, every gasp and whisper echoing their shared connection.

Eventually, they collapsed into each other's arms, breathless and spent, the world outside fading away. Wrapped in each other's warmth, they drifted off to sleep, hearts full and entwined, ready to embrace whatever adventures awaited them in the morning.

Julian's phone alarm buzzed insistently at 6 AM, cutting through the tranquil silence of the early morning. He groaned, rolling over to silence it, then swung his legs over the side of the bed noticing that Marco was up already. The promise of a full day of planning hung in the air, and he felt a mix of excitement and anxiety.

He shuffled to the bathroom, where Marco was already under the spray of the shower. The sound of water splashing echoed off the tiles.

"Hey, sleepyhead! You're up early," Marco called out, poking his head around the shower curtain, droplets glistening on his skin.

"Barely," Julian replied, smirking. "Just trying to avoid the coffee-induced panic later."

"Good plan," Marco laughed. "You know, I should've set my alarm for 5:30 to make sure I had enough time." Julian said, "Maybe I'll just skip the shower and dive straight into the coffee."

"Please don't. I'd hate to be seen with a coffee-stained, unshowered version of you," Marco teased, turning off the faucet and stepping out of the shower with his soaked body glimmering in the bathroom light. The water made his body look even more ripped, if that was even possible.

"We've got a big day ahead with Liam, Eleanor, and Victoria," Julian growled as he stepped into the shower of hot water.

As Julian lathered his hair, Marco continued, "Do you think Liam's going to be as organized? I still remember that color-coded presentation he did at a symposium in Milan a few years back."

"Let's hope he's toned it down a bit. It was impressive but slightly terrifying," Julian chuckled, rinsing off.

After finishing dressing for the meeting, they moved to the sofa where the aroma of freshly brewed coffee wafted through the air smelled amazing. Julian poured two mugs, taking a moment to breathe in the rich scent.

"Thank you Marco for making this

coffee for us," Julian smiled.

"No problem. Do you think we'll actually stick to the agenda today?" Marco asked, taking a sip of his coffee.

"Honestly, probably not. But it's good to have a roadmap, even if we take a few detours," Julian replied. "Let's just make sure we cover the key points."

Making sure they had their satchel's containing papers and personal belongings, they headed out the door, the anticipation building as they made their way to the Montague only 5 minutes from their hotel.

24.

The Montague Summit

The Montague was buzzing with early-morning activity, the lobby filled with travelers and staff bustling about. Julian and Marco approached the front desk, where a friendly receptionist greeted them.

"Good morning! How can I assist you?" she asked, her smile warm and welcoming.

"We're here for a meeting with Liam Chen. Could you direct us to the meeting room?" Julian inquired.

"Of course! You're in the Brighton Room. Just take the elevator to the second floor, and it's the first door on your left," she replied, pointing to the elevator.

"Thank you," Marco said as they headed toward the elevator, a sense of anticipation in the air.

As the doors opened on the second floor, they walked down the hall, finally arriving at the Brighton Room. Julian pushed the door open and stepped inside, only to be greeted by a familiar sight.

Liam Chen was already there, a meticulous array of notepads, pens, and other materials laid out on a large table. A spread of breakfast—pastries, fruits, and coffee—was just being delivered, the aroma a delightful addition to the atmosphere.

"Look who's here!" Liam exclaimed, glancing up and grinning. "I was starting to think you'd sleep in."

"Not a chance. We wouldn't miss this for the world," Julian replied, taking in the setup.

Just then, Eleanor and Victoria strolled in, their energy infectious. "Hope we're not too late!" Eleanor said, brushing her hair back.

"Perfect timing! Breakfast is here," Marco announced, gesturing to the spread, as he passed out a copy of the meeting agenda.

AGENDA
Auction Planning Meeting
Brighton Room
The Montague on the Gardens, London
October 1-2, 2024

1. Overview of the Auction
   - Selection of the artwork & cataloging
   - Marketing and promotion
   - A preview auction
   - Auction Day

2. Market Analysis
   - Discussion on current market conditions and trends.
   - Identification of potential buyers and target demographics.

3. Lot Selection
   - Criteria for selecting items for auction.
   - Review of preliminary lot list.

4. Marketing Strategy
   - Strategies for promoting the auction.
   - Discussion on advertising channels and materials needed.

5. Logistics and Operations
   - Venue arrangements and setup.
   - Technology requirements (e.g., online bidding platform).

6. Legal and Compliance Issues
   - Review of necessary permits and regulations.
   - Discussion on terms and conditions for bidders.

7. Budget and Financial Projections

- Overview of auction budget and expected revenue.

- Discussion on reserve prices and commissions.

8. Roles and Responsibilities

- Assigning tasks to team members for the auction.

9. Q&A Session

- Open floor for questions and additional input.

10. Next Steps

- Outline action items and deadlines leading up to the auction.

They all gathered around the table, exchanging light banter as they filled their plates. Julian looked around at his colleagues, feeling a sense of mutual support and excitement.

After a few moments of casual chatter and laughter, Liam clapped his hands together. "Alright everyone! Let's dig into this agenda. Julian, how about you start us off?"

Julian nodded, pointing out the neatly typed agenda that Marco had passed around. "Thanks, Liam. I organized some key points for today's discussion," he said, clearing his throat.

Julian started with the first item on the agenda: "Overview of the Auction Process. We need a review of the auction timeline and key milestones. Victoria, would you like to take this one please," Julian asked? "Absolutely," Victoria acknowledged and accepted.

Victoria began, "As the Auction House Director of Christie's London, this is my view of the processes to create a successful auction. First, there is the selection of the artwork. The auction house curates a selection of artworks, often focusing on a theme or specific artists. The number of paintings can vary widely, but major auctions typically feature anywhere from 20 to 100 pieces."

"Wow, 20-100 pieces? I had no idea organizing an auction is so complex," Marco said, his eyes wide with surprise. Where would we even find 30 paintings for this?"

Julian nodded thoughtfully, "First, we need to choose a theme. We could focus on a specific era, like the Renaissance, or highlight the works of a single artist. That would help narrow down our search. You know who would be perfect to assist us here, is Dr. Andrew Fischer,

Auction Director of the Hermitage in Moscow."

"Next, we need to catalog the pieces," Victoria said, her tone brisk. "Each artwork must be documented and photographed, complete with detailed descriptions, provenance, and estimated values. We'll publish a catalog, either in print or online."

She continued, "The next step is crucial: marketing and promotion. We'll announce the auction through various channels—social media, newsletters, and press releases. Invitations are sent to collectors, curators, and art enthusiasts to ensure a strong turnout."

"We will need to organize a preview exhibition before the auction," Victoria said. "During this preview, potential buyers can view the artworks in person. It often draws media attention and art critics, generating excitement around the event."

"Finally," she added, "there's the actual auction day. On that day, the works are displayed prominently, and the auctioneer will kick off the bidding process, bringing all our hard work to fruition."

Julian said, "Approximately, how much time do we need until the actual Auction date?"

Victoria, looking serious, said, "Not long, we should announce and schedule the auction as soon as possible. I would suggest Wednesday, November 5, 2024. That will give us about one month."

"Thank you Victoria, Julian said.

"Julian and Liam, would you like to tackle market analysis--discussion on current market conditions and trends and the identification of potential buyers and target demographics, Victoria added?"

Julian agreed, "Absolutely, I'll compile

data on current trends and potential buyers."

Victoria seemed excited, said "Great! Liam, your extensive knowledge of the art market would be a huge asset here. Can you collaborate with Julian on this?"

Liam nodded, "Of course! I'll bring in some recent reports and insights to support our analysis. With Julian's extensive knowledge of the art markets, it makes him a valuable asset for this discussion. I am sure he can provide insights into buyer behavior, as well. What are the current trends in the art market? Who are the emerging buyers?"

Victoria nodded and said, "Marco, could you work on the lot selection? Your experience with various styles will help us curate a strong auction lineup."

Marco looked up with excitement in his voice, "I'll start looking into what's trending in the market. It is imperative for this auction, especially, that the lot selection and categories of art (e.g., Renaissance, Impressionist), that will be featured at the auction, are perfect and will bring in the right bidders.

Marco offered, "If we all agree, with my knowledge of various art styles, I am confident that I can help in curating the selection."

Victoria, said, "As a seasoned auctioneer, I can provide insights on what has sold well in the past. We need to look at which categories have the most potential for profit? Are there any up-and-coming artists worth considering?"

Victoria kept running with assignments, and said, "Eleanor, I'd like you to focus on logistics and operations. You have a good grasp of how to ensure everything runs smoothly."

Eleanor nodded in agreement with Victoria. "I'll coordinate with Lily and Roland to establish best practices for transport and display. I would like to suggest that we seek assistance from Lily Serrano, an art dealer, who fully understands the intricacies of transporting and displaying art." Further, I would suggest, Roland Kovac, his expertise in security systems can ensure the artworks are protected during transport. We should determine what are the best practices for handling and displaying the artwork? What security measures need to be in place? I will reach out to Lily and Roland."

Lily Serrano is a charming and successful art dealer who runs a trendy gallery in a bustling urban area of Manchester. She has an eye for spotting undervalued art and has built a network of wealthy collectors. However, beneath her glamorous exterior lies a complex web of deceit. Lily is deeply involved in the underground art market, often using her gallery as a front for illicit transactions. Her upbringing in a family of forgers has equipped her with skills that blur the lines between authenticity and deception.

Lily is charismatic and persuasive, often using her charm to win over clients. She is quick-witted and fiercely independent, but her ambition can lead her to make questionable choices. She has a penchant for manipulation, easily playing people against one another to achieve her goals.

At 32, Lily is motivated by a desire for power and recognition in the art world. She seeks to outshine her competitors and is willing to take risks, including possible ties to criminal activities, to elevate her status. Her connection with undercover agent Marcus Wells adds a layer of complexity to her character.

Roland Kovac, at 34, is a tech-savvy security expert who works for Victor Salvatore. With a background in cyber security and a degree in engineering, he specializes in motion detection systems and surveillance cameras. Roland's expertise makes him invaluable to Victor, ensuring the safety of high-value pieces during auctions. However, his fascination with technology can lead him into ethical gray areas, especially when it comes to information security.

Roland is introverted and intensely focused on his work. He possesses a brilliant mind but struggles with social interactions. His obsessive nature often leads him to be overly cautious, which can frustrate his colleagues. However, his loyalty to Victor is unwavering, stemming from a past where Victor helped him out of a tight spot.

Roland is driven by a desire for mastery in his field. He wants to create the most foolproof security system for the auction house, but his curiosity about the darker side of technology sometimes tempts him to cross ethical lines.

Marcus Wells, 39, Undercover FBI Agent, works for the FBI's art crime division, specializing in undercover operations. He's ruggedly handsome and adept at blending into high-society events. His past is shadowed by a personal tragedy; his father, a respected art historian, was implicated in a scandal involving stolen artifacts. Fueled by a desire for justice, Marcus took up the mantle of fighting art crime. While he's dedicated to his work, he harbors suspicions about his own past, as he once crossed paths with shady characters during an earlier investigation.

Marcus is a determined and resourceful agent, known for his keen instincts and analytical mind. He is often conflicted between his undercover persona and his true self. Though he's a man of principle, he struggles with the moral ambiguities of his profession.

Marcus seeks to uncover the truth behind art thefts and forgeries, driven by a personal vendetta against those who exploit the art world. His relationship with Lily complicates his mission, as he must balance his growing feelings for her with his duty to enforce the law.

Julian stressed, "We need to very careful with these people we do not really know." Julian looked directly at Eleanor and said, "I believe in another art crime I worked on several years in Venice, Roland Kovac was under suspension by Interpol for having ties to Victor Salvatore. What do you know about that Eleanor, if anything?"

Julian emphasized, "We need to tread carefully with these individuals; we don't know their full capabilities." He then turned to Eleanor, saying, "I recall another art crime I worked on a few years ago in Venice. Roland Kovac was under suspicion by Interpol for having connections to Victor Salvatore. He's highly tech-savvy, with expertise in cyber security motion detection, and surveillance systems. I'm curious, Eleanor, do you know anything about him?"

Eleanor looked taken aback, her brow furrowing in concern. "I… I know Roland Kovac. I've spoken to him before, and I had no idea he was connected to Victor Salvatore's team," she admitted, her voice wavering slightly. "This changes everything for me. I don't know what to do—should I keep him in the loop, or should I be cautious and distance myself? I feel torn, and I'm not sure what's safest for our investigation."

Julian replied thoughtfully, "I'm conflicted here too. I'm sure you all feel this way. It could be beneficial to keep him under close watch, but there's a risk he might tip off Victor about our moves while we try to gather intelligence from him. We need to carefully consider our next steps before making any decisions." Everyone simply nodded, unsure of what to say or think.

Victoria with warmth in her voice said, "Mark Thompson will be perfect! Eleanor, please ask Mark if he can help you lead the legal and compliance discussion? We want to make sure everything is above board."

Liam offered, "Mark's background in law enforcement can help navigate legal complexities. As far a legal consultant, perhaps Mark knows a legal expert in art transactions than can be invited for guidance. I will reach out to Mark."

Agent Mark Thompson, 42 years old, is a veteran FBI agent from New York, specializing in financial crimes linked to art theft and forgery. He has a degree in economics and a keen understanding of how money moves through illicit channels. Mark has worked on several high-profile cases and is known for his pragmatic approach to investigations.

Mark is analytical and strategic, often approaching problems with a financial mindset. He can be blunt and pragmatic, which sometimes clashes with more idealistic colleagues. However, his dedication to justice is unwavering, and he has a dry sense of humor that lightens tense situations.

Mark aims to uncover the financial networks that support art crime. He is determined to bring down major players in the forgery and theft ring. His focus on the financial side of crime sometimes leads him to overlook the emotional and cultural aspects of art.

Marco spoke up, "I agree with Liam. Are there any specific regulations we need to be aware of? How can we protect ourselves from liability?"

Victoria said, "If we need someone with a wide array of experience in international art markets, Sophia Martinez can provide insights into financial trends. Her knowledge of the art world will help in creating accurate projections. By the way, we need to determine our overall budget? What are the projected costs and revenues?"

Sofia Martinez is 37 years old and an Interpol Agent. She has a multicultural background, having been born in Spain and raised in the U.S. She works for Interpol's art crime division, focusing on international investigations. Her fluency in multiple languages and understanding of different cultures make her an asset in cross-border art crime cases. Sofia has a knack for building relationships with international contacts, which helps in gathering intelligence.

Sofia is charismatic, empathetic, and a natural diplomat. She balances being assertive with a warm demeanor, making her approachable. She believes in the power of collaboration and often acts as a mediator between different agencies.

Sofia is passionate about preserving cultural heritage and believes that art belongs to everyone. She seeks to dismantle the networks of art crime and restore stolen pieces to their rightful owners. Her collaborative spirit drives her to foster connections across the globe.

As the first day of the planning session drew to a close, Julian stood at the head of the table, a satisfied smile on his face. The team had successfully navigated through their categories and responsibilities, identifying key individuals to assist in each area. "Thank you all for your contributions today," he said, his voice filled with enthusiasm. "We've laid a solid foundation for this auction. Each of you has a crucial role to play, and I'm confident that together, we'll make it a resounding success."

The atmosphere in the room shifted to one of camaraderie and excitement as the team members exchanged nods of agreement. With plans in place and a sense of purpose ignited, they gathered their belongings and prepared to leave. As they stepped out of the conference room, laughter and chatter filled the air, signaling their anticipation for a well-deserved dinner together— a chance to unwind, share stories, and strengthen the bonds that would carry them through the challenges ahead.

25.

Team Night Out

The sun dipped below the horizon, casting a warm golden hue over London as Eleanor, Victoria, Liam, Marco and Julian gathered at a charming restaurant just a stone's throw away from the auction house. The air was filled with the tantalizing aroma of roasted herbs and spices, mingling with the sounds of laughter and clinking glasses. They settled into a cozy corner booth, the ambiance inviting and intimate.

As they sipped on their drinks—Eleanor opting for a crisp glass of Sauvignon Blanc, Marco and Julian indulging in a rich Merlot, and Victoria and Liam enjoying a classic gin and tonic—the conversation flowed easily. Memories of past auctions, symposiums, and gallery openings filled the air, punctuated by bursts of laughter that echoed around the room.

"I still remember that time we nearly missed the bidding on Johannes Vermeer's c.1665 painting 'The Girl with a Pearl Earring' at the Amsterdam auction," Marco chuckled, his eyes sparkling with mischief. "We were so engrossed in the wine tasting that we lost track of time!"

Eleanor laughed, her face lighting up. "And you had to sprint across the room, waving your paddle like a madman! I thought for sure they'd toss you out for being too enthusiastic."

Victoria chimed in, her voice warm with nostalgia. "That was a classic Marco moment! But we got the painting, and it turned out to be one of the best decisions we ever made."

Liam asked, "Do any of you know if Anneke Vermeer is a relative of Johannes Vermeer the painter? It's probably a wild coincidence, but I am curious to know."

"Vermeer died in 1675. I highly doubt there's any connection to Anneke there. However, a quick fact is this painting was regarded as Vermeer's masterpiece and is often called the Mona Lisa of the North or the Dutch Mona Lisa. The girl in the painting is believed to be Vermeer's oldest daughter, Maria, who was about 13 years old at the time," said Julian.

As they sipped their drinks, Marco leaned back, a grin spreading across his face. "Remember that time we got stuck in traffic on the way to the Paris auction? We were sure we were going to miss the bidding on that Monet."

Julian chuckled, shaking his head. "I still can't believe you talked your way into the front row when we finally arrived. You had that poor security guard convinced you were a long-lost relative of the artist!"

Eleanor laughed, her eyes sparkling with nostalgia. "And you were right behind him, trying to stifle your laughter while I tried to look dignified. I thought we'd get kicked out for sure!"

Marco leaned forward, his expression turning more serious. "It was moments like that that made the stress worth it. We've faced so many challenges together, but we always seem to come out on top."

Julian nodded, his gaze softening as he looked at Marco. "That's what I love about us—our ability to adapt and overcome. We've built a sort of family in this crazy art world."

Eleanor raised her glass, a mischievous smile on her lips. "To family, then! The art world may be chaotic, but at least we have each other to rely on."

As they clinked their glasses together, Marco caught Julian's eye, warmth blooming between them. "And let's not forget how far we've come. I remember when I first joined the team. I felt like a fish out of water, but both of you made me feel at home."

Julian reached across the table, placing his hand over Marco's. "You fit in perfectly from the start. Your passion for art is infectious. You've taught us all to look at things differently."

Eleanor chimed in, her voice filled with affection. "And your knack for negotiation? That's something I'm still trying to master. I can't tell you how many times I've relied on your expertise to seal the deal."

Marco shrugged his shoulders, a hint of modesty in his smile. "I guess we all bring something unique to the table. It's our differences that make us stronger."

As the evening wore on, the conversation flowed effortlessly, filled with anecdotes and laughter. They reminisced about late nights spent poring over auction catalogs, the thrill of bidding wars, and the friendships forged in the heat of competition.

"Remember that symposium in Florence?" Julian said, leaning back in his seat. "We ended up at that tiny café, and you both insisted on trying every single dessert on the menu."

Eleanor laughed, recalling the experience vividly. "I can't believe we ate our weight in tiramisu! But those moments, the laughter, and the shared indulgence—they're what make this journey worthwhile."

Marco grinned, leaning forward. "And who could forget the art heist we narrowly avoided? I still get chills thinking about how close we came to losing that van Gogh."

Julian's expression turned serious for a moment. "That was a wake-up call for all of us. It reminded us how important our work is—not just for ourselves, but for preserving cultural heritage."

Eleanor nodded in agreement. "Exactly. Each piece we protect tells a story, and it's our responsibility to ensure those stories aren't lost."

As the conversation continued, Marco and Julian's hands remained intertwined on the table, their connection deepening amid the laughter and reflections. They shared knowing glances and quiet smiles, the bond between them palpable to Eleanor, who couldn't help but feel a sense of warmth for their relationship.

After hours of sharing stories and memories, the atmosphere shifted slightly as Julian spoke softly, almost introspectively. "I don't know what I would do without both of you. This journey can be isolating at times, but having you by my side makes all the difference."

Marco squeezed Julian's hand gently, his voice sincere. "We're in this together, always. No matter what challenges come our way, we'll face them as a team."

Eleanor raised her glass once more, her smile radiant. "To friendship, to art, and to the adventures yet to come. May we always find the beauty in the chaos."

As they toasted again, the friendship among them felt like an unbreakable bond, one that would carry them through whatever the auction—and the art world—had in store.

As they reminisced, the connection among them deepened, a shared bond forged through years of navigating the art world's complexities together. Their discussions meandered from favorite artists to the intricacies of various museums, each anecdote layered with affection and respect for the craft that brought them together.

Julian stood up, glancing at Marco with a playful smile. "Well, I think Marco and I will retire to our room at the hotel. I don't know about him, but I'm still feeling jetlagged, and my head is spinning." Marco nodded in agreement, a knowing grin spreading across his face.

"I could definitely use some sleep before our busy day tomorrow," he replied, his voice light yet sincere. "See everyone at 8:30 AM back at the Montague. Good night!"

As they exchanged goodbyes, the warmth of the evening lingered in the air. Just as they were about to leave, Liam pulled Julian aside, an inquisitive look in his eyes. "Julian, can I ask you something?" he began, his tone serious yet friendly. "Are you and Marco a couple?"

Julian's heart raced at the question. He took a moment to gather his thoughts, feeling a mix of vulnerability and excitement. "Well, it's complicated," he started, glancing back at Marco, who was chatting with Eleanor and Victoria. "We've been through so much together in this crazy art world. Our bond has grown deeper over the years, and yes, there's definitely something more between us."

Liam raised an eyebrow, intrigued. "So, you're not just colleagues anymore?"

"No, it's more than that," Julian confessed, his voice softening. "We support each other through the chaos of our work and beyond. I've never felt this kind of connection with anyone else. It's like we understand each other on a different level. After all, we've known each other for over 14 years."

"Sounds like you're in pretty deep," Liam said with a knowing smile.

Julian chuckled lightly, feeling a sense of relief in sharing his feelings. "It's true. Marco brings out a side of me I didn't know existed. He's passionate, driven, and incredibly insightful. Being with him makes the long nights and stressful days feel manageable."

Liam nodded, clearly happy for Julian. "That's great to hear. Just make sure you communicate, okay? Relationships can be tricky, especially in our line of work."

"Thanks, Liam. I will," Julian replied, appreciating the advice. He felt a surge of gratitude for the friendship and support he had found among his colleagues. As they rejoined the others, he caught Marco's eye, and a warm smile spread across his face. In that moment, Julian knew that no matter what challenges lay ahead in the art world, he and Marco would face them together.

After their goodbyes, Marco and Julian decided to stop at a bar just outside their hotel for a nightcap. The dimly lit atmosphere was perfect for quiet conversation, and they settled into a secluded booth. With a couple of drinks in hand—Julian opting for an Cognac while Marco chose a smooth whiskey—they exchanged flirtatious glances, the chemistry between them visible.

"Tonight was a success," Julian mused, leaning closer. "But I think we deserve to celebrate our little victories."

Marco smirked, his heart racing as he leaned back, playfully teasing. "And how do you propose we do that?"

Julian's eyes sparkled with mischief as he leaned in, the warmth of his breath sending shivers down Marco's spine. "I can think of a few ways."

With laughter and light banter, they finished their drinks and made their way back to their hotel room. The door barely closed behind them before they were wrapped in each other's arms, the world outside fading away. Passion ignited as they kissed, the heat between them building with every touch. Clothes fell to the floor in a flurry, and soon they were lost in each other, exploring every curve and contour, their bodies entwined in a whirlwind of desire.

As the night unfolded, the room filled with whispers and laughter, punctuated by soft gasps and the rhythm of their bodies moving together. Time seemed to stand still as they surrendered to the moment, each kiss and caress drawing them deeper into a realm where nothing else mattered but the two of them and the connection they shared.

Outside, London continued its dance of lights and sounds, but within the walls of their hotel room, nothing else existed—just the intoxicating blend of love, lust, and the promise of tomorrow.

Victoria Harrington strode through the cobblestone streets of her upscale London neighborhood, the late afternoon sun casting a warm glow on the historic buildings that lined the avenue. As the Director of Christie's auction house, she was accustomed to the high stakes and glamour of the art world, but today, her mind drifted to the comforts of home.

Her small flat, adorned with a mix of contemporary art and cherished trinkets from her travels, was a reflection of her eclectic taste. She loved hosting dinner parties, where lively discussions about art and culture flowed like the wine. But it wasn't just work that filled her life; it was also the warmth of her boyfriend, Daniel, and their mischievous golden retriever, Milo, who brought a sense of balance to her busy schedule.

As she reached her door, she could hear Milo's excited barks from inside. She smiled, knowing that no matter how demanding her job became, her evenings were reserved for unwinding with her little family.

Hey, you two! Did you miss me?" she called out as she entered, greeted by Milo's enthusiastic tail-wagging and Daniel's playful grin.

"Of course! Milo has been on high alert, waiting for your return. He's convinced you would bring home treats, Daniel said lovingly."

Victoria, excitedly said, "Just a few. But I brought something more exciting—an invitation to the preview in a couple weeks. You'll have to come and see the pieces in person!"

"You know I'm always up for it. Besides, I love seeing you in your element. But remember, no talking shop all night. Let's just enjoy the art and each other's company, Daniel smiled."

Victoria exclaimed, "Deal! But I can't promise I won't slip a few anecdotes about the paintings. They're like old friends, each with their own story."

As they settled in for the evening, Victoria felt grateful for the balance Daniel brought to her life. While she thrived in the fast-paced world of auctions, it was these quieter moments that reminded her of what truly mattered: love, laughter, and the simple joy of being home.

Later that night, as they settled into bed, the air between them crackled with unspoken desire. Their laughter faded into soft whispers, and with each gentle touch, the passion that simmered beneath the surface ignited. They explored each other with fervor that spoke of longing and connection, losing themselves in the rhythm of their bodies. The world outside faded away, leaving only the heat of their embrace, the intimacy of their shared breaths, and the sweet surrender to love that encapsulated them both.

26.

The Montague Summit --
Day Two

The morning light streamed through the tall windows of the Brighton Room at the Montague Hotel, illuminating the faces of the planning team as they gathered for another day of intense discussion. The air buzzed with anticipation, especially as they prepared to delve deeper into the upcoming auction.

Victoria Harrington, the Director of Christie's auction house in London, stood at the head of the table, her presence commanding yet approachable. She cleared her throat, drawing everyone's attention.

"Good morning everyone! I'm excited to continue our discussions today, especially regarding the selection of paintings for the auction. We have an incredible lineup that I believe will attract significant interest," Victoria began, her enthusiasm undeniable.

Marco Rossi leaned forward, a curious look on his face. "I know we've narrowed it down to 17 Renaissance and 17 Impressionist pieces, along with 'Salvator Mundi'. What's the strategy for presenting these works?"

Victoria smiled, gesturing to a large screen that displayed the list of selected paintings. "We want to create a narrative that showcases the evolution of art from the Renaissance to the Impressionist period. Each painting should tell a story, reflecting both historical significance and artistic innovation. Here is our list with the appropriate details."

Auction Lot Catalog:

Renaissance Paintings (17):

1. Equestrian Portrait of Charles I (on Horseback) c.1637-38
   - Artist: Anthony van Dyck
   - Location: National Gallery, London
   - Value: $180 million

2. The Ambassadors c. 1533
   - Artist: Hans Holbein the Younger
   - Location: National Gallery, London
   - Value: $200 million

3. Boy Peeling Fruit c.1593
   - Artist: Caravaggio
   - Location: Private Collection (undisclosed)
   - Value: $210 million

4. A Boy Blowing on an Ember to Light a Candle c.1571-73
   - Artist: El Greco
   - Location: Museo del Prado, Madrid
   - Value: $105 million

5. Self Portrait c.1506
   - Artist: Raphael Santi
   - Location: Galleria degli Uffizi, Florence
   - Value: $100 million

6. The Arnolfini Portrait c.1434
   - Artist: Jan van Eyck
   - Location: National Gallery, London
   - Value: $500 million

7. The Old Man in a Red Cap c.1640-60

- Artist: Rembrandt van Rijn
- Location: The Louvre, Paris
- Value: $190 million

8. Venus of Urbino 1538
   - Artist: Titian
   - Location: Uffizi Gallery, Florence
   - Value: $109 million

9. The Madonna of the Pinks c. 1506-07
   - Artist: Raphael Santi
   - Location: National Gallery, London
   - Value: $150 million
10. The Annunciation c.1438-45
   - Artist: Fra Angelico
   - Location: Museo di San Marco, Florence
   - Value: $165 million

11. Venus and Mars c.1483
   - Artist: Sandro Botticelli
   - Location: National Gallery, London
   - Value: $200 million

12. The Anatomy Lesson of Dr. Tulp c.1632
   - Artist: Rembrandt van Rijn
   - Location: Mauritshuis Museum in The Hague,
the Netherlands
   - Value: $300 million

13. Assumption of the Virgin c.1516-18
   - Artist: Titian
   - Location: Basilica di Santa Maria Gloriosa dei
Frari, Venice
   - Value: $110 million

14. The Yellow Christ c.1889
   - Artist: Paul Gauguin
   - Location: The Albright-Knox Art Gallery,

Buffalo, New York
   - Value: $125 million

15. The Tempest c.1505-08
   - Artist: Giorgione
   - Location: Gallerie dell'Accademia, Venice
   - Value: $80 million

16. St. George and the Dragon c.1605-07
   - Artist: Peter Paul Rubens
   - Location: Museo del Prado, Madrid
   - Value: 70 million

17. The Garden of Earthly Delights c.1515
   - Artist: Hieronymus Bosch
   - Location: Museo del Prado, Madrid
   - Value: $80 million

Impressionist Paintings (17):

1. Les Femmes d'Alger c.1955
   - Artist: Pablo Picasso
   - Location: Private Collection
   - Value: $180 million

2. Umbrellas c.1886
   - Artist: Pierre-Auguste Renoir
   - Location: The National Gallery, London
   - Value: $200 million

3. Portrait of Adele Bloch-Bauer c.1907
   - Artist: Gustav Klimt
   - Location: Neue Galerie, New York
   - Value: $135 million

4. The Card Players c.1890-95

- Artist: Paul Cézanne
- Location: Private Collection
- Value: $250 million

5. Dance at Bougival c.1883
   - Artist: Pierre-Auguste Renoir
   - Location: Private Collection
   - Value: $78 million

6. The Scream c.1893
   - Artist: Edvard Munch
   - Location: Private Collection
   - Value: $120 million

7. Boulevard des Capucines c.1873
   - Artist: Claude Monet
   - Location: Private Collection
   - Value: $100 million

8. Woman with a Parasol c.1875
   - Artist: Claude Monet
   - Location: Private Collection
   - Value: $110 million

9. The Ballet Class c.1873
   - Artist: Edgar Degas
   - Location: Private Collection
   - Value: $85 million

10. The Luncheon of the Boating Party c.1880-81
    - Artist: Pierre-Auguste Renoir
    - Location: Phillips Collection, Washington D.C.
    - Value: $100 million

11. Still Life with Apples and a Pot of Primroses c.1890
    - Artist: Paul Cézanne

- Location: Private Collection
- Value: $100 million

12. Irises c.1889
   - Artist: Vincent van Gogh
   - Location: Private Collection
   - Value: $132 million

13. The Blue Boat c.1881
   - Artist: Pierre-Auguste Renoir
   - Location: Private Collection
   - Value: $70 million

14. Self-Portrait with Grey Felt Hat c.1887
   - Artist: Vincent van Gogh
   - Location: Private Collection
   - Value: $70 million

15. The Dance Class c.1874
   - Artist: Edgar Degas
   - Location: Musée d'Orsay, Paris
   - Value: $50 million

16. The Red Vineyard c.1888
   - Artist: Vincent van Gogh
   - Location: Pushkin Museum, Moscow
   - Value: $75 million

17. The Railway, c. 1873
   - Artist: Edouard Manet
      - Location: National Gallery of Art, Washington, DC
   - Value: $80 million

Auction Highlight Painting:

1. Salvator Mundi c.1500
   - Artist: Leonardo da Vinci

- Location: Private Collection (Saudi Arabia)
- Value: $500 million

Julian had made a note to discuss the 'Salvator Mundi' da Vinci masterpiece, and if available, should they use the authenticated original, or an exact replica? As a master restorer and acclaimed artist himself, who better to construct the replica, than Julian himself and his team of experts.

As Julian sat at the conference table with his esteem colleagues looking on with intrigue, he contemplated the upcoming staged auction, focusing on a specific masterpiece that could drive the entire operation. He leaned back in his chair, allowing his mind to wander to the legendary, "There is no better time than now, to discuss the 'Salvator Mundi,' a haunting painting attributed to Leonardo da Vinci. Dating from around 1500, it shared a time frame with the da Vinci's most famous work, the 'Mona Lisa,'" Julian remarked with complete confidence.

Long thought to have been lost to history, 'Salvator Mundi' was now one of fewer than 20 paintings definitively attributed to the master Renaissance artist, according to Christie's auction house. The painting depicts Christ in a serene pose, holding a crystal orb—a symbol of his role as the savior of the world. Yet, its journey through the art world has been plagued by whispers of controversy and intrigue, and the sheer notion that the masterpiece was missing for many years, make it the perfect centerpiece for the auction," he continued.

Julian, with his deep knowledge of Leonard da Vinci, continued to speak, I can already envision the buzz that will surround the piece, drawing in high-profile bidders and art enthusiasts alike. But with that buzz, danger is eminent. Rumors of forgeries and theft have hung over the painting like a shadow, and I am well aware that it could attract the attention of those with nefarious intentions."

Julian quickly jotted down some notes about the painting's history, considering its dark undertones. The rumors of its destruction and subsequent rediscovery in 2005 added layers of complexity to its narrative, creating an allure that would be irresistible to collectors. But it also made it a prime target for those looking to exploit the auction for their gain.

As he prepared to discuss the painting with the team, Julian felt a surge of determination. "If we successfully stage the auction and use 'Salvator Mundi' as the bait, we might just be able to draw out the criminals behind the forgery ring. I can envision the scene at Christie's: the lights dimmed, the audience hushed in anticipation as the auctioneer unveils the masterpiece, a moment charged with tension and possibility."

Julian stood up from his seat and stated, "We need to make this auction unforgettable. And that means putting the spotlight on 'Salvator Mundi.'" With its history and the air of mystery surrounding it, the painting will become more than just a piece of art; it will be the key to uncovering the truth hidden in the shadows of the art world.

The team broke out in a round of applause after Julian's encouraging and profound speech.

Evelyn Sinclair and Liam Chen agreed to emphasize the importance of including Leonardo da Vinci's 'Salvator Mundi' in the auction, alongside the 34 Renaissance and Impressionist paintings. This combination not only enhances the auction's appeal but also presents a strategic opportunity for both the event itself and the wider art market.

"Here's how it fits into the context of these two groups of paintings, Julian leading off the conversation.

"There is the cultural significance first and foremost. The Renaissance context of the da Vinci painting 'Salvator Mundi' as a pivotal work from the Renaissance period, attributed to one of the most renowned artists in history, Leonardo da Vinci. Its inclusion elevates the auction's prestige and emphasizes the importance of Renaissance art. This painting serves as a centerpiece that ties together the historical significance of the other Renaissance works, reinforcing the auction's theme of celebrating masterful artistry from that period."

Julian continued, "The historical importance of this auction will attract attention not only for the 'Salvator Mundi' itself but also for how it contextualizes the broader exploration of Renaissance themes present in the other 34 paintings, such as spirituality, humanism, and the exploration of light and shadow."

Victoria speaks, "Auction dynamics such as using 'Salvator Mundi' will absolutely attract bidders, with its estimated value at a half billion dollars, it is likely to draw high-profile collectors and investors, potentially increasing interest in the other paintings. The presence of such a high-value piece may encourage bidders to consider purchasing additional works from the auction, elevating the overall sales potential."

Victoria continued, "By creating a sense of urgency with a 'marquee' piece like 'Salvator Mundi', the auction can create a sense of urgency among bidders. The excitement surrounding this iconic work can lead to competitive bidding, influencing the perceived value of the entire collection.

Evelyn interjected, "We absolutely must have thematic marketing components. The auction can be marketed as a rare opportunity to acquire both a masterwork by Leonardo da Vinci and a curated selection of significant Renaissance and Impressionist pieces. This thematic cohesion can enhance promotional strategies and attract a wider audience."

Victoria noted, "The educational component of the auction can include discussions or panels that highlight the relationship between 'Salvator Mundi' and the other works being auctioned. This educational aspect can engage attendees and collectors more deeply, creating a narrative that ties the pieces together.

Evelyn raised the point, "Collaborations with institutions with the inclusion of 'Salvator Mundi' may lead to partnerships with museums or galleries for exhibitions or promotional events surrounding the auction. This can enhance the credibility of the auction and provide additional exposure for the other paintings."

"High-profile networking and relationship building among collectors interested in 'Salvator Mundi' may also engage with the other works, fostering relationships between collectors, institutions, and the auction house that can benefit future sales and exhibitions, Liam advised the team.

Marco, said, "There will be market influence with the sale of 'Salvator Mundi' that could set a new benchmark for Renaissance works and influence the market for the other paintings in the auction. Successful sales of both categories may elevate the perceived value of Renaissance art as a whole, potentially impacting future auctions and sales.

"In summary, Julian stated, "'Salvator Mundi' can serve as a powerful catalyst for the auction, enhancing the appeal, value, and cultural significance of the 34 Renaissance and Impressionist paintings being offered. Its presence not only elevates the auction's profile but also creates a unique opportunity to explore the interplay between iconic masterpieces and a curated selection of art history.

Liam Chen, always the strategist, nodded thoughtfully. "That makes sense. We should highlight key pieces in our marketing materials, drawing parallels between the works. For instance, how do the themes of humanism in the Renaissance resonate with the emotional depth found in Impressionism?"

Eleanor chimed in, her eyes sparkling with ideas. "And we need to emphasize the cultural significance of 'Salvator Mundi' as the centerpiece. It's not just another painting; it's a masterpiece that links our auction to the broader narrative of art history."

"Exactly," Victoria agreed. "And to strengthen our presentation, I think we should bring in Evelyn Sinclair from the British Museum. As the curator of auctions there, she can provide invaluable insights and lend credibility to our collection."

"Good idea," Marco said. "Evelyn has extensive experience with high-profile auctions and can help us navigate any potential concerns regarding provenance."

Victoria nodded, already pulling out her phone. "Let me reach out to her now. I believe her expertise will be crucial in ensuring that our auction runs smoothly and that we maximize the potential of these works."

As Victoria sent a quick message, the conversation shifted back to the selected paintings. Liam pointed to the screen, highlighting 'The Madonna of the Pinks' by 'Raphael' Santi. "This piece, along with our other Renaissance selections, beautifully exemplifies the transition from medieval to modern art. It will resonate with both seasoned collectors and new buyers."

Eleanor added, "And the Impressionist works, like Edgar Degas' 'The Ballet Class', will draw in a different audience. We must emphasize the emotional and experiential aspects that characterize these movements."

Just then, Victoria's phone buzzed. She glanced at it and smiled. "Evelyn is available to join us shortly. Let's prepare to discuss how we can integrate her insights into our auction strategy."

As they continued discussing the details, the team began to envision the auction not just as a sale, but rather an event that would celebrate the rich tapestry of art history. The combination of Renaissance and Impressionism masterpieces, anchored by 'Salvator Mundi', would create an unforgettable experience for bidders and art lovers alike.

When Evelyn Sinclair arrived, the atmosphere in the room shifted slightly, her expertise adding a layer of professionalism and depth to the discussions. She greeted everyone warmly and settled in, ready to contribute to the planning session.

"Thank you for inviting me to be part of this exciting project," Evelyn said, her voice confident. "I'm eager to help ensure that your auction not only highlights these incredible works but also stands as a model for future collaborations between institutions and auction houses."

With Evelyn's input, the team felt more empowered to refine their auction strategy, paving the way for what they hoped would be a groundbreaking event in the art world.

As the sun dipped below the horizon, casting a warm golden hue over the conference room, the atmosphere in the auction planning meeting was a mix of relief and anticipation. The team had spent two intensive days studying the 35 paintings slated for the upcoming auction, each piece a potential cornerstone of art history. Julian, the lead curator, glanced at the clock, aware that time was slipping away.

"Alright, everyone," he said, standing at the head of the long oak table, his voice cutting through the murmur of conversations. "I want to thank you all for your hard work over the last two days. Your insights into each painting were invaluable, and I'm confident we've set a solid foundation for the auction."

The room hummed with appreciative nods and murmurs of agreement. Marco, seated beside Julian, turned to him with a knowing smile. "You handled that beautifully, as always."

Julian chuckled softly. "Just trying to keep the ship steady, especially with so much at stake." He shifted his gaze back to the team. "Before we wrap up, I need to address any open items that need finalization while Marco and I are away. We're heading back to New York tonight, so let's make sure we have everything covered."

Victoria, leaned forward, her brow furrowed. "Julian, do you really think we have enough time? A month feels tight, especially with the logistics involved."

"I understand your concerns, Victoria," Julian replied, his tone calm but firm. "But we've planned meticulously. The curators will coordinate the transport and installation of the artworks. I'll be back in about three weeks with Marco for the auction, and we'll finalize everything then. Trust me; we're in good shape."

The team nodded, reassured by Julian's confidence. He took a moment to scan the faces around the table, each one a vital part of the operation. "Let's stay in close communication. If any issues arise, don't hesitate to reach out."

With the meeting nearing its conclusion, Julian stepped back, allowing Marco to take the floor. "I want to echo Julian's gratitude," Marco said, his voice warm and engaging. "Your commitment to this auction is evident, and I look forward to seeing how it all comes together. Remember, this isn't just about the paintings; it's about the stories we tell through them."

As attendees began to gather their things, a sense of camaraderie filled the room. Julian smiled, offering handshakes and warm farewells. "Thank you all once again. We'll be in touch, and I'll see you soon."

Liam Chen and Evelyn Sinclair have developed a friendship that hints at something deeper. Their shared experiences in the art community created a bond, especially as they navigate the complexities of their roles.

Following such an intense two days of meetings, Evelyn and Liam find themselves seated at a small table in a chic café, filled with art-inspired décor and a warm ambiance, each nursing a cup of coffee, their minds buzzing with the details discussed.

Liam glances at Evelyn, who is sketching something on her notepad, a habit that calms her nerves. "You're quite the artist," he remarks, nodding toward her sketches.

Evelyn looks up, a smile breaking through her focus. "Thanks! It helps me process everything. This auction is monumental for us, isn't it?"

Liam leans back, considering her words, "Definitely. I didn't expect the dynamics of the collection to be so intricate. The politics involved... it's like navigating a minefield."

Evelyn chuckles, "Tell me about it. I thought I was just curating art, but it's also about relationships—some more complicated than the pieces themselves."

As they share their experiences, a connection begins to form. They discuss their backgrounds, revealing shared struggles in the art world—the pressure to maintain integrity while dealing with collectors and critics.

"I remember my first exhibition," Liam confesses, "I thought I had everything under control until the night before when a major piece fell through. I had to improvise on the spot."

Evelyn laughs, her eyes sparkling. "I can relate! I once had a piece go missing just days before a show. The panic was real! But it taught me to be resilient."

Their laughter fills the café, drawing glances from other patrons. It's clear that their shared experiences are weaving a thread of closeness between them.

As their conversation deepens, they start discussing their visions for the future of the art community. Liam expresses his desire to create more inclusive spaces for emerging artists, while Evelyn shares her dream of revitalizing the representation of underrepresented voices.

Maybe we could collaborate on something," Liam suggests, his tone hopeful. "I feel like we could create something impactful together."

Evelyn's eyes widen with intrigue. "I'd love that! Combining our strengths could lead to something really special."

As they finish their coffees, the atmosphere shifts. There's an unspoken understanding that this is just the beginning of a deeper relationship. They exchange contact information, promising to keep in touch about their ideas.

"Who knows," Liam says with a grin, "we might just change the art world together."

Evelyn smiles, her heart racing with excitement. "I believe we can."

Julian and Marco made their way back to their hotel, the evening air cool against their skin. "It feels good to have that behind us," Julian said, his pace quickening as they approached the entrance.

Marco nodded, his expression thoughtful. "But the real work starts now. We have to ensure everything runs smoothly while we're gone. The auction is only a month away."

"Exactly. We'll be back in about three weeks, just in time to iron out the final details," Julian replied as they stepped into the lobby, the buzz of the city echoing outside. "Let's grab our bags and head to Heathrow."

Once in their hotel room, Julian quickly packed his belongings, shoving clothes into his suitcase with practiced efficiency. Marco, on the other hand, took a moment to check his phone, glancing at messages from colleagues back in New York.

"Everything alright?" Julian asked,

noticing Marco's furrowed brow.

"Just some last-minute updates on the logistics," Marco replied, typing quickly. "We need to ensure the paintings are handled with care."

Julian paused, looking at Marco. "You think we should call Clara? She might have insights on the transport process."

"Good idea," Marco agreed, hitting send on his message. "Let's sort that out before we leave."

With their bags packed and final arrangements made, they stepped out into the cool evening air, the city lights twinkling like stars above them.

"Ready for the journey," Julian asked, a hint of excitement in his voice.

"As ready as I'll ever be," Marco replied with a grin. "Let's make this auction unforgettable."

They arrived at Heathrow with plenty of time to spare, the airport bustling with travelers. As they checked in for their flight, Julian felt a wave of anticipation wash over him. This auction was not just a professional milestone; it was a testament to their passion for art.

"Should we grab a light supper?" Marco asked, glancing at Julian. "I'm not that hungry, but it wouldn't hurt to eat something."

Julian chuckled. "Oh, come on. We're in first class. We'll have a late dinner served on the plane."

With a playful smirk, Marco grabbed two pretzels from a nearby bowl. They settled into the first-class lounge, each savoring a cognac while nibbling on the snacks, the warmth of the spirits calming their nerves before boarding their flight at 10:15 PM London time.

"Here's to a successful auction," Marco said, raising an imaginary glass as they headed toward security.

"To a successful auction," Julian echoed, the weight of their plans heavy on his mind, yet the thrill of the challenge igniting his spirit.

As they navigated through the airport to board their plane, their minds buzzed with thoughts of the paintings, the upcoming auction, and the stories yet to unfold. The night was just beginning, and so was their journey.

Julian and Marco stepped outside the airport into the crisp autumn air of New York. The vibrant colors of the falling leaves painted a picturesque backdrop as their car service awaited them at the passenger pickup.

"Finally back in New York," Julian said, taking a deep breath. "I forgot how refreshing the air is here."

"Yeah, it's nice to be home, but we were only gone for three days" Marco giggled, sliding into the back seat of the car. "Manhattan's charm never gets old. Just a short drive and we'll be at your condo."

As the car merged into the bustling traffic, Julian leaned back, feeling the familiar rhythm of the city. "I need to meet with Samuel Grant and Lila Thorne as soon as we get settled. There's a lot to discuss after London."

"Right, the auction's just around the corner," Marco said, glancing out the window. "You think they'll be ready for everything that went down?"

"Samuel usually is," Julian replied, a hint of confidence in his voice. "We've got three weeks to put our plans in place before we head back for the preview. It's crucial we hit the ground running."

27.

The Hideaway – Team Meeting

Nestled in the secluded hills of the Budaörs Mountains, just outside Budapest, stood a grand mansion that appeared almost like a mirage against the backdrop of the lush green landscape. The sprawling estate was hidden from view by thick foliage and the natural contours of the land, providing the perfect cover for Victor Salvatore's operations. Few knew of its existence, and even fewer had ever set foot inside its opulent halls.

As dusk began to settle over the Hungarian countryside, the mansion illuminated softly, its windows glowing like jewels in the twilight. Inside, the decor was a blend of classic European elegance and modern luxury, with high ceilings adorned with intricate moldings, marble floors, and walls lined with carefully curated artwork—some original, but most cleverly crafted forgeries. This was a sanctuary for Victor and his syndicate, a place where they could work in secrecy and style.

Victor's security team had arranged transportation for the BMAS members, a fleet of discreet black vans that wound their way through the narrow, winding roads leading to the estate. As the vehicles pulled up, the team members stepped out, a mix of anticipation and tension evident in the air.

Inside the mansion, Victor stood in the grand foyer, a commanding presence with an air of authority. He welcomed each member as they entered, his sharp gaze assessing their readiness for the task ahead.

"Welcome, everyone," Victor said, his voice smooth yet firm. "Tonight, we gather to discuss our most ambitious project yet."

The team moved into the expansive drawing room, where a long oak table was set up for the meeting. The walls were lined with bookshelves filled with art history texts and tomes on forgery techniques, a testament to the knowledge that fueled their illicit endeavors.

As the team settled in, Victor began outlining the plan. "We're going to create a forgery of Leonardo da Vinci's 'Salvator Mundi,' one of the few remaining pieces attributed to him.

It's crucial that this replica is flawless. I have heard, from a very reliable source, that the British Museum's curator, Evelyn Sinclair, is working with Christie's London Auction House Director, Victoria Harrington. She may possibly meet with the owner, a Saudi Prince, to auction off the painting. The rumor circulating is, the opening bid will be $750 million and they hope to have the first $1 billion sale creating the most valuable piece of art in the world.

Isabelle Dube, the marketing expert, leaned forward, her expression focused, "We need to craft a compelling narrative around the painting's provenance. If we present it as a lost masterpiece that resurfaced in 2012, and has been in storage in Riyadh, Saudi Arabia since 2017, collectors will be eager to pay top dollar."

Martin Falcone, the art restorer, nodded. "I can age the forgery to make it look as if it has been hanging in a private collection for decades. The details will be key to convincing anyone who examines it."

Victor said, "Make that centuries Martin. The painting was completed circa 1499-1510. 'Salvator Mundi' was sold at auction for $450.3 million in late 2017 by Christie's in New York to a Prince on behalf of Abu Dhabi's Department of Culture and Tourism who actually stood in as the bidder on behalf of the Saudi Arabian Crown Prince. The painting has not been publicly exhibited since the 2017 auction. It is said the painting has been in storage in Saudi Arabia awaiting a museum for exhibit or auction.

Simone Leduc chimed in, "I'll ensure our digital references are impeccable. The textures and colors must match exactly with the original."

"Good," Victor replied, his eyes gleaming with determination. "This project will elevate our operation to new heights. If we pull this off, it will not only secure our financial future but also solidify our reputation in the underground art world."

Hidden beneath the mansion was a vast underground complex, accessible only through a concealed entrance in Victor's private study. A series of tunnels led to the restoration and forging area, designed to keep their activities hidden from prying eyes. The air was cool as they descended, a low hum of machinery echoing through the tunnels.

As they entered the main workspace, the team was greeted by a pristine environment filled with natural light filtering through strategically placed lighting. The space resembled an artist's studio more than a factory—a blend of creativity and craftsmanship.

"Here, we can work without interruption," Victor said, gesturing to the expansive area. "We have everything we need to replicate the masterpieces, from high-quality materials to advanced tools."

The team spread out, each member taking their stations. Clara Jensen was already analyzing the security measures in place, ensuring that their underground operations would remain undetected. "I'll run a full risk assessment to identify any potential vulnerabilities," she stated, her tone serious.

As the team familiarized themselves with their workspace, Victor outlined the specifics of the operation. "We must be extremely careful. The task force is looming, and we cannot afford any mistakes. Our timing must be impeccable. Once the painting is in place at the British Museum, we can execute our plan to switch it with the forgery."

Conrad Mercer, the former art thief, spoke up, "I can use my connections to gather intel on the auction and the museum's plans. We need to know when the painting will be on display and how we can make our move."

Victor nodded, pleased with the contributions. "Exactly. We'll create a distraction during the auction—something to draw attention away from our operation. With the right timing, we can make the switch without anyone being the wiser."

The meeting continued late into the night, filled with detailed discussions and fervent planning. Each member of Victor's syndicate understood the risks involved, but the allure of the operation—and the promise of success—fueled their determination.

As the evening wore on and the team delved deeper into their plans, Victor felt a surge of excitement. This operation was not just about art; it was a testament to their skills, their unity, and their defiance against a system that sought to control creativity. With each stroke of the brush and every calculated move, they were not merely forgers—they were artists crafting a new narrative in the shadowy world of art crime

28.

Julian and Marco Back in Manhattan

Once they arrived at Julian's condo, they quickly freshened up, taking hot showers that washed away the remnants of their flight. They had slept well on the plane, so they weren't feeling too jetlagged. Dressed in sharp suits, they looked ready for business.

"It's just past noon," Julian said, checking his watch. "Let's grab a quick bite, then head to the museum."

"Sounds good," Marco agreed, already pulling out his phone to check for nearby restaurants.

After a brief meal, they made their way to the museum. The elegant architecture greeted them as they entered, and the familiar scent of polished wood and art supplies filled the air.

Once inside, Julian headed straight to his office. He took a moment to collect his thoughts before dialing Samuel Grant's number. As the phone rang, he glanced at Marco, who was setting up his workspace.

"Let's see if they're available," Julian said, his excitement bubbling beneath the surface.

"Good idea. They need to be briefed on everything that happened in London," Marco replied.

When Samuel answered, Julian wasted no time. "Samuel, can we meet? I need to fill you and Lila in on the recent developments and our plans for the next few weeks. We have a lot to cover before we head back to London for the auction preview in about three weeks from now."

"Absolutely, Julian, we'll be ready," Samuel replied, his tone professional yet eager.

As Julian hung up, he felt a surge of anticipation. The next three weeks would be crucial, and with the heist looming during the auction, every detail needed to be meticulously planned.

After a brief wait, Julian received a call from Samuel. "Julian, can you meet us in the conference room? We want to include a few other team members who'll be working with you over the next three weeks."

"Of course, I'll bring Marco and any data we need to share," Julian replied, glancing at Marco, who was already gathering files. "When should we be there?"

"Let's say 1:30? That'll give us time to set up," Samuel suggested.

"See you then," Julian said, hanging up. He turned to Marco. "Looks like we're heading to the conference room. They want to bring in some additional people. I have my thoughts on the replication team. I will stress that timing is not on our side. I want the best in the business on replication team."

"Perfect. I've got the list of paintings ready," Marco replied, his eyes gleaming with anticipation.

At 1:30pm, they entered the large conference room just outside Dr. Grant's office. The room buzzed with energy as Samuel and Lila greeted them, flanked by Timothy and a couple of other team members. Julian nodded in acknowledgment.

"Thanks for coming, everyone," Julian began, taking a seat. "I'll give you a recap of what happened during our two days in London."

As Julian laid out the details, the atmosphere shifted from casual to focused. "We've settled on the 35 pieces that will be featured in the auction. And here's the kicker: We are including the 'Salvator Mundi', however, I have decided to replicate the 'Salvator Mundi' for the auction."

Lila raised an eyebrow. "Replicate it? But isn't the original locked away in a vault at the Louvre?"

"Exactly," Julian confirmed. "It's owned by a Saudi Arabian prince, and it's just too precious and vulnerable, especially with the auction coming up. He paid $500 million for it, and the bidding price is expected to soar between $750 million to $1 billion."

"Wow," Timothy said, leaning forward. "That's going to attract a lot of attention. Are we ready for that level of scrutiny?"

"Absolutely," Julian assured him. "This is a joint collaboration with Christie's London Auction House, Interpol, Scotland Yard, the FBI, and law enforcement from London. We will, however, need to ensure our replica is flawless. I have my list of experts that I know and can trust who specialize in high-value art forgeries. They'll be invaluable in this process."

Marco interjected, "And let's not forget about the heist. We need to keep everything under wraps until the auction, especially since it's going to happen right in the midst of the event. So, nothing can leave this room."

Lila smirked, "So, we're not only working on a masterpiece but also planning a masterpiece of misdirection."

"Exactly," Julian said, grinning. "We'll need to coordinate closely. The last thing we want is for anyone to suspect a thing."

"Who exactly do you envision being part of your replication team, Julian?" Samuel asked, his curiosity piqued.

Julian began passing out his list to the group, stating, "I'll be collecting this list back once I've discussed the individuals on my team. Please understand that this information is highly sensitive and confidential—it cannot leave this room. Law enforcement in London is currently running the investigation, and part of this plan involves significant risks." He paused, gauging the reactions in the room.

Lila, visibly anxious, interjected, "Given the sensitive nature of this project, I suggest we ask everyone to leave except for Julian, Marco, Samuel, and myself. We need to go over Julian's replication team in detail." With a nod of agreement, she added, "Thank you all for your time. Please return to your work on the upcoming van Gogh exhibition. We appreciate your understanding."

After the conference room door closed,

Julian began with his credentials as he summarized the members he wanted on his replication team. "I will emphasize my own qualifications, highlighting my extensive knowledge of Renaissance techniques and my well-known passion for preserving art. As a skilled restorer and accomplished artist, I will be responsible for the overall vision and execution of the painting."

Julian continued, after gulping down a full glass of water, "Forgive me, I am starting to fell a bit jetlagged. The next member of my team is Marco Rossi, who will serve as the assistant restorer and color specialist. Marco has a keen eye for blending colors and a deep understanding of the subtleties of paint layers. Marco will support me throughout the painting process, providing valuable insights based on his extensive experience. This isn't our first collaboration; Marco has helped me restore damaged paintings before, and this process shares similarities with creating a forgery."

Julian continued, "As you might be aware, the 'Salvator Mundi' underwent restoration from 2007 t0 2011, during which it was confirmed to be original rather than on of the many copies of the long-lost Leonardo da Vinci painting that have circulated for years. The painting is done in oil on a walnut panel. The wood's surface seems to have been prepped with an unpigmented layer, observed as a discreet under-layer in several cross-sections. We are faced with a challenging yet achievable replication ahead of us in a short time frame.

Julian then introduced a new team member, "Sarah Chen is a digital artist whose expertise would be invaluable to our efforts. She is proficient in digital imaging and software used for art restoration. Sarah specializes in creating digital mockups of the painting. This allows the team to visualize the final product and make necessary adjustments before they begin the actual painting process. Her primary responsibility will be to develop detailed digital representations and conduct an analysis of the original "Salvator Mundi," helping the team grasp intricate details before they start.

With a strong background in art history, Julian continues providing more information on Sarah, "She understands the context and techniques of the original artwork, enhancing her contributions. She is accomplished in tools like Photoshop, Illustrator, and specializes in restoration software, making her an innovative asset who finds ways to leverage technology to support traditional art techniques. Additionally, she communicates effectively with restorers and curators, ensuring that the digital aspects align seamlessly with the physical restoration efforts. Her ability to clearly explain complex digital processes guarantees that everyone on the team understands the vision and execution. I want Sarah on my team," Julian concluded with conviction.

"I have two more members that I want on my replication team. Firstly, Anton Kirov, is an aging specialist with a wealth of experience in art restoration. His role on my team will be crucial, as he will work closely with me to ensure that the replica of "Salvator Mundi" exhibits the appropriate aging and wear to convincingly mimic a 500-year-old painting. Anton is an expert in both traditional and modern methods of restoring aged artwork, bringing a comprehensive skill set to the team."

"With extensive knowledge of various materials—such as varnishes and substrates—

Anton understands how they age over time, allowing him to apply the right techniques to achieve an authentic appearance. Anton's meticulous approach ensures that every aspect of the restoration process looks genuine, and he is adept at crafting innovative solutions for unexpected challenges that may arise, particularly regarding aging techniques."

"Having collaborated with restorers like Marco in the past," Julian added, "Anton is well-versed in navigating the ethical dilemmas that can surface in the art world. His experience enables him to provide guidance on maintaining the integrity of the artwork while achieving the desired results. Working closely with my team, Anton will help replicate the nuanced characteristics of a five-century-old masterpiece, ensuring that the final product resonates with the authenticity of the original."

"Last, but not least, I have Elise Harper," Julian noted. "Elise is a skilled woodworker and frame maker renowned for her craftsmanship in creating historical frames and preparing wooden panels for painting. With years of experience in the art of framing, Elise specializes in constructing frames and wood panels that not only enhance the artwork but also authentically reflect the period style of the pieces they support."

"Her expertise is crucial to this team, as she will be responsible for constructing the wooden panel to apply the oil paints and a frame that matches the aesthetic of the original "Salvator Mundi," ensuring that the overall presentation of the replica is historically accurate. Elise's meticulous attention to detail allows her to select the appropriate materials and techniques, capturing the essence of the era in which the painting was created and," as he glanced at Marco,

"In addition to her framing skills, Elise is knowledgeable about the historical context of various styles, enabling her to make informed decisions that align with the artistic vision of the team. Her passion for woodworking and dedication to preserving the integrity of art makes her an invaluable asset in the replication process, ensuring that every aspect of the final presentation resonates with authenticity.

Julian, with a confident smile, glancing at Dr. Samuel Grant and Dr. Lila Thorne, who sat expectantly, "First, let me emphasize that I'll be leading this project," Julian said, "and I want to ensure you that we have the right people on board to make this a success."

Dr. Grant leaned forward, a knowing grin on his face. "We trust your judgment, Julian. Just remember, even the best artists need a strong support system."

"Absolutely," Dr. Thorne chimed in. "And I think bringing in new talent will only strengthen our efforts.

Before Julian could respond, Marco interjected, arms crossed and a playful smirk on his face. "Well, I hope he's not bringing in anyone who thinks they know more than Julian. We all know how that goes!"

Julian laughed, the warmth in the room engaging, "I assure you, these individuals are highly skilled and will complement our team perfectly."

"Just make sure they know who's in charge," Dr. Grant teased, chuckling. "We wouldn't want any misunderstandings."

"Right," Marco added, nodding dramatically. "Julian's the maestro here. We're just the backup singers!"

As the banter continued, Julian felt a

surge of gratitude. "Thank you all for your support. It means a lot to me." His smile widened, and he looked around the room, feeling the fellowship.

Dr. Thorne clapped her hands together. "Let's get this show on the road! We're excited to see what these new team members can bring."

"Agreed," Dr. Grant said, beaming. "And just remember, Julian, we're all in this together. Whatever you need, just say the word."

Julian's heart swelled with appreciation. "I couldn't ask for a better team. I'm really looking forward to working with everyone."

The atmosphere was charged with enthusiasm and mutual respect, and Julian couldn't help but feel that they were on the brink of something extraordinary.

29.

Coalition of the Committed

Inspector Ellen Hayes is a seasoned investigator with Scotland Yard, specializing in art crime. With a background in art history and criminal justice, she has spent over two decades working to protect cultural heritage. Known for her tenacity and sharp mind, she has built a reputation for solving complex cases. Ellen is respected among her peers but often feels the weight of expectations, especially as she navigates a male-dominated field.

Ellen is determined, analytical, and unyielding in her pursuit of justice. She has a strong moral compass and refuses to compromise her principles. Though she can appear stern, she has a deep passion for art and its preservation, which drives her work.

Ellen wants to make a lasting impact in

the fight against art crime. She seeks to uncover the truth behind the forgeries and thefts plaguing the art world. Her determination to succeed often puts her at odds with her superiors, who sometimes prioritize public relations over genuine justice.

As the task force members began arriving for their early start at 8:00 AM, Detective Eleanor Byrne, an art crime specialist at Scotland Yard, took her seat at the head of the conference table. To her left sat her longtime colleague, Jonathan Walters, also an art crime specialist, while to her right was Detective Claire Bertrand from Interpol. As the last team members entered the room, Eleanor stood to address the group.

"Good morning, everyone. It's wonderful to see you all on this beautiful autumn day. You represent the various law enforcement agencies that have successfully collaborated in tackling art theft and forgery schemes across Europe and the U.S. Today, we gather for a critical mission: to uncover the largest art theft and forgery syndicate in the world, especially with the upcoming auction just over two weeks away."

With that, Eleanor directed, "Let's go around the table for introductions. Claire, would you like to start?"

Detective Claire Bertrand smiled and began, "Thank you, Eleanor, and good morning. I'm Claire Bertrand, an Interpol detective from Lyon, France. I'll be coordinating communications between our agencies and overseeing international leads. Interpol has access to a global database of stolen art and forgeries."

"Hello, I'm Ellen Hayes, an investigator with Scotland Yard. I focus on local investigations and historical art thefts in the UK, leveraging my established contacts within the art community to navigate local laws."

"Good morning, I'm FBI Agent David Cortez from New York City. My jurisdiction covers U.S. citizens and interests, and the FBI is particularly concerned with the financial implications of art crime, including money laundering linked to high-value forgeries."

"Hi, I'm Agent Mark Thompson, also with the FBI. I take a pragmatic and analytical approach, viewing the case through the lens of financial crime and organized syndicates."

"Good morning, I'm Agent Sofia Martinez with Interpol. I'm a multilingual agent with a background in art history, and I focus on bridging communication gaps between our agencies to foster cooperation."

"Hello, I'm Jonathan Walters, an art crime specialist with Scotland Yard," nodding to the group.

"Good morning, I'm Liam Chen, an established art critic with extensive knowledge of the underground art scene," he added.

"I'm Dr. Emily Harper, also an art crime expert," she introduced herself.

"I'm Isabella Rossi, an expert in the European art market, hailing from Venice," she said with a smile.

"And I'm Victoria Harrington, the Director of Christie's Auction House. I'm collaborating with Julian Taylor and his team to plan the upcoming auction," Victoria concluded.

"And I'm Evelyn Sinclair, the Head Curator of The British Museum here in London," she finished, her presence commanding attention.

With the introductions complete, Eleanor felt a surge of determination. The diverse expertise gathered in the room was a powerful asset as they prepared to tackle the challenges ahead.

The conference room at Scotland Yard buzzed with a sense of urgency as the members of the law enforcement task force settled in for a critical all-day meeting. The clock on the wall ticked steadily, a constant reminder that time was running out before the auction. Detective Eleanor Byrne, the lead organizer, glanced around the table at the diverse group of agents gathered from various agencies, each bringing unique expertise to the mission at hand.

"Thank you all for being here today and for your self-introductions," Eleanor began, her voice steady. "With the auction just days away, we need to finalize our strategies to ensure we catch Victor Salvatore and his crew red-handed."

As she spoke, Eleanor noticed the tension in the room. The weight of the impending deadline hung heavily over them. To her left, Detective Claire Bertrand from Interpol nodded in agreement. "We've got to move quickly. If we don't gather enough evidence by the time the auction starts, we risk losing our chance."

Agent Mark Thompson from the FBI leaned forward, a serious expression on his face. "We need to focus on surveillance at the auction house. If Salvatore is planning a switch, he'll likely have eyes on the original 'Salvator Mundi'."

Eleanor turned to Thompson, appreciating his analytical approach. "Exactly. But we also need to ensure that we're not just watching the auction. We have to be proactive in gathering intelligence ahead of time."

Agent Sofia Martinez, a multilingual operative with Interpol, interjected, her diplomatic tone. "Let's not forget about Julian Taylor and his team. If they think they can outsmart Salvatore, it could complicate our operation. We need to monitor both teams closely."

The room fell silent for a moment as everyone considered her words. The interplay of law enforcement and criminal elements was a delicate dance, and they needed to stay one step ahead.

Eleanor sighed, her brow furrowing. "We also need to address the jurisdictional issues we've faced in the past. Each agency has its own legal limitations, which can create friction during operations."

"Exactly," Hayes agreed. "For instance, Scotland Yard may need warrants for searches that the FBI can't obtain in the UK. We must navigate these legal pathways carefully."

Agent Thompson crossed his arms, a hint of frustration in his voice. "And let's not forget the cultural differences. Some agencies prioritize swift arrests, while others focus on gathering extensive evidence for successful prosecutions. This could lead to disagreements when we need unity."

Claire Bertrand nodded thoughtfully. "We must bridge those differences if we want to be effective. We're on the same side here."

Eleanor's gaze swept around the table, taking in the determined faces of her colleagues. "We're all here for the same reason. Let's focus on what we can do together. Claire, what's Interpol's strategy for tracking stolen artworks?"

Claire leaned forward, her fingers steepled. "We'll be utilizing Interpol's international databases to track stolen artworks and known forgers. I'll be organizing meetings with art crime units from other countries to keep the lines of communication open."

"Good," Eleanor replied. "The more information we have, the better. What about the

FBI?"

Agent Mark Thompson shifted in his seat, ready to outline their approach. "We're focusing on the financial investigation. I'll be examining auction house records and tracing any money laundering activities linked to high-value forgeries. The 'Salvator Mundi' is a crucial piece in this puzzle."

"And we propose sending an undercover agent to pose as a wealthy collector at the auction," Thompson continued. "This could give us invaluable insight and possibly catch the criminals in the act."

Eleanor glanced at the other agents, gauging their reactions. "That's a risky move, but it could pay off. We need to ensure that the agent has backup ready in case things go sideways."

The atmosphere in the room was charged with tension as they considered the implications of an undercover operation.

"Let's not overlook the challenges we'll face during the auction," Sofia reminded them. "If we're not careful, we could encounter significant pushback from the criminals involved."

Eleanor nodded, appreciating the caution. "And we also have to be aware of the trust issues among our agencies. Historical rivalries could complicate cooperation if anyone feels their jurisdiction is being encroached upon."

Before the discussion could continue, the door opened, and Jonathan Walters, Eleanor's longtime colleague, stepped in, a stack of files in hand. "Sorry I'm late, everyone. I was gathering intel on recent art thefts in the area."

"Perfect timing, Jonathan," Eleanor said, gesturing for him to join the discussion. "We were just outlining our strategies. What insights do you have?"

Jonathan took a seat, opening one of the files. "I've compiled information on local gallery owners who may have seen suspicious activity. Several have reported unfamiliar faces asking about rare pieces. We need to follow up on those leads."

Eleanor's eyes lit up with interest. "Great work. We need to infiltrate the local art market. Ellen, can you lead that effort?"

Ellen Hayes, the local investigator, nodded vigorously, "Absolutely, I'll interview gallery owners and museum staff to uncover any signs of forgery. We can also rely on informants within the art community."

As the meeting progressed, the dialogue flowed with increasing intensity. They discussed the execution phase of their plan, with each agency determined to play its part effectively.

"Once we gather enough evidence, we have to be ready to act," Eleanor reminded them. "If Salvatore makes a move, we need to adapt on the fly."

Agent Thompson leaned back in his chair, his expression serious. "I'll ensure our undercover agent is in place early. We need eyes on the crowd to spot any suspicious behavior. We must have backup ready to go. We can't afford any slip-ups."

As they wrapped up their discussions, the atmosphere was thick with anticipation. Each agent felt the weight of the mission ahead, knowing that their collective efforts could lead to a major breakthrough in the fight against art crime.

"Let's stay focused and keep communication open," Eleanor concluded. "Time is of the essence, and we're all counting on each other to make this work."

With that, they prepared to leave the conference room, determined to put their plans into action as the countdown to the auction continued.

"Agreed," Martinez said. "And I'll coordinate with local law enforcement to ensure we have their cooperation."

30.

A Weekend to Remember

As the day at the museum drew to a close, the soft glow of the setting sun filtered through the grand windows, casting a warm light across the gallery. Marco and Julian were wrapping up their discussions about the replication project when Marco glanced at the clock.

"Wow, where did the time go? It's almost 5 PM," Marco said, stretching his arms above his head. "What do you have planned for the weekend?"

Julian leaned against the edge of a nearby table, a relaxed smile on his face, "Rest and relaxation, mostly. I want to spend some quality time with my man. We have an extraordinary few weeks ahead of us with the auction and everything."

Marco chuckled, raising an eyebrow playfully. "Ah, so I'm just a weekend getaway for you now, huh?"

"Not just a getaway," Julian replied, laughing as he nudged Marco's shoulder. "You know you're my favorite distraction."

"Good save," Marco said, grinning. "But seriously, do you want to work a bit on Saturday morning? I thought we could put in a few hours at the museum before enjoying the rest of the weekend."

"Definitely," Julian agreed. "I'd like to get a head start on some of the details. Maybe we can brainstorm a bit about the replica before the madness begins."

"Sounds like a plan. How about dinner out tomorrow night? We could hit that new Italian place you mentioned," Marco suggested, his eyes lighting up with enthusiasm.

"I love that idea! Let's make a reservation," Julian replied, his mind already racing with anticipation. "And we can treat ourselves to brunch on Sunday, followed by a Broadway matinee."

"Perfect! It's been ages since we've seen a show," Marco said, his excitement notable. "I can't wait to relax and enjoy some time together."

After a whirlwind day at the museum and a busy week of meetings, Julian and Marco finally returned home, feeling the weight of jet lag creeping in. The sun had begun to set, casting a warm glow through the windows of the cozy apartment. Julian dropped his bag by the door and turned to Marco, a smile breaking across his face.

"Home sweet home," he said, pulling Marco into a warm embrace. They shared a tender kiss, the familiar comfort of each other's presence easing the fatigue from their trip.

"Honestly, I could sleep for a week," Marco replied with a chuckle, rubbing his eyes. "But first, how about we order some Chinese? I'm starving."

"Perfect idea," Julian agreed, already reaching for his phone. "I've been craving dumplings since we landed."

As they settled onto the couch, Julian placed the order while Marco flopped down beside him, stretching out. "I can't believe we're finally back. London was great, but there's no place like home," Marco said, a hint of relief in his voice.

"Agreed, and I missed our Friday night rituals," Julian added, glancing over at Marco with a playful smirk, "You know, takeout and bad movies?"

"Hey, those bad movies are classics!" Marco shot back, feigning offense. "Plus, I think we'll both be too tired to care what's on."

When the doorbell rang, they both jumped up, eager to grab their food. Julian opened the door to find the delivery person holding a large bag filled with their favorite dishes. "Perfect timing!" he beamed, taking the bag and tipping the delivery person before closing the door.

They set the table, and the aroma of spicy Szechuan chicken and fried rice filled the air as they dug in. The conversation flowed easily between them, laughter punctuating their shared stories from the trip. Marco recounted a particularly funny moment from the museum, and Julian couldn't help but chuckle.

After eating, the remnants of the meal lingered on the table, they retreated to the bedroom, ready to unwind. Julian grabbed the remote and flipped through channels until he found a movie that promised some mindless entertainment.

They nestled under the blankets, the soft glow of the TV illuminating their faces. However, as the film played, the exhaustion from the day caught up with them. Julian felt his eyelids grow heavy, and he shifted closer to Marco, who had already succumbed to sleep.

Julian fought to stay awake for a few more minutes, but the warmth of Marco's body and the soothing sounds of the movie lulled him into a peaceful slumber.

Around 3 AM, Julian stirred awake, disoriented as he realized the TV was still on, casting flickering shadows in the dark room. He reached over, turning off the lights and the television, then snuggled back under the covers, feeling Marco's steady breathing beside him.

With a contented sigh, Julian closed his eyes again, surrendering to the comfort of the moment. They slept soundly, wrapped in each other's warmth, the chaos of the outside world fading away until morning.

Saturday morning dawned bright and clear. Julian arrived at the museum early, the quiet ambiance allowing him to focus on the details of the project. Marco joined Julian a few hours later, coffee in hand.

"Hey, are you ready to tackle the day?" Julian asked, smiling at Marco as he took a sip of his coffee.

"Absolutely, let's make some magic happen," Marco replied, setting his cup down and rolling up his sleeves.

They spent the morning immersed in their work, discussing techniques and reviewing plans for the replica. Time flew by, and before they knew it, it was lunchtime.

"Let's take a break," Julian suggested,

glancing at the clock. "We've earned it."

They stepped out for a quick bite, enjoying a casual lunch at a nearby bistro on the west side of 5th Avenue. As they ate, Marco leaned across the table, a teasing glint in his eyes. "So, what's on the menu for dinner tonight? I hope it's not just spaghetti and meatballs."

"Oh, I've got something special in mind," Julian replied, a mischievous smile playing on his lips. "But you'll have to wait and see."

After their lunch, they returned to the museum for a few more hours of work before wrapping up for the day. By evening, they were both eager to unwind.

That evening, they made their way to the Italian restaurant, where the atmosphere was lively and the aroma of fresh pasta filled the air. As they enjoyed their meal, Marco looked across the table, his gaze softening. "I'm really glad we're doing this together, Julian. It makes everything feel more... meaningful."

Julian reached across the table, taking Marco's hand in his. "I feel the same way. I wouldn't want to do this with anyone else."

After dinner, they strolled through the bustling streets of Manhattan, hand in hand, the city lights sparkling around them. The energy was infectious, and they both felt a sense of joy in simply being together.

Sunday morning arrived, and they indulged in a leisurely brunch at a well-known café in the theatre district, savoring every moment. "I could get used to this," Marco said, grinning as he took a bite of his French toast. "Good food, great company."

"Agreed," Julian replied, his eyes sparkling. "And the best part is, we still have the matinee to look forward to."

After brunch, they made their way to the theater, excited to see a new production. The performance was captivating, and they found themselves completely absorbed in the story unfolding on stage. As the final curtain fell, they left the theater buzzing with excitement.

On their way home, they stopped by the market to pick up ingredients for dinner. "What about some steaks for the grill?" Julian suggested, his eyes lighting up at the thought.

"Now, that sounds perfect! I'll make a salad to go with it," Marco replied, his enthusiasm matching Julian's.

Once back at Julian's condo, he led Marco to the large wraparound terrace where the barbecue grill awaited. As Julian prepped the steaks, Marco busied himself washing and chopping vegetables for the salad.

"Want any help with that?" Julian called out, glancing over his shoulder.
"I've got it covered! Just focus on those steaks," Marco replied, a playful grin on his face. "I want them cooked to perfection. Remember, I like mine medium rare."

When dinner was ready, they sat outside on the terrace on this unusually warm October evening, the sunset painting the sky in hues of orange and pink. As they ate, they locked eyes, feeling the connection between them deepen with each passing moment.

"Can you believe how much has changed in just a few weeks?" Marco asked, his voice softening.

Julian nodded, a smile spreading across his face. "It's incredible. I feel like we're building something amazing, both with the project and with each other."

After dinner, they retired indoors, taking

a romantic candlelit shower together. The warmth of the water and the flickering candlelight created an intimate atmosphere, and they couldn't resist getting lost in each other's touch.

Wrapped in each other's arms, they eventually fell into bed, their bodies entwined and unable to keep their hands to themselves. The night unfolded with passionate lovemaking, each kiss and caress deepening their bond. As they slowly drifted off to sleep, they felt a profound sense of contentment, knowing they were embarking on this journey together, both in art and in love.

31.

The Black Market Arts Syndicate (BMAS)

Victor Salvatore stood in the dim light of his enormous studio, the faint scent of oil paint and turpentine hanging in the air. A master forger, he had perfected the art of deception, his exceptional talent enabling him to replicate the styles of history's most revered painters. With a degree from one of Europe's most prestigious art schools, Zurich University of the Arts in Switzerland, Victor had spent years immersing himself in the techniques of the masters, studying every brushstroke, every hue, until he could mimic them with uncanny precision.

His workspace was a carefully curated chaos—canvases in various stages of completion leaned against the walls, while shelves overflowed with paint tubes, brushes, and reference books. Each piece he produced was a meticulous replica, so flawless that even the most discerning eye would struggle to differentiate it from the original. This meticulous attention to detail was Victor's hallmark, and it was what made him the mastermind behind the underground art syndicate known only in whispered tones as the Black Market Arts Syndicate (BMAS).

But Victor was not just an artist; he was a strategist. He understood that to maintain his operation, he needed a team—an ensemble of specialists who could help him execute his elaborate schemes. Each member of his crew brought a unique skill set, and together they formed a tightly woven network dedicated to the art of deception.

Victor had always possessed a keen eye for talent. Over the years, he had cultivated relationships with various individuals from the art world, some of who had fallen on hard times or had become disillusioned with the industry. He approached them with a proposition: join him in a venture that would challenge their artistic abilities and provide financial rewards far beyond what legitimate avenues could offer.

Salvatore's first recruit was Alina Rossi, a talented art historian and researcher who had once worked for a prestigious gallery in Florence. She had grown disenchanted with the commercialism of the art world and was drawn to Victor's vision of reclaiming art for the sake of beauty—and profit. With her knowledge of art history and provenance, Alina became invaluable in identifying pieces that were ripe for replication.

Alina Rossi was born in the heart of Florence, Italy, a city steeped in artistic heritage and cultural significance. From a young age, Alina was captivated by the beauty of the Renaissance masterpieces that adorned the galleries and churches of her hometown. Her parents, both educators, encouraged her artistic inclinations, introducing her to the works of Botticelli, Michelangelo, and, of course, Leonardo da Vinci. Alina's passion for art blossomed, leading her to pursue a degree in art history at the University of Florence, where she excelled academically.

After completing her studies, Alina secured a position at one of the most prestigious galleries in Florence, where she worked as an art historian and researcher. Her responsibilities included curating exhibitions, conducting provenance research, and writing detailed analyses of the artworks. Alina thrived in this environment, surrounded by beauty and creativity, and she quickly became known for her keen insights and meticulous attention to detail.

However, as the years went by, Alina became disillusioned with the commercialism that permeated the art world. She watched as galleries prioritized profit over artistic integrity, choosing to showcase popular works that could be easily sold rather than taking risks on lesser-known artists. The art she once revered felt diluted, commodified, and stripped of its true value. The thrill of unearthing hidden gems was replaced by the relentless pursuit of sales targets and market trends.

Feeling trapped in a system that no longer aligned with her values, Alina started to question her place in the art world. She found herself longing for a deeper connection to art— one that transcended mere transactions. She wanted to reclaim the beauty of art for its own sake, to celebrate creativity without the constraints of commercial viability.

It was during this tumultuous period in her life that she first heard whispers of Victor Salvatore, the enigmatic master forger. Initially skeptical, Alina was intrigued by the notion of someone daring to challenge the status quo. As she delved deeper into Victor's philosophy, she found herself drawn to his vision of art as a living, breathing entity that deserved to be celebrated, regardless of its monetary value.

Their meeting took place in an unassuming café in Florence, where they discussed their shared frustrations over the direction of the art world. Victor spoke passionately about his desire to create replicas that honored the techniques of the masters, while Alina shared her yearning for authenticity in art. A spark ignited between them, fueled by a mutual understanding of the complexities and contradictions within the art industry.

Victor soon recognized Alina's potential as a valuable asset to his underground syndicate, BMAS. Her extensive knowledge of art history and provenance made her an ideal candidate for identifying pieces that were ripe for replication. Alina, in turn, saw this as an opportunity to break free from the confines of the commercial art world and to immerse herself in a project that aligned with her ideals.

As she considered Victor's offer to join the BMAS, Alina felt a mix of excitement and trepidation. She knew the risks involved in forging art, yet the prospect of reclaiming beauty and artistry reignited her passion. This was her chance to work on art that truly mattered to her—to create replicas that celebrated the masters while simultaneously challenging the art world's commercial underbelly.

With a newfound sense of purpose, Alina accepted Victor's invitation. She believed that by joining the syndicate, she could contribute to something greater than herself—a movement that celebrated art in its purest form, even if it meant operating in the shadows. Together with Victor, she would embark on a journey that would test her skills, ethics, and commitment to the very essence of art.

Salvatore's next pick is Marco Rossi, Apprentice Forger. A young, talented artist looking to make his mark, Marco has been drawn into the forgery world. Eager to learn from Victor and the team, he assists with painting and research, though his loyalty is tested as he becomes more aware of the ethical implications of their work.

Marco Rossi, a bright and ambitious artist, grew up in Florence, Italy, surrounded by the rich history and culture that shaped his artistic sensibilities. From a young age, he showed a keen interest in art, often sketching in the margins of his notebooks during school. His passion led him to pursue a graduate degree in Art History and Restoration at Columbia University, where he honed his skills in analyzing and preserving artworks.

After graduating, Marco returned to Florence, eager to make his mark in the art world. He was drawn to the idea of creating pieces that would resonate with collectors and art enthusiasts alike. However, the competitive landscape of the art scene left him feeling disillusioned. Despite his talent, Marco struggled to gain recognition and found himself working part-time as an assistant to Julian Taylor at the Metropolitan Museum of Art in New York City.

Working at the MET provided Marco

with invaluable experience, allowing him to immerse himself in the world of art curation and restoration. He admired Julian's dedication and expertise, often seeking his guidance on various projects. Their professional relationship blossomed into a close friendship, and over the years, they developed a deep bond that transcended the workplace. However, that bond was complicated by Marco's growing frustration with the limitations of the legitimate art world. He yearned for creative freedom and the opportunity to express himself fully.

It was during this time of uncertainty that Marco crossed paths with Victor Salvatore. Intrigued by Victor's reputation as a master forger, Marco found himself captivated by the idea of creating art that could challenge the established norms. Victor's vision of reclaiming art for beauty and profit resonated with Marco's desires, igniting a spark of ambition within him.

Yet, Marco faced a profound internal conflict. His fourteen-year friendship with Julian Taylor weighed heavily on his mind. Julian had always been supportive of Marco's artistic pursuits, and their partnership was built on mutual respect and trust. The thought of betraying that bond to join Victor's underground syndicate filled Marco with anxiety. He feared that by choosing to work with Victor, he would not only jeopardize his relationship with Julian but also compromise his own integrity as an artist.

As Marco navigated this crossroads in his life, he found himself torn between two worlds. On one hand, there was the stability and familiarity of his life with Julian, who embodied the ideals of legitimate artistry. On the other, there was the allure of the underground art scene promised by Victor—a world where he could unleash his creativity without constraint.

In the days leading up to his decision, Marco spent countless hours contemplating his options. He could envision a future where he would become a master forger, crafting replicas that could stand alongside the originals, but he couldn't shake the guilt of potentially betraying Julian's trust. The weight of his dilemma pressed heavily on him as he sought solace in his art, pouring his emotions onto the canvas.

Ultimately, Marco knew he would have to make a choice. Would he pursue the risky path of becoming a forger under Victor's guidance, or would he remain committed to the legitimate art world and the relationship he had built with Julian? The decision loomed over him like a specter, and as he weighed the consequences of each path, he felt the pull of ambition tugging at his heart.

As he considered his options, Marco recognized that regardless of the choice he made, it would shape the course of his life—both as an artist and as a partner. The allure of the underground art world was powerful, but so was the bond he shared with Julian. Would he be able to reconcile these conflicting desires, or would he have to choose one at the expense of the other?

After much contemplation, Marco finally gathered the courage to tell Victor the truth. Sitting across from him, he felt the weight of the decision pressing down on him. "I can't join your team, Victor," he said, his voice steady, but resolute.

Marco's mind raced as he considered the path his life was taking. He had been making significant strides in his career, forging a reputation for himself in the art world that he was proud of. The thought of abandoning that progress felt like stepping onto shaky ground. More importantly, his long-standing friendship with Julian Taylor was something he cherished deeply. The bond they shared had been built on trust, mutual respect, and a shared passion for art. It was a connection he didn't want to jeopardize for the allure of a risky venture.

Victor's expression shifted, a mixture of disappointment and frustration flickering across his face. But Marco stood firm, knowing that some choices could not be swayed by temptation. He was committed to his own path, one that aligned with his values and aspirations. As the conversation unfolded, he felt a sense of relief wash over him. In that moment, he understood that sometimes, the hardest decisions were also the right ones.

Simone Leduc grew up in the bustling streets of Paris, where the art world was as vibrant as the city itself. From a young age, he showed a keen interest in both technology and design, often spending hours at his computer experimenting with graphic design software. His fascination with visual aesthetics led him to pursue a degree in Graphic Design at a renowned university, where he excelled in digital manipulation and creative problem-solving.

After graduation, Simone worked for a prestigious design firm, creating marketing materials for high-profile clients. However, as he honed his skills, he grew increasingly frustrated with the limitations of commercial design. He felt that the industry often prioritized profit over creativity, leaving little room for genuine artistic expression. This dissatisfaction led him to explore the darker side of his abilities, where he could wield his skills in a more thrilling and unconventional manner.

It was during a chance encounter at an art fair that Simone first crossed paths with Victor Salvatore. Intrigued by Victor's audacious reputation as a master forger, Simone was captivated by the idea of creating authentic-looking documents and certificates of authenticity. He realized that his expertise in graphic design and digital manipulation could be invaluable to Victor's underground operation.

Simone's skill set was impressive; he had a knack for crafting documents that could withstand even the most rigorous scrutiny. Whether it was a seemingly vintage certificate or a meticulously replicated signature, Simone could create it with astonishing accuracy. His understanding of both art and technology allowed him to bridge the gap between the two worlds, making him a key player in Victor's syndicate.

As Victor courted Simone to join his team, the excitement for the operation was electrifying. Simone loved the thrill of outsmarting the system, of bending the rules to create something that challenged the very foundations of the art world. The prospect of crafting forgeries that could deceive even the most discerning collectors filled him with a sense of purpose he had long been searching for.

Simone was drawn to the idea of being part of a movement that reclaimed art from the clutches of commodification. He envisioned a world where the beauty of art could be appreciated without the constraints of legality, where creativity could flourish without fear of judgment. Joining Victor's syndicate felt like a rebellion against the commercialism that had stifled his own artistic ambitions.

However, he was also aware of the risks involved. The world of art forgery was fraught with danger, and the consequences of being caught could be dire. Yet, the allure of the underground art scene was compelling, and Simone found himself torn between the safety of his current life and the exhilarating possibilities that lay ahead.

As he considered Victor's offer, Simone felt a rush of adrenaline at the thought of what they could accomplish together. With a team of skilled individuals, they could craft forgeries that not only rivaled the originals but also told their own stories—stories that challenged the status quo of the art world.

Ultimately, Simone Leduc was ready to embrace the thrill of the unknown, to dive headfirst into the world of art forgery, and to prove that with the right skills, even the most secure systems could be outsmarted.

Felix Lombardi grew up in a gritty neighborhood on the outskirts of Rome, where the allure of art was often overshadowed by the harsh realities of life. From a young age, he was fascinated by the intricate designs of classical architecture and the stories told through sculptures and paintings. This passion led him to pursue a degree in Security Management and Technology, where he learned the ins and outs of protecting valuable assets.

After graduating, Felix landed a job as a security specialist for several high-end galleries across Europe. His responsibilities included assessing vulnerabilities, designing security protocols, and implementing advanced alarm systems to protect priceless artworks. Felix was meticulous, often spending long hours evaluating security measures, ensuring that every piece was adequately safeguarded. His work was commendable, and he quickly gained a reputation for his expertise in the field.

However, over time, Felix became disillusioned with the art world. He watched as galleries prioritized profits, often compromising the integrity of the art they displayed. The same institutions he worked to protect were frequently more concerned with maintaining their bottom line than with preserving the cultural heritage they housed. This growing frustration left him feeling trapped in a system that valued commercial success over artistic integrity.

During one of his gigs, Felix encountered Victor Salvatore, who was conducting research on security systems for a project involving forgeries. Intrigued by Victor's audacity and vision, Felix found himself drawn to the idea of using his skills for something that challenged the status quo. Victor's proposal—to join an underground syndicate dedicated to creating flawless forgeries—sparked a flicker of excitement within him.

Felix was aware of the risks associated with such a venture. The world of art forgery was dangerous, and getting caught could lead to severe consequences. Yet, he couldn't shake the feeling that this was an opportunity to reclaim the excitement he had lost in his legitimate career. The thrill of planning heists and outsmarting security measures reignited his passion for art and design.

As he weighed his options, Felix realized that his unique skill set could play a crucial role in Victor's operations. With his insider knowledge of security measures and alarm systems, he could help plan heists that were both ambitious and meticulously executed. His resourcefulness and quick thinking were essential qualities for navigating the treacherous waters of the art world.

Despite his initial reservations, Felix

found himself increasingly tempted by the idea of joining Victor's syndicate. He imagined a world where he could not only protect art but also contribute to its creation in a way that defied the conventions of the art market. The prospect of working alongside other talented individuals, each with their own unique skills, excited him.

Ultimately, Felix Lombardi decided to take the plunge. He approached Victor with a mix of caution and enthusiasm, ready to embrace the thrill of the underground art scene. He understood the risks but felt that the opportunity to work on something meaningful—something that challenged the very foundations of the art world—was worth it.

As he prepared to dive into this new venture, Felix was determined to use his expertise to ensure that their operations remained under the radar. He knew that success depended on careful planning and execution, and he was ready to bring his knowledge to the table. The thrill of outsmarting the system was calling, and Felix Lombardi was eager to answer.

Martin Falcone was born and raised in a quaint village in Tuscany, Italy, where art and history were woven into the fabric of daily life. From a young age, he displayed a remarkable aptitude for craftsmanship and creativity, often found sketching the beautiful landscapes and historic buildings that surrounded him. His passion for art led him to study at a prestigious conservatory, where he specialized in art restoration.

After completing his education, Martin secured a position at a renowned museum in Florence, becoming one of their most talented conservators. He worked tirelessly, applying his in-depth understanding of restoration techniques and materials to preserve invaluable works of art. Martin was meticulous in his approach, often spending hours studying the original materials and methods used by the masters. His expertise allowed him to restore paintings and sculptures to their former glory, ensuring that future generations could appreciate their beauty.

Despite his success, Martin grew increasingly frustrated with the constraints of the conventional art world. He witnessed the bureaucracy that often stifled creativity, as well as the commercial pressures that dictated which pieces were deemed worthy of preservation. The world he had devoted his life to felt increasingly disconnected from the art's true purpose— celebration and expression.

It was during this period of disillusionment that he first met Victor Salvatore. The two crossed paths at an art event, where Victor was discussing his bold vision for creating replicas that honored the techniques of the masters. Intrigued by Victor's audacity and the potential for collaboration, Martin found himself captivated by the idea of creating art that would challenge the established norms.

Victor recognized Martin's talent and proposed that he join his underground syndicate. With Martin's extensive knowledge of restoration techniques, he could create forgeries that not only looked authentic but also aged convincingly over time. The prospect of collaborating with Victor excited Martin; he could use his skills to craft pieces that would pass as genuine, appearing as though they had hung in galleries for decades.

As he considered Victor's offer, Martin felt a rush of adrenaline. This was an opportunity to reclaim the joy of creation, to work on projects that stirred his passion rather than merely preserving the status quo. The thrill of crafting replicas that could deceive even the most discerning collectors was intoxicating.

However, Martin was also acutely aware of the risks involved. The world of art forgery was fraught with danger, and the consequences of being caught could be severe. Yet, the allure of working outside the constraints of the traditional art world was too compelling to resist. He envisioned a new kind of artistry, one that celebrated the beauty of the original works while pushing the boundaries of what was considered acceptable in the art community.

Ultimately, Martin Falcone decided to embrace this new path. He joined Victor's syndicate with the understanding that his expertise would not only provide financial rewards but also reignite his passion for art. As he prepared to dive into this underground world, he felt a renewed sense of purpose. Working alongside Victor and the rest of the team, Martin was ready to craft forgeries that would challenge the very foundations of the art world, proving that art could exist beyond the confines of legality.

With Victor's vision and Martin's expertise, they could create a legacy that blurred the lines between authenticity and imitation—a testament to the enduring power of art in all its forms.

Sophie Chang was born and raised in San Francisco, California, where the tech-savvy culture of Silicon Valley molded her early interests. From a young age, she exhibited a knack for both art and technology, often merging the two by creating digital art on her tablet. Her parents, both engineers, encouraged her to pursue her passions, leading her to study Graphic Design and Digital Media at a prestigious university.

After graduating, Sophie quickly established herself as a rising talent in the world of digital art. She secured a position at a well-known design firm, where she specialized in creating high-resolution digital images of artworks for various clients, including galleries and museums. Her ability to re-create textures and colors with astonishing accuracy set her apart, making her a sought-after designer in the art community.

However, despite her success, Sophie felt a growing sense of dissatisfaction. She often found herself frustrated by the constraints of commercial projects that prioritized profit over artistic integrity. The thrill of pure creativity was often overshadowed by client demands and corporate agendas. As she navigated the confines of the industry, she began to yearn for a project that would allow her to push boundaries and explore art in a more meaningful way.

Her life took a turn when she attended an underground art exhibition in a hidden gallery in San Francisco. There, she learned about Victor Salvatore and his audacious work in the world of art forgery. Intrigued by the idea of using her digital skills to challenge the established art world, Sophie approached Victor after the event, eager to learn more about his methods and vision.

Victor recognized her potential immediately. He saw that her expertise in digital imaging could be invaluable to his underground syndicate. With her skills, they could create hyper-realistic forgeries that not only looked authentic but also had the necessary provenance documents to back them up. Sophie's ability to analyze and replicate the textures and colors of masterpieces would provide the team with accurate references, making their forgeries more convincing.

As she considered Victor's offer to join

his operation, Sophie felt a mix of excitement and trepidation. She knew that by stepping into this world, she would be jeopardizing her career and possibly her safety. The risks of being caught in the act of forgery were significant, and the potential consequences could be dire—not just for her career but for her personal life as well.

Yet, the thrill of creating art in a way that defied convention was intoxicating. Sophie envisioned a role where she could not only use her skills to craft beautiful replicas but also to manipulate provenance documents that could further lend authenticity to their forgeries. The prospect of collaborating with a team of talented individuals, each with their unique skills, filled her with a sense of purpose she hadn't felt in years.

Ultimately, Sophie Chang decided to embrace this new path. She was ready to dive into the underground art world, using her digital expertise to push the boundaries of forgery and authenticity. As she joined Victor's syndicate, she felt a renewed sense of agency—an opportunity to reclaim her passion for art while challenging the conventions of the industry she had grown disillusioned with.

With Victor's vision and her digital prowess, Sophie was determined to help craft forgeries that not only deceived but also celebrated the beauty of art. She knew that the journey ahead would be fraught with risks, but the possibility of creating something extraordinary drove her forward into the shadows of the art world.

Julien Mercer was born in the vibrant heart of New Orleans, Louisiana, a city known for its rich cultural tapestry and artistic heritage. From a young age, he was fascinated by the stories behind the art he encountered, drawn to the allure of the underground scene that thrived just beneath the surface. His charm and quick wit made him a natural at navigating social circles, and he quickly learned how to read people, a skill that would later prove invaluable.

After high school, Julien fell into the world of art theft. What began as a thrill-seeking adventure turned into a career as he became increasingly skilled at planning heists. He developed a reputation for being able to infiltrate galleries and auctions, using his charm and knowledge of the art world to blend in with collectors and curators. His experiences taught him the ins and outs of the underground art scene, where high-stakes auctions often held more opportunities for profit than the legitimate market.

However, after a close call during one of his heists, Julien Mercer realized that the life of an art thief was fraught with danger. He began to see the writing on the wall: one misstep could lead to arrest or worse. It was time for a change, and he decided to pivot from thievery to forgery. The skills he had honed as a thief—his ability to navigate high-stakes environments, his connections within the art world, and his knack for subterfuge—would serve him well in his new role.

Julien first crossed paths with Victor Salvatore during an underground auction, where he was impressed by Victor's audacity and expertise in creating forgeries that could outsmart even the most vigilant collectors. Intrigued by the idea of joining forces, Julien approached Victor with a proposal: he could use his connections to acquire materials, scout for potential buyers, and help infiltrate the art market to sell their forgeries.

Victor recognized the value in Julien's

offer. With his background as an art thief and his insider knowledge of the underground scene, Julien could navigate the complexities of high-stakes auctions and galleries without raising suspicion. He could identify lucrative opportunities and ensure that their forgeries found their way to the right collectors, all while staying one step ahead of the law.

As he considered this new venture, Julien felt a rush of excitement. This was an opportunity not only to continue his involvement in the art world but also to do so on his own terms. He envisioned a future where he could outsmart the system, using his skills to create a legacy that blurred the lines between authenticity and imitation.

However, he was also aware of the risks involved. The world of forgery was dangerous, and the stakes were high. But for Julien, the thrill of the game outweighed the potential consequences. He knew he could rely on his instincts and experience to navigate the treacherous waters of the art world.

Ultimately, Julien Mercer embraced his new role within Victor's syndicate. He was ready to leverage his skills as a field operative, using his connections to infiltrate the art market and find opportunities to sell their forgeries. With Victor's vision and his expertise, Julien was determined to leave a mark on the underground art scene, proving that even a former thief could carve out a new identity in a world defined by deception.

As he prepared to dive into this new chapter of his life, Julien felt a sense of purpose and exhilaration. The art world was his playground, and he was ready to play the game.

Isabelle Dube was born in Paris, France, where the art world pulsated around her from an early age. Growing up in a family of art collectors, she developed a passion for the stories behind the artworks and the narratives that could make them irresistible to buyers. Isabelle pursued a degree in Art Marketing at a prestigious university, where she specialized in the intersection of art and commerce.

After graduation, Isabelle worked for several high-end galleries, where she honed her skills in crafting compelling narratives around artworks. She learned how to present pieces in a way that highlighted their provenance, artistic significance, and emotional impact, making them highly desirable to collectors. Her persuasive skills quickly garnered her a reputation as a top sales expert, able to sell even the most challenging pieces.

However, Isabelle felt constrained by the rigid expectations of the legitimate art world. She grew frustrated with the commercialism that often overshadowed artistic integrity. When she crossed paths with Victor Salvatore at an underground exhibition, she was intrigued by his vision of creating forgeries that celebrated art's beauty rather than its market value.

Recognizing the potential for collaboration, Isabelle approached Victor with an offer to join his syndicate. Her expertise in marketing and sales could help the team craft narratives around their forgeries that would entice buyers willing to pay top dollar. Isabelle saw an opportunity to reclaim the art world for what it should be—an arena for creativity and expression.

Isabelle's ability to weave compelling stories around the forgeries would be essential for their operation. She knew how to highlight the emotional and historical significance of each piece, making them appealing to collectors who might otherwise dismiss replicas. With her on board, the syndicate could elevate their forgeries from mere imitations to sought-after works of art in their own right.

Anton Petrov was born in Kyiv, Ukraine, where he developed a fascination with the intricate logistics of supply chains from a young age. His parents owned a small shipping company, and Anton often spent his weekends helping them organize shipments and manage inventory. This early exposure to logistics led him to pursue a degree in Supply Chain Management, where he excelled in optimizing processes and coordinating complex operations.

After graduating, Anton worked for a multinational logistics firm, where he quickly climbed the ranks due to his exceptional organizational skills and attention to detail. He became adept at overseeing the transportation of goods, ensuring that everything ran smoothly and efficiently. However, despite his success, Anton grew disillusioned with the corporate world, feeling stifled by bureaucratic red tape and the relentless pursuit of profit.

His life took a turn when he met Victor Salvatore at an art-related event. Intrigued by Victor's audacious approach to art forgery, Anton saw an opportunity to leverage his skills in a more thrilling and unconventional way. Victor recognized Anton's expertise in handling logistics and offered him a role in his underground syndicate.

As the logistics coordinator, Anton would be responsible for sourcing materials, coordinating the transportation of forgeries, and ensuring that all operations remained under the radar. His background in supply chain management made him the perfect fit for the role, as he could navigate complex logistical challenges with ease.

Anton was excited by the prospect of working in the underground art world, where he could use his skills to orchestrate operations that would be both daring and discreet. He was determined to ensure that every aspect of the syndicate's activities ran smoothly, allowing the team to focus on their creative endeavors without worrying about logistics.

Clara Jensen grew up in Cheyenne, Wyoming, where her fascination with security began at a young age. Her father was a police officer, and she often accompanied him on his rounds, absorbing the intricacies of crime prevention and safety protocols. This early exposure led her to pursue a degree in Security Management, where she specialized in risk assessment and security systems.

After graduating, Clara worked for a leading security firm, where she gained extensive experience in assessing vulnerabilities in various settings, including galleries and museums. Her keen eye for detail and ability to design effective security plans earned her a reputation as a top security expert. However, as she navigated the corporate world, Clara grew frustrated with the limitations of her role. She felt that the focus was often on profit rather than genuine safety and protection.

Clara's life changed when she attended an art exhibition and met Victor Salvatore. She was drawn to his vision of creating forgeries that celebrated art in a unique way. Recognizing the potential for collaboration, Clara approached Victor and offered her expertise in security.

As the security specialist for Victor's syndicate, Clara would provide insight into how to avoid detection and assess risks associated with their operations. She could identify vulnerabilities in galleries and auction houses, ensuring that the team remained covert. Clara was excited by the challenge of using her skills in a more unconventional context, where she could make a meaningful impact on the art world.

With her background in security and risk management, Clara was determined to help the syndicate operate under the radar, allowing them to navigate the art world without raising suspicion.

Dr. Lydia Chen was born in Toronto, Canada, to a family of academics who valued education and critical thinking. From a young age, Lydia exhibited a passion for the law and a fascination with the complexities of art ownership. She pursued a degree in Law, followed by a doctorate in Art Law, where she focused on the legal nuances surrounding provenance and ownership rights.

After completing her education, Lydia worked as a lawyer for a prestigious firm specializing in art law. Her expertise in navigating the complexities of legal loopholes and art ownership made her a sought-after advisor for collectors, galleries, and museums. However, as she gained experience, Lydia became increasingly disillusioned with the art world's focus on profit and exclusivity. She felt that the legal system often favored the wealthy, leaving smaller artists and collectors vulnerable.

Lydia's life took an unexpected turn when she met Victor Salvatore at an art symposium. Intrigued by his bold approach to art forgery, she saw an opportunity to use her legal knowledge in a more unconventional way. Victor recognized Lydia's expertise and offered her a role as the legal advisor for his underground syndicate.

In this capacity, Lydia would help the team navigate the complexities of art ownership and provenance, providing advice on legal loopholes that could protect them from potential repercussions. Her understanding of the law would be invaluable in ensuring that the syndicate could operate with a layer of protection against legal challenges.

Lydia was excited by the prospect of using her skills to challenge the established norms of the art world. She believed that by joining Victor's team, she could make a difference— creating a space where art could thrive outside the confines of legality while helping to protect the integrity of the pieces they created.

As he built his team, Victor made sure to select individuals who were not only skilled but also fiercely loyal. He knew that trust was paramount in their clandestine activities. He organized meetings in discreet locations, often late at night, to discuss strategies and assign roles.

With a core group now in place, Victor turned his attention to finding additional specialists. He sought out a talented painter named Ingrid Bertozzi, known for her ability to replicate the styles of Impressionist masters. He also recruited Tomás, a master framer who could create ornate frames that would enhance the value of their forgeries.

As the syndicate began to take shape, Victor's confidence grew. Each member brought something vital to the operation, creating a diverse skill set that would allow them to undertake increasingly ambitious projects. They started small, replicating lesser-known works and selling them to unsuspecting collectors, but Victor had bigger plans in mind.

He envisioned high-stakes forgeries—

pieces like Leonardo's "Salvator Mundi," which could fetch millions at auction. With each successful operation, their reputation in the underground art world grew, drawing in potential recruits and eager buyers alike.

Victor understood that the art of forgery was not just about replicating masterpieces; it was about weaving a tapestry of deception that could ensnare even the most discerning collectors. As he prepared for their next venture, he couldn't shake the thrill of the chase—a game of cat and mouse that could lead to unimaginable wealth or devastating consequences.

With his team assembled and ambitions set, Victor Salvatore was ready to dive deeper into the shadows of the art world, ready to orchestrate a symphony of deception that would leave an indelible mark on the criminal underbelly of the art community.

32.

The Replication of da Vinci's 'Salvator Mundi'

Early Monday morning, October 7, Sarah suggested, "Using digital software, we can analyze the original's color palette and textures. It's like having a roadmap before we start."

"Exactly," Julian said. "Let's make sure we capture every detail accurately."

Anton offered, "To mimic five centuries of aging, we'll need to layer certain materials and use specific techniques. It's all about patience."

Marco offered, "Patience isn't my strong suit, but I'm willing to learn!"

Elise turned towards Julian and said, "I'll need specific measurements for the frame. It should reflect the grandeur of the original—nothing less will do."

Julian, happy to hear this from Elise, said

"Absolutely. The frame is just as important as the painting itself."

Julian gathers everyone in his studio to discuss the project. Initial introductions and setting expectations for each team member follows.

Julian, started by saying, "Thank you all for coming. We're embarking on a challenging yet thrilling project. I have my trust in this group and your understanding of how serious and confidential your efforts will be. Our goal is to create a replica of da Vinci's 'Salvator Mundi' that not only looks authentic but feels authentic."

Marco said, "And we have the right people for the job. I'm excited to see how we all contribute."

As the conversation flowed, ideas bounced around the table, each person contributing their expertise. The atmosphere was charged with enthusiasm and a shared sense of purpose as they prepared for the challenges ahead.

Julian's replication underway, minutes ticked by, the hours melted into days, and Julian found himself immersed in a whirlwind of creativity and collaboration with his replication team. Each member brought a unique set of skills and perspectives, creating a dynamic atmosphere that inspired innovation and solidarity.

Julian observed the interactions with keen interest. Sarah Chen, the digital artist, refined her digital mockups, her focus unwavering as she adjusted the colors and textures. "I've finished the digital mockup," she announced during the afternoon, her eyes sparkling with excitement. "It's a great starting point, but we need to adjust the colors here," she pointed at the screen, her voice brimming with enthusiasm.

Anton Kirov, the aging specialist,

nodded thoughtfully as he leaned against the wall, arms crossed. "Once we start painting, we need to think about how to layer the aging process," he said, his tone serious but encouraging. "It's not just about making it look old; it has to feel old. We need to consider the wear and tear, the nuances that come with centuries of history. Every crack and faded hue tells a story."

Marco Rossi chimed in, glancing at the digital mockup on the screen. "Exactly! If we can replicate those subtle details, we'll create something that truly resonates. It's about capturing the essence of the original."

The team continued to brainstorm, bouncing ideas off one another, their dialogue a blend of technical jargon and passionate debate. Hours slipped away unnoticed as they worked side by side, the energy in the room credible. Laughter punctuated their discussions, and there were moments of light-hearted teasing that only deepened their bond.

Elise Harper, the woodworker and frame maker, chimed in with her perspective. "And don't forget about the framing. The frame has to match the period style perfectly. It enhances the overall aesthetic and can influence how the painting is perceived."

As the team spent long hours at the museum, Julian felt a sense of pride swell within him. They were dedicated, often working late into the evening, fueled by pizza and coffee, their laughter echoing through the halls. He marveled at how quickly they had gelled as a unit, each member contributing not just their skills but also their personalities to the collective effort.

By the end of the week, they had logged countless hours of collaborative work. The days were filled with discussions about color palettes, aging techniques, and the historical context of the original 'Salvator Mundi'. Each meeting brought them closer to their goal, and Julian could sense the excitement building.

"Let's recap what we've accomplished so far," Julian proposed one afternoon as they gathered around the table, the digital mockup displayed prominently on the screen. "We've established a solid foundation for the replica, and with each adjustment, we're getting closer to something truly remarkable."

Everyone nodded in agreement, their expressions reflecting a mix of determination and anticipation.

"Here's to the late nights and early mornings ahead," Marco raised an imaginary glass, a playful grin on his face.

"Cheers to that!" Sarah added, her laughter infectious.

As the week progressed, Julian knew they were on the brink of creating something extraordinary—not just a replica but a testament to their teamwork, creativity, and shared passion for art.

One week into their efforts, the atmosphere in the studio was charged with anticipation and creativity. However, that morning, Julian's frustration boiled over. "This isn't going as planned!" he exclaimed, standing at the head of the table, his hands clenched. "I need everyone to be on the same page, please!"

The room fell silent, the weight of his words hanging in the air. Marco exchanged concerned glances with the others. "Julian, we can adjust," he replied, trying to keep his tone calm. "Let's brainstorm solutions together. We've got this."

Elise Harper, sitting nearby, leaned

forward, her brow furrowing. "But we've made significant progress! The digital mockups are solid, and we've outlined the aging techniques. It's just the first stroke of paint that hasn't gone on the canvas yet."

"Exactly," Sarah Chen chimed in, her voice steady. "We're right on track. You're just feeling the pressure because we're nearing the start of the painting phase. It's normal to feel stressed, but we're doing a great job."

Anton Kirov crossed his arms thoughtfully. "Julian, I understand your concern, but we still have time. You're not flying back to London for another two weeks. We'll have this completed well before then."

Julian ran a hand through his thick dark brown hair, his frustration evident. "But what if we don't? I want this to look perfect. We have to layer the paint correctly to achieve that aged look, and I worry that we're not coordinating as well as we need to."

Marco stepped closer, his expression earnest. "You know that's not true. We've been collaborating well. Just because a week has passed doesn't mean we're behind. We're in the creative process, and that takes time."

"Exactly," Lila Thorne added, nodding as she stepped into the workroom. "Art isn't rushed. We need to trust the process. If we focus on each detail now, it will pay off when we start painting."

The tension in the room began to dissipate as Marco continued, "Let's take a moment to regroup. We can set specific goals for the next few days to ensure we're aligned. We'll break it down into manageable tasks, and I promise you'll see progress."

Julian took a deep breath, the supportive

words of his team gradually easing his anxiety. "Alright, you're right. I need to step back and trust that you all have my back. But I want to make sure we're ready by the end of next week. No last-minute scrambles."

"Deal," Marco said, a reassuring smile spreading across his face. "We'll have this done before the end of the second week. There's no need to rush just for the sake of it. Quality over speed; as they say?"

"Right," Julian conceded, his shoulders relaxing slightly. "Thank you everyone. Let's refocus and make sure we're all clear on our next steps."

As the team began to discuss their plans, the atmosphere shifted back to one of collaboration and creativity. Ideas flowed freely, and the slight uproar soon transformed into a productive brainstorming session. Julian felt the tension lift as he realized they were, indeed, stronger together.

Julian apologized, glancing at the clock. "It's 4PM on Friday afternoon. How about we wrap up for the day and head to our respective homes for a well-deserved break this evening?"

As the second week of the replication project unfolded, the atmosphere in the studio buzzed with a mix of anticipation and intensity. On Tuesday, Julian, with Marco closely by his side, began the delicate process of painting. Anton Kirov stood beside them, offering detailed instructions on how to achieve the perfect overlays to create the authentic aging of the painting.

"Remember, Julian," Anton said, guiding Julian's hand as he applied the first strokes, "it's not just about the colors. It's about the texture and layering. Each brushstroke should reflect the passage of time."

Julian nodded, focused intently on Anton's guidance. "Got it. So, we need to build up the layers gradually to mimic how the original would have aged?"

"Exactly," Anton replied, his eyes sharp with expertise. "Start with the base layer in warmer tones, then we can add in the cooler colors for depth."

Marco, observing closely, chimed in, "And don't forget about the small imperfections. That's what gives a painting a sense of being lived in, as if carries a rich history."

As the days passed, the painting slowly evolved through their unwavering dedication. Each session brought new challenges, but the team's collaboration made progress manageable. By Wednesday, Elise was hard at work on the frame, her craftsmanship evident as she shaped the wood into an intricate design that would complement the painting beautifully.

"Almost there!" Elise called out, a spark of excitement in her voice as she sanded down the final touches. "This frame is going to be the crown jewel for the replica."

That evening, Julian and Marco returned home, the weight of the project lingering in their minds. As they settled in, Julian turned to Marco, his expression serious. "We need to talk about what's at stake here," he began, his voice steady but urgent.

Marco looked up, sensing the gravity in Julian's tone. "What's on your mind?"

"If Victor Salvatore realizes the paintings are fake, it could lead to serious trouble. He's not just going to let it slide. He'll either try to steal it or expose us," Julian said, pacing slightly. "We have to make sure that the moment the painting is unveiled, it's locked away securely. I want it shipped to an undisclosed location before the preview night."

Marco nodded, understanding the implications. "And we need to ensure law enforcement is ready to catch him in the act if he tries anything. This is a high-stakes game, Julian."

"I know," Julian replied, taking a deep breath. "But we're creating something truly special here. This replica isn't just a forgery; it's a testament to our skills and dedication. It represents our fight against theft in the art world."

As the week progressed, the emotional stakes for each team member deepened. On Thursday, as they neared completion of the replica, Julian gathered the team for a moment of reflection. "I want us to take a moment to appreciate what we've accomplished together," he said, looking around at the group—Marco, Anton, Sarah, and Elise. "This project means so much to all of us."

Elise smiled, her hands still dusty from working on the frame. "I've poured my heart into this frame, and I can't wait to see how it complements the painting. It's not just wood; it's part of the story we're telling."

Sarah added, "For me, this is about the intersection of technology and traditional art. I've loved creating the digital mockups and seeing them come to life. It's exciting to be part of something that will challenge the status quo."

"Agreed," Anton said, his voice steady. "Every brushstroke we've laid down has been a step towards preserving the legacy of art. This replica might not be the original, but it holds its own significance."

Marco looked around the room, his heart swelling with pride. "We're all on this journey together, and I believe we can pull this off. It's a race against time, but we have each other's backs."

Julian smiled, feeling the weight of their shared commitment. "And remember, this isn't just about the end product. It's about how we've come together as a team, how we've supported one another through this process. The completion of this replica is just the beginning."

As they resumed their work, the energy in the room shifted to one of determination and teamwork. With each stroke of paint and each detail painstakingly crafted, they were not only creating a replica but also weaving a narrative of resilience and artistry. The completion of the painting loomed closer, and with it, the promise of the journey they would embark on next.

On Friday morning at 10 AM, Julian gathered Dr. Thorne and Dr. Grant in the workroom, a sense of anticipation buzzing in the air. He had something significant to reveal, and he wanted to share it with them firsthand. As they entered, they noticed a covered painting standing prominently in the center of the room.

"Thank you both for coming," Julian said, standing beside the covered artwork. He took a deep breath, feeling a mix of excitement and nerves. "What we've accomplished over the past two weeks has been remarkable, and I believe it's time to unveil the culmination of our hard work."

With that, Julian reached for the cloth, his heart racing. "I'm ready to unveil the 'Salvator Mundi.'"

As Julian pulled the cloth away, the room erupted in gasps of joy. Dr. Thorne's eyes widened in disbelief, and applause filled the air. "Oh my goodness, Julian! This is absolutely fabulous!" she exclaimed, stepping closer to admire the magnificent sight before her. "It's amazing—only an expert would dare to believe this is a replica!"

Dr. Grant, equally impressed, stepped forward, his expression filled with admiration. "Julian, I have to commend you for an unbelievable two weeks of hard work. To come up with something as magnificent as this replica is truly impressive," he said, his voice steady but filled with emotion. "The significance of what this will do in helping to catch the notorious thief cannot be overstated."

Julian felt a surge of pride wash over him, his heart swelling at their reactions. "Thank you both. It's been a true team effort. Each of us played a crucial role in bringing this vision to life." He gestured to the intricate details of the painting, the aged textures, and the careful brushstrokes that reflected their dedication.

Dr. Thorne stepped back, her gaze still fixed on the painting. "This is going to change everything," she said, her voice filled with conviction. "With a piece this convincing, we can finally set a trap for Victor Salvatore. You've outdone yourself, Julian."

"Indeed," Dr. Grant added, nodding in agreement. "We now have a weapon in our arsenal, one that will help us reclaim stolen art and protect our cultural heritage. This replica is not just a remarkable artwork; it's a symbol of our fight against art theft."

Julian smiled, feeling the weight of their words. "I couldn't have done this without all of you. We're one step closer to ensuring that justice is served." He glanced around the room, taking in the pride and excitement etched on their faces. "Now, let's make sure we prepare for the next phase of our plan."

The atmosphere in the workroom was charged with energy, each team member uplifted by the momentous achievement. As they gathered around the replica, it was clear that they were not just celebrating a painting; they were celebrating a shared mission and a commitment to preserving art for future generations.

33.

Julian and Marco Return to London

After the meeting where Julian unveiled the stunning replica of the 'Salvator Mundi', the atmosphere in the workshop buzzed with excitement and purpose. Julian and Marco spent the next few days meticulously refining the details of their work. With the unveiling behind them, they shifted their focus to the upcoming plans for their return to London.

As they wrapped up their two weeks of nearly ten-hour days, the fatigue began to weigh on them, but the anticipation of what lay ahead kept their spirits high. "We've come a long way in just two weeks," Marco remarked one evening, glancing at the replica that now stood proudly in the studio. "I can't believe we are heading back to London with some very precious cargo."

"Yeah, it feels like we've been preparing for this moment forever," Julian replied, his mind racing with thoughts of the upcoming auction and the law enforcement investigation that would accompany it. "We'll need to make sure everything is in order for the preview week. There's a lot at stake."

As they finalized their plans, the decision was made to return to the same hotel they had stayed in previously. "It's familiar, and it feels like a good base camp for what we need to accomplish," Julian said, his eyes sparkling with determination. "We'll probably be there for at least two weeks this time, with the planning and then the auction itself."

The two friends packed their bags, organizing their materials for the trip. The weight of their work pressed down on them, but there was also a sense of exhilaration. They understood that the upcoming weeks would be intense, filled with late nights and high-stakes decisions.

On Sunday night, October 20th, they boarded their flight, the familiar hum of the aircraft comforting as they settled in for the journey. As the plane ascended into the night sky, Julian glanced at Marco, who was already reviewing their notes for the upcoming meetings.

"Ready for this," Julian asked, a mixture of nerves and excitement coursing through him.

"Absolutely," Marco replied, his expression serious yet confident. "We've prepared for every scenario. Let's just stay focused and keep our eyes on the prize."

Marco and Julian arrived in London on Monday morning, October 21, the city alive with energy as they stepped out of the airport. Julian felt a rush of adrenaline as they made their way to the hotel, eager to dive headfirst into the next chapter of their journey.

Once they reached their room, a wave of exhaustion washed over them. Julian flopped onto the bed, letting out a contented sigh. "I can't believe we're finally here. London feels electric!"

Marco leaned against the wall, a smirk on his face. "Electric? More like overwhelming. I could use a shower after that long flight."

"Agreed," Julian replied, glancing at the clock. "We've got a busy week ahead with the auction preview on Friday."

"Right, let's get cleaned up, and then we can order some breakfast. Room service sounds perfect," Marco suggested, heading toward the bathroom.

As the water cascaded down, Julian took a moment to reflect. He felt a mix of excitement and nerves bubbling within him. After a quick shower, he stepped out, wrapping a towel around his waist, just in time to see Marco standing at the mirror in the bathroom, looking refreshed and a little mischievous.

"Feeling better?" Julian asked, raising an eyebrow.

"Much. But I think I need a proper celebration for being back in London," Marco teased, stepping closer.

Julian chuckled, "Is that so? Well, we do have the entire day ahead of us. How about a little fun before breakfast?"

With a playful grin, they shared a brief moment, laughter echoing in their cozy hotel room. After their lighthearted exchange, they pulled themselves together and ordered breakfast.

As they waited for room service, they laid out their plans for the week. "I can't wait to see what's at Christie's," Julian said, his eyes sparkling with anticipation. "The auction is going to be incredible."

Marco nodded, leaning back against the bed. "Yeah, and that preview on Friday—it's going to be a whirlwind. We should take notes, maybe even sketch out some ideas for our bids."

Just then, there was a knock at the door. Julian rushed to answer it, revealing a cart filled with steaming plates of breakfast. "Finally, I'm starving," he exclaimed, rolling the cart into the room.

They settled at the small table, the aroma of their eggs and bacon wafting through the air. As they dug into their meal, the conversation flowed easily.

"Remember that auction we went to in Paris?" Marco asked, a grin spreading across his face. "We almost got into a bidding war over that ridiculous sculpture."

Julian laughed, shaking his head. "I still can't believe you wanted it. It looked like a twisted metal pretzel!"

"Hey, it was art!" Marco defended, raising his fork dramatically. "Art is subjective, my friend."

They both burst into laughter, the bond between them clearly evident. After finishing breakfast, Julian leaned back in his chair, feeling content. "Alright, let's head to Christie's. I want to see what they've got lined up."

"Lead the way," Marco suggested, a glint of excitement in his eyes. "London, here we come!"

With that, they grabbed their jackets and headed out, ready to explore the vibrant city and dive into the thrilling world of art auctions once again.

34.

A Visit to Christie's Auction House

The air thick with anticipation, Julian stood in the expansive auction hall of Christie's, Manson and Wood, one of the oldest auction houses in the world. The walls were adorned with the masterpieces that would soon be up for bidding, each piece a silent witness to the history it carried.

"I can't believe we're finally here," Julian said, his eyes scanning the impressive array of art on display. "Let's see the printed catalog. I want to know exactly what we're dealing with."

As they approached the front desk, Julian spotted Victoria Harrington, the Director of the auction house, striding toward them with a warm smile. "Julian, Marco! It's great to see you both," she greeted, extending her hand. "Welcome back to Christie's."

"Thanks, Victoria! We're eager to see what you have lined up for the auction," Marco replied, his enthusiasm evident.

Victoria led them through the elegantly decorated halls, showcasing various pieces that would be featured in the auction. "I hope you're ready for a whirlwind," Victoria said. "The preview starts on Thursday, and we have only three days to finalize everything."

Julian asked, "How many pieces are we showcasing this time? Were you able to secure thirty-five masterpieces like we spoke about in our last team meeting? I know we're aiming for something spectacular."

Victoria, quickly responded: "We've got thirty-five paintings lined up. Each one was meticulously chosen for its historical significance and potential market value."

"When can the public come in to view the artworks during the preview?" Julian asked.

Victoria explained, "The preview opens three days before the grand opening night, and it's essential for generating buzz. We've carefully selected these dates: the preview will take place on Wednesday, October 30, and the grand opening, along with the auction will begin promptly at 6 PM on Saturday, November 2. We anticipate a significant turnout, including coverage from the press and other attendees."

Julian: "Do we expect a lot of collectors this time? The last auction was quite the spectacle."

Victoria: "Absolutely. Knowing our limitations on time, we've already sent out invitations to key collectors and curators. Social media is buzzing with excitement. Once the catalog goes live on Thursday, October 23, it should attract even more attention."

As they discussed the logistics, Julian felt a rush of excitement. The thrill of the auction, the chance to uncover hidden stories behind each piece, was what drove him. But he also knew the stakes were high—art forgery loomed in the shadows of the vibrant art scene, and he was determined to ensure authenticity prevailed.

Julian felt a knot form in his stomach. "Speaking of which, we need to know where we stand with the thirty-five paintings. When will they arrive?"

"Absolutely. Let's head to the planning room," Victoria said, guiding them to a more private area away from the already busy art admirers. The room was lined with photographs of the artworks, each piece carefully documented.

As they settled in, Julian's mind raced. "Do we really have enough time to get everything ready? With all the law enforcement involved, I can't help but wonder how seamless this will be. Are we going to be under a microscope the entire time?"

Victoria nodded, her expression serious. "I understand your concerns. Over the last two weeks, we've been working tirelessly with Interpol, the FBI, and Scotland Yard. They're all on board, but the situation is delicate. Everyone has different roles, but it's crucial that we maintain a façade of normalcy during the auction."

"What about the logistics?" Marco asked, crossing his arms. "How many people are aware of the full scope of this operation?"

"Only a select few," Victoria replied, leaning forward. "We've kept the circle tight to minimize leaks, but it's still a risk. The last thing we want is for anyone to suspect something is amiss while the auction is underway."

Julian felt a wave of anxiety wash over him. "So, if something doesn't go according to plan, how will we manage it? We can't afford to alert anyone that we're onto something."

Victoria took a deep breath, glancing at the array of paintings surrounding them. "That's why we need to be strategic. We've had two weeks to prepare while you were in New York, and I assure you, we're doing everything we can to make this seamless."

Julian exchanged a glance with Marco, both men understanding the gravity of the situation. "We have to be ready for anything," Julian said, his voice steady. "If we're going to pull this off, we need to stay one step ahead."

"I agree," Marco added. "We can't let our guard down, especially with so much at stake."

Victoria smiled, trying to alleviate the tension. "I'm confident in our team. With your expertise and our resources, we can navigate this successfully. Just keep your eyes open and trust your instincts."

As they continued to discuss the details, Julian felt a mix of apprehension and determination. They were on the brink of something monumental, and while the stakes were high, he knew they had to push forward. With the auction just days away, every moment counted.

"We'll do everything we can to ensure this goes smoothly," Julian said, feeling a renewed sense of purpose. "Let's make sure we're ready for whatever comes next."

Victoria nodded, her eyes sparkling with determination. "Together, we can make this work. Now, let's dive into the specifics of the paintings and finalize our strategy."

With that, they delved into the intricate

details of each artwork, aware that the clock was ticking and the world of art—and deception—was waiting.

Victoria led Marco and Julian into a spacious gallery room, where the paintings were meticulously arranged on the walls, each piece illuminated under soft lighting. The atmosphere was charged with anticipation as they stepped closer to examine the artworks that would soon be up for auction.

"Here they are," Victoria said, gesturing proudly. "These are the pieces we've selected, all organized in the order they'll be auctioned. Each one has been photographed for the catalog, and I think you'll find the lineup quite impressive."

Julian's eyes widened as he scanned the room. "Wow, these are stunning! I can't believe how well you've curated this event. Why did I ever doubt you could pull it off, Victoria? You're simply the best." He moved closer to a vibrant landscape painting, its colors practically leaping off the canvas. "This one is sure to attract a lot of attention."

Marco leaned in closer to read the information card next to it. "Look at that opening bid—$100 million! It's Claude Monet's 'Boulevard des Capucines', that's absolutely heavenly!" His voice was a mix of awe and disbelief.

Victoria nodded, her expression serious, "The art market has been thriving, particularly for Renaissance and Impressionist artists--the world's most celebrated creators. We anticipate intense competition for many of these pieces."

Julian moved to another painting, immediately noting it was Renoir's 'Umbrellas'— so magnificent. "And for this one, the opening bid is listed at $200 million!" He shook his head in disbelief. "How are they setting such high starting prices?"

"It's based on recent sales trends and appraisals from experts in the field," Victoria explained, her tone knowledgeable. "These artists have proven their value in the market, and we believe these opening bids reflect that. But the auction can be unpredictable. You never know how high the bidding will go."

Marco pointed to a striking portrait 'Portrait of Adele Block-Bauer' by the great artist Gustav Klimt with an opening bid of $135 million. "But do you think these prices will deter potential buyers? What if the bids don't reach the estimates?"

"That's always a possibility," Victoria admitted. "But with the right buyers in the room, we often see prices soar above expectations. This particular auction has attracted attention from several high-profile collectors."

Julian felt a mix of excitement and apprehension. "So, with the stakes this high, we really need to keep our eyes on everything. If the atmosphere is tense, it could affect the bidding process."

"Exactly," Victoria said, looking between them. "We need to ensure that no one suspects anything unusual while the auction is underway. If people sense tension, it could influence their willingness to bid."

"Got it," Marco replied, still studying the vibrant pieces. "We have to find a way to blend in while staying alert."

As they moved from painting to painting, the weight of the upcoming auction settled over them. Each piece held not just artistic value, but a potential for chaos, deception, and high stakes. Julian felt his heart race at the thought of what lay ahead.

"Let's keep our focus sharp," Julian said, determination in his voice. "We need to be ready for anything that comes our way."

Victoria smiled, appreciating their resolve. "I have no doubt you both will rise to the occasion. Now, let's finalize our strategy for the preview and ensure everything goes off without a hitch."

With that, they continued their tour, the vibrant colors of the paintings surrounding them, each one a reminder of the thrilling—and dangerous—world they were about to enter.

As the meeting with Victoria Harrington came to a close, Julian and Marco exchanged appreciative glances. The vibrant energy of Christie's Auction House still buzzed around them, but they felt a sense of accomplishment after gathering crucial insights.

"Thank you, Victoria, for showing us everything that's taken place in our absence," Julian said, extending his hand. "It's incredibly helpful to see the pieces up close and understand how you've curated them for the auction."

Victoria smiled, her professionalism evident. "I'm glad you found it valuable. We're all in this together, and your expertise will be critical as we move forward. Just remember, time is of the essence."

"Absolutely," Marco added, leaning against the conference table. "The more we understand about the auction dynamics, the better equipped we'll be to anticipate any movements from Salvatore's crew."

Victoria nodded, her expression serious. "Keep an eye on the original 'Salvator Mundi'. If they plan to switch it, it will be during the auction. We need to be ready."

With final words of encouragement

exchanged, Julian and Marco made their way out of the auction house, the crisp autumn air greeting them as they stepped onto the bustling London street. The city was alive with activity, and the evening light cast a golden hue over the buildings.

"Can you believe how much we learned today?" Julian said, his eyes reflecting excitement. "It's like we've been given a front-row seat to the whole operation."

"Definitely," Marco replied, glancing over at Julian. "But it also makes me anxious. There's so much at stake, and we have to stay sharp."

As they walked back to their hotel, the weight of the day settled over them. "Let's make some calls when we get back," Julian suggested. "I want to touch base with a few contacts in the art world and see if they've heard anything about Salvatore's plans."

"Good idea," Marco replied. "I'll reach out to some of my connections as well. Every bit of information counts."

Once they arrived at the hotel, they headed straight to their room. Julian tossed his bag onto the bed and pulled out his laptop, eager to dive into his calls. "I'll grab us some coffee from downstairs. You want anything?" he asked, glancing back at Marco, who was already scrolling through his phone.

"Just some water is fine," Marco replied, his focus still on the screen. "I'll be right here, trying to piece together what we know."

Julian nodded and headed out, the hotel lobby buzzing with guests. He returned a few minutes later, two steaming cups of coffee in hand and a bottle of water for Marco.

"Here you go, caffeine fix," Julian said, handing Marco his drink. "How's it going over there? Hey..ah…Stand up for a minute Marco, please." Marco did as he was asked, and Julian reached his arms around Marco and hugged him tightly, "I just wanted to feel you close and get a much needed hug." Marco pulled Julian close and gently kissed his lips. I needed a hug too Julian. It's so sweet to take this moment for each other. Thanks my love."

"To answer your previous question, Pretty good. I've got a lead on a gallery owner who might have seen something suspicious. It's a long shot, but worth checking out," Marco replied, taking a sip of his coffee. "What about you?"

"I'm following up with a contact who specializes in art authentication. If anyone knows about forgeries hitting the market, it'll be him," Julian explained, his fingers flying over the keyboard. "I'll also check in with Claire from Interpol to see if there's any news on their end."

As they settled into their routine, the atmosphere in the room shifted from tension to relaxation. They shared updates, bouncing ideas off each other as they strategized for the next day.

"Hey, remember what Victoria said about keeping our eyes open?" Marco said, leaning back in his chair. "We need to be aware of everything happening around us, not just the auction itself."

Julian nodded, his expression serious. "Right, it's not just about the art; it's about the people involved. We can't let our guard down, even for a second."

As the night wore on, they continued their discussions, the weight of the upcoming auction looming large. They knew that tomorrow would bring new challenges, but for now, they felt a sense of unity in their mission.

"Whatever happens, we're in this together," Julian said, raising his coffee cup in a small toast.

"Together," Marco echoed, clinking his cup against Julian's.

With renewed determination, they jumped into bed to get some much needed rest. Jetlagged and brain-fogged they turned the lights off and, almost immediately, fell off to sleep in a warm embrace.

35.

Law Enforcement Team Update

As Julian stood at the head of the table early Tuesday morning, he could feel the energy shift in the room. The casual morning chatter faded as everyone focused on him, eager to dive into the planning session.

Julian began by stressing, "While preparing for the upcoming preview and opening night just a little over a week from now, our law enforcement task force must continue the investigation of Victor Salvatore. The task force must unravel Victor Salvatore's network while contemplating how his syndicate adapts to increasing scrutiny."

Victor Salvatore and his team of skilled forgers and operatives have executed many heists with precision, establishing a network of hidden masterpieces across various European cities. Their forgeries are carefully crafted to withstand scrutiny, allowing Victor to continue his operations under the radar.

These hidden pieces not only serve as a testament to Victor's audacity but also provide him with leverage in the underground art world. As he prepares for the upcoming auction, he knows that the stakes have never been higher. The task force's investigation could uncover his past crimes, making it imperative for him to stay one step ahead.

As the task force investigates the recent thefts of 'The Starry Night' and 'House and Figure,' they begin to notice a pattern in the types of artworks that have been stolen. Each piece has a historical significance or a connection to major art movements, suggesting that Victor is not just a forger but someone with a deep appreciation for art. This realization leads them to dig deeper into past thefts, revealing the possibility of several, if not many, hidden masterpieces.

The task force employs forensic art experts to analyze the forgeries currently in circulation. They discover similarities in the techniques used, linking them back to Simone Leduc's digital manipulation and Martin Falcone's restoration methods. This connection allows them to tighten their focus on Victor and his team as they uncover the sophisticated methods that have eluded law enforcement.

As investigators interview museum staff from the various locations where thefts occurred, they gather testimonies that point to a pattern of insider knowledge. Some staff recall suspicious individuals who seemed to have insider access during the times of the thefts. This leads the task force to suspect that Victor has infiltrated various institutions, embedding his operatives within the art world.

The task force investigates the financial implications of the thefts and begins to trace payments made to art dealers and collectors. They uncover transactions that lead back to Victor's syndicate, revealing how he has been laundering money through the sale of forgeries. This financial trail becomes a critical piece of evidence linking the past and present.

As the investigation unfolds, the task force begins to suspect that the hidden masterpieces are stored in various catacombs and underground locations across Europe. They start mapping these locations based on Victor's known patterns of movement and connections, with the intentions of leading them to uncover hidden caches of stolen art.

To combat the increasing scrutiny, Victor may decide to rotate his operatives or bring in new recruits to avoid detection. This could introduce tension within the syndicate, as established members question the loyalty and skills of newcomers. The task force could exploit this tension, trying to turn one of Victor's new recruits against him, leading to leaks of valuable information.

The culmination of the task force's investigation could lead to dramatic confrontations at the auction where Victor plans to showcase his latest forgeries. As they attempt to make a significant bust, the tension mounts, revealing the intricate web of deception Victor has spun over the years.

36.

Reconnaissance Phase—
Final Prep

With exactly one week to go before the Auction Preview, it appears that all of their hard work is paying off. But, as the stakes of the upcoming auction rose, so did the need for a thorough reconnaissance plan. Information gathering became paramount, not just for the success of the event, but for ensuring that all participants were above board. With a diverse team composed of international law enforcement, the operation would draw on the expertise of Scotland Yard, Interpol, and the FBI. Each member brought a unique set of skills and insights, crucial for navigating the complexities of the auction industry.

At the helm of this initiative was Inspector Ellen Hayes from Scotland Yard, known for her sharp investigative instincts and extensive experience in high-profile cases. Partnering with her was Detective Sophia Martinez from Interpol, whose deep understanding of international crime networks made her an invaluable asset. International Criminal Police Organization (ICPO), also known as Interpol, and Scotland Yard in London will be supported by FBI agents Robert Collins and Mark Thompson, both seasoned operatives skilled in handling sensitive operations.

As they convened in a discreet meeting room, the atmosphere was charged with purpose. Each character took a moment to assess the gravity of their mission. With the auction looming, the pressure was on to ensure that every detail was accounted for and that the event unfolded without a hitch.

A great deal of information has been compiled over the last couple years on Victor and his team of thieves and forgers.

No matter how many people Victor Salvatore employs in his gang of thieves, he cannot determine the location of the 'Salvator Mundi'. They only have information indicating that a Saudi Arabian Prince purchased the painting in 2018 for an estimated price of $450-500 million. Victor Salvatore is convinced the painting is housed in one of the world's major museums, specifically suggesting to his crew that it is locked away in the Louvre in Paris. He has numerous associates conducting surveillance operations at the Louvre in Paris, the National Gallery in London, the Museo del Prado in Madrid, and even the National Gallery of Art in Washington, D.C., using drones equipped with cameras to monitor security patterns, guard shifts, and access points. The list of suspected museums worldwide continues to grow, fueled by Victor's extreme paranoia and his relentless determination to obtain ownership of the 'Salvator Mundi'.

Victor employed Roland Kovac, 34 years old, a skilled security and alarm systems contractor who specializes in working with museums. With a solid background in technology and engineering, Roland has developed a reputation for his expertise in designing and implementing advanced security measures, making him an invaluable asset to Victor, but it also places him in a morally complex position.

Roland is highly intelligent and detail-oriented, often fixated on the technical aspects of his work. He can come across as socially awkward, preferring the company of machines to people. However, his loyalty to Victor runs deep, stemming from a past where Victor helped him out of a difficult situation.

Roland is driven by a desire to innovate and improve security systems, but his involvement with Victor places him in morally ambiguous territory. He struggles with the implications of his work, torn between his professional integrity and his loyalty to Victor.

Roland's connections include Victor Salvatore. Roland is one of Victor's closest associates, providing him with insider knowledge about museum security.

As an undercover agent, Marcus Wells, may cross paths with Roland during investigations. Roland's knowledge could either aid Marcus or complicate his mission, depending on Roland's choices.

If Ellen Hayes becomes aware of Roland's connections to Victor, she may seek to leverage his expertise to gain insights into Victor's operations.

Salvatore's team discreetly gathers information about the auction process, focusing on key details such as who will be in attendance, potential bidding strategies, and the auctioneer's methods. However, despite their efforts, they have been unable to obtain any intel on the specific paintings that will be up for auction, leaving a crucial gap in their knowledge as they prepare for the event.

Victor Salvatore seeks to uncover what Julian Taylor and his team of experts were planning at The Met in the lead-up to the auction. Victor has not yet uncovered Julian's replica team on any of their tactics as they position themselves to manipulate the situation to their advantage.

37.

Auction Preview Night

The grand hall of Christie's Auction House exuded opulence, with crystal chandeliers casting a warm glow over the polished wood floors. Exquisite artworks adorned the walls, each piece a silent invitation to the wealthy and discerning art aficionados gathered within. The air was thick with anticipation as the exclusive preview night for the 'Masters of Light: The Renaissance and Impressionist Collection' unfolded.

Victoria Harrington stood at the entrance, elegantly dressed, her demeanor a blend of professionalism and warmth. Beside her, Marco and Julian, looking quite debonair in their black tuxedoes, greeted guests, their eyes scanning the crowd for any signs of trouble. The preview ran from 6:30 PM until 8:30 PM, a carefully curated event designed to entice potential buyers to bid on the coveted artworks.

"Welcome, everyone! Please enjoy the evening and feel free to ask us any questions about the pieces," Victoria announced, her voice ringing with enthusiasm. "This is an incredible opportunity to view these masterpieces up close before the auction."

As attendees moved through the hall, the sounds of admiration, critique, and animated conversation filled the space. "Look at the brushwork on Cézanne's 'Still Life with Apples and a Pot of Primroses'!" a woman exclaimed, her eyes wide with excitement. "It's almost as if you can feel the texture of the fruit!"

Nearby, a group of bidders debated the merits of a Raphael's 'Portrait of a Young Man'. "I don't understand the fuss," one man scoffed, crossing his arms. "It looks like something an amateur could have painted. Why on earth is this piece valued at $100 million? You'd have to be out of your mind to pay that much for it."

"Oh, come on!" another retorted. "It's all about the emotion! Raphael captures the essence of his subjects in a way that's unparalleled. Valued at $100 million, the piece is truly worth it, and as an investment, it could be worth $110 million or more the very next day."

Evelyn Sinclair, the curator from the British Museum, moved gracefully through the crowd, engaging with guests and sharing insights about the historical context of the paintings. "Van Gogh's 'The Red Vineyard' was painted during his time in Arles," she explained to a small group. "He was deeply influenced by the vibrant colors of the landscape."

Meanwhile, Julian caught sight of David Cortez, the FBI agent, mingling discreetly among the guests, his keen eyes observing the interactions. He approached David, lowering his voice. "How's it looking? Any sign of Salvatore's crew?"

David shook his head, a slight frown creasing his forehead. "Not yet, but we're prepared for anything. My team is positioned in plain clothes, blending in with the crowd, ready to act if needed."

Liam Chen, the well-known art critic, joined them, a glass of wine in hand. "This is quite the event," he said, his voice rich with enthusiasm. "The buzz around these paintings is substantial. I've written extensively about the importance of these pieces in the art world."

Julian smirked. "Just be sure to keep your critiques constructive. We don't want anyone getting too heated tonight."

As the preview continued, Vincent Blackwood, the distinguished auctioneer, made his entrance, exuding charisma and authority. His presence commanded attention, and the crowd shifted to make way for him. "Ladies and gentlemen," he announced, his voice smooth and captivating, "I trust you're enjoying the evening. The anticipation for the auction is noteworthy, and I can assure you, these masterpieces are worth every moment of your attention."

"Vincent!" Victoria called out, waving him over. "We were just discussing the excitement surrounding the auction."

"Ah, Victoria," Vincent replied, his eyes sparkling. "The energy in this room is intoxicating. I can feel the excitement building for the 'Salvator Mundi.' It's the jewel of the collection."

Julian interjected, "We're hoping to see some serious bidding. The stakes are high, and the interest is fierce."

"Absolutely," Vincent agreed, his tone serious. "But we must also be vigilant. With great art comes great risk. We can't afford any distractions tonight."

Just then, a ripple of excitement coursed through the hall as two prominent collectors entered the room, drawing attention with their presence. "The buzz is definitely building," Liam remarked, a gleam of interest in his eyes. "This will only heighten the stakes for everyone."

Suddenly, a commotion near the entrance caught Julian's attention. A group of students advocating for more funding for the arts had appeared outside, their voices raised in protest. "This isn't the time for protests!" Julian murmured, frustration evident in his tone. "We don't need distractions tonight."

Victor Salvatore's absence was noticeable, but Julian knew that his crew could still be lurking, ready to exploit any opening. "Let's keep an eye on those outside. We can't risk any surprises."

As the evening wore on, the atmosphere charged with energy, guests critiqued the paintings passionately, their voices rising and falling like the ebb and flow of the tide. "What a travesty! They're treating these masterpieces like commodities!" one attendee exclaimed, his face flushed with indignation.

"Art is meant to be appreciated, not hoarded," another countered, waving a hand dismissively. "This auction is a celebration of beauty, after all!"

Evelyn, overhearing the conversation, chimed in. "Art is both a treasure and a responsibility. We must ensure that these pieces are preserved for future generations, even if it means selling them to the highest bidder."

As the clock ticked down to the end of the preview, Victor's team remained a constant shadow in Julian's mind. He felt the weight of the evening hanging heavy in the air, an unspoken tension that suggested danger lurked just around the corner.

"Let's regroup at the end of the night," Julian suggested to Marco and Victoria. "We need to debrief and ensure everything is in place for the auction."

As they continued to engage with the guests, the excitement swirled around them like a heavy perfume, intoxicating yet fraught with potential peril. And as the lights dimmed slightly, signaling the evening's conclusion, Julian couldn't shake the feeling that the real drama was still to come.

As the evening drew to a close, the lights in the grand hall began to dim, signaling to the guests that it was time to leave. A soft murmur of conversation rippled through the crowd as attendees gathered their belongings and exchanged farewells. Victoria Harrington stepped to the front, microphone in hand, her expression warm yet professional.

"Ladies and gentlemen," she called out, her voice echoing softly in the now quieter hall. "Thank you all for joining us this evening. Your presence means a great deal to us, and we hope you enjoyed the opportunity to view these extraordinary works of art. We look forward to seeing you at the auction on Saturday, November 2, at 6:30 PM. Have a wonderful night! The auction begins promptly at 7 PM. Have a wonderful night!"

As the last guests filtered out, Victoria, Julian, and Marco remained behind with Evelyn Sinclair and Liam Chen. The atmosphere was charged with a mix of relief and excitement, the energy of the evening still electric.

"Well, I'd say the preview was a success," Victoria remarked, her eyes sparkling. "The turnout exceeded my expectations, and the enthusiasm for the pieces was fantastic."

Evelyn nodded in agreement, a smile spreading across her face. "Absolutely! It's always thrilling to see how people react to the art. I believe we've managed to create a buzz that will carry into the auction."

Liam chimed in, his voice thoughtful. "The discussions were lively, and I think we've stirred interest in some of the more challenging pieces. That's a win for all of us."

Julian felt a wave of gratitude wash over him. "It's reassuring to see such engagement. I think it bodes well for the auction. If the bidders feel this invested now, they'll be ready to compete when the gavel comes down."

As they shared their reflections, Marco leaned back against the table, a satisfied grin on his face. "I'm just glad everything went smoothly. The last thing we need is any drama before the auction."

With their discussions concluded, Julian and Marco exchanged glances, silently agreeing it was time to unwind. "Shall we head back to the hotel?" Julian suggested, his voice lightening as he took Marco's hand.

"Definitely," Marco replied, a playful glint in his eyes. "I could use a little downtime after all that excitement."

Once back in their hotel room, the atmosphere shifted from the high-stakes world of art to a cozy sanctuary. They kicked off their shoes and sank into the plush chairs, the city lights twinkling outside their window.

"Can you believe we only have a couple of days before the auction?" Marco said, leaning back and letting out a contented sigh. "It feels surreal."

Julian smiled, his heart swelling with affection. "It's been a whirlwind, but tonight was a reminder of why we do this. The art, the passion—it's all worth it."

As the night deepened, they settled into a comfortable silence, the weight of the upcoming auction lingering in the background but momentarily forgotten. The world outside faded away as they shared stories and laughter, cherishing the quiet moments together before the storm of the auction arrived.

"Whatever happens next, I'm glad we're in this together," Marco said softly, reaching for Julian's hand.

"Always," Julian replied, squeezing his hand gently, feeling a sense of peace amidst the chaos. They knew that whatever challenges lay ahead, they would face them together.

38.

The Countdown to the Auction Event

The excitement of the evening lingered in the air as they relaxed in their hotel room. Julian glanced at his watch. "We have a lot to do before Saturday. Let's make a plan."

"Agreed," Marco replied, settling onto the couch. "What's first on the agenda?"

"First, I need to make some calls to New York. Lila and Samuel will want updates on everything," Julian said, pulling out his laptop and firing it up. "I'll fill them in on the auction details and any last-minute changes."

As Julian began typing, Marco leaned back, stretching his arms. "I can take care of a few things here. Maybe proof the auction catalog one more time and double-check the reserve prices?"

"Perfect. Let's ensure every detail is

covered," Julian said, grateful for Marco's support. "We can't afford any slip-ups."

Over the next couple of days, the pair worked tirelessly. Julian made calls to New York, providing Dr. Thorne and Dr. Grant with updates. "The preview went incredibly well," he informed them. "The interest in the paintings is high, and we're expecting fierce bidding on Saturday night."

"That's excellent news!" Dr. Grant replied, his voice crackling through the line. "Keep us posted on any developments. We want to be ready for anything."

"Will do," Julian assured him, hanging up and feeling a sense of accomplishment.

By Thursday night, the weight of the auction preparations began to lift slightly, and Julian suggested they take a break. "What about some bar-hopping in London? We could use a little fun before the big night."

Marco's eyes lit up. "That sounds perfect! A chance to unwind and enjoy the city sounds like exactly what we need."

They spent the evening exploring quaint pubs, laughing and sharing stories over pints of local ale. The vibrant atmosphere of London invigorated them, and they felt free from the pressures of the upcoming auction.

"Cheers to us!" Marco said, raising his glass. "To art, love, and the thrill of the chase."

"To us," Julian echoed, clinking his glass against Marco's. As the night wore on, their laughter turned into whispers, and they found themselves wrapped in each other's arms back at their hotel, the world outside forgotten.

Friday dawned bright and crisp, the autumn air invigorating. After a leisurely breakfast, they dove back into preparations. Julian made final calls to Victoria, David Cortez, and Claire Bertrand.

"Hey, Victoria," Julian said when she picked up. "I am just checking in. Are there any last-minute concerns on your end?"

"Everything is on track," Victoria replied, her voice efficient yet warm. "The security detail is in place, and we're ready for anything. Just keep me posted if anything changes."

"Will do. And I appreciate everything you're doing," Julian said sincerely before hanging up.

Later, Julian and Marco met with David and Claire at a nearby café, their conversation serious yet hopeful. "We're all set for tonight," David assured them, a hint of anticipation in his eyes. "The task force is on high alert. We've got people positioned at strategic points."

Claire added, "We can't afford any surprises. Victor's crew is still a threat, but we're ready for them."

With their plans solidified, Julian and Marco turned their focus to the evening ahead. They had made dinner plans at a renowned steakhouse in London, inviting Victoria, her husband, Evelyn Sinclair, and Liam Chen to join them.

As they sat down in the elegant restaurant, the atmosphere was lively and filled with laughter and clinking glasses. Julian raised his glass of red wine, "To a successful auction and a wonderful night with friends!"

"Cheers!" everyone echoed, their spirits lifted as they enjoyed the delicious food and engaging conversation.

"This steak is incredible," Marco declared, savoring every bite. "I can't remember the last time I had something this good."

Evelyn smiled, "London Steakhouse Company is the best in London, and only serves dry-aged British beef from their private cutting room at the King's butcher. You have to indulge before the big night."

As the evening progressed, stories flowed freely, with Liam recounting amusing anecdotes from his years in the art world. "You'd be surprised at the lengths some collectors will go to acquire a piece. I once saw a bidding war escalate to a ridiculous level over a supposed 'lost' Van Gogh!"

The laughter continued late into the night, a welcome distraction from the pressures looming ahead.

On Saturday, the day of the auction, Marco and Julian awoke to a beautiful autumn morning. The golden leaves danced outside their window, and the sun bathed the city in warmth.

"Today's the day," Julian said, excitement threading through his voice as he pulled on his tuxedo. "Are you ready?"

"More than ready," Marco replied, adjusting his cufflinks in the mirror. "Let's make this night unforgettable."

By 5:30 PM, they were dressed to the nines, both looking stunningly handsome and every bit the part of the confident auction participants they were. Julian felt a mixture of nerves and anticipation bubbling within him. "This is it, Marco. All our hard work leads to tonight."

"Together, we can handle anything that comes our way," Marco reassured him, his eyes filled with determination.

As they stepped out into the lively London streets, the energy of the city mirrored their own. The night ahead was filled with possibility, and the stakes had never been higher. They were ready to face whatever challenges awaited them at the auction, united in their commitment to each other and their passion for art.

39.

"Masters of Light: The Renaissance and Impressionist Collection"

Christie`s, the grand auction house in London, exuded opulence, with crystal chandeliers casting a warm glow over the polished wood floors. Exquisite artworks adorned the walls, each piece a silent testament to history and creativity. The air was thick with anticipation as wealthy bidders mingled, their voices a low hum, blissfully unaware of the chaos brewing beneath the surface.

In preparation for the evening, Christie's had made the Auction Catalog available well before the event, a beautifully designed booklet showcasing a curated selection of 35 masterpieces from the Renaissance and Impressionist eras. Each entry featured high-quality photographs, revealing the intricate brushwork and vibrant colors that made these works so coveted. The catalog not only highlighted the artist's name and year of creation but also provided insight into the rich cultural backgrounds of the pieces. It was more than a guide; it was a celebration of the masterpieces that had shaped the art world.

At the podium, Vincent Blackwood, the renowned auctioneer, stood confidently, ready to command the room. Charismatic and articulate, Vincent was known for his captivating voice and unparalleled knowledge of art. Yet, whispers of his mysterious past lingered, rumors suggesting he was once part of an art theft ring known as "The Phantom Curators." Now, after a close call with law enforcement, he sought redemption, though his darker inclinations still haunted him.

"Ladies and gentlemen," Vincent announced, his voice rolling like thunder, "welcome to tonight's extraordinary auction, 'Timeless Visions: The Renaissance and Impressionist Collection.' I assure you, the 'Salvator Mundi' is the highlight of our evening. Without further ado, let the bidding commence!"

As the auction progressed, the atmosphere buzzed with excitement. Bidders raised their paddles with enthusiasm, the rhythmic clicking of glasses and the murmur of conversations creating a lively backdrop. Vincent stepped forward, his presence magnetic. "Our first piece tonight is 'Still Life with Apples and a Pot of Primroses' by Paul Cézanne. The opening bid is $100 million."

A hush fell over the crowd, and paddles shot up as eager bidders vied for the iconic piece. After a tense moment, Vincent declared, "Sold to Mr. Carrington in the front row for $130 million!" The room erupted in applause, energy soaring.

"Next, we have 'Portrait of a Woman' by Amedeo Modigliani. Opening bid starts at $80 million," he continued, the excitement palpable. The bidding intensified, wealthy attendees exchanging competitive glances. "Sold to Mrs. Carrington for $95 million!" Blackwood announced, the crowd cheering once again.

Finally, Vincent presented the exquisite Van Gogh landscape. "And now, 'The Red Vineyard.' Opening bid is $75 million." The bids flew, and with a flourish, he concluded, "Sold to Lord Harrington for $172 million!"

Amidst the excitement, detectives from Scotland Yard and Interpol were strategically positioned throughout the room, blending seamlessly with the crowd while keeping a watchful eye for any suspicious activity. Inspector Ellen Hayes of Scotland Yard stood near the entrance, her keen gaze scanning the attendees, aware of Victor Salvatore's notorious reputation. Agent Sofia Martinez and her colleague Robert Collins, both from Interpol, were also in attendance, disguised as wealthy art collectors. They knew Salvatore and some of his gang members might be lurking among the bidders, acting as if they were undetected.

In the shadows, Victor Salvatore strategically learns his team's positions, biding their time for the heist. Julian and Marco were hyper-aware of the tension, their instincts on high alert. "Keep your eyes peeled," Julian whispered to Marco, scanning the crowd. "I have a bad feeling about this."

Ellen whispered to Sofia, "I am sure Salvatore is here. We need to keep our eyes peeled. He won't be able to resist the spotlight."

"Agreed," Sofia replied, her expression tense. "But we must blend in; we can't draw attention to ourselves."

Meanwhile, FBI Agent Mark Thompson monitored the auction from a discreet vantage point, ready to intervene at a moment's notice. The stakes were high, and as the auction continued, the room crackled with the potential for chaos.

The atmosphere in Christie's Auction House was electric, excitement coursing through the crowd as the bidding for the 'Salvator Mundi' approached. Guests mingled, their conversations a low hum, unaware of the storm brewing just beneath the surface. Vincent Blackwood stood at the podium, poised and charismatic, ready to command the room.

"Now as we promised," Vincent announced, raising the tension in the room, "the pièce de résistance—the 'Salvator Mundi,' attributed to Leonard da Vinci. Bidding will start at a staggering $500 million!" The atmosphere shifted. Victor saw his moment and sprang into action. "Do I hear $500 million, Blackwood called out?"

"$500 million!" came from a voice in the crowd, a paddle raised high.

"$510 million!" another bidder shouted, caught in the competitive spirit.

The bids continued to soar higher, captivating the audience. While in the shadows, Salvatore's gang readied themselves for the heist, their eyes locked on the painting as they planned their next move.

Undercover Agent Marcus Wells moved through the crowd, gathering intel while keeping an eye on the auctioneer and the coveted painting. "I'm positioned near the front," he whispered into his earpiece. "No sign of Salvatore yet, but the tension is building. They're pushing the bids up—

$550 million now."

"Stay alert," Mark Thompson replied on the other end. "We can't let any distractions slip through. If Salvatore makes his move, we need to be ready."

The stakes felt higher with every bid. The audience remained oblivious to the impending crime as Blackwood expertly played the crowd, drawing them into the frenzy.

"$600 million, ladies and gentlemen!" Vincent declared, his voice soaring above the chaos. "This is an extraordinary investment in history! Do I hear $650 million?"

"$675 million!" came a frantic paddle raise from a bidder.

"$700 million!" shouted another, the excitement peaking as the bids escalated.

Suddenly, a thunderous crash shattered the elegance of the auction hall as one of Salvatore's crew members sent a display tumbling to the ground. The sound reverberated like a gunshot, igniting chaos as panic surged through the crowd. Gasps of disbelief turned to frantic shouts, and in an instant, the atmosphere shifted from poised anticipation to sheer terror. Amidst the chaos, Salvatore's crew moved like shadows—swift and determined—ready to exploit the confusion for their daring heist.

Panic rippled through the room as guests turned to see the commotion, and in that instant, Agent Wells sprang into action, racing toward the original 'Salvator Mundi'. Meanwhile, Salvatore's crew seized the opportunity, slipping through the chaos, determined to remain unnoticed as they executed their audacious plan.

"Not so fast!" Agent Wells called out, his voice stern and commanding. "You're not getting away with this!"

Victor's maniacal grin widened as he shouted back, "You really think you can stop us now?" With a quick gesture, he signaled to his team, and pandemonium erupted.

Wells' heart raced as he realized that Victor was holding a forgery crafted by Julian's team in New York. For now, the authentic 'Salvator Mundi' rested safely in Saudi Arabia, under the vigilant gaze of the Prince. Victor was unaware that he was about to steal a Julian Taylor crafted forgery.

In an instant, law enforcement sprang into action, but Victor's crew was ready. The room erupted with the sounds of shattering glass and terrified screams as guests scrambled for safety. Julian's heart raced as he caught sight of Victor, moving with calculated precision toward the display.

"Stop right there, Salvatore!" yelled FBI Agent David Cortez, bursting into the room with his team. "You're surrounded!" But Victor merely laughed, his voice dripping with audacity. "You really think you can stop me? This is our night!"

Chaos erupted as a police officer responded to the threat, firing at one of Salvatore's men. The bullet hit its mark, and the injured man crumpled to the ground. Before anyone could process the moment, another member of Victor's crew brandished a weapon, the air thick with impending danger.

A deafening shot rang out, and Julian turned just in time to see Marco stagger back, clutching his side, his eyes wide with shock. "Marco!" Julian cried, rushing to his partner's side as he fell to the floor, blood seeping through his fingers.

"Stay with me, Marco, please!" Julian urged, his heart racing amidst the chaos. The sound of wailing sirens echoed in the distance, blending with the screams of guests scrambling for safety. What seemed like an eternity, the paramedics rushed in, and Julian felt himself being pushed aside as they assessed the situation.

"Clear some space, we need to stabilize him!" one shouted, urgency lacing their voice.

"Marco, just stay with me! You're going to be okay," Julian pleaded, his voice trembling. "Help us her, please!"

"Just hold on sir, we are doing our best!" As the paramedics worked swiftly, Julian felt helpless, the chaos around him fading into a blur. A stretcher was brought over, and Marco was lifted up and rolled away, tubes and equipment surrounding him.

"No! Don't take him!" Julian cried, desperation spilling from him. "Please, don't take him! God! I love you, Marco!" Tears streamed down his face as he watched the paramedics whisk Marco away, his heart shattering with every passing second.

The last image burned into his mind was Marco's eyes, filled with pain yet still holding a flicker of their shared love. The weight of the moment crashed over him like a tidal wave as the ambulance doors slammed shut, sealing away the one person he couldn't imagine living without.

As chaos continued to unfold, Victoria Harrington, the house director, and Vincent Blackwood, the auctioneer, found themselves swept into the maelstrom. Victoria's heart raced as she assessed the situation, instincts kicking in. "We need to secure the paintings!" she shouted to Vincent, who was already moving to protect the artworks.

"Follow me!" Vincent urged, his authoritative voice cutting through the turmoil.

They ducked behind a nearby display just as a shot rang out, sending guests into a frenzy. Victoria's mind raced—she had to protect the integrity of the auction house and its priceless treasures.

"Is everyone accounted for?" she asked, scanning the room for staff. "We can't let any of Salvatore's men near the art!"

"We'll manage the crowd," Vincent replied, his tone steady despite the chaos. "But we need to ensure our own safety first. We'll regroup once things settle."

Together, they navigated through the frantic guests, determined to maintain control in the face of disaster. Despite the peril, Victoria felt a surge of adrenaline. She was determined—her hard work would not unravel in an instant.

The night had transformed from a celebration into a nightmare. Outside, Victor Salvatore slipped away through a secret exit he had previously scouted, relishing the chaos he had orchestrated. He believed he had successfully stolen the original 'Salvator Mundi', confident that he held the real treasure—a perfect forgery left behind in its place. Amid the chaos, the remaining members of Victor's crew make a hasty exit, dragging the semi-conscious injured man with them.

Inside the auction house, law enforcement scrambled to regain control, their professional demeanor cracking under the pressure of utter turmoil. "We managed to stop his immediate plan, but Salvatore is somehow getting away with this again," Ellen Hayes reported, frustration evident in her voice as she scanned the room for any sign of the fugitive.

David Cortez, the FBI agent, nodded gravely. "We need to put him under full-time surveillance. He won't stop until he gets what he wants."

Claire Bertrand from Interpol chimed in, her expression steely. "I agree David, but we need to find him. He seems to have disappeared into thin air. We should also track his known associates. If he's escaped, they might help us pinpoint his location."

Ellen's gaze hardened. "Every minute we waste gives him a head start. We need to coordinate with all available units and establish a perimeter around the city."

As they spoke, Julian's mind was elsewhere, haunted by the image of Marco's eyes, filled with pain as he was whisked away in the ambulance. The urgency of the moment pressed heavily on him, amplifying his desperation to find Victor and hold him accountable.

Liam stepped closer to Julian, his expression one of unwavering support. "Come with me, Julian. I'll drive you to the hospital. I know you want to be with Marco, and you should be by his side. I am praying for him. Let's go!"

They rode to the hospital in complete silence, broken only by Julian's soft moans and whimpers as he fought against the overwhelming fear and despair.

As Julian and Liam stepped into the hospital, the sterile smell of antiseptic hit them like a wave. Julian paced anxiously in the waiting room, his heart pounding in his chest. The upheaval of auction night felt like a distant nightmare, yet the reality of Marco's condition loomed heavily over him, a dark cloud that wouldn't lift.

After what felt like an eternity, a doctor finally emerged from the operating room, her expression serious but not grim. "Mr. Taylor?" she called. Julian rushed forward, his breath hitching in his throat. "Is he okay? What happened?" Desperation laced his voice, each word tinged with fear.

"The bullet went straight through Marco," the doctor explained, her tone professional yet reassuring. "It exited through his lower back, narrowly missing his liver. Fortunately, it caused only minor damage to his stomach, but there's more significant damage to his upper intestines, and he has lost a considerable amount of blood."

Julian felt a wave of anxiety wash over him as the doctor's words sank in. "We'll need to operate again," she said, her expression serious. "We need to ensure that there's no tear in the large intestines and check for any internal bleeding."

"Will he be okay?" Julian asked, clinging to hope despite the grim news. "Can you stabilize him?"

The doctor nodded, her demeanor reassuring. "We're doing everything we can. He's currently in recovery, and we believe we can stabilize him. Fortunately, the injuries aren't life-threatening, but he will require close monitoring in the coming hours."

As relief washed over Julian, it was tempered by lingering anxiety. He felt the weight of the night's events pressing down on him, but his focus remained on one thing: finding Victor Salvatore and ensuring he paid for what he had done. The battle was far from over, and Julian was determined to uncover the truth.

Leaning forward, urgency in his voice, he asked for the second time, "When can I see him?"

As the investigation unfolded, agents spread out through the auction house, meticulously combing for evidence. They reviewed security footage, looking for any sign of Victor Salvatore's escape route. The video was grainy, but there were moments when they could make out the shadows of Victor and his crew slipping through the chaos.

Meanwhile, an evidence team collected the spent shell casings from the scene. "We'll need to analyze these to determine the type of weapon used," one officer said, carefully placing them in evidence bags. "If we can match them to a registered firearm, it might lead us to whoever fired the shot."

Ellen watched as the team worked, her mind racing with possibilities. "We need to establish a timeline of events. What time did the chaos begin? How long did it take for law enforcement to respond?"

Another agent chimed in, "The chaos started right after Victor made his move. We need to interview the auction staff to get a clearer picture of the timing."

"Also," Ellen added, her expression tense, "we need to find the man who was shot. If he's alive, he could provide crucial information about Salvatore's escape and his operations. We have to track him down."

As they continued their efforts, it became clear that Salvatore's men had taken their injured accomplice with them during their escape. The realization hung heavily in the air: unless they found Victor, they might never uncover the whereabouts of the man who could expose their entire operation.

"Alright, people, we need to gather all available information," Agent David Cortez commanded, his voice cutting through the noise of the bustling room. He stood at the center of the makeshift command post, surrounded by evidence boards and maps detailing the auction layout. "We know Salvatore was here, and we need to figure out how he slipped through our fingers."

"Agreed," Eleanor replied, turning to the group assembled around her. "Who can verify the events leading up to the shooting?"

"We're still interviewing witnesses," one officer reported, frustration evident in his tone. "But so far, no one has given us a clear account of who fired the shot that hit Marco Rossi."

Ellen shook her head, trying to piece together the chaos. "That's concerning. We need to track down everyone who was in the vicinity of the shooting. Someone must have seen something."

"I believe Marcus Wells fired at Salvatore's man," David interjected, recalling the events of the night. "He was positioned near the front, and his team should have a clear account of their actions."

"Where is Wells? Someone find him and bring him here for questioning," Eleanor said, her determination palpable. "We need his perspective on what happened and who he saw in the moments leading up to the shots fired."

As the investigation unfolded, agents spread out through the auction house, meticulously combing for evidence. They reviewed security footage, looking for any sign of Salvatore's escape route. The video was grainy, but there were moments when they could make out the shadows of Victor and his crew slipping through the chaos.

The thought of Salvatore escaping with the authentic 'Salvator Mundi' hung heavily over them like a dark cloud. "Thank goodness for Julian's magnificent replication. Not even

Salvatore knows that he has a forgery on his hands," Ellen smiled.

Julian's boyfriend was in critical condition, and they needed to act fast. The stakes had never been higher. "Let's set up a perimeter around the city," David ordered, his voice steady. "We know Salvatore has connections, and he could be trying to slip away. We need eyes everywhere."

Ellen nodded, her determination unwavering. "We'll also need to inform our international contacts. Salvatore's network stretches beyond London, and we can't underestimate his reach."

As agents continued gathering evidence, one detective reported back to David and Ellen. "We've identified a car that matches the description of a getaway vehicle seen leaving the scene during the chaos. It was caught on a nearby traffic camera."

"Great work," David said, his resolve strengthening. "Let's track it down. If we can find that vehicle, it might lead us directly to Salvatore or at least give us a clue about his next move."

The investigation was relentless, each piece of information serving as a steppingstone toward the ultimate confrontation with Victor Salvatore. As the sun began to rise outside the auction house, illuminating the chaos of the night before, the team knew their battle was just beginning. They weren't just fighting to reclaim stolen art; they were fighting for justice, for Marco, and for the integrity of the art world that Victor threatened to destroy.

In the sterile hospital room, Julian grasped Marco's hand tightly, his heart racing with a mix of fear and determination. The beeping machines around them faded into a blur as he focused on Marco's pale face, willing him to wake up and fight. Outside, the police were mobilizing, strategizing their next move against Victor, each revelation heightening the stakes. With the shadows of the past still looming over them, Julian felt an unwavering resolve grow within him. He couldn't let Victor win—not now, not ever.

As dawn broke, illuminating the path ahead, Julian braced himself for the confrontation that lay ahead. He knew the danger was far from over. The team was united in purpose, ready to face whatever Victor had planned, but the questions lingered: Would Marco pull through? What dark intentions did Victor harbor? The fight for their future had only just begun, and the stakes had never been higher.

THE END